Jerusalem
in the days of Lehi

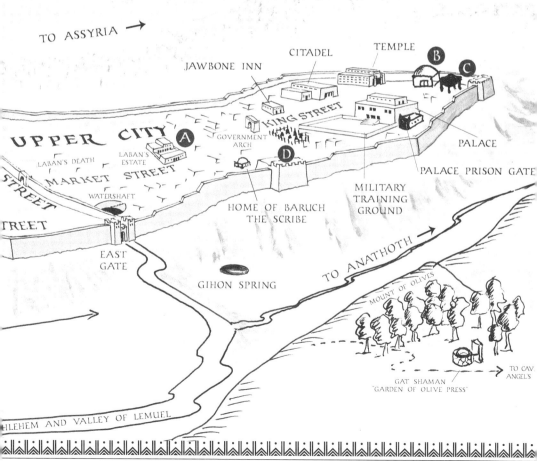

TO ASSYRIA →

JAWBONE INN

CITADEL

TEMPLE

B

C

UPPER CITY

A

GOVERNMENT ARCH

KING STREET

LABAN'S DEATH

LABAN'S ESTATE

MARKET STREET

D

PALACE

WATERSHAFT

STREET

PALACE PRISON GATE

HOME OF BARUCH THE SCRIBE

MILITARY TRAINING GROUND

TREET

EAST GATE

GIHON SPRING

TO ANATHOTH →

MOUNT OF OLIVES

TO CAV ANGEL'S →

GAT SHAMAN "GARDEN OF OLIVE PRESS"

HLEHEM AND VALLEY OF LEMUEL

DAY *of* REMEMBRANCE

OTHER BOOKS AND AUDIO BOOKS
BY DAVID G. WOOLLEY:

The Promised Land Series:

Vol. 1: Pillar of Fire

Vol. 2: Power of Deliverance

Vol. 3: Place of Refuge

VOLUME 4
THE PROMISED LAND

DAY *of* REMEMBRANCE

A NOVEL

DAVID G. WOOLLEY

Covenant Communications, Inc.

Cover image: *Father Lehi* © Glen S. Hopkinson.
Please visit www.glenhopkinson.com for more information.

Cover design copyrighted 2008 by Covenant Communications, Inc.

Published by Covenant Communications, Inc.
American Fork, Utah

Printed in Canada
First Printing: September 2008

14 13 12 11 10 09 08   10 9 8 7 6 5 4 3 2 1

ISBN 10: 1-59811-478-6
ISBN 13: 978-1-59811-478-2

In the seventh month, in the first day of the month, shall ye have . . . a memorial of blowing of trumpets.

LEVITICUS 23:24

Author's Note

Day of Remembrance is a split novel based on two major historical events. The first follows the return of Nephi and his brothers to Jerusalem in search of the brass-plate record as recorded in the opening chapters of the Book of Mormon. The second follows the events surrounding the coming forth of the Book of Mormon recorded by the Prophet Joseph Smith in his history found in the Pearl of Great Price. Though separated in time by more than two thousand years, these two stories are brought together through the timeless significance of the Day of Remembrance.

Since the day Moses returned from the summit of Mount Sinai with the celebrated stone tablets, Jews have memorialized the first day of the seventh month on the Israelite calendar by blowing horns in memory of the receipt of revealed covenants from heaven, petitioning God through prayers and the playing of trumpets to awaken their spirits after many millennia to a remembrance of those ancient promises given the seed of Abraham.

Among the covenant blessings revealed to Moses was an understanding that it was the work and glory of God to bring to pass the immortality and eternal life of His children and preserve forever the eternal nature of family ties—a timeless principle lost for centuries after the Babylonian occupation of Judah, but kept alive in a lesser-known, brass-plate record sequestered deep in the treasury of Laban, captain of the Israelite guard at the turn of the sixth century before Christ.

Present-day Jews observe *ha-Teurah,* the Feast of Trumpets, on a day known as *Rosh Hashannah,* meaning the "turning of the year"—a holiday that has evolved within modern Jewry into a "Jewish New Year." It was on that feast day in 1827 that Joseph Smith Jr., like Moses before him, brought down from a hill in upstate New York an ancient record he referred to as a New Covenant. The sacred text was etched on plates of gold by ancient Jews who migrated to the New World, and it was later deposited in a subterranean stone box about four hundred years after the birth of Christ—sealed in the ground for centuries in a hill south of what would one day be nineteenth-century Palmyra, New York. Fourteen hundred years later, Joseph Smith Jr. translated the record from its ancient reformed Semitic dialect and published the translation as the Book of Mormon, fulfilling ancient biblical prophecies that the God-given covenants revealed to Moses would, in the last days of the earth, speak out of the dust.

On September 22, 1827, the Jewish celebration of *Rosh Hashannah* marked the beginning of a prophetic call for Joseph Smith Jr. to do a work unlike any in the modern world. Early in the morning of the Jewish feast day, Joseph Smith Jr. ushered into existence additional Judeo-Christian scripture appropriately subtitled Another Testament of Jesus Christ. Thus began a dispensation of revelations destined to reach beyond the community of Palmyra Township and touch the lives of men and women across the earth who would listen to this modern prophet tell of a latter-day Restoration when God remembered again His ancient covenants with Israel. The significance of *ha-Teurah*—the Feast of Trumpets—remains somewhat unfamiliar to readers of the Book of Mormon. The Hebrew Holy Day on which this feast is celebrated did not always bear the name *Rosh Hashannah* as it did in Joseph Smith's time of the late 1820s. When the prophet Lehi lived at Jerusalem six hundred years before the birth of Christ, the day set apart for celebrating the Feast of Trumpets was known among Jews as *ha-Zikkaron*—The Day of Remembrance.

The task of producing *Day of Remembrance* has drawn me to reflect on the establishment of the Church of Jesus Christ in our time and the modern-day restoration of ancient covenants through the Prophet Joseph Smith that began with the coming forth of the Book of Mormon. May God bless your life as you come to appreciate living in the days of the fullness of times.

David G. Woolley
Springville, Utah
December 6, 2006

List of Characters

HISTORICALLY BASED CHARACTERS

<u>The Family of Lehi the Olive Oil Merchant</u>
Lehi, *Olive Oil Merchant*
Sariah, *Lehi's Wife*
Rachel*, *Eldest Daughter*
Leah*, *Daughter*
Laman, *Eldest Son & Pressmaster*
Lemuel, *Son & Stablemaster*
Sam, *Son & Caravanmaster*
Nephi, *Youngest Son & Keeper of the Oil*

<u>The Royal Family of Judah</u>
Zedekiah, *King of Judah*
Miriam*, *Queen of Judah*
Mulek, *Prince and Heir Apparent of Judah*
Dan*, *Prince of Judah*
Benjamin*, *Prince of Judah*

<u>The Family of Lord Yaush, Exiled Governor of Southern Judah</u>
Lord Yaush, *Former Commander of Fort Lakhish*
Sophia*, *Wife*
Setti*, *Son & Former Captain of the Night Watch*

<u>The Family of Ishmael the Vineyard Master</u>
Ishmael, *Vineyard Master*
Isabel*, *Ishmael's Wife*

Nathan*, *Eldest Son & Master of Olive Culture*
Seth*, *Son & Watermaster*
Nora*, *Eldest Daughter*
Abigail*, *Daughter*
Hannah*, *Daughter*
Mary*, *Youngest Daughter*

The Family of the Prophet Jeremiah
Jeremiah, *Prophet of God*
Eliza*, *Jeremiah's wife*
Zoram, *Keeper of the Keys*

Other Historical Characters
Baruch, *Scribe to the Prophet Jeremiah*
Zadock, *Chief Elder of the Jews at Jerusalem*
Shechem, *King of Robbers*
Ebed-Melech, *Ethiopian Sailor & Jailer of the Palace Prisons*

While this is a work of fiction, and all of the characters have been fictionalized, many are based on what we know of the historical figures of the time period. In cases where the names of historical characters are not known, the author has created names. These are marked with an asterisk (*).

FICTIONAL CHARACTERS

The Family of Jonathan the Blacksmith
Jonathan, Blacksmith
Ruth, Wife & Weaver
Elizabeth, Eldest Daughter
Aaron, Eldest Son & Firemaster
Daniel, Son & Forgingmaster
Sarah, Youngest Daughter
Joshua, Youngest Son

The House of Josiah the Potter
Josiah, Second Elder of the Jews

Rebekah, Josiah's Only Child
Mima, Rebekah's Ethiopian Handservant

The House of Moriah, the Scribe
Moriah, Former Apprentice Scribe at Fort Lakhish
Hagoth, Boat Builder and Uncle to Moriah

The Family of Reuben Kessler the Clock Maker
Reuben Kessler, Clock Maker
Danny Kessler, Clock Maker Apprentice & Calendar Maker

The Family of Avram Weiss
Avram Weiss, immigrant Hassidic Jew
Katerina Weiss, only surviving child

HISTORICALLY BASED CHARACTERS

The Family of the Prophet Joseph Smith
Joseph Smith Sr., *Wheat Farmer*
Lucy Mack Smith, *Wife & Oil Cloth Maker*
Alvin Smith, *Eldest Son (born 1798)*
Hyrum Smith, *Second Son (born 1800)*
Sophronia Smith, *Eldest Daughter (born 1803)*
Joseph Smith Jr., *Third Son (born 1805)*
Samuel Harrison Smith, *Fourth Son (born 1808)*
Ephraim, *Fifth Son (Born 1810, Died 1810)*
William Smith, *Sixth Son (born 1811)*
Catherine Smith, *Second Daughter (born 1812)*
Don Carlos, *Seventh Son (born 1816)*
Lucy Smith, *Third Daughter (born 1821)*

Other Historical Characters of the Early 1820s
Joshua Stafford, *Wheat Farmer*
John Stoddard, *Carpenter*
Isaac Hale, *Boarding House Owner*
Emma Hale, *Daughter and Housekeeper*

Jerusalem
598 years before the birth of the Anointed One

CHAPTER 1

—*Late Summer, 598 B.C.*
Jerusalem

"Answer me!"

Ebed-Melech knelt on the cold prison floor, his thick, black-skinned frame hovering over the well of the prison. Where was Jeremiah? It was impossible to see him with only the glow of a single lamp finding its way through the narrow opening and casting little light on the reason for the silence below.

A rope disappeared into the well, and somewhere in the shadows the prophet Jeremiah lay tied to the end of it like an ox in a harness. Ebed pulled on it with both hands. There was no play—nothing but dead weight taking out the slack.

"Do you hear me?" The stench of rotted mire stung tears from Ebed's eyes, and he turned his ear to the muddy chamber. There should at least be a whimper, a sigh, or some sound of life rising from this hellish place, but the only answer was the relentless drip of water seeping through the subterranean foundations of the palace. Something had gone terribly wrong. Ebed balanced his feet along the edge of the hole, took hold of the rope and—

"Not down there!" The former jailer—the man Ebed replaced by order of the king—held a torch ahead of his stride. Since the day Ebed took the man's post, he did nothing but wander in the shadows of the prison, following Ebed wherever he went, watching him like a spirit that never slept. The man never offered a word of advice, never showed Ebed about the prison; he didn't even bother to introduce Ebed to the prison guards. The old jailer could be of help—he knew the prison better than any of the guards or prison hands—but how could he trust eyes that burned with vengeance?

Ebed said, "He's not stirring."

"That's how they all go. Real quiet. Not much life left in them after so long in the well." The old jailer walked with his shoulders hunched forward, his words whistling through the wide gaps in his teeth. He held the torch to the opening, close enough that the searing heat flashed across Ebed's face. "It won't be long. Another day or two and the chills and sickness will have him." The old jailer sidled in next to Ebed and tugged on the end of the rope. "Lift the corpse out with this."

"We can't leave him to die."

"Fool. That's why they sent him here."

"Then why not a sword and be done with him months ago?"

The old jailer lowered his chin onto his chest and whispered, "For fear of his spells."

"He's no sorcerer."

"Tell that to the Chief Elder."

"Give me that." Ebed snatched the torch from the old jailer and forced the flame through the opening in the floor. Dirty water pooled around the form of Jeremiah. His legs were entombed in a layer of mud, his body slumped forward, and his face stuck in the mire. He lay still, without the rise and fall of breath in his shoulders, and Ebed shoved the torch back into the old jailer's hands, took hold of the rope, and stepped to the edge of the pit.

"Go down there, and you'll curse us both." The old jailer took Ebed by the arm. "You weren't in Jerusalem the day Jeremiah conjured a curse of death."

"Faith is the only curse Jeremiah cast on anyone." Ebed pulled free of the jailer's grasp. "That isn't anything to fear."

Ebed scaled down the rope, landing in mud up to his knees. He struggled across the dark pit to Jeremiah and pulled him out of the earthen tomb, his mouth and nose stopped by the foul mire. He steadied Jeremiah's frail frame over his shoulders before climbing the rope, his powerful arms slowly lifting them cubit by cubit, his feet working against the wall, and his toes finding the crevices in the mortared seams between the giant foundation stones.

"Free we are." The old jailer waved the torch over the opening in the floor. "Free of his curses."

Ebed laid Jeremiah's thin, mud-covered body on the floor.

"Breathe!" Ebed pressed against Jeremiah's chest, emptying and then filling his lungs with air. "For the love of heaven, live!"

"Leave the dead be." The old jailer started down the corridor. "I'll fetch the help to bear away the body."

Jeremiah's arms lay lifeless at his side. His eyes remained shut and his body still, but when Ebed set the wooden ladle to the prophet's lips and the first drops of cool water fell on his tongue, his heaving lungs sprayed water from his mouth.

"Curse you. Look what you've done." The old jailer limped back to Jeremiah's side. The breath of life filled the prophet's body, chasing away the gray in his cheeks and replacing it with a red hue. "You'll anger the Chief Elder by this."

"Better him than God." Ebed removed the harness from around Jeremiah's slight frame and lifted him from the floor, the prophet's body hanging limp in his arms. He started through the catacombs past a lamp. The brightness startled Jeremiah's eyes open. He reached for Ebed's hand and said, "The time is come."

"It's another of his curses." The old jailer hurried alongside Jeremiah and leaned his head in. "What time is come?"

Ebed said, "Ask him once he's bathed and fed and resting in the upper prison."

"There isn't time to rest." Jeremiah tightened his grip on Ebed's arm. "The day for God to begin to remember His covenant with Israel is come."

"We've done nothing to you." The old jailer hurried around in front of them and back-stepped ahead of their walking, his gaze shifting between Ebed and Jeremiah. "Tell him we're innocent. You. Me. We've done nothing but follow orders. Tell him before he curses us with something more terrible than the affliction he sent Hananiah."

Jeremiah's mud-soaked hair fell down into his lips, and the ends played over his words. He said, "God will do a marvelous work among his people."

"There was nothing marvelous about it." The old jailer shook his head. "They found Hananiah dead in his house."

"Yea, even a marvelous work and a wonder." Jeremiah spoke with a trembling voice, telling the old jailer of the covenant given to Moses and recorded on the brass plates locked away in Captain Laban's treasury. He insisted the record was to be taken from the city and copied by another prophet into a record fashioned of plates of gold. He said, "In the last days, the covenant will be read upon the housetops, and all things shall be revealed unto the children of men which ever have been among them and which ever will be, even unto the end of the earth."

"Mad he is." The old jailer pulled back. "Mad enough to curse us all."

"Let him alone." Ebed held Jeremiah close.

"You haven't heard him when he's lost in one of his deluded fits." The old jailer stood in the center of the corridor with the torch raised in the air, blocking Ebed's way through the shadowy catacombs. "He's possessed by Captain Laban's relics; thinks he's going to steal them."

Jeremiah said, "Twenty-eight days shall pass away, and then God will remember his covenant written on the brass plates."

The old jailer counted the days on his fingers before slowly lifting his gaze and whispering, "What evil do you plan for the Day of Remembrance?"

Jeremiah said, "It is written in the Hebrew calendar."

The old jailer spat on the ground. "Curse the calendar Moses invented."

"Moses didn't invent it. God revealed it to him." Jeremiah raised his voice enough to cut through the wheezing in his throat. "God gave him a vision of the great time-keeping orbits and revolutions of the planets in the heavens. Every feast celebrated among the Jews was appointed its day according to that which was ordained in the council of heaven before this world was created, and the Day of Remembrance holds a sacred place among the most holy of days." He leaned higher in Ebed's powerful arms, his gaze moving slowly about the dark ceiling of the prison, like a wise man scanning the night sky. "The heavens with all their planets and stars and the revolutions of this earth are a great timepiece, more accurate than the most precise water clock, and the time appointed to preserve the records of the covenant is come." He took Ebed by the forearm. "Every feast among our people was calendared in the heavens. The Babylonians and the Egyptians and the Chaldeans have their calendars, but they do nothing more than track the passing seasons and the rising and setting of the sun." Jeremiah held his hand to his mouth and coughed before saying, "Hidden in the calendar given to Moses is the appointed day for the record to come forth in the fullness of times." Jeremiah lay back in Ebed's arms. "I must ready the brass plates to have part in that future Day of Remembrance, and curse any man who seeks to stop me—curse him to death."

"He's threatening Captain Laban." The old jailer raised his torch higher, the flickering orange-yellow light casting over the prophet's frail frame. "Just as he threatened the prophet Hananiah. He killed the man. No one knows how, but he did it."

Ebed said, "He isn't well."

"He's well enough to curse us." The old jailer backed toward the entrance to the catacombs, the torchlight growing faint with each step. "Curse us all, he will."

"Jeremiah hasn't the strength to harm anyone." Ebed held the prophet close.

"His strength comes from another world." The old jailer fumbled for the key to the prison, pushed open the iron gate with his boot, and started up the circular stairs, but before he disappeared around the turn he pointed the end of his torch at Jeremiah and spoke through the oil smoke rising from the flame.

"Twenty-eight days, and we're all cursed!"

CHAPTER 2

—September 5, 1823
Old City of Jerusalem

Danny Kessler, son of Reuben the clock maker, pushed the finely crafted steel springs to the side of his clock-making table and placed the intricate timing gears back into a cotton-padded case. He set aside the gold-plated pendulum and weights without inserting them into the casement of the finely crafted, freestanding, long-case clock. There wasn't time for any of that if he was going to finish calculating the Jewish feast dates on the Gentile calendar for the customer who hired the work done. He should have started on the project weeks earlier, but because he was good with numbers, he had waited until early this morning to begin a calendar due for pickup today at first light.

The oval faces and metal pendulum tails of a hundred hanging clocks lined the thick limestone walls of this underground clock-making shop. Silver and gold-plated pocket watches tied with chains of every length and three-legged, round-faced clocks filled the shelves, the tick of their springs reverberating off the centuries-old walls with the tin sound of their timekeeping. And over in the center of the shop beneath a glass case sat the most valuable clocks—a solid gold pocket watch imported from relatives of the Kessler clock-making clan in Switzerland, a square-faced timepiece crafted by Papa with diamonds embedded in the hour and minute hands, and an heirloom wall-hanging clock made by the first clock-making Kessler in Germany and passed down from father to son for generations until it arrived at this shop in the Old City of Jerusalem. Danny and his father, Reuben, weren't the only clock makers in Palestine, but they were the only Kesslers, and every Jew, Arab, and Gentile knew that the finest clocks and the most reliable repairs were only to be found at the shop of *Kessler and Son.*

Danny spread a sheet of expensive parchment over the table, the paper curling back along the edges. Clock making was his legacy, but calendar conversion was his passion. His mind processed numbers with the efficiency of a perfectly balanced clock spring, and calculating dates was a simple matter of understanding the difference between the Gentile and Jewish calendars. And with immigrants trickling into the city from Eastern Europe where they used the same calendar as the Americans and British, there was money to be made by converting the Jewish feast dates onto the Gentile calendar. In less than two hours and for a fee of two shekels, Danny calculated thirteen months' worth of Jewish holy days onto a twelve-month Gentile calendar faster than any of the time-keeping scholars at the synagogue. Not that the Rabbis didn't do a perfectly accu- rate job with their calendaring of the ancient festivals, but they didn't have a mind for numbers like Danny, and he could do the conversions for a tenth of what the Rabbi and his scribes charged for a New Year's calendar, and he could do it for any year since the beginning of time through the end of eternity.

Danny leaned forward on his work stool, the wooden legs creaking under the weight of his tall frame, his long, steady clock-making fingers working a pen over a pad of scratch paper. He dipped his pen in the well, tapped the extra ink away, and wrote the name of the Jewish seventh month, *Tishri,* under the heading of the Gentile ninth month "September" before quickly blowing the ink dry. As soon as he finished with the feasts in the month of Tishri he'd have the calendar ready for the customer, and not an hour too soon. The man insisted Danny have it done this morning in time to celebrate today's Feast of Trumpets—he said it was a family tradition to pass *Rosh Hashannah* with a new calendar, and since Danny wasn't about to tread on tradition he agreed to make the calculations and meet the man here on a feast day—a day when the shop was usually shuttered for the New Year celebration.

Danny wrote today's date, *1 Tishri 5,584,* at the top of a writing pad— the first day of the seventh month, 5,584 years since the creation of the world. In the column below the date, he calculated the phases of the moon for each year since the beginning of time, carefully recording in a sequence of numbers the beginning of each of the thirteen Jewish months. And next to the string of numbers for the phases of the moon, he correlated the numbers to the revolution of the earth around the sun. Near the end of the number-filled page, he added two days for each Jewish deficient year since the creation and one more day for each regular Jewish year before reaching the final mathematical calculation. That was it. Danny set aside his pen. Today's Feast of Trumpets fell on the fifth day of the Gentile month called September in the American year of 1823, and every Jew across the world was preparing to celebrate *Rosh Hashannah* today. The hanging clocks on the wall ticked away the time. It was half-past six in the morning in Jerusalem, which was half past two in London, and it was still late in the evening of September 4 in New York City—still too early for American Jews to be making a memorial by the blowing of trumpets and offering prayers for God to remember His covenants with Israel. The Jews in Jerusalem celebrated *Rosh Hashannah* well before their brothers in Europe and America, and Danny wrote *ha-Teurah*—Feast of Trumpets—on the calendar next to the date September 5, 1823.

Footsteps sounded above the time-keeping rhythm of the clocks, and Danny turned on his work stool to see if the customer had arrived to collect his calendar. There was no one standing at the door and no boots descending the stone steps from the narrow, cobblestone street above. The poured glass windows next to the entrance framed nothing but the gray of early morning outside the shop, and there was still time to finish converting the last two feasts. The stir of footsteps filled the shop, but there was no telling who was making the noise until he heard the high-pitched click of the safe over beyond the shelves on the far side of the shop.

Danny spun around on his stool and pushed his visor back off his brow. "Papa, is that you?"

Reuben Kessler stood on the other side of the shop, his tall, thin frame visible between the shelves of clocks. He stood in front of a two-inch-thick metal door, turning the gears in the combination lock. The safe was made of high-tempered steel shipped from Toledo, Spain, and hinged in place into the centuries-old stone with long, metal rods drilled a good three feet into the wall with a tedious hand drill and bit. They'd never had trouble with thieves, not in this basement shop with only a single outside entrance down narrow stairs, a thick metal entry door reinforced with iron bars, and the thickest foundation stones of any structure on this ancient, winding street in the Upper City. It was old enough that most of the homes and shops in the neighborhood were believed to be built on the foundations of buildings destroyed more than two thousand years ago when Babylon leveled Jerusalem and took the Jews captive. The locksmith who helped Papa hinge the safe door in place didn't have to cut out any limestone. The interior was already chiseled to the perfect dimensions by ancient stone masons, and when they dug out the foundation and built their home on top of these limestone blocks, they found a hole in the wall for a vault to store their most valuable possessions—an heirloom family prayer shawl embroidered with gold thread and a handwritten copy of the Torah scrolls with all five books of Moses meticulously preserved by generations of scribes for Papa to read when he performed his singing and reciting duties at synagogue. They were Kesslers, and the family worshiped at the Sephardic synagogue, a ten-minute walk up the winding cobblestone street from the shop. What Danny didn't know was that 2,421 years ago this vault guarded a copy of the law on brass plates. This basement clock-making shop was once the ancient treasury of Laban, captain of the Hebrew guard.

Reuben Kessler turned the circular gear on the combination lock until the last number clicked in place and the vault door fell open. He reached into the small, chest-high chamber and took out the heirloom copy of the Torah. The long wooden dowel sprouted from the leather scroll nestled against Papa's waist and ran up along his arm to well above his shoulder. Reuben arranged the white and blue-striped *talis* prayer shawl around his neck and hung the gold watch by a chain from his coat pocket. He didn't need the watch to perform his duties as cantor at synagogue, but he was a watchmaker before he was ever a singer of the songs of Jewish worship, and the neighbors expected him to wear the watch and chain from the pocket of his finely tailored suit when he sang the words of the Torah at synagogue. He was a tall man, about the same height as Danny, and when he stood straight with the *talis* prayer shawl over his shoulders, the wide bands of white and blue cloth highlighting his features, he was king of this clock-making shop, selected by the rabbi to sing the songs of scripture and bring music to the verses of the Torah. They called him

Reuben, the time-keeping cantor, and there was not a finer day for Papa than the weekly observance of *Shabbat* or a feast day like today when he rendered in song the words of the covenants written in the Torah by the prophet Moses.

"Ready for synagogue, are you, son?" Reuben walked down between the clock shelves and came around next to Danny's work-table. His voice was filled with the brogue of Jews from the south, his tongue precisely clipping the words as they escaped his mouth, the sound of his speech resonating from deep in his belly like a tenor in an Italian opera. "The rabbi, I promised him the songs of the covenant, and a promise we will keep." He began to hum a melody, softly going over the words that Israel would awaken to a remembrance of her covenants with God. They fell from his lips in an effortless rise and fall of song that filled the shop with the fullness of his powerful voice. He cleared his throat and sang another short verse before saying, "Along you go, and get your coat. A cool morning it is for a feast day, yes? You don't want to make your singing father late. If I'm not in my place when the synagogue fills, the rabbi, he becomes a very nervous man."

Danny set aside his pen. "The rabbi can sing Torah, Papa."

"You call the noise he makes singing?" Reuben clucked his tongue like he did whenever he disagreed. "Blessed the rabbi is with a good mind." He shifted the Torah scroll onto his other arm and peered over the glasses perched on the end of his nose. "The vocal cord is a musical instrument, and the good rabbi was not blessed with a tuned one. No matter how keen his mind, he'll never think a well-pitched song."

Papa was right. The rabbi sang with a rasping voice that scared the children at synagogue, and the man had learned to depend on Papa for the music, especially on feast days.

"I won't be much longer." Danny turned back to the calendar. "I promised Avram I'd have this for him."

"The Russian?"

Danny hurried his pen over the calendar, filling in the last feasts of September. "Is that where he emigrated from?"

"Emigrate, he didn't, son. Avram escaped." Reuben came around in front of Danny's table. "The uprisings in Russia didn't end thirty years ago; you know about that, yes?"

"Only what you've told me."

"It was bad for him, very bad. A tax collector for the royal family he was, in a small village in the south, near the Polish border. Have I not told you this?"

Danny nodded. He'd often heard Papa speak about the Jews in Russia hired to collect the taxes, keep the keys of public buildings, and represent the Tzarist ruler in every corner of the kingdom. But all Danny's nodding didn't keep Reuben from going on about the awful past one more time, reminding him of the plight of Russian Jews. They were nothing but second-class residents, though they ran the government. And under their stewardship, Russia flourished until thirty years ago when a peasant uprising turned against the men who collected the taxes.

Reuben said, "Avram was the caretaker in his village. He kept the keys for three churches and a hall on the main square." Reuben clucked his tongue against the roof of his mouth. "He was lucky to save the life of any in his family." He slowly shook his head. "Only Avram and his daughter, Katerina, survived, and he brought her here. A very nice little girl."

Danny said, "I hardly noticed an accent."

"Hassids they are, Danny. They recite the Torah every day, and all of it in Yiddish, not Russian. Strict they are, very strict about living the law."

Danny said, "Avram speaks Hebrew well enough."

"His name is Mr. Weiss to you, yes? You treat him with respect, no matter what you hear in the street about his Judaism. I don't want you to—"

The shop door swung open, and the appearance of Avram Weiss silenced any discussion of the man's Hassidic Judaism. He ducked beneath the chimes attached to the top of the door, stood on the welcome mat, and wiped the morning dew from his feet before offering Papa a nod and a quick bow. A black *caftan* hat capped his head of graying hair. He removed it, turned it in his hands, and replaced it, the brim pressing the long locks of braided hair against his sideburns and the curious curls winding down past his cheeks and mixing with the hair of his beard. The end of a *tzit-zit* cloth hedged out from beneath his coat, and he wore it like a good Hassid should—against the skin, the white linen undershirt hidden beneath his black coat, the hem sneaking out from beneath the tails where the four corners were tied into a fringe of 613 knots, each one representing one of the 613 commandments in the Torah. Avram was a short man with narrow shoulders, penetrating blue eyes, and a square chin. He waited quietly until Papa welcomed him to the shop before turning to Danny and saying, "You are finished, yes?"

Danny gathered the twelve sheets of the Gentile calendar, but before he could roll them into a scroll and tie them off with a string, Avram reached over the table and set his finger on the fifth of September. He said, *"Ha-Zikkaron* falls today, yes?"

Danny said, "You mean *Rosh Hashannah,* sir?"

"The feast days, do you not know them, son?" Avram tapped his finger on the calendar. "The Babylonians celebrated the New Year in the fall, never the Jews." Avram began to sway like a Hassid in prayer. "A single generation the Jews were captive in Babylon, and they come back to Jerusalem with a new name for the day we celebrate the Feast of Trumpets." He raised his hands in the air. "Fifty-seven years I live on this earth, and I still remember my name. But the Jews, they're gone from Jerusalem for seventy and they forget the proper name for the *Day of Remembrance.* God should have kept the Jews in Babylon another generation until they remembered to remember."

Danny said, "I didn't know, sir."

"A good Jew doesn't celebrate the turning of the New Year on the first day of the seventh month." Avram gathered the twelve sheets of the Gentile calendar under his arm before stepping to the door and holding it open to let the sound of the first blasts of morning trumpets echo down the street from the synagogue, calling Jews to come remember their covenants with God. He said, "Good Jews celebrate *ha-Zikkaron.* We never forget to remember the Day of Remembrance."

"Papa." A soft voice filtered down the steps from the street before the black polished leather of a woman's shoes appeared in the window, touched by the hem of a red skirt, which was topped with white sashes and a blouse sewn of a humble—

"Katerina." Avram stepped aside and let her into the shop. "You were to wait in the street."

"The trumpets, Papa. It's time for the celebration to begin." Katerina pulled on her father's arm. "We should be off now."

Katerina wore her black hair without any braids, the long strands falling down about her shoulders. Long lashes accented her wide, blue eyes, and her narrow nose and cheeks were red from the cool of early morning. Danny slid off his stool, straightened the creases out of his clock-maker's apron, and removed his visor. Where did Papa get the notion that Avram's only living daughter was a child? Katerina was a young woman—a very stunning one at that.

Danny quickly ran his fingers through his hair before replacing the visor. "Good morning, Katerina."

"Hello, Danny."

How did she know his name?

Katerina said, "My father says you're good with calendars."

"Come daughter. It's time we were gone." Avram reached for her hand, but she stepped away from his reaching and said, "You're the son of the clock maker, yes?"

Danny started toward her, but Avram stepped between them. "The trumpets, daughter. This is no time for idle conversation." He held up the calendar. "I have what we came for."

Avram led her up the steps and onto the street, and her smile slowly disappeared with each step. Danny followed them out the door and stood halfway up the stairwell, his head level with the cobblestones. Katerina was a beautiful girl, the same age as Danny—seventeen—and he couldn't help staring long after she disappeared beyond the horizon of the street.

"Let her go, son." Reuben stepped out of the shop with Danny's coat in hand, the prayer shawl over his head, and the scroll of the Torah balanced against his shoulder. He locked the shop door and handed the coat to Danny. "She's the daughter of a Hassid."

"But Papa, I only wanted to ask her—"

"Let her go."

Danny followed Reuben up the steps from the shop entry. The street was empty without any sign of Katerina's red dress brightening the winding street leading down the rise toward the lower city.

"Synagogue is this way, son." Reuben started him walking up the hill in the other direction. They were off to celebrate the *Rosh Hashannah* New Year, but this wasn't a new year, not according to Mr. Avram Weiss. Today was *ha-Zikkaron*—the first day of the seventh month—and Danny would not soon forget it. How could he not remember this day?

September 5, 1823—the Day of Remembrance—was the day he first met Katerina Weiss.

—16 Days Later, September 21, 1823
Palmyra Township, State of New York

Joseph Smith Jr. hurried down the last stretch of moonlit road this side of home, climbed the timber fence bordering the Smith family property, and landed on his good right foot. The ache in his left leg begged him to stop, and he pulled up beside the tallest tree along the north end of the maple grove and leaned against the smooth bark. The leaf-covered branches were beginning to wither in the cool fall evenings—nights he'd come to love since moving onto this land five years back. Joseph held the trunk with one hand and rubbed his shin with the other. No one would ever force them to leave this land like they did in Norwich. He was only ten years old when they lost the Vermont farm, back when he couldn't help his parents raise any money for the mortgage after doctors cut an eight-inch incision between his knee and ankle. They had pulled back the bloody flesh and bored holes on both sides of his shin, weakening the bone enough so they could pry out three pieces from his diseased leg.

Seven years had passed since surgeons hacked away at his leg, with only the sedative of his father's arms wrapped around him to help him manage the pain. It had taken this long to get the strength back and work out the stiffness from the surgery. Mama said he might have to endure a limp the rest of his life, but he refused to be a hobbled son unable to earn his keep, and he forced himself to hide what limp was left from the surgery and work alongside his older brothers without complaining of the subtle pain that gnawed at his shin.

There was a reason they settled in Palmyra Township on this farm northwest of the highest drumlin in the county—a good-sized hill not too far distant from their home. It was the tallest landmark in the township, good for getting bearings and finding one's way about the fields and woodlands south of Palmyra. It didn't matter why their crops failed three years in a row back in Vermont and forced them out. They were here now on new land. They'd not endured a single drought or early frost in four harvests, and with another crop coming under the sheath, there was no telling what promises the virgin soil of upstate New York held for them.

Joseph found his way around three small maple saplings, past a sturdy stand of aging maples, and over to a clearing where the skeleton of a new frame house came into view, the outline rising through the tree branches on the other side of Stratford Road. The light of a full moon filtered down over the split planks of what would someday be the second-floor bedroom, the moonlight shining through the open beams and into the parlor on the main floor like a lamp hanging from invisible rafters that had yet to be nailed in place. His brother Alvin started building the home last year on the highest point of land lining Stratford Road; he said Father and Mother should have a house to keep them comfortable as they grew older. But Papa didn't have a mind to build a larger, finer house than the log cabin they called home—not with them struggling to meet the mortgage on the farm—and Alvin set to building the frame house himself, regardless of their situation. It wasn't until he finished the foundation in midsummer that the rest of the family joined him in his venture. The frame of the second story was taking shape, and the timbers cast long shadows across the road in the moonlight. If winter didn't set in too early, they'd square the roof beams, nail them in place, and wrap them with canvas to keep them from splintering until spring when they could fashion some shakes from felled trees in the maple grove and nail down a rain-worthy roof.

Joseph started through the last stand of trees toward the family's log cabin home. These maples were the only ones left standing on the family's hundred-acre farm that straddled both sides of Stratford Road. It was syrup that spared these trees from Papa's clearing axe and rooting chains, the sugary sap paying a portion of the hundred-dollar mortgage and keeping them from losing this land when all about them, farmers were losing theirs.

Money was scarce, but they were going to keep this land—Joseph wouldn't let it slip away when they were so close to owning it outright. They weren't going to end up like the hordes of other farmers who lost their property only to rent back the land they toiled to clear and plant.

Papa needed cash, and Joseph was out late earning what he could—tonight it was money digging for Joshua Stafford.

Old farmer Stafford claimed treasure was buried on his farm, said he dreamed Indians hid it there before the war with Britain, and for ten cents an hour—nearly half a full day's wage for a canal hand on the Erie docks at Palmyra—he hired Joseph to dig in his wheat field before fall turned to winter and the ground froze. Farmer Stafford was like most other unschooled men in these parts, chasing after rumors of gold buried by fleeing Indians, Spanish conquerors, French invaders, British officers, and the like. All this digging through the soil without clearing the land for a crop or planting a single seed bordered on indolence. Farmer Stafford's notions of hidden treasure were certain to prove disappointing when he had neither a barn filled with wheat nor a chest of gold to show for a season of hard work.

Tonight Joseph finished digging a trench twenty feet long, a few inches shy of eight feet wide, and a good seven feet deep. They didn't find even a plug nickel, but Joseph indulged Farmer Stafford's obsession for the hourly wage. Papa had a yearly debt on the land deed, and tonight's wages would go toward the one hundred dollars cash due at the end of the month. That's all the land agent accepted. No credit against the wheat they were harvesting and no potash from the trees they cleared and burned on the back twenty acres. The leftover supply of maple syrup from last spring's sap harvest wasn't enough to cover what they owed for the year. Not even a taste of William and young Don Carlos's sugar cookie and confection business—supervised by their older sister Sophronia—could sweeten the bitterness of the land agent's claim to one hundred dollars cash. The thought of losing the farm filled Joseph with more dread than the memory of the surgeon's knife cutting into his leg. Everyone in the family except little Lucy worried over the property. She was hardly two years old and not long enough out of diapers to be concerned about anything beyond running through the house in a fit of smiles. The rest of the family didn't pass a day without wondering if they were going to earn enough for the land payment.

The small, two-room log cabin with an upstairs loft sat along the southeast edge of the maple grove, back off Stratford Road a good two hundred feet. A light flickered in the window of the cabin, welcoming Joseph home from his second job—the only welcome he could expect with the rest of the family gone to bed. He was home, and he could forget the fancies of money diggers searching for buried treasure and sleep a while before sunrise, when he would be back to harvesting wheat with his brothers.

Joseph slowly opened the door to keep the creaking from waking the family. The girls—his older sister Sophronia, Catherine, and two-year-old Lucy—slept in the room next to the kitchen. The door leading to the new addition on the back of the cabin stood ajar—wide enough for light from the lamp to filter in past the doorpost and over the form of Mother and Father asleep in their bed. There was no stirring in the loft above the main room where all five of Joseph's brothers—Alvin, Hyrum, Samuel, William, and Don Carlos—had long since gone to bed. Joseph stepped to the hearth and dished out a helping of stew from the kettle Mama had left simmering over the coals, poured himself a drink of water from the bucket hanging from a hook on the wall, and sat at the long table in the center of the main room, hurrying the spoon to his mouth to savor what he could of Mother's potato-and-carrot stew with far too few bits of beef hidden in the thick gravy. Between bites, Joseph rubbed the tiredness of his second job from his shoulders. Working a shovel wasn't the easiest way to pay off the family's land debt after a full day of reaping wheat with Papa, Alvin, and Hyrum, but his earnings along with mother's oil-painted tablecloth-making business and a good wheat harvest was going to keep them from falling delinquent come the end of the month.

"Joseph, is that you, son?" Lucy stepped from her bedroom. Her long, brown hair was tied together in a sleeping cloth to keep it from troubling her rest, the ends of it playing over the shoulders of her white broadcloth nightgown, which she sewed from remnants collected from the seamstress in Palmyra in exchange for a jar of maple syrup. She came alongside the table and laid her hand on Joseph's shoulder. "Thank heavens you're home. I don't like you out late at night. You know what they say about night walks and such."

"You mean what the clergy in the township say."

"They have nothing good to say over the pulpit about men who pass their evenings in loud laughter. Not with the imbibing that accompanies it, and with the company you're keeping, it's no wonder Reverend Lane says what he says."

"It isn't a sin to earn a living."

Lucy reached for his plate. "Did you get enough to eat?"

"I'm fine, Mother."

"That's all you ever say, no matter how hungry you are." Lucy ran her hand through his hair, and a faint smile played about her lips. "You'd starve yourself if you thought it would help with the mortgage, and you'd tell me you were fine right to your grave, you would. Now eat up."

"Joshua Stafford paid me for five hours of digging." Joseph handed her the coins. "That's fifty more cents for the land agent."

"Thank you, son, but . . ." Lucy wrapped her palm around the money and pressed her hand to her lips.

"What is it, Mother?"

"We don't need this if it means you have to keep company with the men Farmer Stafford hires to dig on his land."

"It's hard work." Joseph turned back to the table and cleaned the last of the stew from the plate. "And there's no better pay, not even on Canal Street."

"Mercy, you're not thinking of hiring out with those dock hands, are you, son?"

"No, Mama, not unless you tell me to."

"You know me better than that." Lucy came around the table and stood opposite Joseph. "I was in town today. I ran across Reverend Lane from the Methodist church speaking with some of the other clergy. Minister Chase and Deacon Jessup were there along with a few of the preachers from the Presbyterian church. All right there on Main Street."

"I don't put much stock in what Reverend Lane or any of the other professors of religion say. Not anymore."

"Mr. Lane inquired after you."

"He can't do you any harm. You have a pew in the Presbyterian church, not with the Methodists."

"He didn't mean any harm, son."

Joseph lowered his voice. "You don't know him like I do."

"He was warning the other ministers against dreamers and visionaries and money diggers, but it was like he was speaking directly to me. He said if anyone tells tales of conjuring spirits to help them find riches in the ground, it was the work of the devil preying on the uneducated souls in this township."

"Reverend Lane is only trying to frighten you into thinking I'm a lost soul for hiring out to dig for Farmer Stafford."

"What ever happened between you and the good Reverend?" Lucy leaned against the table, her shadow casting across him. "It wasn't but three years ago that you attended his meetings at the Methodist church."

"I didn't know any better. I was fourteen back then, hardly much older than William."

"Why, you nearly joined his congregation, and now he speaks of you like all the uneducated farmhands of the county, chasing after treasure and the like."

"Do you think I'm uneducated, Mother?"

"It isn't your doing, son." Lucy slowly shook her head and spoke quickly, her long hair playing about her shoulders. "We've not had the good fortune of sending you or any of your brothers or sisters to school."

"Hyrum attended academy."

"That was for a single winter." Lucy sat on the bench seat across from Joseph and set her hands on the table, her sturdy frame silhouetted by the dying embers in the hearth. "That's hardly an education."

"I write as well as the next lad."

"What have you ever written?"

"You've taught me to read the Bible."

"That isn't writing, son, and you don't read your Bible."

"Not clear through, but I read when I can."

"What troubles me is Reverend Lane's words. He had nothing but meanness to say about you. And Deacon Jessup and Minister Chase, bless their souls, didn't have anything good to say, either." Lucy played with the sash around the collar of her nightgown, untying the string then retying it about her neck. "They spoke of you like they do when they're speaking ill of the revivalists who attend camp meetings and itinerant preachers who lure converts away from their congregations. You know the stories they tell of dreamers and visionaries doing the work of the devil and preaching false doctrines and the like.

They said anyone who throws in with money diggers is no better than revivalists."

"Reverend Lane never had anything good to say about visions." Joseph kept his head down and worked his spoon over the empty plate. "Said if there were anything to know about heaven or hell the good Lord would have made it known to the Apostles when they were penning the Gospels. That's what he told me. Said visions were of the devil, that there was no such thing as revelations in these days; that all such things ceased with the Apostles and there never would be any more of them."

"When did you last speak with the man?"

"It's been a few years. Not long after . . ." Joseph played with his spoon.

"Not long after what?"

"Not long after the morning I told you I knew Presbyterianism wasn't right. Do you remember? It was in the spring during maple harvest, three years back. I can never forget it, Mother." Joseph slowly shook his head. "I went out into the grove for a time to pray over the matter and . . ."

"What is it, Joseph?"

"I came inside and leaned against the stone . . ." He tipped his head toward the bricks in the hearth. "You were worried. You said I looked tired, and I told you I'd found out for myself that Presbyterianism wasn't right."

"What you told me was that I should never mind—that you were well enough off." Lucy leaned over the table. "I can't keep never minding, son. Not when men like Reverend Lane speak ill of you. Heaven knows you spent a good deal of time with the man. You were preparing to join his congregation before you lost interest and he started speaking ill of—"

"I didn't lose interest, Mother." Joseph raised his gaze from staring at his empty plate. "I told Reverend Lane that none of the religious sects were right, not a single one, and I told it to the good deacon and the minister as well."

"Mercy, Joseph." Lucy let go of the sash around her nightgown. "No wonder Reverend Lane has nothing good to say about you." She reached across the table and took him by the hand. "What on earth possessed you to say such a thing?"

Joseph took back his hand and sat rigid on the bench, his shoulders straight and his head down. He'd not told Mother any of the details of his vision three years earlier in the maple groves behind the log cabin. That was back when he was thinking seriously of joining with Reverend Lane's congregation in Palmyra. No one but the good Reverend knew he'd found a secluded spot among the trees, over where Papa left an axe in one of the stumps, and offered a simple prayer, asking heaven for wisdom to know which of all the churches he should join. It was a personal vision, meant for him and him alone, and it wasn't right to go about sharing it with anyone; and hopefully Reverend Lane hadn't broken his promise and shared it with the other preachers in town. A minister of the gospel wasn't to share the conversion of a congregant, and there was no greater story of conversion than what Joseph received back when he was a young lad of fourteen. It was on a beautiful, clear morning, early in the spring of 1820, the same week they were harvesting maple syrup from the grove. If Reverend Lane were an honorable man he wouldn't speak of what Joseph shared with him in confidence. Wasn't that what ministers were for—to hear the confessions of their parishioners and help them find God?

Joseph pushed back from the table, his head still down and his shoulders forward. He'd confided his conversion to Reverend Lane, told him he'd found God in the middle of a maple grove. And instead of congratulating Joseph for seeking a spiritual witness from heaven, the man had nothing good to say about his vision. Joseph told him he'd received a promise that his sins were forgiven, and Reverend Lane told him that no one but God could forgive sins. Joseph told him he'd been blessed with an intense feeling of joy that filled his soul and lasted for a good many weeks after his vision, and Reverend Lane told him that he was deluded by an unbridled heart. Why did the Reverend treat Joseph's vision with such contempt? The man was Joseph's minister, shepherding him into the faith of the Methodists, and it was only right he share the experience with the man. That's what Reverend Lane told him he should do, and he had Joseph promise to share his conversion in preparation for membership in his church, but when he told the good minister that God the Father and His Son Jesus Christ appeared to him in a grove of trees behind their log cabin, forbidding him to join any of the sects, the Reverend called Joseph a fool like all the other foolish seekers and revivalists in the region. He labeled Joseph as a diviner, said his vision was the work of the devil, and told him he was like all the other uneducated folk in the county. He went on to tell Joseph that if he didn't repent of this awful sin and never speak of it again he'd end up in hell with all the other money diggers, visionaries, and spirit seekers.

Joseph released his hold on the table, the rough timbers brushing his fingertips. He'd actually seen a light, and in the midst of that light he'd seen two Personages and they did in reality speak to him, telling him that the professors of religion in Palmyra drew near to God with their lips but that their hearts were far from him. And though Reverend Lane hated and persecuted him for saying he'd seen a vision, yet it was true, and he could not deny it.

Joseph left the dirty plate and glass on the table and turned toward the ladder leading up the wall to the loft above the kitchen. He said, "I'm fine, Mother."

"Fine?" Lucy set her hands on her hips. "That's not the report I heard from Reverend Lane."

Joseph turned on the first rung in the ladder, his thick arms holding him up off the floor. "What did he say about me?"

"That you were given to loud laughing in the company of jovial men. That you were always out late at night, and you were given to telling lies that were certain to damn your soul." Lucy came around the table and took Joseph by the arm. "Tell me the man isn't right; tell me I haven't lost my son."

"Don't worry yourself, Mother."

"What is it, Joseph? Is everything well with you?"

Joseph pulled himself up to the second rung in the ladder. It had been three years since he'd felt the joy of the vision in the maple grove behind the house—a vision that was his personal conversion, assuring him his sins were forgiven and telling him to join with no other sects. He was an outcast, deprived of attending church meetings with his mother and the rest of his brothers and sisters. He wanted to get religion too—wanted to feel and shout like the rest—but he couldn't. God had forbidden him, and unless he was given more direction he would forever remain an outcast. Maybe Reverend Lane was right; maybe he'd become what the Methodists called converts who returned to their sins. Had he become a backslider? In the three years since his vision, Joseph mingled with all sorts of society and jovial company, but at least the money diggers and uneducated farmhands in the county could be counted as friends—something the good Reverend would never be. There was only one thing Joseph could do. He started up the ladder to the loft above the kitchen, and Lucy's hand fell away from his arm. He had to find some forgiveness of his sins, but before he disappeared from Mother's view beyond the rafters in the ceiling, he repeated what he told her the morning he returned from his vision in the maple grove three years ago. "Never mind, Mother. I'm well enough off."

The light filtering up from the kitchen cast a dim glow over the two beds in the loft. The frames were hewn of rough maple, lashed together with leather straps, and the down-feather mattress fell over the sides. They were wide, strong beds with enough strength in their construction to hold twenty men, but thankfully only three brothers had to sleep in each. Alvin's twenty-three-year-old stature filled nearly half the bed closest to the ladder. He was nestled beneath a red-and-white-checkered comforter, but there was no doubting it was Alvin. He was the only brother who snored, and it was a shame Joseph wasn't already asleep. He was going to have to ignore the sound of his brother's heavy breathing if he hoped to get some rest. Samuel slept on the other side of the bed, his spindly, fifteen-year-old legs hanging out from under the comforter. The small, black-haired head of five-year-old Don Carlos lay on the pillow between the two.

Joseph stooped over to keep from banging his head on the rafters angling down either side of the roof and quietly stepped around the post and frame to the second bed. Thankfully, his twenty-one-year-old brother Hyrum had the sense to sleep nearest the wall with twelve-year-old William in the middle, the two of them leaving the side nearest the floor open with enough room for Joseph to slide under the quilts without bothering the others.

Joseph pulled off his boots and set them against the wall before kneeling beside the bed and softly petitioning God to see beyond his seventeen-year-old youthfulness, and forgive him for . . .

What was that? Joseph leaned back and raised his head to find a light gathering in his room. It was like a fire burning in the air, but there was no heat, at least nothing Joseph could feel against his face.

It was intense enough to wake his brothers, but Alvin's snoring didn't stop, William didn't turn over, and Hyrum lay still against the wall of the loft not ten hands from where Joseph knelt.

The column of light grew brighter until a man stood in the brightness, defying the pull of earth. It was like the manifestation he'd had in the maple grove, but tonight only a single personage visited him, and he looked nothing like his other visitors. He wasn't dressed with nearly as many sashes to cover his body. The angel wore a loose-fitting robe—the sleeves reaching down to just above the wrists, the hem ending near his ankles, and the lapels open enough so that Joseph could see the man's chest. But this was no man, not with the brilliant whiteness of his skin. His robe was of the most exquisite white color—whiter than any linen sold in Palmyra's finest shops.

The angel lifted both hands as he spoke and said his name was Moroni. His voice was gentle but firm, and clear as the finest orator, and still Joseph's brothers remained asleep in their beds. Moroni said, "God has a work for you to do."

A work for him? Joseph leaned back from the bed frame. This wasn't like his first vision, where his questions on the matter of religion were answered and he had a promise of forgiveness. Moroni told him that because of the work he was called to do, men in every nation on earth would speak both good and evil of his name. But what work could he do that would be known any farther than the confines of Palmyra Township? He was a seventeen-year-old son of a wheat farmer with hardly enough money between the eleven members of the family to make the land payments. He could read, but not quickly. He could write, but not with much skill. He had no money to help the poor, and he spent his evenings with money diggers searching for treasure in the earth.

Moroni spoke with a steady urgency, but for all Joseph's concentration, it was difficult to understand everything. There was something about a book written on gold plates telling about former inhabitants of this continent and where they came from—he called it the source from whence they sprang. What book was he talking about? Joseph didn't remember any plates of gold in the Gospels of the New Testament, at least not the parts he'd read. Mother was right. He'd not read his Bible with much diligence, and if he had, maybe he'd understand more. He was certain the Bible didn't speak of the inhabitants of the Americas. It was all very confusing, and if that wasn't enough, the angel said this book of gold plates contained the fullness of the everlasting gospel delivered by Christ to these ancient people. Joseph brushed away the line of sweat forming across his brow. What did he mean by the fullness of the gospel? And what was this about Christ visiting America? That certainly wasn't anything he'd ever read in the Bible.

Moroni stepped around in front of Joseph, his body suspended directly above the bed and the hem of his brilliant white robe swaying about his ankles. He paused for a moment, letting the sound of his words fall silent against the far wall of the loft before he told Joseph that along with the gold-plate record there were two stones attached to a set of silver bows called a Urim and Thummim. He raised his hand in front of his eyes like a man adjusting his spectacles and explained that these stones were known as "seers" in ancient times and they were deposited along with the gold plates, and he would need them to translate the book. Joseph slowly shook his head. That couldn't be. Joseph could write his name well enough, but how could he translate a book from another tongue when he wasn't well-versed in his own?

Moroni raised his voice, his words demanding Joseph's careful attention to these strange things. The angel said the seer stones were deposited with the plates, but deposited where? Joseph cleared his throat and started to ask where he could find this gold book, but Moroni began reciting scriptures—some Joseph knew from his time with the Methodists, while others were less familiar. Moroni said that the prophecy in the second chapter of Joel was soon to be fulfilled—that young men were to see visions. Joseph reached for the bed frame. Was he one of the young men the prophet Joel saw in his visions? Before Joseph could ask, Moroni went on quoting more scriptures. He spoke of Moses' prophecy of Christ— calling him a great prophet that God raised up for all men to hear in all things. Joseph ran his fingers through his hair. He'd not ever remember all of this with Moroni quoting the Apostle Paul and telling him that Moses knew of Christ, preached of Christ, and had faith that through Christ all the families of the earth would be blessed if they were faithful to their covenants. Moroni quoted Isaiah, explaining the passages in the greatest of detail and telling Joseph that his work would fulfill many of the prophecies of these ancient prophets like a stone cut from a mountain without hands. Fulfill prophecies? That couldn't be. Not Joseph. He was a farmer, not a prophet. Moroni began quoting the last verses of the Old Testament—a passage Joseph had heard a hundred times from the ministers in Palmyra—and he spoke it with such force that Joseph could feel the words penetrate deep into his soul. He said God would plant in the hearts of the children the promises made to the fathers, and the hearts of the children would turn to their fathers. If it were not so, the whole earth would be utterly destroyed at His coming.

Moroni said, "When you get the plates, you're to show them to no one but those you're directed should see them." His voice took on a deep, solemn tone, and while he explained the importance of keeping the plates out of the public eye, the view of the drumlin two miles south of the farm—the highest hill in the county—flooded Joseph's mind. It was as clear as if he were standing right there on Canandaigua Road looking up at the hillside, and he could see in his mind the place where this gold-plate record was deposited a little below the top of the hill on the western slope, half hidden in a stand of trees.

The light gathered around Moroni, leaving the walls and corners of the room in shadows until a conduit of light opened in the air above the angel, like a lighted path leading to another world, and he ascended up into it until he disappeared. The room fell dark with only the light from the lamp downstairs filtering up past the ladder and playing an uncertain yellow light across the rafters. Joseph fell back against the slanted wall of the loft, the rough wood of the roof beams digging into his back. He was with his brothers—all five of them—but they slept on, a deep sleep sealing their eyes shut and keeping them from the slightest movement about their beds. None of them were disturbed by the brilliant light or the sound of Moroni's visit that lasted a good while longer than any sermon by the ministers in town. Joseph ran his fingers through his hair. How was he to remember all this? The messenger told him things he'd never supposed, prophecies he'd never imagined would be fulfilled in his lifetime. Did Moroni really mean that Joseph had a work to do? There was a book of gold deposited in the drumlin south of the farm—that much he remembered, what with the image of the hill firmly rooted in his mind. But all those scriptures he'd quoted were difficult to remember, and everything Moroni said about the fullness of the gospel and the fulfillment of ancient prophecies were a blur beyond what he could hope to remember unless he could hear them again and keep them firmly planted in—

"Joseph." Moroni stood in the air above him just as he had the hour before. He was dressed in the same robe, the loft filled with the brightness of his sudden return. He stretched his arms out and said, "I am Moroni, sent from the presence of God." He spoke with the same gentle but firm voice as he did in his first visit, assuring Joseph that his sins were forgiven, and then he said, "God has a work for you to do."

Moroni repeated the scriptures and prophecies from the first visit, carefully explaining when they would be fulfilled and affirming Joseph's part in their fulfillment. And then he added that there were wars and judgments and pestilence that were to come upon the earth in the last days. Then he ascended up a conduit of light, and he was gone the same way as when he left the room before.

Joseph fell back against the wall, his hands bracing him against the floor. Was he the only one of all his brothers who could see this visitor? They were still asleep in their beds, but there was no sleep powerful enough to shut Joseph's eyes, regardless of the fact that he'd spent the day with his brothers harvesting wheat and the evening hours digging for Joshua Stafford. How could Joseph sleep after seeing an angel and hearing him tell of a book he was to translate? Was he to be a scribe like the ancient writers of the Bible who copied down prophecies and passed them from generation to generation? Why him? Why did the angel choose Joseph for this work? He wasn't a good writer, not by anyone's imagination. Joseph held up his hands, and in the dim light flickering up from the kitchen below the loft he examined the callouses. He was a farmer, not a scribe, and he had to earn money, however he could, to keep from losing this farm. There wasn't time to write a book, even if he had the skills of an author, or what was it the angel called it? Translate. That was it. He was to translate a record with the help of stones called a Urim and Thummim. If these plates deposited in the hill were made of gold, they had to be worth a wagonload of money. He could translate the record and then sell off the gold. That would be a decent wage for spending his time translating instead of digging for the likes of Farmer Stafford. Joseph slowly raised his gaze from his calloused hands. Was the old farmer right? Were there really spirits leading men to treasure buried in these parts? It was all so very strange, and if he couldn't sleep, he could at least go downstairs and get a drink of water. Joseph started to pull himself off the floor when the same messenger stood beside his bed, engulfed in the same bright light, and wearing the same loose-fitting robe. He repeated all he had said the first two times, then said, "Because of the poverty of your family, Satan will tempt you to use the plates for the purpose of getting rich. You can have no other object in getting the plates beyond building the kingdom of God. If you have any other design, you will not get them."

Moroni repeated the warning that Joseph's preoccupation with the poverty of his family would tempt him to the very limits of his understanding, then he ascended for the third time up the conduit of light and disappeared into heaven. The room faded to shadows, and as soon as it fell dark, the cock in the barnyard across Stafford Road crowed loudly enough to wake Alvin. He stirred in his bed, rolled out from beneath the comforter, and stumbled to the ladder. He was a tall, sturdy man, and his sandy brown hair stuck up off his head like the crown of a rooster. He matted it down with his hand, pulled on his trousers, and strapped his boots. Before disappearing down into the main room, he mumbled something about rousing Hyrum and hoping that Joseph had a good night's rest—they had to harvest a full acre of wheat before the end of the day if they hoped to finish reaping before the frost took their crop.

Joseph sat on the end of his bed and slowly buttoned his shirt. The visits from the angel had lasted the entire night, but the wonder of it all was turning quickly to weariness. He climbed down into the kitchen where Mother was busy preparing an early breakfast. The girls were still sleeping in their room, and Joseph downed three cakes off the griddle and chased them with a glass of water.

Lucy said, "Did you sleep well?"

Joseph peered across the room at her, the lack of sleep blurring his sight. Should he tell her of last night's vision? His soul told him he should, but he'd not mentioned his first vision to her. Reverend Lane forbade him to share it with anyone, and how could he explain something that he barely understood? If Mother didn't believe him, then who would? He couldn't tell her or anyone else about either of his visions. They were far too out of the ordinary to be believed. They'd call him a visionary—or worse, they'd think him possessed by spirits like all the money diggers in the county, and then what would he do if his own family didn't believe him?

"Son, are you feeling well?" Lucy crossed the kitchen, pushed Joseph's hair back, and ran her hand across his brow. "You're white as a sheet, and your eyes are red as a fire poker."

Joseph took another cake from the griddle and headed out the front door, but before the wood planks hit against the post he said, "I'm well enough, Mother."

The family wheat fields stood behind the unfinished house, and when Joseph turned past the wood frame of the first story he found Papa and Alvin taking turns working a scythe through the stand of golden brown wheat still wet from the dew of morning. The rising sun brightened the eastern sky, but the sun hadn't come up over the trees beyond the rise at the back of the wheat fields. Joseph slowly climbed over the timber fence edging the field and started down through the already-harvested section, gathering the felled wheat into stacks to keep it away from the moisture on the ground. He reached Papa's side and waited for his turn with the reaper. The impression that he should stop them from their harvesting and tell them of his vision filled his soul. It was the same impression he'd gotten inside with Mother, but he couldn't tell them. What if Papa didn't believe him? What if he sided with Reverend Lane and told him that he was a backsliding sinner and he should give up his work with the money diggers or risk suffering the folly of their company?

Papa finished another pass through the wheat, but when he handed the reaper over to Joseph, he lost his grip on the wooden handle, and it fell to the ground, the long, heavy blade driving into the moist soil and missing Alvin's foot by a hair.

"Joseph!" Alvin pulled the reaper out of the ground. "You nearly shaved off my toes."

"Son, you're not well." Papa stepped to Joseph's side and studied his face. "Not well at all. You've lost all your color. Go inside and rest. Alvin and I can get along a while without you."

Joseph trudged back across the field, his boots dragging in the rich black earth, his shoulders slumped forward and his head down. He reached the timber fence, but when he climbed the rungs, his head started spinning, the dizziness sending him to the ground. He fell face-down, and when he rolled onto his back he found Moroni standing in the air above him. The angel repeated everything he told Joseph during the night and then ordered him to get off the ground and go to his father, informing him that these revelations were no longer personal visions. Joseph had a work to do—a marvelous work prophesied by all the holy prophets since the beginning of time when all things were to be restored to the earth, even a marvelous work and a wonder prophesied by Isaiah and Jeremiah—and if his name were to be had for good and ill across the entire earth, he was going to have to begin sharing his visions. For now they were to be kept within his family, but soon they would go to the entire world like an angel flying through the midst of heaven, sounding a trumpet and having the everlasting gospel to preach to all men. Moroni said, "Now go. Tell your father what I've told you."

Joseph dusted off his shirt, brushed the wheat stalks from his hair, and started back across the field. When he told Papa what had happened during the night, Papa didn't rebuke him, didn't say a word about visionaries or backsliders or revivalists or money diggers. He lowered the reaper to his side, laid his arm on Joseph's shoulder, and said, "Go right away and see to this thing."

Joseph found his way onto Stafford Road and headed south a mile past a forested plot of land before turning off the road and cutting across two farmers' fields and onto Canandaigua Road—the main highway leading south from Palmyra. He could see the hill from here, the summit rising above the horizon like a beacon above the lay of the land, and the closer he got, the faster he strode. There was a book of gold in the hillside—there had to be. He could see in his mind's eye the place where it was hidden, the vision of where it lay riveted into his memory like a map of buried treasure.

The drumlin stood nearly two miles from home, back a few hundred feet off Canandaigua Road. The steep northern slope was an open pasture dotted with grazing milk cows. The south slope was hidden under a thick stand of oak and maple, but up there, near the top of the west-facing slope, there were some scattered trees exactly as Joseph had seen in his mind. He scaled the hillside, the excitement of finding the treasure pushing his tired legs. He rounded a small rise near the top, worked his way across the summit through thick grasses and down through a run of tall trees until he came across a flat stone the size of a wagon stoop, half hidden in the growth. He fell to his knees and cleared away the soil and brush, exposing the width and length of the capstone. It was too large for him to lift alone; he found a fallen branch among the trees, pried it under the lip of the stone, and pushed on the end of the lever.

The capstone came up off its moorings, and the ancient air sealed for centuries inside the cemented vault rushed out in a soft gasp. The light of morning filtered down into the box and spread over the golden hue of metal plates in the center of the underground receptacle. It was exactly as the angel had told him. Three rings held the plates together, the metal sheets filled with curious ancient characters. Next to the record sat a silver bow with two clear stones cradled in the center like spectacles, but far too large to be fastened about the ears. And that wasn't all. There was a double-edged steel sword with a gold hilt decorated with jewels, and next to it was a tarnished spherical ball with spindles like a compass. There were some scratches in the brass ball and a small dent along one side, but the three spindles were perfectly balanced on the fulcrum of the compass. And next to the metal ball, set just inside the edge of the stone box, was another record, this one a darker greenish-orange, like copper or possibly some sort of aged brass.

Joseph knelt along the edge of the stone box, the Palmyra sun casting the first light over these relics in two millennia. The treasures could do more than purchase the farm from the land agent. There was enough precious metal here to make the family wealthy beyond their dreams, and just at the perfect time when Mother and Father were getting older and past the days when they should spend so much time in hard labor. This was an answer to prayers. It could be the end of their troubles—a passage to a better life.

As Joseph reached into the stone box to take out the gold plates, a violent shock pulsed through him with the power of a lightning strike strong enough to throw him back into the tall grasses. He shook his head and pushed aside the green blades. What was that? There wasn't a storm brewing in the sky above the drumlin with enough power to send a bolt to the earth. He crawled back to the edge of the stone box and reached inside, but the lightning hit him again, throwing him farther back, the sting of it shaking his limbs. What power protected these relics? The plates were right there in front of him, their golden color shimmering in the morning sun and mixing with the precious silver of the Urim and Thummim and the brilliant shine of the sword, the light bending around the curious spherical compass and the stately reflection of the brass plates. What an awful twist of fates. These were treasures that money diggers wagered their lives to find. Just last night he tried to talk Farmer Stafford out of searching for buried treasure, told him he was wasting his time; and now he'd found what the poor man couldn't. He was close enough to touch the plates, and he extended his hand one more time to see if he could take the gold record out of the—

The powerful surge of lightning hit him a third time, forcing him onto his back and numbing his arms. He held his hands to his head, rubbed the throbbing pain from his skull, and in the quiet of this hilltop he cried, "Why can I not obtain this book? What force is it that keeps me from—?"

"Joseph." Moroni stood in the air above the stone box, his white robe brighter than the midday sun. "You cannot get the plates because you have not kept the commandments of God."

Joseph struggled back onto his knees and inched to the edge of the stone box. The warnings the angel gave him last night flooded his mind. He was to have no other design than to build the kingdom of God, but he'd gotten carried away. He'd gone against the commands of an angel no less, and there was no way he'd be forgiven for trying to take these treasures out of the box to see how much money he could earn by selling them. Joseph lowered his gaze from Moroni, but instead of a fierce rebuke from the angel, his mind was filled with a vision of the evil working against him. For a moment, the veil of his mind was lifted, and he could see the darkness of the adversary—a man dressed in terrible flowing black robes tempting him to be like the money diggers and seek after riches.

"All this is shown to you." Moroni raised his hands, the wide cuffs of his white robe falling away from his wrists. "The good and the evil, the holy and the impure, the glory of God and the power of darkness—all this is shown to you that ye may know hereafter the two powers and never be influenced or overcome by that wicked one."

Moroni told him that he was to return in one year without fail, and when he said the date, it was as if he were speaking of the precision of a heavenly calendar, the timing of his next visit calculated in the heavens and fitted carefully into the hourglass of eternity. Joseph was to return here next September twenty-second, and no other day would suffice. The angel reiterated that he was to come back in twelve months' time, precisely on the same day, telling Joseph that he was not prepared to receive the record—he had much to learn and much to do before it was entrusted to him. Moroni said, "The time appointed since before the foundation of the earth to bring forth this record of the covenants comes quickly, and then you will have these plates of gold."

A bright conduit opened in the air like the drawing back of an invisible curtain, and Moroni departed up into it, the brilliance gathering around him until Joseph was left standing beside the opened stone box with only the dullness of the midday sun to illuminate the precious relics that lay at his feet. This small plot of rich, grassy soils in upstate New York held treasure far richer than the greatest discoveries on earth, and it was no wonder Satan was abroad in this countryside, spreading rumors of riches buried beneath the ground. What a fool he was to believe the stories of money diggers. Spanish invaders and British soldiers from the revolution didn't bury these records. They were sacred relics left here by the prophet Moroni before he passed from this life, and Joseph was just now beginning to understand his part in this ancient story. He ran the toe of his boot along the edge of the box and let the possibilities of the past rise up from inside this stone arc like an ancient voice from the dust rising out of the ground. He'd been called to do a work. What was it that Moroni called it last evening? Translate. That was it. Joseph was called to the work of translating this ancient record, but not now, not until the day when God would awaken to a remembrance of His covenants with Israel and set His hand a second time to gather His people. That's what Moroni called it—a remembrance of God's covenants with Israel. He didn't entirely understand what that meant, but if Moroni wanted him to come looking for this book of plates atop this drumlin next September twenty-second, then that's exactly what he'd do. One year from today Joseph was to come back and collect the gold record and begin the work of translation. He was a seventeen-year-old lad with no more schooling than what he gleaned from Mother's winter reading and writing lessons around the hearth when she taught him his letters, but he had no other choice than to do as Moroni instructed. In one short evening his entire life was turned on its head. Yesterday, Joseph was the fourth son of a wheat farmer. Today he was a modern-day Moses.

Joseph lifted the capstone on its edge, leveraging it out of the grass with help from a gnarled tree branch, the side of the flat stone balanced on the edge of the ancient box. He steadied the capstone, his shoulder pressed against the rough surface, his hands holding it back from falling into place and allowing him one more examination of the treasures. The codex of brass sat in the corner directly below his right boot, the tarnished record overshadowed by the brilliance of the gold plates, the wonder of the silver spectacles, the allure of the spherical metal compass, and the might of the ancient sword kept bright these many years. What Joseph didn't know was that the brass record was the link tying him to a story that began 2,421 years earlier when the codex was guarded in the vaults of Captain Laban's treasury. Moroni's visit made Joseph part of that ancient story. Joseph slowly tipped the capstone into place, shutting away the brass plates inside their ancient hiding place with a loud clap of stone on stone like the thunder atop Sinai at the first celebration of *ha-Zikkaron,* sealing Joseph's destiny with them.

Joseph Smith Jr. was the prophet of a latter Day of Remembrance.

CHAPTER 3

—Late Summer, 598 B.C.
Jerusalem

Captain Laban stood near the main doors of the Citadel Building, half hidden behind the giant, stone-entry columns. He adjusted the collar of his tight-fitting black tunic against the cool evening air. It was informal attire for a meeting in the council chambers, but the Chief Elder had warned him to come after dark and to dress down—no captain's shirt, no cloak, no riggings, and no breastplate.

The doors swung open, and Lieutenant Daniel stepped out into the night. His wide shoulders spanned the distance between the doorposts, and the light from inside silhouetted his sturdy frame. He wore a thin beard trimmed to the same length as Laban's, and the narrow band of hair colored his chin black. The only flaw in the boy's appearance was the black patch over his left eye. Curse Daniel's brother, Aaron, for blinding him. He'd killed Aaron for his foolishness, but how could he have a half-sighted officer as his second in command? There wasn't another with Daniel's strength or skill with a sword, and hopefully that was enough to preserve the loyalty of the soldiers under the boy's command.

Daniel adjusted the patch over his eye and said, "It's all clear inside, sir."

Laban quickly stepped past Daniel and ducked inside. The hanging lamps burned low this late in the evening and cast long shadows over the main chamber. There were no accountants or lawyers doing business, no merchants paying their tax, no one but Laban and Lieutenant

Daniel to divide the emptiness between them. Laban climbed the first flight of stairs with Daniel beside him, and when they reached the door to the council chamber on the fifth floor he said, "See that I'm not disturbed."

A bright fire burned in the hearth along the far wall, the reflection of firelight dancing on the polished marble floor and lighting the ground around the Chief Elder's sandal-shod feet. Zadock sat at a table near the balcony, the silk curtains rising and falling around him on a warm, late-summer breeze. His red cushioned chair was pushed up next to the table, and his long fingers were running over a leather accounting scroll. A gold amulet hung from his neck like a carpenter's plumb, swaying with the subtle movement of his reading.

"Where's your sword?" Zadock spoke without raising his gaze from the scroll.

Laban pulled the door shut, sealing Daniel in the quiet of the hallway and stopping the breeze from streaming in off the balcony. He waited for the silk curtains to still before saying, "I never take it out in public."

"This is hardly a public meeting." Zadock turned to another leather parchment and continued reading. "Is the weapon secure?"

"What sort of question is that?"

"And the brass record?"

"Tell me you didn't summon me at this hour to fret over my relics."

"You should worry more and drink less."

"I'll do as I please with my wine."

"The relics aren't yours, Captain."

"We agreed never to mention Lehi."

"The relics are the inheritance of a king, not a military captain."

Laban lowered his voice to a whisper. "You're a fool."

"Do you know of another king in this city beyond Zedekiah?"

"I said, no more."

Zadock set aside his reading and peered down the length of the table. "You're to turn your sword over to Zedekiah the first day of next month during the feast celebration."

"I can't believe I'm hearing this."

"Neither will the princes and nobles of the city when Zedekiah makes a bizarre claim to your relics."

Laban slammed his fist to the table. "Have you lost your mind?"

"It isn't my mind that will suffer a loss." Zadock set a small linen cloth on the table and pulled back the ends of it, exposing a white powder with the texture of salt, the crystals hanging together in small clumps. Laban poked his forefinger though the mix and held it to his nose. It had the sickly smell of sour goat's milk, and when he touched his tongue to the end of his finger, the stinging taste shot through his mouth like the juice of a rancid lemon.

"It's opium," Zadock said in answer to Laban's scowl. "It loses its edge when mixed with mint tea. Did you know Zedekiah takes a cup three times a day?"

"I don't make a habit of noting the tea-drinking conventions of the royal family."

"You inherited the relics from your father, and he from his father." Zadock covered the powder with the edges of the linen. "And they from Hoshea, the last king of the Northern Kingdom."

Laban rubbed his finger clean on the tail of his tunic. "I didn't come here for you to point out my genealogy."

"The point is, Captain, there isn't a Jew in Jerusalem who doesn't believe the relics are your royal birthright. And when a half-crazed, hallucinating Zedekiah demands that you bring him your sword, insisting it belongs to him, there isn't a prince or noble in the city who won't believe the man's gone mad enough."

"Mad enough for what?"

Zadock pushed the chair back from the table, the legs grating over the stone. "Enough to murder his sons before turning the blade on himself."

"There isn't enough of your white powder in all Israel to turn Zedekiah into a murderer."

Zadock slammed his fist to the table. "It's better that Zedekiah and his sons should perish than that this nation should dwindle and perish under his rule."

Laban straightened his shoulders, his tunic pulling taut across his chest. Zadock was right. Laban was better suited to rule this kingdom. He was a warrior, and Zedekiah was nothing more than an educated noble. Laban was decisive where Zedekiah wavered. He was proven on the field of battle while Zedekiah was without any experience leading a nation against Babylon.

Zadock said, "The king will be making a feast at the palace on the eve of *ha-Zikkaron*. Every prince and noble in the city will be in attendance." He leaned over the table. "You're certain the relics are safe?"

"They never leave my treasury."

"What about the watch?"

"I have two men assigned day and night."

"That isn't enough."

"No thief has ever gotten in."

"There's never been a threat like this."

The doors to the council chamber swung open, and the old jailer stood in the entry, the sudden draft lifting the silk curtains on the balcony. Lieutenant Daniel stepped around in front of the man. "He insists you sent for him. He says you—"

Zadock said, "Let him pass."

The old jailer wore a long, gray beard, and he walked with a limp, the heel of his left sandal dragging across the stones. He stopped in front of Laban, raised his gaze from the floor, and said, "It's Jeremiah, sir. He thinks to steal the brass plates from your treasury."

Laban said, "What foolishness is this?"

"Jeremiah's no fool, sir." The old jailer pushed a scraggly strand of hair back off his brow. "The man cursed Hananiah to death." He tipped his head toward Daniel. "Your lieutenant here found the man dead in his bedroom, and now Jeremiah sits in prison for the murder, but no one knows how he did it. It was a curse, I tell you—the curse of a prophet."

Zadock said, "What the good jailer is telling you, Captain, is that your relics aren't the only thing in danger."

"What sort of curse did he utter?"

Zadock lowered himself into the angle of his chair and turned his head back into the scrolls. "Death to any man who stops him from taking your plates of brass."

"I heard the curse fall from his lips, I did." The old jailer stepped closer to Laban. "Said he was going to thieve the plates in twenty-eight days, and he cursed to death the man who tries to stop him. Said he'd take them on the first day of the seventh month."

Laban said, "Then kill him before the end of the sixth month and be done with him."

The old jailer said, "I wouldn't, sir. Not if you don't want his blood to haunt you the rest of your life."

Laban lowered his voice to a whisper. "Twenty-eight days?"

"That's right." Zadock slowly nodded. "The same day you deliver your sword to the palace."

"Then we find a better day for Zedekiah to claim my sword."

Zadock said, "There isn't another day when the nobles will be gathered to the palace."

Laban rubbed his thinly bearded chin between his thumb and fore-finger. He had to protect his relics from the foolishness of Jeremiah's claims—and they were foolish to be certain. The old prophet's curses were nothing more than delusions, but to be sure the man didn't ruin their plans for the relics, he said, "There's a stone mason in the lower city." He marched to Daniel's side. "Hire him to chisel a vault in the wall of my treasury and have your blacksmith father forge an iron door for a vault. I want my relics sealed away before the feast day."

Daniel stood to attention. "Shall I double the watch in the treasury?"

"Triple it. And keep a watch on the palace prison." Laban turned to the old jailer. "If Jeremiah attempts an escape, kill him."

The old jailer said, "But sir, he's—"

"Watch him."

Zadock stood from his chair and walked to Daniel's side. "Assign a watch to look after Captain Laban until after the Feast of Trumpets."

Laban said, "I don't need an escort."

Zadock said, "I want you alive when this is finished."

"I can look after myself for twenty-eight days."

"Remember Hananiah, sir?" The old jailer limped around in front of Laban and ran a finger across his throat. "He tried looking after himself."

"Enough of this." Laban pushed the old jailer aside and started out of the chamber. "I'll behead anyone who stands between me and my plates of brass."

CHAPTER 4

Lemuel tested a pile of camel dung with the toe of his sandal. Curse his bad luck! It was the only pile in the entire corral and far too fresh to fuel the cooking fires. Why did good fortune never smile on him? He never beat his brothers at horse racing. He didn't possess Sam's quick wit or Nephi's steady bow-arm, and it was nothing short of a miracle to beat Laman in a game of chance. Thankfully he had nothing to wager beyond the clothes on his back, or Laman was certain to . . .

Where was Laman, anyway? He was to help collect fuel for the fire. Lemuel kicked at the dung, and the rotten-smelling stuff stuck to his sandal. See there, he was cursed with a fool's luck. He shook his foot until the dung came loose, flew through the air, and landed at the foot of—

"Laman? Where have you been?"

"I have a wager for you," Laman said.

"That isn't what I asked." Lemuel pointed across the river. "Stack the dried dung near the fire pit."

"It's a harmless gamble," Laman persisted.

"None of your ventures are harmless."

"What's there to lose in this desert?"

"I never beat you at numbers, I don't win at pitch and toss, and I won't let you talk me into—"

"You know what the wise men say about luck." Laman reached into the leather pouch at his waist and pulled out two smooth stones. "God decides the lot of men by how these fall."

"Those are soothsayers, not wise men."

"I see good fortune for you this time."

"I won't do it." Lemuel pushed Laman's lot-bearing hands aside. "I'm finished losing."

"Look around you, brother. We've lost everything." Laman raised his hands to the desolate rock cliffs. "This God-forsaken valley is two hundred miles from nowhere, and Father keeps us here on the notion he's saving us from the destruction of Jerusalem. You can at least entertain yourself with a wager."

Lemuel rubbed the sleeve of his robe between his fingers. "What sort of wager?"

"If they end like this, you win." Laman held both stones with the marked sides facing up. "And if they fall like this, you win again." He turned them over exposing the two unmarked sides.

"Win what?"

"You sit in the shade of the date palms, sip cool spring water, and watch me collect the dung."

"And if I lose?"

"There's hardly a chance of—"

"None of your speeches. What's my lot if I lose?"

Laman turned the marked side of one stone up, then turned up the blank side of the other. "If they fall like this, you gather dung for the fires until the day Father comes to his senses and we leave this forsaken place and return to Jerusalem."

Lemuel shook his head. "I won't hear any more of this."

"The odds favor you."

"I won't have you speaking of Father like he's gone mad." Lemuel glanced down at the river, and the memory of the rainy day when Lehi followed them down the granite canyon to the shores of the fountain of the Red Sea flooded his mind. Papa begged Lemuel to be as steadfast and as immovable as the towering granite walls in the canyon, and he warned Laman to be like this river, continually flowing into the fountain of righteousness.

Laman said, "The sooner you forget the past, the sooner we'll gain Father's ear and convince him to return home."

"You can say whatever you want about going home, and I'll agree with all of it, but no more talk of Father losing his mind." Lemuel stepped back from his brother. "You were the one who was mad."

"I was tired."

"You had a knife."

"We'd been traveling for days."

"I was right behind you when you went down in the river and the dagger fell from under your shirt."

"I was cold. Both of us slept on an outcrop in the middle of a raging torrent."

Lemuel lowered his voice. "You were going to murder Father."

"Do you want to wager or not?" Laman shook the lots, and the sound drew Lemuel back to him. Could he trust his brother? He was cleverer than any of the others, but his genius wasn't encouraging. Laman was a shrewd man, and though it was better to be with him than against him, he'd lost to Laman's treachery before. Thankfully, the odds were in his favor, and what harm could be done if he had to collect dung for the fire a few times each month? Laman was offering two out of three chances to win. He snatched the stones and ran his fingers over the smooth surface. There were no markings on one side, and when he turned them over, the tip of his finger traced along the deep etching of the "X" engraved into the granite. They were weighted evenly, exactly the same size with the "X" cut in the center. He shook them, but when he cocked his arm to cast, Laman grabbed his fist and kept him from letting go. He said, "I do the casting."

Laman forced open Lemuel's fist and took back the lots before clearing the ground with his boot and exposing the canyon bedrock.

Lemuel leaned over with Laman behind him. "Be good to me, stones."

Laman didn't cast the lots immediately, and Lemuel said, "Go on, throw the stones." He shook his fists at the spot of ground in front of him, but still Laman didn't cast the lots, and when he glanced over his shoulder he saw his brother adjusting the pouch on his belt before tossing the first one into the air. It spun end over end in a high arc and clapped onto the hard ground with the unmarked side showing.

Lemuel said, "Now the other."

The second lot landed with the deep-cut etching of the X facing up.

"Curse my lot." Why did he ever believe he could win? He kicked the ground, the toe of his sandal flicking the stone over and exposing another identical etching of an "X." He fished the blank stone off the ground, and it was without markings on either side. His brother had switched the stones. There was no other explanation. Lemuel threw the lots at Laman's feet and ran at him with fists swinging.

"You cheated me!"

River water seeped into the clay pit and pooled around Sam's ankles. It was a curse that the finest clay stood at the mouth of the canyon. Cool air streamed through two miles of sheer granite walls from the fountain of the Red Sea and chilled his mud-soaked body. He went to his knees and dug an armful of clay. How did he ever let himself fall so low? He was caravan master of Jerusalem's finest camel herd, not a clay digger. They should be trafficking in gold, or silver, or olive oil—anything but mud. Sam peeled a layer of red earth off his fingers. Mucking through clay was nothing like reading maps and plotting a course across the deserts of Sinai. He was neither a clay digger nor a potter, but in this forsaken valley there was nothing to trade. All of Sam's training—the years he studied in the map room, apprenticed in the animal corrals, and drove the camel herd over the trade routes to Egypt—was wasted unless he returned home where his skills and business sense were sure to win him a comfortable life.

Sam carried an armful of mud to the edge of the pit and threw it on a growing pile. Was he condemned to exchange his caravanning for the life of a clay digger? He shook the mud from his arms and spattered red earth across the backs of the other diggers. Thankfully they didn't complain, what with all of them bathed in clay. Commander Yaush and his son Setti had arms as red as the ground. Nephi's hair was spattered with clay. Moriah's dark brown skin was now a shade of bright red, and Hagoth's beard had lost all its black color. They were desert nomads, dressed in nothing but kilts, scraping the clay from the bottom of the pit with no tools beyond their bare hands.

Sam walked another load of clay across the pit, his toes pressed into the slippery earth to keep him from going down. In Jerusalem, they purchased their pots at market, but there was no going back to make a purchase. For the love of heaven, there was no going back for anything. It was an awful twist of fates. They were among Judah's wealthiest families, condemned to live out their days in the shadows of this forgotten valley, digging mud with their hands like Hebrew slaves in the mud-brick pits of Goshen.

"Cheer up, son." Hagoth stood along the edge of the pit with the only shovel among them—a make-shift scoop hewn from the dead limbs of a date palm. He leaned on the handle. "There's plenty of clay for our needs."

Sam didn't answer. How could he tell Hagoth he wished the man was wrong? There was enough clay along with fresh water, dates, and grains growing along the edge of the river to keep them supplied for however long they stayed.

Hagoth said, "Did you hear me, son? Cheer up, there's more than—

"He heard you, Papa." Moriah stepped between Sam and Hagoth with a load of clay.

"I was only cheering the boy."

"He doesn't need your cheer right now."

"He was always a lively lad until we reached the valley." Hagoth shoveled clay to the top of the pile and let the water drain out of the wet earth. "Now he hardly speaks a word." Hagoth pointed his shovel at Sam. "I don't mean to pry, son, but you're not your usual self, not by any measure. You've lost your sea legs."

Sea legs? Sam started back across the slippery clay pit for another load of mud without answering the old boat builder. This was no sailing voyage. It was a desert, and their journey would never take them across any waters beyond the puddles that formed in the bottom of this pit. Sam had trained all his life to run caravans halfway across the earth, and if he didn't find a way to return to the life he left behind he was going to suffocate in the stifling confines of this narrow valley. No matter how many times he heard Papa speak of a promised land, they were going to live like nomads in this place, die like bedouins, and be buried like paupers in unmarked graves. Sam wanted nothing to do with that future, though he kept silent his longing to leave. Silence was the only way to avoid the angry conversations with Laman and Lemuel, and he couldn't discuss the future with Lehi, not with Father insisting they stay in this valley until they were directed to leave. What sort of insanity was that? It wasn't like Lehi not to have a plan, but he said he didn't know when they would venture from this valley and he knew even less about where they would go if they decided to leave, except that there was another land of promise for them. Every time Sam pressed him on the subject, Lehi told him they would act as soon as God made it known to him exactly where they should go. Sam knelt on the wet floor of the pit and scraped together an armful of clay. There was no need to wait on direction from heaven. God already told the Jews where to find the promised land. Moses came to these forsaken deserts of Midian a thousand years earlier, and God told him the land of promise was north of here at Jerusalem. That was direction enough, and Father didn't need any more.

"Right over here, son." Hagoth pointed the end of his spade along the edge of the pit and told Sam to dump his next load there. He was a stout man with thick, calloused hands from years of boat-building. "You could at least let us know what's eating at your soul, boy. I'd never set sail with a man on my crew who didn't speak his mind. You can't trust a man who doesn't—"

"Papa." Moriah crossed the pit and threw his load down at Hagoth's feet. "Let him alone."

"It isn't good to fester in silence." Hagoth leaned over the edge, close enough to reach his hand onto Sam's shoulder. "You brood long enough, son, and it'll canker your soul." He slapped Sam on the back. "You were never anything but full of life before we arrived here, but something's soured your temperament. You've got to get over this or you're going to—"

"Enough."

"I hear you." Hagoth raised both hands to Moriah. "Leave the boy alone." He turned back to his shovel, whispering softly enough that Moriah couldn't hear him tell Sam it was for his own good and the good of everyone in camp for him to find whatever joy he could in their situation. But Sam found no cheer living in this wilderness. He was a prisoner, trapped by the will of a father he wasn't certain he could trust with their future—not with Laman questioning Lehi at every turn and Father never providing an answer beyond what he learned from his dreams. What sort of madness was this? If things didn't change soon, Father wouldn't be the only one losing his mind.

Sam had turned back across the pit to gather another load when he slipped. He grabbed Nephi's arm, but his reaching knocked both of them off balance, and they fell against Moriah and Setti, the four of them going down, the red-colored soup washing over them with a coat of clay from head to foot. Setti and Sam tried to stand, but the slick ground sent them down again.

"You're worse than a regiment of untrained soldiers." Commander Yaush walked an armful of mud past the tangle of arms and legs. "If I were commanding this patrol, I'd have you all assigned to dig out the sewer channel. And then I'd send the lot of you to—"

Setti caught his father by the ankle and tripped the commander to the ground. Hagoth jumped into the pit to help Yaush to his feet, but when the man's steady boat-builder feet hit the slippery clay, he lost his balance and fell into the heap.

Aaron marched down the path calling to them with news about a vein of coal in the cave up along the north rim, but when he found them lying in the mud, he began to laugh, telling them they were likely the worst gang of diggers to ever set foot in a clay pit. Aaron wore the same smile he had the day Sam first met him at the blacksmith shop in Jerusalem when he offered him work in their smithy at Beit Zayit. That was back when Aaron's feet were burned and he walked with a limp that hobbled his stride, but he was well enough now that he could . . .

"Run, blacksmith." Sam threw a handful of clay at him, landing it on Aaron's shoulder and spraying mud across his face.

Aaron threw a return volley, and Sam and Nephi ducked, the clay shooting past their heads and hitting Setti in the chest. Setti took aim at Aaron, but just as he released the mud, Moriah crossed his line of sight, and the clay ball hit the scribe in the back of the head. Moriah spun on Setti, fired a shot at him, and the pit erupted in a battle of flying clay. They were like children at play, and for a moment Sam forgot they were living in a lonely corner of the world. He threw another handful at Aaron, the mud splattering across his clean tunic. Sam was a great warrior, sighting his targets, his arms firing mud about the pit like he did when he was young and the rains softened the earth in the olive groves and he and his brothers played for hours on the land that was their inheritance, the land they left . . .

Sam lowered his throwing arm. He took a hit in the chest without returning a throw. The mud slid down his belly and fell into the puddle at his feet. He backed into the deepest, water-filled part of the pit, his feet stuck in a layer of mud.

"Sam?" Aaron lowered his aim. "What is it?"

He took two more hits—one from Moriah and another from Setti—before the clay pit fell silent, the laughter dying against the towering cliffs at the mouth of the lower canyon, the cool morning breeze rushing over them, chilling the silence. This wasn't the olive grove of Sam's childhood. It was a prison without any hope of escape, and Sam took another step back, his foot slipping but not sending him to the ground. He steadied himself, his feet half covered by a soup of red-colored water and his toes sinking into the muck. He tried to clean his hands, but it was hopeless; the red earth of this valley was stuck to him like dried mortar between heavy bricks and he may never get it off. He wrapped his arms around himself to warm him against the chilling breeze. "We never should have come here." His body began to tremble. "Father's a dreamer, and he has led us to the land of his dreams to die."

Nephi said, "He'd never do that to us."

"You'd best get used to this place, son." Hagoth pulled himself out of the pit. "Otherwise your father's dreams will become your nightmares."

"Papa." Moriah waved his hand at the boat builder. "Let him alone."

Sam said, "How do you know Father hasn't gone mad?"

Nephi said, "You've been listening to Laman again."

"I hear what Father says. He doesn't know where we're going from here."

"See this." Nephi opened his hand and held out a ball of red mud. "The prophet Isaiah wrote that we're all clay, and God is the potter, and we're the work of His hands."

"Isaiah didn't know of this madness."

"Lehi's our father. He's the potter and we're the clay, and a good potter would never lead the work of his hand into this wilderness to die. Lehi brought us here to save us."

Sam said, "Do you really believe that?"

"I prayed to know if I could trust Father." Nephi pressed the clay into Sam's hand. "The Lord softened my heart."

Sam slowly raised his gaze from staring at the clump of clay.

Nephi said, "We were led here by God."

"How can you be so sure?"

"I was visited by the Holy Spirit." Nephi leaned closer. "Heaven is watching over us."

There was no reason Sam should listen to his younger brother—this boy with dark curly hair gone red with a covering of mud. Wasn't Nephi the same boy who believed Sam when he told him he could climb the olive trees of the old vineyard to get to heaven? But Nephi wasn't a young boy any longer. Somehow, without Sam noticing, the youngest of all the brothers had become a man. He was always strong and stout beyond his years—a fine wrestler, a hardworking soul, and a studious lad—but somewhere in the run of years Nephi had stored up a reservoir of wisdom that was just now beginning to spill out of him. He was the one assigned the tasks about the estate that others refused to take, the funny toddler, the long-legged, awkward boy. But this morning he was nothing if not noble, covered with red clay from head to foot and standing with Sam in the middle of this cold clay pit, buoying Sam's spirits and helping him see what he could not see on his own. For the first time in his life, Sam understood that Nephi was more than Mother's youngest child. They were brothers, and he couldn't deny the power of Nephi's words, his certainty in chasing away the confused mix of anger and fear that had gripped him since abandoning their inheritance at Jerusalem. Nephi's deep brown eyes were filled with the intensity of his words, and his steady voice filled Sam with a peace he'd not known since before they left Beit Zayit. A tear burned in Sam's eye, and he quickly brushed it away. He threw the ball of clay to the ground. "I hope there's a land as fine as the one we left behind."

"There is, Sam. Somewhere there has to be a land of promise for us. God doesn't tell lies."

A cry from the corral echoed through the valley. It was Lemuel's voice, and it pierced the quiet scene like a call to war.

Commander Yaush said, "There's trouble with the animals." He climbed out of the clay pit and started up along the stream like a general marching to battle. "To the corral, boys."

Nephi ran through the river ahead of the others, the water washing away the red mud on his legs. He turned up the bank past the last date palm grove to find Sariah, Rebekah, and Sophia looking on as Lehi tried to stop Laman and Lemuel from struggling in the sand. Laman landed a blow across Lemuel's face, but when he raised his fist to swing again, Lehi took him by the arm and said, "Stop this."

Setti, Moriah, Yaush, Josiah, and Hagoth joined Sariah, Rebekah, and Sophia in a circle around Laman.

Sariah said, "What's the cause of all this?"

"He cheated me." A line of blood ran from Lemuel's nose and splattered off his lips as he spoke. "We cast lots, and Laman tried to—"

"Hold your tongue." Laman pulled free from Lehi's grasp and snatched the stone lots from Lemuel's hand.

Lehi said, "Is that what this is about? A wager?"

"It was a misunderstanding." Laman hid the stones in the palm of his hand before turning the full force of his gaze onto Lemuel. "Isn't that right, brother?"

Commander Yaush said, "A misunderstanding over camel dung?"

Lemuel wiped the blood from under his nose, and when he spoke he kept his gaze riveted on his older brother, the two of them locked in a silent battle. He slowly said, "It's over now."

Laman said, "It won't be over until we're gone from this place."

Sam said, "That's all you ever talk about."

"Someone has to remind you about what we left behind." Laman turned about the circle. "The rest of you are too frightened to speak of it in front of Father Lehi, but you think it. You all want to leave this place and return to the land of our inheritance, all of you."

"We can't go back." Nephi stood next to Lehi. "It isn't safe there."

"Then we make it safe." Laman worked the smooth stone lots between his fingers. "I can soften Captain Laban's heart."

Nephi said, "What about the Babylonians?"

"Ask him." Laman took Hagoth by the arm and stepped the boat builder forward. "Go on. Tell them what you told me. Tell them what you think of the Babylonian threat."

Hagoth pulled free of Laman's grip. "All I know is Inspector Tobit was a reasonable fellow."

Laman said, "That isn't all."

Hagoth said, "You were there. You know he treated us well."

Laman said, "Go on."

"He released us without any harm, and he made certain not to map the directions to this valley."

"What did he tell you when he let you go?"

"He said he wanted us to live our lives in peace as free men."

"You see there?" Laman raised an open hand to the others. "Father Lehi's talk of the Babylonians destroying Jerusalem is meant to frighten us, to keep us from returning to our homes."

Nephi turned to Lehi. "You wouldn't lead us from our lands unless it wasn't safe there."

"I've told you why we came here, son, but my words will never be enough." Lehi laid his hand on Nephi's shoulder. "Have you inquired of God about our coming to this wilderness?"

Laman said, "We don't need to pray to know that Captain Laban isn't hunting us any more."

Nephi said, "Tell them, Father. Tell them what you wrote in your journal about the destruction of Jerusalem and the promise of an inheritance of new land."

Laman came around in front of Nephi. "What parcel of land in this God-forsaken wilderness do you want to inherit?"

"Laman." Sariah stepped to her son with one hand on her belly and the other raised to her eldest son. "I won't hear any more of your harshness."

Nephi took Lehi by the forearm. "Tell them what you told me about your visions."

Laman said, "Reasonable men aren't led about by visions they see in the night." He held one of the stone lots between his thumb and fore-finger and pointed it at the men and women surrounding him. "When were any of the rest of you blessed with a vision?" He stopped the stone lot on Nephi. "Tell us, brother, have you been dreaming of the future? Can you lead us to this promised land, or is this valley as good as our inheritance will get? And why aren't the rest of us haunted by dreams of the destruction of Jerusalem?" He came back to Lehi. "We don't share your nightmares because there's no reason to fear the Babylonians. Hagoth told you how it is. The Babylonian inspector left us to live as we please."

Nephi said, "Father is a prophet."

Laman said, "He's an olive oil merchant."

Nephi said, "He saw a pillar of fire."

"Have any of the rest of you seen lights in the sky or heard voices from heaven?" Laman raised his hands to the circle of family and friends. "Have you?"

"Enough of this." Sariah walked to her husband's side and took his hand. "You were there when Lehi came down off the cliffs at Raphia a changed man. Don't you remember when he lay on his bed for three days, and we thought he was dying, but he was only sleeping for a time—lost deep in a vision of the council of heaven?" She took Aaron by the arm and pulled him over next to Lehi. "He healed this boy's feet. Isn't that enough for you?"

Laman turned his back on Aaron and faced Lehi. "Do you still believe Jerusalem will be destroyed, or can we reason with you, show you that the Babylonians are sensible men with no desire to destroy our land?"

Lehi said, "Our lives were in danger. That's why we left our home in Jerusalem. None of you doubt that, but many of you hope we'll return." He turned his gaze over the faces in the circle. "The Babylonians will not always be kind—not when the Jews at Jerusalem practice so much evil."

Laman said, "What's the real reason you're keeping us in this wilderness?"

"I brought you here to preserve your lives and our faith."

Laman said, "What faith?"

"I've told you of the Messiah." Lehi lowered his voice. "That six hundred years from now the Lord will raise up a Son to redeem us from our lost and fallen state."

"We're not lost." Laman turned to the gathering. "We know the way home."

Sariah took Laman by the arm. "Hold your tongue until your father is finished."

"You want to know the reason we're here, son?" Lehi's words settled over the gathering. He walked in front of Moriah and Setti, past Hagoth, Yaush, and Sophia over to where Rebekah stood with Aaron, the boy's muddy hand pressed in hers, and both of them listening to Lehi tell the story of the Messiah who would be baptized in the Jordan River—the

Lamb of God who would come to take away the sins of the world. Lehi pulled up beside Laman, explaining that this Redeemer would be slain for claiming He was the Son of God, but that He would rise from the dead. Lehi started back around in front of the gathering, telling them that their coming into this wilderness fulfilled the words of the allegory of the olive tree—that they, like many other Jews, would be scattered across the whole earth. Some had already ventured into the lands north of Jerusalem, and others would be taken to Babylon, but for them there was another land of promise. They were to be some of the branches of the olive tree planted in the nethermost parts of the vineyard, and they were going there to preserve the covenants given to all the prophets before them—preserve them for a generation living in the last days of the earth.

"Why do we listen to this foolishness?" Laman raised his hands to the valley around them. "Do you want to live here the rest of your lives?"

Nephi said, "If it was the will of heaven, I would."

Laman said, "My little brother, the zealot."

Lehi said, "If we return to Jerusalem we're all dead men."

Laman said, "You're the only man Captain Laban wants dead."

"Laman!" Sariah stood in front of him, her gaze turned up into his dark eyes. "It's true, isn't it? I didn't want to believe it before."

"Go back to your resting, Mother."

"How can I rest with this memory haunting me?" Sariah took Laman by the arm and pulled him back to her. "You were going to kill your father, weren't you?" She turned her gaze down toward the river. "You stood right over there with a knife under your shirt, trembling in the cool water, confounded by the very spirit of God that you reject." She let go of him. "And once you murdered your father, what then? Did you think to convince me to return to Jerusalem? And if I refused would you put a knife in me as well?" She turned to the others gathered around her. "And what of our friends? Would you run them off at the point of a knife, or would you slay all of us?" She lowered her head into her hands. "My son. My dear, firstborn son."

"You don't know my heart, Mother. And no man can know the future six hundred years from now." Laman spit at Lehi's feet. "That's what I think of Father's Messiah and his words of redemption and—"

"How dare you!" Sariah slapped Laman across the face hard enough that his head snapped to the side. She slowly backed away, her gaze shifting between her stinging fingers and her eldest son, the distance between them growing wider with each step. She tried to speak, but the words caught in her throat, and she turned away and started up along the stream, heading out of the valley in a stride made slow and labored from carrying her unborn child.

Nephi started after her, but stopped when Laman said, "Where do you think you're going?"

Nephi came back to Laman and stood close enough to feel his brother's breath on his face. If there were any reason to strike Laman, his words against his father's vision of a promised land, his mockery of the Messiah, and his harsh words toward his mother were more than enough, but Nephi kept his hands down, his fists pressed against his side. He leaned his head in and said, "I'm going to pray for you."

CHAPTER 5

—*Late Summer, 598 B.C.*
Upper Valley of Lemuel (Wadi Tayyib al-Ism)

Sariah reached the top of the canyon, up where their hidden valley leveled into a wide stretch of sand east of camp. The high canyon walls gave way to the open expanse of the main valley. And on the far eastern edge of the wadi, the morning sun rose above the inland chain of Border Mountains. She found a small outcrop, lifted herself onto a flat shelf, and leaned back against the rock before rubbing the sting out of her hand. She never should have struck Laman—no matter that he was growing more difficult the longer they tarried in this valley. Until now she couldn't bring herself to believe he would ever think to harm her husband. The morning they arrived here, Lehi warned her of Laman's temper, but when the boy stood trembling in the middle of the river, shaking and unable to speak—confounded by Lehi's words commanding him to stay back—she believed him distraught, confused, possibly sick from fever, but she never thought him a murderer. How could she? She was the boy's—

"Mother?" Nephi cleared the rise from camp and stood in the middle of the wadi, searching the empty sands. His clothing was stained with red clay, and his hair stood on end.

"Here." Sariah leaned up on the rock and waited for him to find her nestled against this east-facing outcrop, sitting in the warm morning sun that grew more uncomfortable with each passing moment. Nephi picked his way along the rocky crags marking the entrance to their hidden valley, up where they never ventured—at least not since coming here. If the Babylonian Inspector Tobit could find this place, then so could Captain

Laban. So they stayed out of the main run of this wadi to remain hidden from the eyes of men.

"You've gotten yourself dirty this morning." Sariah untied the head-band on Nephi's brow, combed his hair with her fingers, and matted down what she could of his curling locks that stood stiff with red clay. She patted him on both shoulders, but before she could tell him he was an obedient, patient child he said, "You shouldn't be up here."

Sariah set her hand over her womb and turned her gaze out across the open expanse of the wadi to the chain of mountains to the east— the mighty Borders near the Red Sea running out of the north, past the entrance to their camp and trailing off into the deserts to the south.

"Let me help you down from here." Nephi reached for her hand, but she pulled free of his firm grip—a grip that was stronger and more powerful than she ever remembered. He was growing older, his voice was deeper, and he had the thick frame of a man—a man who looked very much like his older brother Laman, and, heaven help him, a man with the same appearance as Captain Laban. "Let me sit a while longer." She turned her gaze out over the mountains, their rugged peaks rising and falling along the horizon. "I want to look across this valley and remember what I've not ever seen."

Nephi sat beside her and pointed to the highest peak in the chain northeast of camp. It had a wide base, and the peak was squared near the top with a rugged, horizontal summit reaching up into the mid-morning sky like an altar amid the clouds. He said, "Is that the one, Mother—the mountain you told me about when we first set eyes on this range?"

"The Israelite nation began there." Sariah leaned in next to him and sighted down his arm. "The same mountain where Moses spoke with God face-to-face."

Nephi said, "Can you find your way to camp?"

"Why do you ask such a thing?"

Nephi left her side and picked his way down the outcrop to the sands below.

Sariah said, "Where are you going?"

"There's something I must do."

Nephi started across the wide expanse of sand, headed toward the ridge on the other side where a narrow canyon traversed out of the wadi and into the valleys of the inland mountain range of the Borders near the Red Sea.

"Son?" Sariah slowly let herself down the rocky outcrop. "You're not to travel about these mountains. It isn't safe. What will I tell your father?"

Nephi turned in the warm sand made even warmer by the midday sun. "Tell him I'm searching for what Moses found."

"That was six hundred years ago." Sariah raised her voice loud enough that it echoed across the sands and died in the heat of late morning. "Come back before you get yourself lost and die of thirst in this desert."

"Never mind, Mother." Nephi started across the wadi. "I'm well enough off."

Well enough off? Heading out into the desert without even a water skin didn't conjure the notion of being well enough off, not by any measure. Where did the boy get such a foolish idea? He was headed into a land without a single charted well to keep him from thirst, and little if any shade from the hot afternoon sun that was sure to burn his mind senseless. He was a seventeen-year-old boy marching into the desert without any preparation or the sense he was born with. Sariah leaned against the outcrop, her hand over her brow, shielding her eyes from the brightness of the sun. She never should have told him about the history of these mountains. Her stories only stirred the depths of his soul. He was an obedient son, but when his heart called, no amount of motherly advice had power to turn him from his course. What was she to do with this boy who had the strength of Samson in his arms, but the heart of Isaiah in his breast? He was unlike any of her other sons. She could count on Laman's calloused manner, Lemuel's temperamental ways, and Sam's business sensibilities, but her Nephi was nothing short of impossible to understand. He was a hardworking son, and for that she was grateful. He understood the ways of his father's business, and for that the boy should be grateful—his industry was certain to bring him the comforts of this world. He was obedient without question, thrifty to a fault, and responsible beyond his years, but he was filled with a spirit that was out of place in the heart of a practical soul. He was a contradiction, a mix of traits that lay hidden these many years and were just now surfacing, marshaled into service by the harsh life in the rugged valleys and waterless climes of this desert. Sariah ran her hand over the rough sandstone outcrop. This wilderness was a sparse place to live, but it had power to tutor Nephi in the ways he should go, and she couldn't help but believe that they came to these waters of Moses, deep in the Borders nearer the Red Sea—the same valley where some of the Israelites camped more than six hundred years earlier—to school her youngest son in the same way that God prepared the Israelites to enter the promised land. Sariah steadied her hand on the rocky ridge. No matter how often Nephi claimed to be well enough off, she couldn't "never mind." This desert was doing more than transforming her youngest son into a man— Nephi was quietly becoming a man of God.

"Sariah, is that you?" Aaron cleared the sandy rise from camp, his long-legged stride quickly carrying him over the rugged stone from the sands below. He uncorked a water skin and handed the drink to her. "You worried us."

"It isn't me you should worry about." Sariah refused the water. "Take it to Nephi." She pointed out across the wadi. Nephi's blue-vested frame was a small speck against the towering ridge on the far side. "Follow him and see that he has enough water to get to the mountain and back again."

"Which mountain?"

Sariah raised her hand toward the highest peak in the range and softly said, "Sinai."

CHAPTER 6

—Late Summer, 598 B.C.
Jerusalem

Zoram climbed the steps out of the subterranean passages of the treasury and waited for the new watchmen assigned to the back door to let him out into the night. There was no reason to have two soldiers stationed here. No one but Zoram used the entrance, and he could let himself in and out on his own. The men stood at the top of the stairs with swords sheathed at their hips. Daggers sprouted from their belts, and their spears leaned against the doorpost next to a quiver of metal-tipped arrows and a wooden bow. These men were outfitted for a war in a treasury where never a thief dared enter.

Only a fool would think to steal from this treasury. The estate was guarded more heavily than Jerusalem's East Gate, but Lieutenant Daniel insisted on doubling the number of soldiers in the underground passages and adding a watch to the back door. And what was worse, there was no privacy. Zoram couldn't leave without a soldier wanting to know where he was going and when he was coming back. He couldn't bring out a broken repository jar for repair without the watchmen searching it to make certain Zoram wasn't taking anything of value from the vault. When did Zoram ever steal from his master? He was Laban's trusted servant, sworn to protect everything in the treasury, down to the very last shavings of gold and silver, and he wasn't about to break his oath. Laban's treasures were safe under his watch. And what did it matter if these watchmen treated Zoram like a thief? As long as Captain Laban lived, Zoram was sworn to be faithful.

Zoram said, "I have a key."

The watchmen nodded, but they didn't allow Zoram to let himself out. They unlocked the latch, and a rush of evening air slipped past the door post.

The first watchman said, "Are you taking anything out of the treasury this evening?"

Zoram raised his empty hands. "I have all the captain's silver and gold."

"That's what you said last night, sir."

"I'll share it with you if you agree not to search me."

The second watchman said, "Turn around, sir."

"Must we do this every time I pass?"

"Lieutenant Daniel's orders."

Zoram raised his arms and slowly turned around while the watchmen ran their hands down the vents and pleats of his white coat, feeling along his waistline and patting their hands down his leg. Zoram removed his sandals and let them check the leather insoles before taking them off the floor and carrying them in his hand.

The first watchman said, "Are you done with your work for the night?"

"I haven't the patience to have you check my robes more than once a day."

"So you won't be coming back this evening?"

"You ask the same question every night."

The second watchman came in beside his mate and nodded. "And you always say you'll return if you have a need."

The first watchman said, "Will you be having a need this evening?"

"When I come back for the captain's relics, neither of you will be searching me." Zoram took out the key hanging from a chain about his neck and let it dangle in the dim light of the passageway. "I'll walk them right past you, and you'll never suspect I'm stealing them."

"You've been saying that every day for a week, sir." The first watchman stepped aside to let Zoram pass, and before shutting the treasury door behind Zoram and leaving him in the darkness of the yard he said, "Enjoy the gold, sir."

It was a quiet evening without a breeze blowing over the high walls surrounding the property. Zoram latched his sandals to his feet and stepped down along the path behind Captain Laban's estate to his quarters—a small, single-story building attached to the back of the main house. He pushed open the door, ducked beneath the beam, slowly stepping his way through the shadows over to the table where he left the . . .

Where was the lamp? He felt about the rough surface of the small table, but it was gone. The oil lamp wasn't where he left it, and the flint was missing. He started across the room to the shelves along the wall, but bumped into a stool and—

"Is this what you're looking for?" A flurry of sparks shot through the darkness, and the lamp burst into flame, the orange light gathering around the stout, black-skinned frame of the new palace jailer, Ebed-Melech, the man who foiled their plot to free Jeremiah from prison. His shaved head glistened with a coat of olive oil, as did the skin on his arms and chest. He wore nothing but two straps over his thick shoulders, the leather cords attached to the waistband of his kilt. His legs were thick stumps, and his feet were shod with worn leather sandals, the laces frayed at the ends. His deep voice filled the dwelling. He said, "Your father, Jeremiah, sent me."

How did the jailer know he was Jeremiah's adopted son?

"You can trust me." Ebed set the lamp on the table, so close that Zoram could feel the flickering heat rise off the flame. "I'm a friend to your father."

That was impossible. He was the man who prevented Jeremiah from escaping the prison.

Ebed stepped to the half-open door and checked the yard before pulling back inside and setting the bolt. "It's about your father's prophecies." He latched the shutters on the windows. "The ones your father wants recorded in brass."

Zoram stepped to the shelves over against the far wall and retrieved a clay repository jar. He broke the wax seal, pulled up the lid and handed Ebed a single virgin sheet of brass, the orange metal reflecting the flickering light of the lamp.

"I smithed that to record my father's prophecies."

Ebed turned it over, searching the smooth finish. There were no writings on the plate, no etchings in the metal, nothing but a shimmering brass surface.

Ebed said, "There's nothing written here."

"I can't record the prophecies of a man shut up in prison."

"I'll let you in through the underground passages."

"You don't understand."

"Your father needs your help."

Zoram raised his voice. "There's nothing I can do."

Ebed stepped closer, his breath pulsing over Zoram with each word. "You can honor your father's wishes."

Zoram took back the brass plate and fitted himself into the angle of the chair. "I was never trained to write on metal." He leaned against the back rest. "It will take me years to etch Jeremiah's prophecies onto brass, and we haven't more than—"

"You have twenty-five days, boy."

Zoram leaned forward in the chair. "Did my father tell you that?"

"He said the time has come for the brass relic to leave the city and that you'd know what to do."

"I won't steal Laban's relic." Zoram removed his white turban, and the white cloth bands unraveled in his hands. "I've sworn an oath to the captain. As long as he lives, I'm to protect his plates of brass."

"Will you deny the will of God?"

"Would you have me sacrifice my honor?" Zoram pushed his chair away from the table, but the new jailer took him by the arm and said, "Your father cursed any man to death who has a hand in stopping the brass plates from leaving the treasury." He tightened his grip. "Deny me, and you fall under your father's curse."

Zoram pulled free. "Are you threatening me?"

"I'm warning you. Your allegiance to your father is stronger than anything you owe Laban."

"You misunderstand my loyalties."

"You can't serve two masters, boy."

Zoram hid the brass plate under his tunic, pushed past Ebed, and started for the door.

Ebed said, "Where are you going with that?"

Zoram unlatched the bolt, but before he headed out into the night he said, "To serve my other master."

CHAPTER 7

Zoram knocked until the sound of footsteps filtered through the thick cedar planks. The hinges turned in the pivot stone, and Baruch the scribe stood in the dim light of his porch, dressed in a plain brown evening robe. His cheeks glistened with perspiration from the warmth of the summer evening, and his hair sat atop his head in deep, gray furrows. He lowered his voice to a whisper and said, "We agreed never to meet." He scanned the darkness beyond the reach of the lamplight. "Not until the memory of Jeremiah's failed escape has passed."

Zoram handed over the brass plate, and Baruch ran his fingers over the surface before holding it up to the light and measuring its thickness. "Where did you get this?"

"You're trained in the art of writing on brass."

"Leather parchments and potsherds are less costly." Baruch pressed the plate between his fingers. "Why metal?"

"It has the same dimensions as the ones in Captain Laban's treasury."

"Tell me he isn't altering the relic." Baruch stepped closer. "Do whatever you can to convince him otherwise. The record is more precious than—"

"I'm the one altering the relic." Zoram stepped back from Baruch. "It has to be readied before it's taken."

"I won't let you steal the plates. It's a record of our past."

"It's a record of hope for the future, sir. What's written on the brass plates will be added to another record written on plates of gold to come forth in the last days of the earth."

"Where did you get such a notion?"

"Jeremiah's been telling me that since I was—"

Baruch held his hand to Zoram's lips and stopped him from saying more. He checked the darkened street before escorting Zoram inside and quickly closing the door. "I was afraid this was about your father." He lowered the plate to his side. "Laban will have your head for plotting to steal the relic from his treasury."

"I'm not the one taking the plates."

"Then who?"

"All I know is that I'm to prepare the plates with my father's prophecies before they're taken."

"This is absolute foolishness." Baruch tightened his grip around the virgin plate. "Have you read the brass record?"

"Laban doesn't allow it."

"If you had, you'd know what great loss you speak of." Baruch locked the front door. "Come with me."

The cool limestone walls of the corridor were adorned with the aging leather scrolls of Baruch's making—the same ones Zoram remembered viewing the last time he came here, though in his previous visit he didn't notice the flawlessness of Baruch's flowing script filling parchment after parchment with his artistry. The first two were copies of the words of Isaiah on goat leather. There was another of the prophet Micah's words written on gray ox hide, one containing the prophecies of Elisha, and two more quoting the words of the prophet Zenos. A run of royal letters graced the opposite wall of the hallway. There was a letter copied from the original border dispute between King Solomon and the Assyrians, another letter of psalms copied from the personal effects of the ancient King David, and letters from every monarch down to the reign of Josiah, the father of King Zedekiah—all of them copied onto newly tanned lambskin hides. This man was much more than a skilled keeper of documents or a gifted manipulator of a stylus. His home was the repository of the finest writings to grace the Hebrew nation since the days of the first Passover.

"Are you coming?" Baruch stood at the end of the hall, his long, thin fingers motioning Zoram to follow him inside. A large oil lamp hung from the rafters and cast a strong light over the shelves of scrolled documents and sealed urns filled with generations of scribing. The sheer volume of records enshrining this writing room were the efforts of a lifetime.

Five scrolls of the Law of Moses sat atop a pedestal near the entrance. Red tasseled cords lay across the Hebrew characters and hung over the edges of the partially opened parchments. The ends of the documents were darkened with age, and the fibers were worn thin, but they weren't coming apart. The surface was polished with oils to preserve the ancient words, the light reflecting off the leather like the polish on the stone tablets Moses first brought down off Mount Sinai.

"Every jubilee year the temple priests select a small number of scribes to make a copy of the law from the temple scrolls kept in the Ark of the Covenant before the aging scrolls wear away to dust." Baruch sat Zoram down in a cushioned chair in the corner of the writing room before standing next to the pedestal. "I was a young temple scribe back then, not nearly as well-known as some of the other scribes in the city, but I had the good fortune of being selected. And after copying down a good portion of the words of Moses with my own fingers, I thought I knew the law better than any man on earth until, of course, Jeremiah unlocked the mystery of these writings for me." Baruch ran his fingers carefully over the writings. "I never understood why the Creation was included here with the law until Jeremiah taught me that we were created in the image of God because it was the work and the glory of the Creator to bring to pass our immortality and eternal life." He stopped his fingers in the middle of the scroll. "Do you understand what that means? All men are the children of God; we're His offspring—His posterity—and these covenants will bring us back into His presence." He slowly raised his finger from the scroll and turned to Zoram, his hands folded in front of him. "Do you know what Jeremiah told me about his call as a prophet?" He turned his gaze out through the window. "He said that before he came forth out of his mother's womb as an infant babe, God sanctified him and ordained him in the heavens to be a prophet to the nations. Jeremiah understood what Moses and Abraham and all the holy prophets knew." He nodded slowly. "The covenants have power to keep us from being cast off forever, and the brass-plate relic in Laban's treasury is the last original copy of the Law left in the city; it is what points our souls to the Anointed One."

Zoram said, "Begin with that."

"With what?"

Zoram took the brass plate from Baruch. "Write on this metal that before God formed Jeremiah in the belly He knew him, and before he came forth out of his mother's womb He sanctified him a prophet."

An odd-shaped stylus with a thick wooden handgrip, along with a small hammer made of fine steel, sat on a shelf next to the writing table. They were the instruments of writing on metal plates, and Zoram handed them to Baruch. "Help me record my father's prophecies on brass and preserve them along with the writings of Moses."

Baruch refused the tools. "I'll teach you to write on metal."

"The plates are to be readied by the Feast of Trumpets."

"That soon?" Baruch laid both his hands atop the pedestal next to the aging parchments of the law. "How extensive are Jeremiah's writings?"

"There aren't any." Zoram slowly shook his head. "You'll have to record them as Jeremiah speaks them."

"How can I record the words of a man shut up in prison?"

"Ebed-Melech will let you in."

"Laban's men will be watching."

"No one will question what you do. You've recorded the words of more prophets than any scribe in the city."

"None of the others were the king's prisoner." Baruch slowly lowered himself onto his writing stool and rubbed his beard between his fingers. "How many visits will this require?"

"Until Jeremiah's finished."

"Your father's not short on words." Baruch leaned forward on the stool. "Do you have any idea how dangerous this is? If Captain Laban gets word I'm sneaking brass plates into the prison identical to his, he'll—"

"Copy Jeremiah's words onto leather parchments, then bring them here to your writing room and etch them onto brass."

"I'm old, son." Baruch slowly raised his hands. "My fingers aren't as strong as they once were. Can't you find another scribe?"

"What other scribe could I trust with this?"

Baruch set his hand on the writing table. "If word gets back to Zadock or Laban, there will be soldiers on my doorstep within the hour."

"We'll be protected."

"Where was our protection when we tried to free Jeremiah?"

"I'll send a messenger to fetch the finished plates and deliver new ones."

Baruch pushed the brass plate across the table toward Zoram. "How many plates can you smith?"

"Then you agree to help me?"

"How many plates, son?"

"As many as you need."

Baruch turned back to the pedestal bearing the scrolls of the Law. He ran his hand over the old polished leather, the words of Moses passing beneath his long, skillful fingers. "You have no idea the risks we're taking."

"What we do is worth any risk." Zoram stood next to Baruch. "Those who come after us must know what great things the Lord has done for our fathers."

"You really believe that, don't you? You believe this record will go to all nations."

"I don't know exactly how it will come about, but the brass plates will inspire a marvelous work that will rise out of the dust in the last days of the earth." Zoram handed the writing stylus and hammer back to Baruch. "My father calls it what Isaiah called it—a marvelous work and a wonder."

"Then for your father, and for Isaiah, and for all the holy prophets before them, bring me the finest plates of brass you can smith." Baruch retrieved a long key from a box atop the shelf and pressed it into Zoram's palm. "This will let you inside."

CHAPTER 8

—*September 22, 1824*
Palmyra Township, State of New York

Lucy Smith washed the tin plate in a basin of warm water and set it to dry on a linen towel spread over the table. Dinner was finished and still no sign of Joseph Jr. The boy's father, Joseph Sr., lingered in the main room, arranging the chairs and benches around the hearth like they did last year after their son told them about his visit with an angel and the finding of an ancient record written on gold plates buried in a hill not too far from their home. Lucy washed two more dishes and set them to dry with the others. Of all the young men in the township, why was her cheerful Joseph chosen to see such a marvelous vision? There was no doubting his word. Only an angel could have schooled her eighteen-year-old son to quote scriptures of the last days recounting the establishment of the kingdom of God on earth, and explain covenants recorded in the Bible that had power to turn the hearts of children to their fathers. Lucy certainly didn't teach him such things. The boy knew which Bible prophecies had been fulfilled, which ones were yet to come to pass, and he knew things he couldn't possibly have gotten anywhere but from heaven.

The front door of the cabin swung open, and twenty-two-year-old Hyrum pushed past the doorpost. He was dressed in his work clothes, the smell of freshly cut wheat filtering inside with him. He was out of breath from running across the fields. "Where's Joseph?" he asked.

"He's not here, son." Joseph Sr. lowered himself into the rocking chair near the hearth.

"It's been a year—a year to the day since he told us of the angel's visit."

Joseph Sr. stared into the cold, black belly of the fireplace. "I've never been good with numbers."

"You know it's today." Hyrum paced in front of the benches and chairs his father had set in a circle facing the hearth. "You're expecting him to come home with more stories, aren't you? Or maybe he'll bring us the gold Bible to see for ourselves." He stopped in front of Joseph Sr.'s rocking chair. "Did he tell you where he was off to when he left the fields?"

Joseph Sr. rocked back, the chair creaking under his weight. "Said he had things to see to."

"He went to the hill."

"It isn't any of our business where he's gone, son." Lucy cleaned the last dish and dried her hands on a towel. "This is between your brother and heaven."

The girls emerged from their room; twelve-year-old Catherine was followed by her older sister Sophronia holding young Lucy by the hand, the four-year-old running to keep step with the other girls. They no sooner sat on the bench seat facing the hearth than the door flew open, the planks banging against the inside wall of the cabin. Eight-year-old Don Carlos and thirteen-year-old William rushed inside, chased by their brother Samuel.

"Samuel Harrison!" Lucy threw the drying towel down next to the clean dishes and removed her apron. "In sixteen years of life I've taught you better. There's to be no romping in this house."

"Where is he?" Samuel pushed in front of William and Don Carlos. He pulled the wool cap from his head and sopped the sweat from his brow before refitting the cap. And when he didn't see Joseph among his brothers and sisters he started for the door. "He could be on Stafford Road right now headed this way carrying the—"

"Son." Lucy stepped in front of Samuel Harrison, blocking his escape from the cabin. "Your brother asked you not to speak of the gold record."

Samuel Harrison said, "There's no one here but us."

"Wait here a little longer." Lucy stood next to the boy and straightened the opened collar of his white shirt. He could use three shirts, the way he wore through them. He was growing like a weed, and they couldn't afford to supply him with more than one shirt at a time until he finished his growth. "Joseph will be along soon enough with word about—"

"About the plates?"

Lucy pointed to the bench. "Sit over there."

The day was ebbing toward evening, the warmth of the sun giving way to the cool of September nights, and Lucy latched the door before Samuel Harrison could take it into his mind to go searching for his brother about the dark countryside. There was no telling if Joseph had gone to visit the hill again. He could be fishing in the creek or gone to town for winter wheat for all she knew, but the angel told him to report back in one year's time, and this evening was twelve months to the day when Joseph was first directed by his angel escort to a hill not too far distant from their home. There he was shown the buried records and informed that he would translate them from their ancient Semitic tongue into English. It was nearly too incredible to believe—her son a translator of ancient records like a great scribe from days of old—and today could well be the day they laid eyes on the plates they'd heard so much about.

Lucy untied her apron and hung the cloth over the back of the chair next to her husband before sitting down. This wasn't a tale of money digging, or of buried treasure, or of spirits whispering of riches in the earth. There was something heavenly about the way Joseph described the visits of the angel, and there was no doubting it was of God—not because of the histories or prophecies and such that the angel-visitor related to her son, but by a still, small voice that spoke peace to her soul, telling her she could believe Joseph Jr. Not less than a month ago, back when Deacon Jessup was going about affecting a union of the different churches, Joseph told her he didn't want to keep her from going to meetings, but he wasn't interested in attending with her and the rest of the family—said he could take his Bible into the woods and learn more in two hours than she could in two years of going to meetings, and there was no doubting where that learning was coming from. Her son walked with angels.

Joseph Sr. pulled up two more chairs next to the bench seat alongside the girls, one for Samuel and the other for William, and he let

Don Carlos sit on the wood floor playing with the turkey feather he found in the pasture. Lucy arranged the pleats of her dress over her knees, took the knitting needles from the basket under her chair, and started them working on a sweater for little Lucy. They were all together in the main room like they were the first night after Joseph returned from the hill a year ago, all seated in a circle—father, mother, sons, and daughters—and they presented an aspect as singular as any that ever lived upon the face of the earth while waiting for Joseph to return and tell them about the angel and the plates, just like the last time when they were all melted to tears. That was back before Alvin, her eldest child, died. He was as enthusiastic over Joseph's visions as anyone in the family, begging his brother to go on at length and fill the days and weeks after Moroni's first visit with endless conversations about the angel. Then on the nineteenth of November last year, Alvin had suddenly taken ill and died with no more notice than telling Lucy late that afternoon he didn't feel well. The doctor was out of town, but his office sent an assistant to administer to the boy, and he prescribed calomel. Lucy slowed her knitting needles, lowered her head, and brushed away a tear. Poor Alvin told the man the oil was certain to kill him, but the good doctor's assistant persisted, and not less than two weeks after he drank a half bottle of the awful stuff, the boy died of gangrene in his bowel—his food impacted by the calomel prescribed to save him.

Lucy turned her gaze about the room until it rested on the empty chair in the circle on the other side of her husband's rocking chair, the one they left vacant in memory of their dead son. They hadn't met like this since Alvin's death—she simply couldn't bear to hear Joseph Jr. speak about the angel Moroni and the plates. It only reminded her of Alvin's enthusiasm for Joseph's visions. But ten months was enough time to lessen the sting of his passing, and they were gathered here again, hoping beyond hope that Joseph would return with the plates, though she didn't dare show her eagerness in front of the children lest she find that Joseph was gone chasing wild turkeys or nailing boards in the still-unfinished frame house across Stafford Road and had nothing to tell other than a report on the work of construction or the hunting of wild animals.

Hyrum crossed the main room to the chair next to his father, but before he could sit, Lucy said, "Not there, son. You know we don't sit in that chair." It was Alvin's, and it was to stay empty for when Joseph returned to talk of his visions. Alvin would have wanted to have the closest chair for himself right next to the hearth, close enough so he could reach out and touch his brother's sleeve and beg him to go on longer and tell them more.

Lucy shot to her feet when she heard a man whistling a tune outside the front door. Footsteps sounded along the path, but when the door inched open and Joseph Jr. stood in the entry cradling a sack in his arms, she quickly fell back to her seat and started the needles working furiously through the yarn.

Lucy said, "Have you had your dinner, son?"

"Don't worry yourself, Mother. I'm well enough."

Well enough? Lucy missed a stitch and quickly plucked out the mistake with her fingers. That was it. The sack had to have the plates inside. "I traded some of our wheat with a farmer selling oats down the road on the way to South Bainbridge." Joseph Jr. walked the sack to the kitchen table and it fell over like sand from the creek bottom. "He gave me his best grain."

"That's it?" Hyrum stood from his chair. "You spent the afternoon and evening trading for a sack of oats?"

Joseph patted his hand along the base of the sack. "It was a good trade."

"Nothing could be as good as—"

"A visit with an angel?"

"I was right." Don Carlos jumped to his feet. "Today *is* the day."

Samuel Harrison said, "You see, I told you, Papa."

Joseph came around and stood in front of the cold hearth. The girls leaned their heads in, and even little Lucy sat without stirring while he began telling them that the angel had instructed him further about the record hidden in the hill. He lowered himself into Alvin's empty chair, and Lucy didn't stop him, not with him telling them that the covenants preserved on these gold plates gave them a more perfect knowledge of the plan of salvation and the redemption of the human family. He went on to tell them that the covenants contained in the record had power to bind families together through all eternity. The sweetest happiness pervaded the house, and tranquility reigned. At last, Lucy had some hope for her dead son Alvin—something upon which she could ease her mind.

Hyrum said, "What about the plates?"

Joseph said, "There are troubles ahead."

Lucy said, "What trouble could come of this?"

"You must promise me." Joseph pointed his finger around the circle, stopping on each of his brothers and sisters. "You will tell no one about the plates. Do you understand? Not a soul."

The girls nodded, young Don Carlos swore on his turkey feather, and William and Samuel Harrison agreed.

Hyrum said, "What about the plates? Where are they?"

"Promise me you'll say nothing?"

"You know me well enough." Hyrum stood next to Joseph's chair. "I'll always be by your side."

"The world is a wicked place. I saw a glimpse of it when I was digging for the Staffords, but I never thought they would ever do such things."

Lucy said, "What things?"

Joseph Jr. lowered his voice. "The angel warned me that the Staffords and men like them are all over these parts. Once they get word of the plates, they'll kill us for the sake of the gold. Our names will be cast as evil, and we'll be made out as fools." Joseph turned in his chair to his father. "I'm sorry, Papa. I don't mean to burden your house with this."

"It's your house as well, son. You do whatever you're told to do." Joseph Sr. rocked back in his chair, his hands folded across his middle. "All will be well with the rest of us."

"What of the plates?" Hyrum gripped the backrest of Joseph's chair. "No one would kill us for gold we don't have."

Joseph Sr. said, "Did you get them, son?"

"I couldn't."

"Did you see them?"

"I did, but I couldn't take them."

"I would have taken them." Joseph Sr. sat forward. "If I'd been in your place I would have taken them right away and gotten on with the translating of the record."

"You don't know what you say." Joseph Jr. righted himself in his chair. "The angel wouldn't allow it."

"How can you translate a book that lies in the ground?" Lucy set aside her knitting needles. "All this waiting, son. I don't understand it."

Joseph Jr. said, "I'm to return to the hill again next year on this very day."

"Why then?"

"The angel didn't say, except that . . ."

Joseph Sr. said, "Except what?"

"I don't understand all the timing of heaven, but in the divine calendar of things, the day appointed for me to receive them has yet to arrive."

—Two Days Later
Old City of Jerusalem

Katerina Weiss stood with her father, Avram, at the top of the steps above the entrance to Kessler & Son's clock-making shop in the upper city of Old Jerusalem. The light was on, but there was no sign of Danny seated at his work table near the window, and in the gray light before dawn she retied the red ribbon into her long, black hair and straightened her checkered dress. It was pressed and cleaned for synagogue this morning, but with the cool, mist-filled late September breeze blowing inland from the Mediterranean it was impossible to keep the starched pleats and the white laces of her blouse from sagging.

"I don't like this, daughter." Avram hid in the shadows of the gates to the Kessler home. The newer stone in the walls of the two-story home were cut to the same dimensions as the ancient ones in the foundation, the new structure sitting squarely atop the remains of the old one. Poured glass windows graced the front of the building, and inside the kitchen, near the back of the home, the Kesslers' cook worked beneath the light of a kerosene-fueled flame preparing loaves of double-twisted challah along with basted veal and fish, pies, cakes, and candies to celebrate the day with a traditional meal after synagogue. The light of a many-flamed chandelier filtered out the largest front window and into the darkness of early morning, casting long shadows across Katerina and mixing with the light filtering up the stairs from the doors to the basement clock-making shop. Katerina brushed her hair back over her shoulders and rubbed rouge across her cheeks. She could fit their two-room apartment into the entry of this house. This was one of the grand estates in the city, and they should be grateful the Kesslers had taken a liking to them, or they'd have precious few friends in their new home.

"None of that primping, daughter. It's to synagogue that we go, not to a wedding dance." Avram buttoned the top button on his black coat, fitted the *caftan* hat over his long, gray earlocks and started down the first step when a loud mournful blast like the horn on a street vendor's cart greeted them from inside the clock-making shop. The trumpeting shook the small glass windows on either side of the entrance, echoing up the stairs and reverberating in the narrow stairwell cut through the ancient stones of the foundation. Another run of short staccato blasts sounded inside the shop, rattling the wood door against the post, the sound forcing Avram back onto the cobblestones in the street. He reached for the railing at the top of the steps and steadied himself with the iron rod. "What in the name of Jericho?"

"Oh, Papa. It's only Danny."

"The clock maker's son?"

"He's practicing. I told you they invited us to attend their synagogue this morning to hear Danny blow the *shofar*. It's his first time."

"He's to blow the *shofar* to celebrate the feast, not bring down the walls of the synagogue, daughter."

"Not a word about his horn playing, do you hear me?" Katerina nudged him in the back to start him down the stairs, but he would not budge. "You'll offend the Kesslers with your humor. They don't know you like I do."

"It's Danny you don't want to offend, yes?"

Katerina took him by the arm. "I'll suffer none of your wit this morning."

"We buy calendars from the Kesslers, and now we go to synagogue with them? I should have known this wasn't going to be a good New Year."

"We don't turn down an invitation from the Kessler family."

Avram wagged his finger at her. "The invitation was to you from Danny."

"Fine." Katerina let go of his arm. "I'll go with Danny."

"You'll do no such thing." Avram patted her on the cheek. "I'm not so old I don't remember what it's like to be you."

"You were never a woman."

"I won your mother's hand, God bless her soul."

"Papa, not here in the street."

"It takes an audience to make a scene. Do you see a crowd gathered around, daughter? I see what happens when you speak with Danny Kessler." Avram removed his *caftan* and ran his fingers through his graying hair before refitting the hat. "You laugh for his jokes more than they deserve, you smile more in his presence than I should ever allow, and you forget there's anyone else for miles around. You're in a room full of Jews and think you're alone with the son of the clock maker." He took Katerina by the hand. "The Kesslers aren't like us, daughter."

"Papa, there's hardly anyone in Jerusalem like us."

"You miss my point."

"Which is?"

"We should celebrate today with the other Hassids in the city, not with these, these . . ."

"They're Jews, Papa. We're all Jews. You, me, Danny, Mr. Kessler. What does it matter if we don't share the same customs?"

"Living the Law is not a custom."

"The Kesslers live the Law."

"They don't wear the covenants." Avram grabbed the fringe that hedged out from under the tail of his black coat—the 613 knots tying the corners of his undershirt together filled his hand with white linen.

Katerina lowered her voice to a whisper and said, "They don't need to wear them, Papa, not as long as they live them."

"It isn't proper. You should be with your own kind." Avram dropped the knotted fringe to his side and patted her on the back of the hand. "There's certain to be a clock maker among the Hassids in this city."

"I'm not interested in a clock maker."

"You're interested in Danny Kessler, yes?"

"I wouldn't care if he were a street sweeper. Must I ignore every young man in the city?"

Another loud blast on the trumpet shot out the entrance of the shop, followed by a run of nine staccato blasts—three of which were sharp and powerful, but the rest cracked when Danny held onto them. He was still having troubles, and there was no time to practice.

"You see there." Katerina brushed some lint from Avram's sleeve. "He's getting better. He has the *teruah* down nicely."

"She knows the names of the trills and runs of the trumpet notes played on the feast day." Avram raised both hands in the air. "You've been coming here to listen to the Kessler boy practice."

"Only enough to know he's improving."

Avram straightened his cuffs. "There are Hassidic men in the city that haven't a wife."

"No, Papa." Katerina shook her head. "Not Jonah the butcher."

"And what's wrong with a butcher?"

"The poor man has no teeth."

"He doesn't have need of them. He grinds his food in his meat-grinding machines."

"Oh, Papa, you don't want me to grind my food for the rest of my life."

"When have I ever not meant what I say?" Avram held her by both hands. "The young clock maker is all you ever speak of."

"Is that such a bad thing?"

"How can I arrange a marriage with the butcher if you're always talking about Danny Kessler?"

"If speaking of Danny Kessler will keep the toothless butcher away, I'll speak of the clock maker in every breath."

The horn sounded again with three resounding blasts before falling silent long before the run of notes was complete. The door to the shop swung open, and Danny Kessler poked his head around the doorpost, his hair falling down over his brow. "I thought I heard voices." He stepped into the stairwell, his long *shofar* horn hanging at his side. He combed his hair back before waving them down the stairs, inviting them into the shop and wishing them a happy first day of the seventh month.

Katerina stood just inside the door with her father hovering over her, his wide frame separating the couple. Danny leaned around him to greet her with a warm good morning and offer a reserved smile before removing his apron, revealing a freshly pressed white shirt with long sleeves. A black bow tie sat uncomfortably over the top button, and Katerina reached past her father to adjust it, her small hands quickly untying and retying the bow on his long neck. She brushed against his chin, and her touch raised a smile across his lips. She helped him with his coat, tucking the chain of a silver pocket watch in place, and then he put on his *kittel*—the long white robe that reached from his shoulders down to the soles of his black polished shoes. It was the costume the horn blower wore to synagogue to celebrate the Feast of Trumpets and remember the appearance of Elisha come to announce the Messiah and the blessing of eternal life promised to those who keep their covenants. And Danny did look like an angel with his red cherubic cheeks and his light brown hair brushing against the top of his ears and the high collar of his shirt—simply the most heavenly young man in all the Old City, and Katerina leaned up on her toes and kissed him on the cheek. "You'll play very well today. I'm sure of it."

Danny reached under the white robe and fished the timepiece from his coat pocket before calling across the shop, past the shelves of ticking clocks. "Papa, we can't be late."

Reuben Kessler stood at the safe door, turning the dial on the lock and reaching his long arms inside the chest-high vault. Katerina stepped past her father to see down beyond the shelves of clocks to where Reuben stood, but there were too many shadows playing across the opening of the ancient receptacle to see inside and get a glimpse of what lay safeguarded there. Danny had told her that the foundation of their home—the thick limestone forming the walls and floor of this clockmaking shop—were original stones from a centuries-old estate chiseled by pickax and hammer. If that vault could speak, what tales would it tell? What sorts of relics were guarded inside the walls of this estate thousands of years ago?

Katerina leaned her head forward as Reuben took out a copy of the Torah, rested the end of it in his hand, the length of it fitted against his arm, and the top coming alongside his cheek. That was odd. The man kept valuable gold and silver clocks on the shelves in plain view, but he sealed the family copy of the Torah away in his vault. Reuben was the guardian of a Torah scroll passed down through a noble family of cantors for generations. The scripture was well more than a hundred years old with hardly any cracking or chaffing in the leather, and Mr. Kessler treated it with more safekeeping than any of the gold and silver in his shop.

Danny gathered a stack of papers from his worktable and walked them over to Avram. "Just as you ordered." He handed him the calendar for the year 1824. "Today's Feast of Trumpets falls on September twenty-fourth."

Avram rustled through the papers. "Calculate them all, did you?"

"I finished the conversions early this morning." Danny waited for him to check his math against the dates on the Gentile calendar before saying, "Happy New Year, sir."

"Day of Remembrance, boy, and forget it you will not." Avram nodded. "A proper name the day has." He stuffed the calendar under his arm before turning his gaze onto Katerina. "And may it be a good day for us all."

Danny clicked open the face of his pocket watch. "We don't want to arrive late."

"Arrive late, he says." Carefully holding the Torah scrolls, Reuben Kessler walked down between the shelves. He draped his prayer shawl over his head, covering his gray linen suit and bowtie with the blue-and-white-striped cloth and started out the door ahead of them. "Punctuality. When did my son ever concern himself with it? More than ten years now I sing the songs of the Torah, and never does he worry about the hour of synagogue until it's his turn to blow the *shofar* horn." Reuben glanced at the clocks on the shelves. "For the love of Moses, Danny, it doesn't require thirty minutes to walk three blocks."

Of the four Sephardic synagogues in the Old City, the Kesslers attended the largest. It stood on the hill in the Upper City, hardly a five-minute walk up a steep, centuries-old street wound around two wide turns and beneath three archways. It was a limestone building with a rounded dome for a roof. There were no elegant steeples, no parapets or cathedral towers, nothing but a thick, double-planked door that stood open to welcome the gathering Jews.

Katerina was first inside the crowded main room. She pushed through the throng and opened a way for the others in their small group until a woman called out that the trumpeter had arrived. Then the congregation parted to let Danny and Mr. Kessler pass to the front to stand beside the rabbi—an older gentleman with graying hair, a small black *yarmulke* on the crown of his head, and a white prayer shawl with blue stripes draped over him like the one Mr. Kessler wore. There was no room on the old wooden benches, and Katerina found a secluded place to stand in the shadows along the far wall with her father, though the darkness didn't keep the worshippers from staring at them. The quick glances and curious stares stung her father more than they bothered her. She could feel him stiffen next to her, his shoulders pulling back and his head going down behind the cover of his *caftan.* Hassids didn't come to this synagogue with their black coats and black pants and a fringe of knots hanging about the hip. Thankfully, Danny raised his trumpet without waiting for the rabbi to begin the service, and Katerina nodded to him, silently thanking him for turning the eyes of so many in another direction.

Danny spoke with a confident voice, offering the blessing over the *shofar* to begin the celebration of the Feast of Trumpets. He said, "Awake, ye that are sleepy, and ponder your deeds, remember your Creator, and go back to Him in penitence. Waste not your years seeking after vain things that neither profit nor deliver. Look well to your souls and consider your deeds." He turned his gaze back to Katerina. "Return to God, so that He may have mercy on you and bless your life with goodness."

The rabbi raised his hands, his prayer shawl cascading down over his arms, and explained that the *shofar* recalled how the children of Israel received the Ten Commandments and the covenant at Mount Horeb. Mr. Kessler stood next to the rabbi and announced the first note on the *shofar*—the *tekiah*—and Danny pressed his lips to the mouthpiece and sounded a long, mournful blast on the trumpet. And when he finished, Mr. Kessler's resonating voice filled the chamber with the sound of his singing prayer, inviting Israel to awaken to their covenants with God and reminding them of the creation of the earth.

The congregation repeated the song. They didn't sing well, but it was like hearing the voices of angels with so many faithful Jews remembering their covenants. And they were faithful, no matter how much Papa insisted otherwise. Katerina took Avram by the hand and leaned over and wished him a happy New Year. He held his fringe of 613 knots with his free hand and wished her a blessed Day of Remembrance.

Mr. Kessler announced the *shevarim*—the second portion of horn playing in the service—and Danny played three shorter blasts followed by the *teruah,* the nine quick, sharp notes echoing about the chamber and repeated in a flurry of different sequences, all paired in groups of nine blasts. Danny's horn-playing was bright and strong without any of the cracking notes that plagued his practice, and Katerina nodded at the completion of each set of nine-note runs. He was doing a fine job, and she closed her eyes while the rabbi spoke, and imagined what it must have been like to stand at the base of Mount Horeb when Moses received the Law from heaven. And she kept her eyes closed while Mr. Kessler sang a song begging God to awaken Himself to a remembrance of His covenants with Israel. Papa squeezed her hand, but she didn't open her eyes. She listened while the rabbi concluded the service, reminding them that the *shofar* carried to their hearts the promise of redemption, the coming of the Messiah, and the time when God would send the prophet Elijah, bearing the covenants—the same covenant given to Abraham that through his posterity all the nations of the earth would be blessed. He said, "From the tops of the mountains will sound the mighty *shofar*."

Katerina opened her eyes, and when her gaze fell on Danny smiling down at her, a thrill passed through her. He was the trumpeter sounding the *shofar*, and if not for the crowd separating her from him, she would have stepped to his side and begged him to take her to the tops of the mountains and find the promise the rabbi spoke of for both of them—the promise that they could marry, no matter what Papa said, and see that their marriage was blessed by heaven to endure forever.

CHAPTER 9

—Late Summer, 598 B.C.
Jerusalem

"Back away from the oven, son!"

Jonathan pushed Joshua away from the hot metal door before opening the oven with tongs and shoveling in a load of coal. With Joshua hardly a week into his tenth year, Jonathan wasn't about to let the boy suffer the same injury that burned Aaron's feet. They'd endured enough pain in this family to last a thousand lifetimes, and Jonathan's youngest was not going to add to that misery. Joshua's blacksmithing skill included nothing more than listening to his brothers speak about their days in the shop, and now he was living those stories without anyone but Jonathan to divide the work between them. Joshua's light brown hair was the image of Aaron's, and his bones were beginning to lengthen out like his older brother. He was going to be a tall lad—maybe taller than Aaron—with the same blue eyes and quiet but confident ways. Hopefully they didn't share the same naive obsessions. Aaron would have been an ideal eldest son if not for his blind friendship with the fools from Beit Zayit, and it was Jonathan's duty to see that Joshua didn't mix with similar company and suffer the same terrible fate.

Joshua reached for the bellows, but Jonathan deflected his hand, took the leather contraption, and pumped air over the coals. "You're not to work near this door until you're old enough."

"How old is that?"

"Ask your mother. She's the one who worries more than she should."

That wasn't entirely the case. Jonathan may never allow his youngest to take on the task of firemaster. Joshua could wield a forging hammer if he liked, try his hand in the cooling vats, and see if he had a liking for other work in the shop, but Joshua was not to follow in Aaron's footsteps. No one would replace his dead son as firemaster. No one ever could.

Joshua stood behind his father and peered over his shoulder, the boy's slow breath passing over Jonathan's ear, and the wonder of his gaze focused on the fiery coals of the smelting oven. The boy had a good mind, and he learned his duties as fast as Aaron ever learned them. Thankfully he didn't ask if this was the place where Aaron burned his feet or beg him to recount the story of Aaron's healing. How could he tell a story he hardly believed himself? Jonathan worked the bellows harder, venting the oven with enough air to fire the ingots of hard coal to a white heat. Aaron wasn't healed. His burned skin may have grown back more quickly than seemed possible, but Jonathan would not recount any claim to miraculous healing. If Lehi had power to call down a blessing from heaven, why did he save Aaron only to have him die at the point of Captain Laban's arrow? Lehi the olive oil merchant and his cousin Ishmael the vineyard master were imposters of the worst ilk, and it was their foolish beliefs that killed Jonathan's eldest son.

The wood and coal inside the oven burned down, leaving the hard ingots to fire the oven hot enough to smelt iron ore into steel. They had an order for three door latches and a single-edged sword, but there was no telling if Jonathan could smelt a good grade of steel without the ovens at the right temperature—a task he had left to Aaron all these years. With the boy dead, Jonathan was relearning forgotten skills after so long away from tending the fires. He ruined a round of steel last month, and if he didn't find a way to keep the heat constant, he may never put out quality steel again.

Jonathan filled the clay mold with iron ore, set it into the oven, and shut the door with his foot. It was like rolling a stone over the opening of a sepulcher, the life of the fire sealed away inside the oven along with the memory of Aaron's fire-making skills.

"Good morning, Papa."

Jonathan turned from the oven to find Daniel standing in the doorway. He was dressed in a military tunic, the silver stripes on his sleeve glimmering in the morning sunlight. A cord held a black patch tight against his left eye. Daniel never said how he lost his sight, and Jonathan didn't press him for the details. The boy grew angry whenever he asked.

"What are you staring at?" Daniel adjusted the patch over his eye.

"Your mother will be happy to see you." Jonathan turned his gaze from Daniel's blind eye and walked the shovel over to the door. "I'll have her set another plate for evening meal."

"I didn't come for a visit."

Zoram stepped inside behind Daniel. He was dressed in a white coat and turban—nothing like the tattered tunic he wore about the shop when he worked here last year in a trade for Daniel's services in the military. It was a shame Zoram's time here had ended. Jonathan could use the help. He said, "Elizabeth was wondering why you've not been by to visit, son. You can find her at home."

Daniel said, "He's with me. I ordered him to come."

Ordered him? When did any of them order Zoram to do anything? Jonathan handed Joshua the shovel and asked him to stow it over beyond a stack of wood at the far end of the forging table and away from their conversation.

Zoram nodded. "We came to see about a door."

"This is a blacksmith shop, not a carpentry."

"A steel door." Daniel spoke quickly, the words snapping off the end of his tongue.

Zoram said, "It's for a vault in Captain Laban's treasury."

"For the love of heaven, he doesn't need a vault. Laban's treasury is guarded by an army."

Daniel said, "Must I find another blacksmith?"

"There aren't any others."

"I haven't forgotten the art."

Jonathan looked away from his son without speaking. Why did he ever encourage his son to leave the shop and join Captain Laban's military?

Daniel said, "Is that your answer?"

Jonathan slowly raised his gaze. "Can the treasury walls bear the weight of a metal door without cracking?"

Zoram said, "I'm not certain."

Jonathan wiped his hands on his apron. "I'll have to examine the vault."

Zoram said, "There isn't one to examine, sir."

"The stonemason begins his work in the morning." Daniel stepped closer to Jonathan and spoke with his head pushed forward. "He's chiseling a compartment in the foundation of the treasury." He set two pieces of gold on the forging table.

"Why so much for a metal door?"

Daniel said, "Laban wants it finished by the Feast of Trumpets."

"That's only a month from now."

"Twenty-one days."

"We should talk about this." Jonathan removed his smithing apron and hung it over a hook on the wall before coming back to the forging table. "I'll tell your mother you'll be by for dinner."

"Not tonight." Daniel started for the shop door. "You can come to the treasury for measurements as soon as the stonemason finishes."

"Ruth will want to see you."

Daniel didn't reply, didn't say anything about Ruth. It was as if he'd forgotten he had a mother. He tipped his head and marched into the street.

Zoram paused at the door, his gaze shifting between the street and the ovens inside the shop.

Jonathan said, "What is it, boy?"

Daniel called from the street, ordering Zoram to hurry along. It was time they headed back to the treasury to meet the stonemason.

Jonathan said, "That boy is insufferable."

"Don't judge him too harshly. It's the relics. He worries over them a good deal. Maybe more than he should." Zoram didn't move from the entry, didn't go into the street.

Jonathan said, "Is there something more?"

"I did some smithing in the morning hours last year, do you remember?"

"Some sort of brass plate, wasn't it?"

Zoram nodded and kept his voice low, hardly audible above the cracking of the fire in the smelting oven. "I'm in need of fashioning some more, and I was hoping . . ."

Zoram fell quiet, and when he didn't continue with his asking, Jonathan said, "You want to use my ovens."

"If you don't mind."

"A single plate like before?"

"Six."

"That's a good deal of silver and copper, son." Jonathan scratched the side of his head. "Why does Laban need so many plates of brass?"

"This isn't for the captain." Zoram stepped to the door and told Daniel he was coming right away before he turned back to Jonathan and said, "Another man engaged me to record some of his thoughts on metal, preserve them for those who come after him."

"Six plates of brass is a costly way to preserve a man's reminiscences."

"I'll pay for the ore and the wood for the fires."

Jonathan set his hands on the forging table. "This patron of yours must have a fetish to preserve himself to generations unborn."

"I wouldn't call it a fetish."

"Obsession then. Wealthy nobles are always wasting their money."

"He isn't wealthy." Zoram removed his turban and held the white bands of cloth between his hands, his dark hair falling into his eyes. "He doesn't have the money to pay for them immediately, but he's determined to have his words preserved on brass."

"If he doesn't have the money, he shouldn't engage you. Let me speak to him. I'll see that he understands the costs."

"A meeting isn't a good idea."

"Does he really think to hire the smithing of six plates of brass without any money?" Jonathan leaned over the table. "You can't bear the cost, son."

"I don't want to turn him away just yet."

"Smith the man a single plate, and if he doesn't pay what you're due, you won't be left without remedy."

"He needs them all before the end of the month."

"Six plates of brass in twenty-one days?" Jonathan returned his forging hammer to the rack on the wall and hung the bellows from a rope above the smelting oven. "Why is everyone in such a hurry?"

"I'll do the work late in the evening after you retire."

"You'll need this." Jonathan handed over the shop entry key along with one of the pieces of gold Daniel gave him for the steel door. "This won't cover the entire cost, but it's a start."

"I can't take this."

"It's a loan, and I expect usury along with the payment of debt."

"How high a usury?"

"Elizabeth is home weaving a white veil." Jonathan walked to the door and stood next to Zoram. "Do you know why women weave white linen veils?"

Zoram nodded. "I believe I do, sir."

"You're alone in this world, without a father to make arrangements for your future. I'll expect a repayment of uprightness, a sober mind, and a usury of providing for my daughter as best you're able. You're a fine man, and my Elizabeth is a fine woman. I'd like to tell her that you and I are discussing her future."

"With all due respect, sir . . . " Zoram wrapped his fingers around the piece of gold. "I'd like to tell her myself."

Elizabeth sat in front of the Egyptian foot loom along the back wall of the main room. The worn pedals were soft against her bare feet, and when she pushed down, the levers came to life, the wooden arms quickly passing over the beginnings of a white linen veil and stitching the threads into a perfect . . .

Oh, dear! Look what her eagerness wrought. She'd moved the pedals too quickly and stitched a line of thread without feeding a counter thread to tie off the weave. She let the levers go still before picking out the half-done stitch with her fingers. Why did mother insist she weave a wedding veil? Zoram hadn't proposed marriage, and it didn't appear he ever would. And despite her unmarried status, Elizabeth could never hope to work the foot loom for the precise stitching required for an intricate cloth.

Elizabeth started the pedals moving more slowly, feeding the loom with a steady stream of thread. This veil was going to take her days, maybe weeks, but Mama was adamant she learn to weave a wedding veil. It had been more than a week since the man who gave her reason to learn the delicate art passed by the house. Zoram's work in the treasury was his excuse for now, but what would it be next time? She never should have hoped to find a suitor—especially one as well suited to her as Zoram. Had he found another, more suitable woman with the proper skills of motherhood? Elizabeth's talents were for reading and writing—not stitching. Could it be that Zoram's heart had wandered and she was destined to forever endure the snide remarks and the stings of the stares from women in the market who had nothing better to do than wonder why she was without a husband at her age? She should be weaving a horse blanket, not the subtle pattern of—

Dear, no! Look at that. She'd pushed too hard on the foot pedals and pulled up a row of stitches.

"Mama, I can't do this." Elizabeth sat back, her feet pulled up under the stool, and her hands at her side. It was no use. She'd never weave a wedding veil for anyone.

"Don't give up so soon, girl." The sound of Ruth stacking plates fell silent, and her calm voice filtered in from the kitchen. "A gift of the heart requires a delicate touch."

Delicate? Elizabeth leaned over the loom and slowly started the levers moving. There was no touch that could warm a heart gone cold after so many months of dashed hopes.

Oh, bother. The thread on her spool was running down. There was still enough to keep her feet busy operating the pedals, but she couldn't reach for another in the basket and keep the loom working. "Mama, I need a new spool." There was no answer from the kitchen, and Elizabeth kept weaving, adding another swath to the growing veil before she said, "Mama, please." There were two, maybe three passes of thread left on the spool, and she said, "I need more thread."

A spool appeared over her shoulder, and she was about to thank Ruth for coming so quickly when she saw Mama standing on the other side of the room. Ruth smiled an odd smile before returning to her dish cleaning. Whoever handed her the spool had ink-stained fingers and a long white coat sleeve covering the arm.

"Zoram?" Elizabeth spun around on the foot stool. "What are you doing here?"

That wasn't the finest welcome she could offer. Why did she always speak before she weighed her words? She should be more careful, but that was the question that she most wanted answered. Zoram wore a long, white tunic with buttons along the front—nothing like the pleated robes of other scribes—and the high collar came up around his dark-skinned cheeks, hiding his neck like a stiff shawl. He was bathed in perfumes, the sweet smell of his presence filling the main room, his dark skin glistening with olive oil. This wasn't one of Zoram's casual visits, not with his coat freshly pressed, his sandals polished in beeswax, and a single red rose in his hand.

"I'm hardly presentable." Elizabeth quickly fitted her feet into her sandals, pushed her long black hair back over her shoulders and pressed the wrinkles out of her robe. "I didn't expect you, what with your work in the treasury taking so much of your—"

"That's what pressed me to come and speak with you."

"These clothes?"

"My work."

"Is there a problem?"

Zoram was without his usual smile, and it could only be a dreadfully serious thing that brought him to speak with her dressed as he was and bathed in perfumes. He handed over the red rose, but Elizabeth didn't take a breath of the blossom's scent. When had he ever brought her flowers. She could only guess what awful thing this bode. His work in the treasury was going to take him from her; she could tell by the way he handed her the flower, his hand stiff around the stem, and his voice intoning an apologetic tenor. Elizabeth ran her hand over her robe again, but all her pressing wouldn't remove the wrinkles from the cloth. A strand of uncombed hair fell down in front of her face, and when she tried to push it away, a handful of black curls covered her eyes.

Zoram said, "There's something I need to tell you, but I see this is a bad time. Shall I come back when you're more comfortable?"

Comfortable? Elizabeth was never more at ease than in his company, but considering the seriousness in his manner, he was right about her comfort. There was no controlling the frantic pace of her heart.

"There's no better time than now." Elizabeth pushed her uncombed hair back. "Tell me what it is you came to tell me."

"Do you recall the brass plate we fashioned in your father's smithy?"

What did that have to do with telling her he wasn't to be coming around anymore? Zoram took a seat on the bench in the middle of the room, and Elizabeth sat on the end farthest from him, her hands folded in her lap. She spoke in a monotone without any of the rise or fall of emotion that usually colored her speech. If she allowed even a hint of disappointment to taint her words, she'd become a whimpering fool. "We should have added more copper."

Zoram stared at her, confused by her words. "More copper?"

"That's right. You were going to tell me that the color of the new plate didn't match the others, and then you're going to tell me that you . . ." Elizabeth cleared her throat to keep the pain from stopping her speech. She straightened her shoulders against the back of the bench.

Zoram inched forward. "Have you discussed this with your father?"

"I shouldn't have need to confer with anyone but you."

"Then you agree?"

Elizabeth turned away from his gaze. "Do I have any other choice?"

"I'll only proceed with your permission."

Tears burned in her eyes, and she brushed them away, but that only unleashed a flood of tears. "Oh, Zoram." Elizabeth dropped the rose and ran toward the kitchen; Ruth appeared at the entry, and Elizabeth fell into her mother's arms.

"Dear, what is it? What's wrong, girl?"

Elizabeth tried to speak, but the words wouldn't come, and she nestled her head in Ruth's shoulder, the cloth of her mother's robe sopping up her sadness.

Ruth said, "Zoram, what's wrong with my Elizabeth?"

Before he could answer, the front door swung open, and Jonathan stood in the entry, his smithing apron over his shoulder. He stepped inside with Joshua following him, the boy's cheeks smudged with black coal and his sandy brown hair standing on end after a long day at the smithy. Jonathan smiled at Ruth and offered a good evening to Zoram. He said, "I see you've told the girl."

Ruth said, "Told her what?"

Zoram removed his turban and set it under his arm. He stepped closer to Elizabeth and extended his hand, but she refused to leave the comfort of Ruth's arms.

Jonathan said, "This wasn't meant to be such a torturous thing, daughter."

Ruth said, "Let her be for a moment."

Elizabeth collected herself enough to say, "You knew, Papa, and you didn't tell me?"

"I would have, but . . ."

Ruth said, "But what?"

Jonathan threw his smithing apron over the bench seat. "I agreed to let Zoram speak to the girl about it."

"Oh, Papa, how could you?"

Zoram said, "This isn't going well."

"Of course it is." Ruth patted Elizabeth on the back of the head, her gentle touch unable to rid Elizabeth of the pain that festered deep in her soul. "Everything's going just fine. Isn't it, dear?"

Jonathan said, "This is for the best."

Ruth said, "Best?"

"The least she could do is be agreeable and accept this." Jonathan leaned over and picked the rose up off the floor. "Zoram didn't go to the trouble of coming to see the girl for her to fret so. We'll get this over with and she can move on with her life." He motioned to Zoram. "Go on, son. Finish this and be done with it."

Elizabeth pressed her head deeper into the cloth of Ruth's robe. How could Papa be so cruel?

"I haven't much money." Zoram stood next to Elizabeth. "I'm consigned to work in Captain Laban's treasury for five more years before I'm free to pursue my own employ."

Elizabeth kept her face pressed against the warmth of her mother's body.

Zoram said, "I don't have many bad habits."

That's not entirely true, Elizabeth thought. Coming here and telling her in front of her family was the worst of habits. He could at least be more discreet when discarding her.

Zoram tightened his grip on the cloth of his turban. "I can provide a decent living. Nothing like your father's house to be sure, but with time I'm certain I could do well by you."

Elizabeth rubbed her stinging eyes.

"This belonged to my mother." Zoram held out a small silver charm dangling at the end of a chain. "It's all I have to remind me of her, and I want you to wear it on our wedding day."

Elizabeth dried her cheeks. "You want what?"

"The charm. Will you wear it?"

"She will." Ruth prodded Elizabeth closer to Zoram.

"I promise to take care of you." Zoram took Elizabeth by the hand. "If you'll have me." He drew Elizabeth's hand to his lips and softly kissed the back of it. Was this really happening? Was what she'd hoped for since the day she first met Zoram unfolding squarely in front of her?

Jonathan said, "Then it's settled?"

Ruth waved her hand at him. "Let them finish."

Elizabeth returned the kiss and said, "I wouldn't have any other." She brushed a tear from her cheek. Zoram was to be her husband, and they would raise a family together. They could buy the abandoned home next door and build a gate between the properties. They could add a library and a reading room, and Zoram would have a table to do his writing. Elizabeth combed her hair behind her ear. She could feel the happiness swelling up inside and passing over her soul, and she prayed it would never end. Nothing could ever change this blessed feeling.

What Elizabeth didn't know was that the coming Feast of Trumpets had power to change everything.

CHAPTER 10

—*Late Summer, 598* B.C.
Jerusalem

Bel pushed the scraggly bands of gray hair from her eyes and shoved the pan filled with pink poppy blossom over the flames. Finest harvest in three years. The heat slowly dried the petals on the open fire in front of her home—a wooden lean-to pieced together from the dead tree branches collected along the edges of the quarter-acre of poppies growing up behind the shanty. No one knew where she did her potion making, not with her shack hidden down a narrow path behind a stand of scrub oak. Poppy cooking was her secret, and no one in this city was going to steal it from her so long as she had breath. Without these poppies, she was an old woman living in a shanty, but the powder from these flowers gave her powers she'd never imagined. She was Bel the magician.

Juices simmered from the poppies, and Bel gently bobbed the pan over the fire, stirring the blossoms like a cook preparing a fine fare. No need to offer incantations or beg the blessing of an idol god. The power of these poppies covered her lack of uttered chants. A thick brown residue collected in the bottom of the pan and clumped into grains like the sands on the Great Sea. Only ten blossoms, and look at how much powder—nearly a palm full. More than enough to cure the aches and pains of her customers and see that they forgot their troubles in a blissful world. No chanting or banging on drums to persuade her customers. Once a man was under her spell, all she need do was suggest whatever dreams he desired and let his mind craft the fantasy. And no jumping about in a fit or wild dances. With a few pinches of her powder she could make a man king of Judah for a day, convince him he could fly like a bird, or send him off into a deep sleep. And her customers always came back for more. When the magical powders weakened, despair settled in—a hopelessness deep enough to rouse wild delusions—and the only escape was more of her powders. A little sprinkle persuaded men to believe in her magic, a spoonful turned them into babbling fools, and large doses drove a man to the edge of insanity—something she dare not try and risk losing her customers to death.

Bel shuffled back a step and pulled the hem of her long black robe away from the edge of the fire pit. Bad omen it was to singe this robe. She'd never get another like it. Bel rolled the wide cuffs back off her wrists to keep them from falling into the flames. Her newest customer gave her the robe in exchange for her silence, and silent she'd be. It was the perfect dress to inspire the myth of her mystic powers, and she wore the expensive costume whenever she left the shanty. The robe along with her new name brought her more money than she ever made begging in the streets. Praise be to the Babylonian god. She took the name *Bel* after one of the Babylonian idols, and in less than two weeks, her sales of powders increased three-fold.

The scrub oak along the path rustled, but there was no breeze this late in the evening, and Bel turned from the fire to see a black-robed man turn down the last stretch toward her shanty. His head was covered with a pointed cap, and there was no mistaking the rigid stride of her newest customer. How did he find her? The Chief Elder was not allowed here. She had arranged with Zadock to deliver the powders to his estate in the Upper City and keep secret the location of her shanty.

Bel said, "You're not to come here."

"I've run out." Zadock held out a piece of silver.

"You had enough for two weeks." Bel snatched the silver from his long-fingered hand and slipped it into a purse she kept tied around her middle before scraping the last of the dried juices off the surface of the pan.

Zadock said, "I'm using larger doses."

"Not a wise thing, not wise at all." Bel pointed her long finger at Zadock. "Take too much, and your heart races out of control. Are you eating? What about your head?" Bel leaned forward. "Lose your mind to gloom, you will. Feel hopeless enough you'll want to kill yourself and everyone around you."

"How large of a dose for that kind of despair?"

Bel smiled. "You like my powders."

"I asked how large."

"Don't get near such nonsense." Bel poured the powder from the pan into a small leather pouch. "One pinch in the morning for the aches and pains, and one more in the evenings with your tea to surrender your mind to a fantasy for a time, but no more than two pinches a day. Do you hear?" She came around in front of Zadock and peered into eyes so dark she couldn't read the effect of her powders on the man. "This should last you a good while." She dangled the pouch in front of him. "There's not a finer powder in the city."

Zadock reached for the pouch, but she pulled it back and said, "That will be one piece of silver, sir."

"I gave you your money."

"That was your due for coming on my land uninvited." Bel tightened her hand around the pouch. "Do you want my powders?"

Zadock paid her another piece of silver, and she handed over the potion. "Remember, a single pinch in the evening is more than enough for what troubles you."

"You have no idea what troubles me, woman."

CHAPTER 11

—Later That Same Day
Jerusalem

Zadock tucked the powder-filled pouch under the pleats of his black robe and turned down the palace corridor, the draft of evening following him through the main doors. It wouldn't be long before he could venture about the city in the middle of the day without suffering this cursed heat, but until the shorter months of winter arrived, he would do his business in the cool shadows of evening and leave the heat of the Judean sun to fools. He daubed his brow with a cloth and turned past a stone column to find a maidservant stepping out of the dining hall with an empty tray. She was a robust woman with a cloth over her arm; her hair was pulled back and tied with a ribbon behind her head. They passed in the hall, and Zadock nodded to her before asking, "Is the king taking his tea this evening?"

The maidservant lowered the tray to her side. "He always takes it before dinner."

"And the queen?"

"You're always here about this time of day, sir. You know she doesn't come to the dining hall until dinner is served." The maidservant clucked her tongue, and the soft ticking against her palate echoed about the hallway. "The poor woman hardly ever takes tea with him anymore." She glanced about before lowering her voice to a whisper. "Not since the king's been acting so strange."

"Strange?"

"Something isn't right with the man. He carries on for no reason, and those sullen fits of his, surely you've seen him staring at the wall for long bouts before dinner. I don't blame the queen for not joining him until dinner is served. He always seems at his worst this time of day. I've tried different herbs." She raised the tray a little higher on her hip. "It's no use. It doesn't matter what kind of tea I serve, he only gets worse." She slowly shook her head. "It's the dinner bell I hate most. When he rings it, he isn't calling the cooks for another ladle of soup or a round of bread. It's tea he wants, and it has an awful effect on him." She glanced down the hall toward the dining chamber before returning her gaze to Zadock. "It isn't good to be in the same room with him until well after he's had his tea. His ill-tempered moods I can endure, but those downcast dispositions of his are insufferable."

"Have the cooks served his dinner?"

"You didn't hear the bell did you? I took him two cups of tea. If the queen doesn't come early to dinner, he'll be awhile until he drinks them both. His passion for tea is out of control. He's possessed by it. He asks for it all the day long, but it never soothes his mind until evening—about the time you stop by each day. And thank heaven you're here tonight. He's in one of his moods." The maidservant raised the tray in front of her with both hands, and before continuing down the hall she said, "How I hate the ringing of the dinner bell."

Zadock waited for her to turn through the double kitchen doors at the end of the hall before entering the dining room. The palace cooks scurried about the far side of the chamber, preparing two place settings at opposite ends of the long cedar table. And over beyond their scurrying, on the darker side of the room, two chairs stood before an empty hearth without any fire to brighten the shadows. Zedekiah sat in the first chair, his lean, stiff frame fitted against the backrest, and his gaze turned toward the hearth. A small table occupied the narrow space between the chairs, and two identical teacups sat atop the table. They were filled to the brim, a line of steam filtering up into the chamber and scenting the hall with the aroma of roasted herbs. Zedekiah added four drops of honey and stirred the brew with a silver spoon.

"It's for what ails me," Zedekiah said in answer to Zadock's staring.

Zadock crossed the room. "Exactly what ails you, sire?"

"I go a day without my tea, and I have headaches, and poor vision and—"

"And fits of despair?"

"Do you suffer from the same malady?"

"I need a good tea now and then." Zadock sat in the chair beside the king and leaned over the armrest. "It calms unexplainable fears, rids me of cold sweats in the middle of the night, and helps with voices others don't hear."

Zedekiah turned his gaze back into the dark, cold depth of the hearth and nodded.

Zadock set a leather pouch filled with powders on the table next to the tea cups. "Whenever you need something to soothe your mind, mix a spoonful of this with your drink, and it's certain to lift your spirits."

Zedekiah sniffed at the opening and peered inside. "An herb?"

"The finest you'll ever mix with your teas. Very costly."

"You're a good man." Zedekiah settled back into his chair, his hands clutching the armrests. "I'll see that the maidservants mix some with every cup of—"

"Not the maidservants." Zadock poured a heaping spoonful into Zedekiah's cup, and the crystals quickly dissolved in the hot liquid. It was twice his usual dose, but the Feast of Trumpets was growing near, and it was time that Zadock increased the measure of the king's insanity. "I wouldn't let on to the help that you have these powders. Once the reason for your joy is known, the entire palace will sneak a pinch, and there's hardly enough for you."

Zedekiah reached for the potion-laced cup. "Will you join me?"

"I wouldn't think of squandering your powders, sire."

Zedekiah raised the teacup to his lips and drank it dry. He held the empty cup in one hand while he added another spoonful of powder to the second cup and drank it down. He let out a nervous laugh. "A good tea keeps the spirits of the damned from haunting the mind, and your new herbs are certain to—"

"Rid you of your headaches?"

"Nightmares. Your powders must save me from the darkness and the falling and the terrible despair of . . ."

Zadock waited for the King to finish his rambling, but when he fell silent and stared into the darkness of the hearth, the Chief Elder said, "What is it, sire?"

"Nice. Very nice indeed." Zedekiah leaned against the backrest. He opened his silver-trimmed tunic down to his stomach and fanned air over his chest. There was no flame kindled in the hearth, but he said, "Have the butler put out the fire."

Zadock peered into Zedekiah's eyes, searching for the faraway look that accompanied the taking of these powders, and when he was certain the man was lost in another of his delusions he said, "Tell me sire, what are your thoughts on executing traitors?"

"That's an odd question."

"It troubles your mind."

"How do you know what troubles me?"

"Close your eyes and listen to the rise and fall of my voice."

"I hear you well enough."

"Listen with your mind." Zadock spoke in a rhythmic cadence, his voice as low and devoid of rasping as he could force it, the sound lulling the king back into his chair and calming the stiffness in his posture. "I speak from the depths of your thinking. Can you hear me?"

"It's dark here." Zedekiah bit on the end of his collar and spoke with his lips wrapped around the cloth like a babe sucking its thumb. "I dread the darkness."

"You can hide in the shadows."

"Is that you again?" Zedekiah turned his head toward Zadock, but his eyes stayed closed. "It is, isn't it? I know your voice. Why do you bring me here every night?"

Zadock leaned closer and whispered. "You know the answer."

"Tell me again."

"I've told you again and again."

"Traitors?"

"They want your throne."

"Who's taking my kingdom from me?"

"Where's your son Mulek?"

"It isn't him or any of my sons. They wouldn't take my—"

"The sword of kingship is the only way to stop them."

"My sons?"

"Laban keeps the weapon in his treasury. You must have the relic to defend your throne." Zadock waited for the cooks to leave the dining room before he pulled a dagger from under his robe and held the blade in front of the king's face. "Look at this."

Zedekiah slowly opened his eyes, the reflection of the sharp edge dancing across his face, and his gaze slowly moving from the point, down along the edge to the hilt, and then back up the shimmering metal to the tip. He set his finger on the blade and pushed it aside, a laugh escaping his lips, the silliness bubbling from deep inside his bosom and filling the chamber with the giddiness of a child. The powders were doing their blessed work, transforming the king into a fool without a care for anything beyond his laughing. Zedekiah dropped the teacups, and they broke against the stone floor. "Off with their heads."

Zadock said, "Swear an oath to defend your throne from any who dare take it from you, even your own flesh and blood."

They were alone in the dining room, but the king placed his hand to the side of his mouth and lowered his voice like a child repeating a secret. He said, "You'll bring me the sword, won't you?"

"Laban has it." Zadock reached over and took Zedekiah by the hand. His skin was cold, but there was a film of perspiration wetting his palm. The powders were beginning to ebb. "I'll see you have an audience with the captain." He started out of the chamber, and when he passed the dining table he took the bell from beside the king's place setting and rang it loud enough to startle Zedekiah from his blissfulness.

Zadock said, "Dinner is served."

The dinner bell sounded in the hallway, and Miriam hurried the last few steps toward the dining room, careful not to catch her feet in the hem of her new silk robe imported from Egypt and scented with perfumes from southern Arabia. Her long braids were tied back with colorful oriental scarves, her lips accented with red pomegranate oils, and her ears sparkled with new silver earrings minted in the mines of Elephantine. Her dress should be more than enough to attract the notice of her husband and soften his heart that grew harder after every meeting with Zadock.

Miriam stepped aside as the Chief Elder brushed past her without offering a word in greeting or lifting his gaze to give her notice. What was he doing here again? He walked with a quiet step, his shoulders forward. The soft rustle of his robe about his ankles was like the creeping of a jackal in the shadows of a forest. She should have asked the reason for his frequent visits. The man was gone, but he always left Zedekiah with a poor temper, and her husband never remembered the reason why Zadock should call on him so often.

Miriam took her seat at the far end of the table, the long boards of finely carpentered and polished cedar separating her from Zedekiah's eating. He sat with his head forward, his hands working a knife through the steaming slab of lamb. His face was pale, but there was no reason for his sickly look. He never coughed, and beyond the fiery outbursts that plagued his once cheery temperament, he claimed to be content. His hair had gone uncombed for a good many days, and the collar of his robe was ruffled up off his neck. His silver-trimmed tunic was open, revealing far too much chest for a proper dinner in this chamber.

Zedekiah shook his unkempt hair out of his eyes and cut another slice of lamb with a vicious stroke of the knife. He was acting odd again, but he'd committed a number of feral acts since Zadock and Laban became his trusted counselors, and she added his unkempt appearance to the growing list of peculiar behaviors that soured his temper. He glanced up from his plate, peered through long thatches of hair covering his bloodshot eyes and worked a piece of meat between his teeth. Couldn't he at least smile in her direction? There was a time when, if she entered a room dressed like this, his eyes lighted with the brightness of her coming—a boyish smile she'd not seen for more than a year now. His cheerful manner was only a memory, and Miriam had no recourse other than to endure his harsh disposition and pray she would find a way to cure him from whatever poison cankered his soul.

Miriam pushed aside her food, set her hands on the table in front of her, and stared back at her husband. If she were to save him, she had to find the cause of his boorishness. There was a day when Zedekiah sided with her on the matter of the prophets, but that was before she was compelled to send Mulek away to save him from the retribution of the Chief Elder and Captain of the Guard. Those men were not her husband's friends, and she had to protect him no matter how blind he was to their twisted thinking.

Zedekiah said, "You don't like the Chief Elder."

"I can only tolerate so much of his badgering."

"The man doesn't harass." Zedekiah turned his gaze back onto his food. "We sat before a raging fire and drank tea."

Miriam glanced at the hearth that stood dark and cold along the far wall with two broken cups shattered on the stonework. "What sort of business did he bring this evening?"

"Mulek." Zedekiah wiped his lips on the back of his hand, and between bites he said, "What evil does our eldest think to conjure against me?"

Miriam played with the silverware beside her plate. "Our son has been missing for months."

"I don't trust the boy." Zedekiah set aside his knife and leaned over the table. "It was his pigeons that betrayed me during Uriah's trial."

"He was hardly old enough to plan betrayal."

"He's nearly fourteen years."

"Mulek isn't working against you." Miriam broke a round of flat bread and laid half beside her plate. "He was helping the prophets."

"He should obey me."

"He's never disobeyed you."

"He kept his heart from me, and there's no telling what sort of treachery lies in the hearts of his younger brothers." Zedekiah pointed his cutting knife across the expanse of the dining table at her. "You know what we do with traitors in this kingdom."

"Zedekiah!" Miriam dropped the flat bread to the table. How could he say such awful things about his own flesh and blood? He was acting like a wild animal, and the more she shook her head in disgust, the more his stern look melted into a smile; then he began to laugh, the same awful, high-pitched laughing that plagued their conversations these past weeks. He leaned back in his chair, his body shaking with laughter, and he banged the armrest with his fist. He said, "Off with their heads."

What a ghastly thing to say. If he were speaking of their sons, then he wasn't well—not well at all. No matter how often he denied his sickness, something wasn't right in her poor husband's head. This was neither the sweet man she'd known for going on fifteen years, nor the father of three beautiful boys. There had to be something terribly wrong, and Miriam came down along the table and reached to feel for the fever in his brow, but he grabbed her hand and said, "Don't touch me unless I ask to be touched."

"You're hurting me." Miriam tried to pull free of his grasp, but he wouldn't let go.

"I won't let you take my throne from me."

"You've been drinking."

"I don't want your mothering." Zedekiah let go of her hand. "I want that cursed sword."

Miriam stepped back. She should have run from this horrible scene and found a place to hide until her husband returned from his nightmare—well and kind and without the lost look that clouded his gaze. The sunny company of the man she married was gone, and if she had any hope of feeling the warmth of his presence in this household again, she was going to have to draw back the curtains of his mind, push open the shutters on Zedekiah's dreadful disposition, and save him from this awfulness. She stayed at the table beside him and said, "What sword?"

"Laban keeps it in his treasury."

"What right do you have to—"

"It belongs to me, and I will have it."

There was no reason he should think the sword his. It was a relic of a lost kingdom, passed down from king to prince in the Northern Kingdom of Israel along with the ancient writings recorded on the brass plates. But Israel was destroyed more than a hundred years ago, and all the Israelites who lived in her borders were scattered among all the nations along the shores of the Great Sea, leaving behind the relics in memory of a kingdom that was no more. There had to be a reason her husband was consumed by the sword, and if it had anything to do with his dreadful behavior, then she had to know why. Miriam leaned over the table, but before she could inquire after his interest in the relic, the stout frame of Ebed-Melech, the new jailer, turned into the dining room.

Thick leather belts ran over his shoulder and tied together in the center of his chest, knotted around a metal ring before running down his belly and fastening to studs pounded into the waist of his kilt. His leather boots were strapped up to his knees, with the butt of a dagger sprouting out the top. Why did her husband have to replace the old jailer with this Ethiopian? He was not someone she could persuade to treat Jeremiah kindly—not after the man stopped the prophet from escaping.

"What is it now?" Zedekiah daubed his lips clean with a cloth and leaned back in his chair.

"Jeremiah, sire."

"Is he dead?"

"He's recovering in the upper prison."

"I condemned him to the well." Zedekiah stood and steadied his unbalanced stance against his chair. "Who ordered this?"

"You did. Last week."

Zedekiah used both hands to balance himself. "Then why trouble me with it again?"

Ebed stepped closer. "Jeremiah spoke a curse."

"Against whom?"

"Anyone who interferes with Captain Laban's relic."

"The sword?"

"The plates of brass. He cursed to death any man who stops the record from leaving Captain Laban's treasury."

Zedekiah lowered himself back into his chair. "Nothing about the sword?"

"He didn't mention the weapon."

"You're feeding him, aren't you?"

"He's well fed, but I fear someone may try to harm Jeremiah."

"I won't allow it." Zedekiah fitted himself back into the angle of his chair. "Double the man's guards and keep him away from the other prisoners. I don't want him harmed. Do you hear? Give him whatever comforts he asks, and keep him from cursing me or my sword. I'll not face the same fate as Hananiah."

"Very well, sire." Ebed turned out of the dining room. Miriam left her husband to finish his dinner alone and followed the jailer down the corridor. There was no reason to go after him. He was one of her husband's trusted servants, but something deep in her soul prodded her to pursue him. She turned into the hall, but he was gone with not even the fall of footsteps echoing in the passageway. She hurried past a run of pillars when Ebed appeared from behind the last one. He took her by the arm and said, "You can trust me."

"I hardly know you." Miriam struggled against his powerful grip.

"Your son carried messages to the prophets." Ebed leaned in so close she could feel his breath rush past her face. "He wears a serpent charm around his neck to remind him of his baptism."

Miriam stopped struggling. How did he know so much about her son? She said, "You betrayed Jeremiah to my husband."

"I had no choice." Ebed pulled her into the shadows of the columned hallway and checked in both directions before saying, "I need more palace guards to protect him."

"From what?"

"Laban." The white of his teeth was bright against his dark lips. "I believe the captain may try to kill him."

Miriam lifted the hem of her robe and started from behind the pillar. This was a trick, and she would not betray her friends without something more than the jailer's words.

Ebed stepped in front of her, blocking her escape. "You must believe me."

"Why should I?"

"You were here the day the Babylonians invaded the city and took the Ark of the Covenant from the temple. Do you remember?"

How could she forget the day the King of Babylon besieged Jerusalem? It was in the days before her husband was made king, and she didn't need the jailer to remind her. Miriam remembered it as clearly as if she were standing in the temple courtyard again, surrounded by Babylonian soldiers. Miriam let go of the pleats in her robe and lowered her head. Ebed-Melech's words conjured up the past fear that had gripped her soul with the uncertainty of what was to become of her family, and she remembered gathering Mulek, Dan, and Benjamin close, her arms draped over them and the long skirts of her robe covering their shaking frames. Would they end up like the blacksmiths in the city, deported with their families to Babylon and their shops destroyed? Or worse, would the Babylonian General Nebuchadnezzar have them all killed for their ties to the royal house?

The image of General Nebuchadnezzar standing on the top step of the temple entrance was riveted in her mind. His tall, slender frame towered over the captives in the courtyard. He was dressed in a blue tunic with silver threads weaved into the fabric, the precious metal shimmering in the afternoon sun. He wore a silver-plated helmet that came to a point at the top and was strapped beneath his chin with a silver-studded leather piece.

Nebuchadnezzar came around on the steps, and his dark-eyed gaze stopped on Zedekiah. He ordered his soldiers to bring her husband to him. Mulek ran after his father, and Dan and Benjamin began to cry, their faces hidden in the skirts of Miriam's robe. Zedekiah ordered Mulek back to her, but the boy stood in the open expanse of the courtyard, watching his father being escorted up the steps to stand beside the Babylonian general. There were other cousins, nieces, nephews, and a host of distant royal relatives gathered here. Why did the conquering general want her husband to stand before him?

Nebuchadnezzar unsheathed his sword and raised it in the air. Dear no, not this! Her husband was the next in line to the throne, and the general was going to kill him for his ties to the deposed king. She started for the steps, but the Babylonian soldiers held her back. She struggled against their powerful arms until Nebuchadnezzar declared that all the rights, privileges, and authority of kingship belonged to Zedekiah. Miriam stepped back from the double-file line of soldiers. Did she hear right? Was Nebuchadnezzar appointing her husband king in place of his seventeen-year-old nephew, Jehoakim? And if Zedekiah was to be king, did that make her Queen of Judah? How could this be? She was a commoner, born of a vineyard owner and now, amid all this war and turmoil, in days when the hearts of her people were filled with fear of these Babylonians, she was to be queen.

Nebuchadnezzar ordered the deposed boy-king Jehoakim, her seventeen-year-old nephew, and his immediate family to the chariots to begin their journey to Babylon, leaving her husband to rule the kingdom. But before Nebuchadnezzar escorted them to the street he had the royals stay and watch his soldiers remove the spoils of war from the temple, telling them they could keep their altar and their brass washing pool on the backs of twelve oxen. He wasn't interested in destroying their religion, and he wouldn't force the Jews to worship the gods of Babylon. Jerusalem was to remain a home for the Jews. They could have their incense burners, their brass bowls and silver spoons. He left the veil hanging in the temple without tearing it from its valance. The Jews were vassals, and they could keep their fields, flocks, and grains and live a prosperous life under the rule of Babylon. But so that the Jews would see that Babylon was all powerful, he turned to the four soldiers standing at the doors of the temple and said, "Bring me the Ark of the Covenant from the innermost room."

The soldiers disappeared inside and returned carrying a large chest crafted of fine woods and inlaid with gold and silver. Miriam had seen the Ark of the Covenant once each year when it was removed from its resting place and paraded about the temple grounds to the beat of drums and the blowing of horns on the first day of the seventh month, and she pushed past the other royals to stand near the gate when the Ark went out into the street. The Babylonians could have taken the gold cherubim statues, the brass bowls, the expensive woods and ivories adorning the temple, but instead the conquerors took all the blacksmiths in the city along with this book of the covenant. Within the wooden chest lay the scrolls of the Law—the five books of Moses—and Miriam reached for the gold trimmed Ark, but didn't touch its surface as it disappeared into the street under heavy guard. She was the newly appointed Queen of Judah, but how could she and her husband rule over a people who had lost their covenants? How would they ever remember what great things the Lord had done for their fathers? Miriam slowly descended the steps of the opened temple gate and watched their guide to eternal life—sealed inside the Ark of the Covenant—hoisted onto the bed of a mule cart, and she couldn't keep her hands from trembling. The Jews at Jerusalem had lost the record preserving the knowledge of blowing of trumpets on the first day of the seventh month, and without that, her people may never celebrate another Day of Remembrance.

Ebed took hold of Miriam's hand, his calloused palm pulling her from her troubled memories, his deep, steady voice reverberating off the marbled walls and columned passages, telling her that they must protect Jeremiah long enough for him to finish the brass plates. His thick Ethiopian accent reached into her memory and returned her from reliving the day when the King of Babylon conquered their city. He said, "The record is the last chance we have to preserve the covenants."

Miriam ran her hand through her hair. All the ancient prophets since the beginning of time prophesied that God would remember His covenants with Israel in the last days of the earth. Was it possible that Ebed's request for help was the beginning of God's remembrance?

Miriam took Ebed by the arm. "When will the plates leave the city?"

"Seventeen days."

Miriam let go of the pleats in her robe, and the hem fell down around her feet. If Ebed knew so much about the future of the brass plates, could he help her find the reason Zedekiah was possessed by Laban's other relic?

"I'll help you if you'll help my husband." Miriam took Ebed's powerful hands in hers. "God save our king."

"Save him from what?"

"From himself."

CHAPTER 12

―*Late Summer, 598 B.C.*
Mt. Sinai

Nephi emerged from the shadows of a rocky gorge that led through the Border Mountains and came out on the level plain of a valley at the base of the highest peak. Rugged cliffs graced the slopes along the north side, and the late-afternoon sun cast an orange glow across the rocky face. If this mountain could speak, what tales would it tell of the day Moses sounded his trumpet and gathered the Israelites here?

The pilgrimages to Sinai ended centuries ago, the location lost to a remembrance of the elders at Jerusalem, and Nephi was left with nothing but folklore and his mother's directions to guide him to this place. Sariah had told him the story of the first day of the seventh month countless times in his youth. It was a day of blowing of trumpets, a day of memorial, a day for all Israel to make a Feast of Trumpets and remember the covenants given to Moses high on this mountaintop. Mother was certain this peak was the same summit where Moses celebrated the first Day of Remembrance, but how could she know with any certainty—how could any of them know for certain?

The sun pushed toward the western horizon, but the promise of nightfall didn't keep Nephi from starting up the slopes. He'd gone a full day without water. His throat was dry and his tongue parched, but there was no thirst powerful enough to keep him from climbing to the summit to ask God the question that plagued him since coming to this desert. If God could lead Moses to a land of promise, couldn't He do the same for Nephi and his family?

A warm breeze hurried past these quiet haunts, and in the whistling of the wind Nephi could hear the faint call of the trumpet sounding from centuries before. Did Moses stand somewhere along this ridge 686 years ago and sound a run of short, high-pitched staccato notes on his *shofar* horn—the same spirited trumpeting that for centuries had been the call of the Jews to gather and offer prayers for Israel to remember their covenants with God?

Nephi reached the last switchback, but before climbing higher, he turned back to see down the mountain's face. Was he standing where Moses stood so many centuries earlier? The prophet's ancient writings told of four hundred priests standing shoulder-to-shoulder along the base of the mountain, each of them with a *shofar* and repeating the same run of notes played by Moses, their trumpets pleading with heaven to do for Israel what God had done for their fathers and restore the forgotten covenants that had power to keep them from being cast off forever. It was a plea to God to help them remember what they had forgotten during so many years in captivity—that it was His work and His glory to bring to pass their immortality and eternal life.

The trumpeters would have been dressed in white robes washed in spring water and scrubbed clean with fuller's soap, their long, black locks falling out from beneath the white caps adorning the crowns of their heads. They were no older than Nephi, and they would have been better suited to the life of desert warriors than priests of God—hardened by months of wandering through the sands of the Sinai Peninsula and defending their camp from wild beasts and roving bands of bedouin robbers. And when the threat of chariot-riding Egyptians came against them in the deserts of Sinai and they were certain to be captured by the armies that had enslaved them for centuries, the Lord parted the fountain of the Red Sea, and these fearless, faithful youths led Israel over on dry ground to make camp in these desert mountains of Midian while Pharaoh's soldiers were drowned in the depths of the sea.

The sound of the *shofar* horns would have summoned the Israelites into the valley, the quiet sound of their reverent march muted by the clap of thunderheads along the higher elevations, the massive cloud rumbling against the rock cliffs and lightning striking loose a shower of rock down the steep face. What a scene it must have been for Moses to look out over this valley filled with thirty thousand Israelites in a sea of brown and white robes. It would have been an endless congregation filing through the rock passages, the Israelites entering the valley hand-in-hand with their families, young children riding on the shoulders of their fathers, infants in mothers' arms, and the tribe of Joseph carrying the mummified remains of their long-dead prophet leader along with two royal relics given to Joseph's sons Ephraim and Manasseh—an ancient sword passed down from father to eldest son, and a record written on plates of brass.

Nephi backed down from the cliff, climbed through a fissure in the rock, and pulled himself up over a ledge to a plateau—up where the mountain reached into the cool of the sky and a run of grasses took refuge from the desert heat below. It was quiet here, with only a lone rock dove soaring across the summit and dividing between them the memory of what happened here so many years ago when the Israelites came to this mountain in search of a land of promise, but received instead an inheritance in eternity. This was Sinai—the place where Moses spoke face-to-face with God. It had to be Sinai, just as Sariah said it was—the sacred place where Israel made covenants with God.

Nephi found a waist-high run of flat stone like an altar gracing a temple courtyard. He was not Moses, and he hadn't come to this mountain to receive the Law, but he needed an answer to the trouble brewing in camp. Was there a land of promise prepared for them—a land to replace the inheritance they left behind in Jerusalem? Or were they left to fend for themselves in this wilderness? Nephi removed his sandals and fell to his knees beside the table of stone. Dear God, he had to know if Father was right. Could he trust Lehi to lead them to a land of promise?

Aaron turned down through a narrow gorge and into a secluded valley along the north face of Mount Horeb. He called Nephi's name, but there was no answer. The footprints led this far, but with the sun setting there was little light left to track his wanderings. Aaron traversed over the rise and fall of the sand running along the base of the mountain until Nephi's footprints disappeared up an outcrop and he lost them in the twisted rock foothills. His friend could be anywhere on this mountain—over along the low-lying ridges, or up along the middle plateaus, or even at the summit. There was simply no telling where.

Aaron climbed past a run of switchbacks to an alcove among a run of brown grasses and scrub oak. The sun was gone, and a stiffening breeze carried the cool of the summit down toward the valley floor. There was enough tinder here to start a fire in the shelter of the foothills, and in the retreating shadows of dusk he quickly pulled up the grasses, cut away an armful of dried branches, and kindled a fire inside a hastily fashioned ring of rocks. The flames crackled sparks into the air and danced an orange light across the darkening mountainside. Aaron uncorked the water skin and lifted it to his lips.

"Can you spare a drink?"

Nephi stood at the edge of the firelight. His blue tunic was soiled with clay, and bits of red earth lingered in his dark hair, but there was a light in his eyes—brighter than the orange glow of the fire that lighted the distance between them. Nephi came around the fire pit, took a long drink from the water skin, and devoured the dates, eating them as quickly as Aaron could get them out of his satchel.

Aaron said, "You never should have gone off like that."

Nephi took another handful of dates and chased them with a long drink before handing the water skin back to Aaron. "Do you know the history of this mountain?"

"I must have heard your mother wrong." Aaron took a drink. "She called it Sinai."

"You didn't hear wrong." Nephi sat next to Aaron and stared into the fire. The crackle of burning wood and grass filled the silence. Aaron knew the legends telling of Mount Horeb hidden somewhere in these Border Mountains, but the location was lost to Jews centuries ago. Aaron cleared his throat to ask how Nephi knew this was the same mountain, but before he could speak his friend softly said, "I spoke with God today."

Aaron leaned forward, the heat of the fire warming his face. Did Nephi say what Aaron thought he said?

"I climbed to the summit and spoke with God. Not face-to-face like Moses, but I asked for guidance, and He answered me."

Nephi's words spilled out in a rush, telling Aaron that there were no clouds gathered into a swirling mass on the offering of his prayer. There was no thunder and no pillar of smoke rising up from the brightness of a fire atop the summit, but in the quiet of this mountain he heard a still, small voice that penetrated to the center of his heart, assuring him he was blessed because of his faithfulness and promising him that if he was obedient he would be a ruler and a teacher over his people and lead them to a land of promise—a land God had prepared for them—while Laman and Lemuel, if they rebelled, would be cut off from their new inheritance.

Nephi's words slowed, and his voice turned to a whisper telling Aaron it wasn't really a heavenly promise. It was more of a warning that if his children and his grandchildren and the descendants of any who came with them to inherit this new land rebelled against God, they would suffer at the hands of the children of Laman and Lemuel. The descendants of his elder brothers would carry ancient grudges for centuries, allotting all their misfortunes to Nephi's posterity, and they would rise up against them to be a scourge to Nephi's seed, stirring them up to a remembrance of their covenants with God. It was an odd warning. Nephi had no children, and neither did Laman or Lemuel, but if that was the promise of heaven in exchange for guidance to a new land of promise, then when he did have a family, he would see they were faithful in living the Law of Moses and keep them from ever suffering the fruits of rebellion.

A flock of rock doves nested in the rocks above the alcove took to flight, the birds gliding on the warm up-current of orange firelight before disappearing into the night. Nephi's voice grew louder as he told Aaron that today was not the first day of the seventh month. There were no blowing of trumpets atop this mountain and no tribes of Israel had come to make a memorial of this day, nor to celebrate a Feast of Trumpets to remember this revelation, but he'd heard a voice from heaven telling him they would be led to a new land of promise.

Nephi turned his gaze into the fire. His face was brighter than the flickering flames, and his eyes were filled with a light Aaron had only seen once before—the day Lehi climbed down the cliffs at Raphia and told him that he'd seen a pillar of fire. Was it possible that the youngest son of the olive oil merchant had heard the voice of God on this mountain? When Nephi spoke, Aaron was filled with the same powerful spirit he felt when Lehi laid his hands on Aaron's head and gave him a blessing that healed his feet from the terrible burns he'd gotten in the blacksmith shop. Aaron pulled his knees close to his chest and wrapped his arms around his legs, his hands falling down toward his feet. God healed him that day—the same day he called Lehi to be a prophet—and now his friend Nephi was drawing the attention of heaven.

Nephi said, "There's a reason we stopped our journey and made camp in these Border Mountains nearer the Red Sea."

Aaron said, "We stopped because Captain Laban ended his chasing."

"There's a reason he withdrew."

"He lost our trail." Aaron threw a handful of dead twigs on the fire, and a spray of orange sparks rushed into the air. "Isn't that reason enough?"

"You don't understand."

"I understand we live in peace."

"We'll find no peace without a record of the covenants." Nephi picked up a thin, gnarled branch of scrub oak, the twisted wood like the graft of an olive tree. He stirred the end of it through the hot coals, recounting to Aaron that after Moses returned from this summit with the covenant written on stone by the finger of God, he wrote the rest of his revelations onto five scrolls, recording for generations unborn the Law that would point their souls toward the Messiah. And he enlisted the help of carpenters and constructed a chest of fine woods inlaid with gold and silver trim to protect the stone tablets and the five leather scrolls of the Law, and he called the holy coffer the Ark of the Covenant. And since animal-hide scrolls did not bear the passage of time as well as stone tablets, nor endure in their perfect form after passing under the altering hand of scribes copying them from generation to generation, Moses found the brass-plate record kept among the descendants of Joseph and etched into the metal a second copy of the five books of the law, preserving the covenant on plates of brass to come forth in the last days of the earth as another witness of the Anointed One.

The rapid pace of Nephi's voice ran over the alcove and filtered up into the dark night with the rising smoke of the campfire, telling Aaron that the Ark of the Covenant containing the Law written in Moses' own hand was kept in the temple at Jerusalem until the Babylonian war two years ago when it was taken by the conquering army as the spoils of war. Nephi raised the glowing red-hot end of the stick and blew on the end of it. "We brought the records of Isaiah with us into this desert and some of the writings of other prophets, like Zenos, but if we're to live the Law of Moses we need a copy of his writings." Nephi slowly shook the stick, the red glow dancing in the night air. "We could never return to Jerusalem to get the brass copy of the Law. Father would never allow it." He stirred the branch in the coals again, heating the end of it until it caught fire. "It's too dangerous."

Aaron said, "We know the trade routes."

"The danger isn't in the journey. It's the brass plates." Nephi tossed the twisted, burning branch into the fire pit. "They belong to Captain Laban."

CHAPTER 13

—Late Summer, 598 B.C.
Jerusalem

Baruch adjusted his writing satchel over his shoulder and waited in the dark corridor for Ebed-Melech to open the upper prison. A rush of musty air streamed around the door, and Baruch stepped past the Chief Jailer. Two empty chairs stood near a writing table. There were no prisoners milling about—no one but Ebed with whom to divide the light of a single cauldron lamp.

"You have until sunset," Ebed said in answer to Baruch's staring. The Ethiopian was a stout man, his upper arms strapped with metal bands, his bald head glistening in the flickering light of the lamp. He disappeared down the circular stairs leading to the catacombs, latching the door behind him and leaving Baruch in the silent chamber with only the trickle of water running through a pipe and into the bathing pool. Baruch lowered himself into the angle of the first chair and spread a leather parchment, an ink well, and three clean pens on the table before him. Why did Ebed leave him here alone? The Ethiopian could have at least stayed with him until . . .

Something stirred in the shadows along the far wall. He squinted in the dim light until he made out the form of a man dressed in a long robe. There were no shackles about his feet or hands. His long, graying hair was clean and combed back off his brow.

"Jeremiah?" Baruch leaned forward in his chair. "Is that you, sir?"

"You forget a friend so quickly?" Jeremiah lowered himself into the chair opposite Baruch.

"Your face . . ." Baruch reached his hand to the prophet's gaunt cheeks and sunken eyes, his fingertips passing close but not touching the man's unrecognizable form. "What did they do to you?"

"I'd be dead if not for the Ethiopian." Jeremiah took a deep breath, and the wheezing sound of sickness festered in his breathing. He nodded at the inkwell, tapped his long, bony forefinger to the leather parchment. "Shall we begin?"

"Are you able?"

Without answering, Jeremiah began uttering his prophecies, the words spilling out of him like a river rushing over a fall, his voice echoing up through the columns in the chamber. He was born to a poor vineyard keeper, the son of Hilkiah, a priest at Anathoth, and he was known of God before the world was created—ordained and sanctified that his prophetic words would go to all nations. Jeremiah said, "Did you get that?"

"Born to Hilkiah. I have it."

"To all nations."

"Yes, right here." Baruch pointed to his hastily written Hebrew characters.

"Write that the word of the Lord came to me." Jeremiah motioned with his hand as he spoke of hearing the Lord's voice, and when he described it, Baruch could almost hear the perfect mildness of the voice of God telling Jeremiah that the judgments against Israel began 120 years earlier when the kingdom of Northern Israel was destroyed, and they wouldn't stop until judgment was visited at the gate of Jerusalem. He went on about the Jews forsaking God and worshiping the works of their own hands. The late afternoon hour rushed past with Jeremiah speaking of the Messiah, the fountain of living waters and the only way to salvation. He condemned idol worship, saying that the King of Babylon would surely come and destroy this land, and he spoke at length about the prophets that had been rejected and murdered in the city. He paused for a moment, his gaze turning about the prison chamber. "Do you hear that?"

Baruch set aside his pen. "Hear what?"

"Dead prophets. Their blood cries from out of the pit of this prison."

"You mean Uriah?"

"He wasn't the first to die at Captain Laban's hands." Jeremiah stood from the chair, his brown robes hanging limp from his gaunt frame. "Nahum was murdered here." He came around the small writing table. "Habakkuk would still be alive if the people of Jerusalem had had enough courage to put an end to the slaughter of the men of God, and there isn't a soul who knows what happened to Zephania. They say he was taken up in a chariot of fire like Elisha, but the only chariot to take him came from Captain Laban's stables. They took him from his bed in the darkest hours of night and delivered him here. The only fire came from the hot coals they used to silence his tongue."

Baruch said, "You've been spared."

"God made me like a defenced city and an iron pillar with brass walls." Jeremiah motioned for Baruch to take up his pen again. "Go on, write that in your parchment." He waited for Baruch to dip for more ink before saying that God was with him and he would deliver him from this—

Jeremiah coughed, his lungs heaving to clear his throat, and Baruch wrote the word "place" at the end of the phrase. That's what Jeremiah intended to say, wasn't it—that God would deliver him from this awful place?

Baruch said, "Are you well enough to go on?"

"I haven't time to be ill."

They were alone in this chamber without anyone to hear them, but Baruch's next question was filled with enough treason that he lowered his voice to a whisper. "Tell me, sir." He shifted in his chair. "Are you plotting to steal the brass relic?"

Jeremiah turned his gaze about the chamber, stopping on the shadows in the far corner, then over to the darkness beyond the door before coming back to Baruch. He softly said, "Laban's plates of brass were never intended for the Jews at Jerusalem."

"But why take them?"

Jeremiah sat up straight. "They're to show unto a remnant of this people what great things the Lord has done for their fathers."

"What good could come of you stealing them?"

"It isn't I."

"Then who?"

"What we do here will convince Jew and Gentile that Yeshua is the Anointed One, the Eternal God, manifesting Himself to all nations."

Baruch started his pen moving, recording that the brass plates would convince Jew and Gentile that—

"Don't write that." Jeremiah reached for the pen. "Those words are for another prophet to write—a man many years from now in a distant promised land. He'll prepare my words on plates of gold to go to all nations and be read upon the housetops."

Jeremiah began to cough, and he wrapped his arms around himself.

Baruch said, "I'll come back tomorrow when you're feeling better."

"Nonsense. The Lord put forth His hand and touched my lips, and I have His words in my mouth." Jeremiah cleared his throat. "We must finish this before the first day of the seventh month is come."

"Are you certain of the date?"

Jeremiah leaned forward in his chair. "What do you know of the Hebrew calendar?"

"Moses established it among the Jews. What else is there to know?"

"He didn't establish it, my friend. God revealed it to Moses, gave him a vision of the great time-keeping orbits and revolutions of the planets created in the heavens." Jeremiah stood next to the flame burning in the crucible, the brightness casting light over his face. "God tracks the passing of every moment. Nothing happens without His knowledge. He's aware of everything, down to the flight of the smallest sparrow, and of all the events in the history of man there are few greater than preserving the covenants written on the brass plates. I'm not certain of the date when Laban's relic will leave the city." Jeremiah laid his hand on Baruch's shoulder. "God is."

CHAPTER 14

—September 12, 1825
Old City of Jerusalem

Avram Weiss sat at the head of the table. It was an uncomfortable place, not because the chair wasn't constructed out of the finest hardwood, and certainly not because the seat was cushioned by hand-sewn leather covers imported from the west. This chair was uncomfortable because Avram never should have agreed to eat the *ha-Zikkaron* feast in the home of Reuben Kessler—a Sephardic Jew. He should be eating in the kosher comfort of their two-room apartment in the Lower City in company with his daughter—his only family left on earth—not sitting at the head of the table where Mr. Kessler should be seated. It didn't matter that the clock maker insisted Avram sit here and preside over the meal. Something odd was going on. He could feel it in the air, and he didn't like it, not one bit.

There was no reason not to enjoy the meal. They were attended by a maid to serve the food, a butler pouring wine, and a cook with a delicate touch—at least this first course of tomato and cucumber soup had the perfect balance of garlic, onion, rosemary, and basil. The dining room was bright with holiday candles lit at dawn, and the flickering light mixed with the light of the kerosene chandelier hanging over the table made this a more festive sight than he'd seen in all his years celebrating *ha-Zikkaron* in Russia. The vase in the center of the table was filled with red and yellow roses, and beside each place setting of silverware, crystal, and china stood a greeting card of the most exquisite making, trimmed in gold and silver and wishing Avram and his daughter a most happy New Year. Avram removed the *caftan* from his head, and the long earlocks fell down past his gaunt cheeks and mixed with the gray hair of his beard. He brushed them back and started on the soup.

Danny sat on the window side of the table, the large frame silhouetting his long body with the darkness of nightfall and the glow of a full moon. The boy hardly touched the first course. He was dressed in a fine gray suit, his black bow tie perfectly affixed on the turned-up collar of his elegant shirt, the white cloth reaching up around his neck. A silver spoon hung from his hand, the end of it still clean and shimmering in the candlelight without the least bit of broth spoiling the reflection. He stared across the table at Katerina, and there was good reason to stare at the girl. Before they left home for this meal, his daughter insisted on painting her lips with a deep red lipstick reserved for the most important occasions. She wore a black dress with a border of red, yellow, and blue pansies embroidered across the hem—a dress she purchased from the seamstress with money saved for nearly a year. A red rose decorated the part in her black hair, and she wore a white lace shawl around her neck, the ends of it swaying with each of her hurried glances, looking up at Danny and smiling before going back to stir her spoon through her soup. But for all the girl's stirring, she'd not taken a solitary bite. Her dress was kosher, all of it well within the modesty required of Hassidic Jews, but Avram couldn't keep from leaning over his bowl, waving his spoon between the two youths and lecturing them.

"We should bless the main course." Reuben Kessler sat at the opposite end of the table, working his spoon through the green chives and mushrooms topping his soup. He finished the last of his soup, and handed the bowl to the maid. The woman disappeared into the kitchen and returned with two loaves of fresh-baked white challah bread. It was prepared exactly as it should be, with the double strands of dough twisting together reminding them of the binding hope that the prayers they offered today at synagogue—the ones asking God to awaken to a remembrance of His covenants with Israel—would reach heaven. The twisted ladder bread announced that on this holiday each year men were judged—some destined to climb and prosper, while others were condemned to descend and fail. A bounty of confections, cookies, and cakes sat on the side table waiting for them to finish their main course, and the smell of simmering meats filtered in from the kitchen, and there was no doubt how heaven viewed the clock maker. It was certain Mr. Kessler was destined to climb and prosper in this New Year like he had for so many years before.

Reuben said, "Avram, will you offer the blessing?"

Avram tore away a piece of challah bread and dipped it in the small bowl of honey beside his plate before raising his gaze to the ceiling and quickly reciting, "May it be thy will, O Lord, to renew unto us a happy and pleasant year." The others dipped their bread in the honey and repeated the words of his prayer, and as soon as they finished, the maid and the cook burst through the doors, the women humming a happy melody and serving the main course—brown trout from the Sea of Galilee. It was just as it should be for the celebration of *ha-Zikkaron*, the fish reminding them of fruitfulness and plenty. But since Danny Kessler's interest in his daughter was far more than he wanted for the girl, Avram raised his wine glass in the air, held it out in front of the boy to keep him from seeing into his daughter's eyes and offered a toast that this baked fish with all its garnish would make for them a year of plenty. There was not a word about fruitfulness. That was a toast reserved for a newlywed couple, and there was no one at this table who needed that blessing or the promise of such. Avram said, "May it be a year of prosperity for all."

Avram started into his fish, and Mr. Kessler joined him, but Danny and Katerina hardly touched their food. Avram had to say something, but what? They'd already spoken of the weather, offered wishes for a prosperous New Year, and sung the songs of the season—and oh how the Kesslers could sing. It was no wonder Reuben was cantor at the synagogue, and if Danny ever gave up his trumpet playing, he could follow in his father's footsteps without a single lesson in the art of voice. Avram said, "What day is it, boy?"

Danny turned in his chair, but his gaze remained fixed on Katerina. "What was that, sir?"

"The day, boy. What day is it?"

"*ha-Zikkaron*, sir." Danny didn't look at him.

"The Greek date." Avram held up the calendar Danny had prepared for the coming year and shook it until he drew Danny's attention away from his daughter. "In the west, what day is it?"

"It's right here, sir." Danny shuffled through the papers and found the month of September hidden among the pages of the calendar. He set his forefinger on the twelfth day. "The holiday falls on the twelfth of September this year."

"Certain you are of it?"

Katerina said, "Papa, when have any of Danny's calculations been wrong?"

Avram straightened the papers into a neat stack. "The calendar, Danny. Did I pay you for it?"

"It's a gift, sir."

"Cards we exchange on *ha-Zikkaron*." Avram lifted the gold-embossed greeting card off the table. "Not gifts."

Danny said, "I was hoping to speak to you about that before dinner."

"A fine job you've done with the calendar this year." Avram reached into his pocket, searching for the money to pay for the boy's work.

"Papa, let him explain." Katerina reached across the table and patted Danny on the hand. "Go on. Ask him."

Danny tapped the tabletop with his finger, his gaze shifting between Katerina and Avram.

Reuben said, "I'll fetch another bottle of wine from the cellar."

"Stay here, Mr. Kessler." Katerina turned back to Danny. "Go on; everyone's listening."

Avram said, "What are we to listen to?"

Danny said, "I was going to speak to you in private, sir, but . . ."

"A few errors I can forgive, son." Avram held up the calendar.

"The dates are fine, but in an odd sort of way, it is about the calendar." Danny took it from him, turned past September, October, and November, the papers rustling in the silence of the dining room. He kept sorting through the months until he came to the end and set the calendar on the table next to Avram's plate. "Here it is. I calculated the date for next year's celebration."

Avram adjusted his glasses on the end of his nose and leaned over the calendar to see the date for the first day of the seventh Jewish month one year from then, when they would again celebrate *ha-Zikkaron*. Below Danny's careful pen strokes recording the day for the celebration was a note indicating the details of the wedding of

Katerina Weiss, daughter of Avram, to Danny Kessler, son of Reuben. Avram removed his glasses, wiped the lens on his cuff and replaced them on his nose, but his rubbing didn't change the words. They were still there in bold black ink. The wedding was set for midday under the canopy in the gardens of the Sephardic synagogue where the Kesslers prayed every *Shabbat*.

Avram handed the calendar back to Danny.

"Papa." Katerina set her fork down. "Hear Danny out."

"Mr. Weiss." Danny forced a smile. "Ever since the first day I met your daughter, I've not thought of much else."

"Too young you are for this."

"We're both nineteen." Katerina worked the napkin between her thumb and fingers.

Danny said, "I met Katerina two years ago today, do you remember, sir?"

"How can I forget?" Avram raised his hands in the air. "Every day my daughter reminds me of it."

Danny said, "We thought it a good thing to marry on the anniversary of that day."

Katerina said, "We'll both be twenty years old by then, Papa."

"A good boy you are, Danny. A fine clock maker, and the calendar— you calculate it better than any in the city." Avram reached his hands toward Danny and Reuben. "You are my good Sephardic friends, but we're not like you. We have our traditions, our ways of doing things." He turned his gaze over the fine furnishings in the dining room. "We came from the ghettos of Russia. Little money we have, and less education. We know no other way."

Katerina came around the table. "You don't have to answer Danny right now."

"There's no other answer, daughter."

"Please, Mr. Kessler." Danny came down the other side of the table. "Allow me to marry your daughter."

"Like oil and water we are." Avram stood and took Katerina by the hand. He nodded to Reuben, thanked him for the lovely dinner before removing the napkin from under his collar and backing away from the table, leaving the half-eaten fish and the untouched garnish on his plate. Katerina resisted, but Avram would not relent. He kept a firm hold on her trembling hand, and before turning into the hall and going out the front doors to the street, he leaned his head in next to Katerina and said, "We don't mix with other Jews."

—Ten days later
Palmyra Township, State of New York

Joseph Sr. worked the sheath along the edge of the wheat field behind the unfinished white frame house while Samuel Harrison, William, and Don Carlos gathered the felled stalks in his wake. He held the blade level with his hips and swung away, the metal cutting through the golden stalks of wheat like a ladle through churned butter. With Alvin dead nearly two years, Hyrum away searching north of Palmyra for some land to contract and settle before his upcoming marriage to Jerusha, and Joseph Jr. disappearing after lunch, he was left without anyone to spell him on the blade and only the help of the younger boys to gather the wheat into bundles. Samuel was a strong, hardworking lad of sixteen, and he gathered the harvest into tall, neat stacks. William's thirteen-year-old body was able to keep up with the fast pace of cutting under the heat of the afternoon sun, but nine-year-old Don Carlos struggled to keep the wheat from falling from his arms, his head sprouting above a bundle that hid him from chest to waist. Joseph Sr. called to the lad, telling him to put down the wheat and head across Stratford Road and help his mother put out the wash on a rope strung between the trunks of two large maples, but he shook his head and said he was big enough to work alongside his brothers, no matter the unusual heat of late September.

Joseph Sr. reached the far end of the field and came around, slowly cutting his way back in behind the white frame house where the sound of sawing and hammering echoed out the back entrance of the unfinished dwelling that still waited for a door to seal it from the elements. The carpenter from Palmyra, a Mr. Stoddard, was busy finishing some work he had contracted with Alvin before the boy passed away. Work on the house slowed considerably when God took Alvin from them, and it was good to hear the sound of a carpenter filling the air with the memory of his dead son's enthusiasm. Joseph Sr. kept the sheath working from side to side. Alvin wanted this frame house finished, and he hired Mr. Stoddard on credit to do some of the work they couldn't do themselves, but Joseph Sr. was going to have to tell the carpenter that as soon as he finished the moldings and the split beams they wouldn't be hiring any more work on credit. It was odd he'd show up to do more after so long an absence. They already owed him a tidy sum, and they were going to have to defer payment on what they did owe until next year. The land payment was due at the end of the month, and the frame house was going to have to wait a while longer.

The sound of the hammer fell quiet, and Stoddard stepped out onto the unfinished stone on the back porch and wiped the sweat from his brow before walking down the rise and into the wheat field. He came alongside Joseph Sr., careful to stay far enough away not to take the blade across the thigh. "Afternoon, Smith."

Joseph Sr. nodded and turned the blade through the stalks, throwing down a wide stand of wheat.

Stoddard said, "Farming's hard work."

"No harder than carpentering." Joseph cut another swath before pulling up long enough to direct Don Carlos to carry his load to the shortest stack in the field where he could reach it to the top. "Samuel, help him, would you? And have William glean the last row and gather anything Don Carlos missed." He wiped his brow with the sleeve of his work shirt before turning back to Mr. Stoddard.

"There's still work to do on the beams." Stoddard hung his hammer on his pant pocket. "I'll start on the moldings along the stair railings come morning and then see to finishing the upper rooms."

"I'm afraid not." Joseph stood the sheath handle on the ground. "We won't be hiring you for a time. We haven't the money."

"I work on credit."

Joseph Sr. ran his hand over the blade. "As it stands now, it'll be a year before we can start paying on the debt we owe."

"I hear you didn't make your mortgage payment on time last year and you're behind this year."

"The land agent's been good to work with us."

Stoddard's voice went low, and he fixed his gaze on Joseph Sr. He said, "The Evertsons in New York City own this farm, isn't that right?"

"Why do you ask?"

"They hired a new agent." Stoddard adjusted his hammer. "The man arrived in Canandaigua last week. I hear he isn't as easy to work with. Have you met him?"

"I'm sure he'll be by to collect soon enough."

"You'd better hope he's as kindhearted a soul as was the last agent. You have enough to pay the man, don't you?"

"A man's debts and credits, sir, are his own business." Joseph started the sheath moving again, cutting the stalks to the ground. "Why do you care so much about the details?"

"I like to know something about a farm before I make an offer." Stoddard walked behind Joseph's slow pace through the wheat field. "I'll give you fifteen hundred dollars for it and forgive what you owe on my carpentry work."

Joseph kept the sheath swinging through the wheat. "Fifteen hundred dollars for a cabin, a frame home, seventy acres of cleared farmland, and thirty more acres in sugar maples?"

"It's cash, Smith. You'll not get an offer like this anywhere in the county. Not in these troubled times. Three-quarters of the farmers have lost their land."

"We don't aim to lose ours. Two more payments, and we'll own this land free and clear."

"You don't have the money, Smith."

"I'm not selling."

"Sell it to me, or lose it to the land agent." Stoddard came around in front of Joseph and stood in the uncut wheat ahead of his sheath, stopping him from swinging the blade. "You got too many debts, and I ain't giving you no more credit. What you owe me is due now, and you got one year from today before the law says I can bring the sheriff with a warrant. You best think twice about selling your farm. You're going to need the money."

"I'm fifty-four years old, Stoddard." Joseph tightened his grip on the sheath handle. "I know what it takes to build a farm on unsettled land. I've done it more times than I like to remember, and I don't have the strength to do it again." He turned a slow circle, his gaze passing over the wheat field, across the unfinished rafters of the white frame house rising up along the road like a monument to Alvin—his eldest son who lay in a grave along the north end of the property behind a white picket fence—then across Stratford to the cabin where Lucy and the girls busied themselves hanging out wash near the edge of the maple grove. He came around full circle, the sheath spanning the distance between his hands. "We've seen more than our share of disappointments over the years—droughts, frost, the kind of struggles that ruin a farmer—and we're not thinking to lose this land and put upon our children in our later years because we haven't a place to call our own. This is where Lucy and I plan to live out our days, God willing."

"And if God ain't willing?"

"We'll make do."

"Is that how you folks plan to make do?" Stoddard pointed over beyond the north side of the frame house, up along the dusty path of Stratford Road. Five men stood in the shadows of the tallest trees at the far end of the property. It was the Stafford clan—old farmer Stafford leading the pack with his son, Doctor John Stafford, on his left hand and two cousins and a nephew trailing a few strides behind the doctor.

"Samuel." Joseph Sr. set aside his sheath. "Take William and Don Carlos over to help your mother."

Samuel dropped an armful of wheat onto the stack. "She don't need any help with the wash."

"Take your brothers and go." Joseph Sr. turned back to Mr. Stoddard. "If you'll excuse me."

"You're that desperate are you, Smith?"

"Stay out of this."

"Fifteen hundred dollars cash. Then you don't have to go working for money diggers like the Staffords." Mr. Stoddard folded his arms across his chest, the hammer hedging out below his hands. "You ain't going to go chasing after any buried treasure, are you? That ain't going to raise you even a plug—"

"Good day, sir."

Joseph Sr. left his sheath in the field and walked through the uncut wheat toward the Stafford men while the carpenter went back inside the frame house, the rhythmic pounding of his hammer carrying on the humid summer afternoon air.

"Afternoon, Smith." Old man Stafford took off his hat, wiped his brow, and replaced the head covering while the other four men gathered around. He turned his gaze past Joseph Sr., out over the wheat field. "Could we have a few words with your son?"

"I have five sons, sir."

"Joseph Jr. We be looking for that particular son."

John Stafford said, "The money digger."

The Stafford cousin said, "The one who dug himself gold plates out of the ground."

Joseph Sr. said, "Where did you hear that?"

Old man Stafford spoke with a gruff voice, his fat cheeks lifting and falling with his words. "It's the right time of year, Smith. The long, hot days of summer pull the Spanish treasure close to the surface. There's no better time to be digging about than early fall."

"No better time." The shorter Stafford cousin leaned his head in. "No better time in the whole year."

"Joseph isn't here." Joseph Sr. shook his head. "He left sometime after lunch."

"Where'd he go?"

"The boy didn't say."

"He wouldn't be out looking for treasure on his own now, would he?"

"Look there." The Stafford cousin pointed his long, dirt-soiled finger at a man approaching from the south. "There's the digger now."

Joseph Jr. walked with a slight limp that only Joseph Sr. detected—a subtle limp the boy had tried to hide ever since his surgery nearly ten years earlier. He wore a wide-brimmed hat that shaded his face from the sun, and a white shirt with brown suspenders strapped over his shoulder. And when his head came up and he saw the Staffords gathered in the wheat field, he crossed the road to the other side and kept walking, his stride picking up and carrying him at a good clip until he reached the cabin. He ducked past the hanging laundry and quickly disappeared inside.

Old man Stafford said, "We were hoping the boy would—"

"My son doesn't dig for money. It's been two years since he worked a spade for you or your kin. I thought he told you not to come asking."

"He did, but . . ." John Stafford stepped in front of his father. "We heard talk of plates of gold and such, and we thought maybe he'd changed his ways."

"There's been no change."

"Look here, Smith." Old man Stafford took Joseph Sr. by the shoulder. "There aren't many farmers with the good fortune of owning their own land in this county. I just happen to be one of the lucky few, and I can afford to hire you and your son. You need the money, and I'm willing to pay you ten dollars to get the boy to help us dig, plus double the wage they pay at the Palmyra docks."

Joseph Sr. slowly shook his head. "He won't agree to it."

"Go on, ask him." Old man Stafford handed him ten silver dollars—more money than he'd earn from weeks of harvesting and hauling his wheat to market. He said, "We'll wait right here."

Doctor John Stafford said, "And if he won't do the digging, see if he'll tell us where to dig." He turned to his father. "We'll pay him ten dollars for directions and give you a share of the treasure, won't we, Father?"

Old man Stafford shook his fist. "I'll give you a fourth of what we find."

Joseph Sr. left them along the edge of the wheat field and started down past the white frame house. Carpenter Stoddard peered out the unfinished window, and when Joseph Sr. walked past, he came out onto the porch, tapping his hammer in the palm of his hand in rhythm to Joseph Sr.'s steps, watching him cross the road like a hawk watches its prey. The carpenter was right. They needed more money to pay the new land agent when he came calling the end of the month, but Joseph Sr. wasn't going to sell this farm to Stoddard, no matter how many threats he spewed about calling his credit due and demanding payment for his work. He'd have to try for another loan on the wheat harvest, and maybe he could convince the new land agent to delay a few months until they had the entire sum.

Joseph Sr. glanced back at the Stafford men. Was this lot of money diggers his only hope to keep from losing the farm and falling into tenancy? Dear God of heaven, how were they to meet their obligations on the mortgage in these down times? Joseph Sr. crossed the road, walked slowly up the stone path, and pushed open the front door of the cabin.

Lucy sat on the edge of the rocker, the chair tilted forward, her hands clasped around Joseph Jr.'s hands. The boy leaned over his Mother's chair, speaking of some strange ancient prophet. The hill? Is that where Joseph Jr. disappeared after lunch? The year passed so quickly, and with so many concerns about money begging his attention, Joseph Sr. had nearly forgotten Joseph's duty to return to the hill on September 22. Joseph Jr. never shared the exact location with them, and there was no telling where he went each of the last two years to spend hours in the company of an angel. Joseph Sr.'s heart begged him to take up a chair and listen to his son's account of another visit, but there were other matters that demanded his attention, and when he didn't move from standing in the doorway Joseph Jr. fell silent, the last phrase about brass plates and gold plates and a prophet named Lehi with a son named Nephi fading against the far wall.

"You didn't tell me you were leaving after lunch." Joseph Sr. closed the door and walked to the dipping bucket hanging on the wall. He poured water over his neck, but it didn't have power to cool him, and he dropped the ladle on the kitchen table.

Joseph Jr. said, "I didn't tell anyone, Papa. It's best that way."

Joseph Sr. stepped to the cabin window. He gripped the sill and peered out at the Staffords across the road. "Did you get the plates?"

"No, sir."

"How much longer?"

"When I'm prepared."

"Prepared for what, son?"

"Tell him." Lucy stood from the rocker, the wooden backrest swaying on her sudden departure. "Tell your father what you were telling me."

"There's so much that I never supposed, Father." Joseph Jr. stepped in next to the window and laid his hand on Joseph Sr.'s shoulder, his voice calm and steady as a stream, telling of his afternoon visit to the hill where he spent the day under the tutelage of Moroni instructing him on the contents of the gold-plate record, telling him of ancient prophets that lived on this continent, and the account of ancient inhabitants recorded in the gold-plate record. There was a prophet Lehi who brought from Jerusalem an ancient record of brass plates containing the covenants God made with the House of Israel—the same covenants recorded in the Bible, and many more that were lost over the years. The brass plates guided these ancient American prophets, and they transcribed the covenants and prophecies given to the House of Israel from the brass plates into their own writings on plates of gold—the same record Moroni was preparing Joseph to translate.

Joseph Sr. lowered his head, his hand still gripping the sill. "I don't know how much longer we can go on like this."

"I'm to return to the hill one year from now."

"That's what you said last year." Joseph Sr. pulled on the windowsill with both hands, the boards creaking under the strain. "What are we to do? We haven't the money to keep the farm."

Lucy said, "Mr. Smith, this isn't the time to lose faith."

"I haven't been a good husband." Joseph Sr. rubbed his brow. "I haven't provided like I hoped to when we were first married."

"You're the finest husband a woman could hope to have." Lucy stepped in next to the window and took him by the hand until his fist softened and fell away from the windowsill. "The very finest."

Joseph Jr. cracked the door and peered out at the five men gathered on the north edge of the wheat field. "What does the Stafford clan want with us?"

Joseph Sr. said, "They're wanting you and me to hire on for some digging."

Joseph shut the door, and the latch clicked in place. "I told the Staffords I was through digging for them."

"They'll pay ten dollars a day for any help you give them."

"No, Papa."

"They know you found treasure buried in the ground once. They think you can find more."

"I didn't find anything. I was led to the place where the plates were buried."

"Could you send them towards where you found the gold plates? There's bound to be more treasure in that part of the county."

Joseph Jr. backed away from the door. "I can't tell them anything."

"They already know, son." Joseph Sr. lowered his head. "They think you have magical powers for treasure hunting."

"That isn't so." Joseph ran his hand through his hair, his gaze shifting between the door and his father. "Who told them such lies?"

"Son." Lucy crossed the room and reached for his arm, but he refused her reaching. "We've been talking about these visits for two years now. All your brothers and sisters know the stories of an angel and ancient peoples, their travels, their cities, and every particular right down to their wars and their type of worship. One of the children must have said something to a neighbor. You know how stories spread in this township."

Joseph Jr. ran both hands through his hair, his light brown locks poking between his fingers. "I never should have said anything."

"Of course you should have, right down to every detail." Lucy stepped to his side. "You've a work to do, son—a work every man and woman on earth will hear about. And no matter what calumny rages against you, there's no evil that can stop it. Do you hear me?" She glanced out the window. "This is the work of God, and no mob from the Stafford clan can bring it down."

"You don't know them like I know them, Mother."

Joseph Sr. said, "Why don't you go out and talk to them, offer them some advice?"

"The angel forbade me to do any such thing."

Joseph Sr. pressed his fist against the rough wood in the cabin door. "Give me something I can tell them—anything."

"They can go home and dig in their own fields if they like."

"Will they find treasure there?"

"Oh, Papa." Joseph Jr. took him by the hand. "Tell them to put away their lust for money."

"I'm sorry, son. I shouldn't trouble you with this right now. You have your own worries." Joseph Sr. broke free of his son's grip and reached for the latch, but before he went out Lucy said, "Mr. Smith, where are you going?"

"I'll be home late." Joseph Sr. fitted his hat over his head, straightened his suspenders on his shoulders, and turned out onto the porch. "I have a land payment to raise."

CHAPTER 15

▼▼▼

—Late Summer, 598 B.C.
Valley of Lemuel (Wadi Tayyib al-Ism)

Sariah sat up, and the lambskin blanket fell from her shoulders. Nephi? The first dim light of morning filtered around the seams in the tent flaps. She leaned forward listening for the sound of her youngest son's footsteps, the steady sound of his voice, anything to announce his return, but there was nothing beyond the chirp of a rock dove. Sariah lowered herself back onto the hard ground, gathering the blanket around her and searching for the courage to pass another day not knowing if Aaron had found Nephi.

Lehi lay asleep beside her. He pulled the blanket from her grasp and turned on his side before coming back onto his stomach. He punched his pillow and grumbled something about his dreams. He didn't usually sleep with such fury, but last night he did nothing but stir like a man with fever. He was fine before retiring—no complaints of sickness or chills—but not less than three times during the night she held his arm until his stirring calmed, and twice more she called his name loud enough to wake him from whatever tumult his dreams caused. But no matter what she did, he returned to the same restlessness. Another night like this, and she was going to have him sleep in the sand. He was a dreamer, but until now he did his dreaming without depriving her of her own. She shouldn't complain. Lehi's restlessness kept her from reliving the nightmare that troubled her own sleep—a vision not fit to recall, and she was thankful for her husband's stirring that would not let her mind drift away to wander over such awful possibilities. Why was she troubled with fearful night visions of her four sons? Laman, Lemuel, and Sam weren't lost on a trek across the desert. It was Nephi who hadn't returned from the mountain where Moses saw God. Sariah rubbed her brow, but the images from her sleep would not leave.

Lehi tossed about, and Sariah felt beneath the blanket until she caught hold of his hand and said, "Dear, are you well?"

There was no answer, but her touch calmed him enough that his stirring ceased, his frame relaxed, and his breathing turned to a more restful rhythm.

The night was gone and she should be up preparing the morning meal or at least helping the other women as much as an expectant mother could. Thankfully Sophia—the wife of Commander Yaush—told her that with the child coming today or tomorrow or possibly as late as the following day, she should do nothing but rest while the other women in camp saw to preparing the meals. Bless that woman. Sophia was a midwife in a camp with far too many men who did not understand the pains of carrying a child.

Sariah reached for the tent pole and struggled to her feet. There had to be something she could do to take her mind off Nephi's absence. Water. That's what needed doing. She could gather drinking water before the others in camp stirred, and—

A spasm flashed through her womb strong enough to force a gasp from deep within. She leaned against the tent pole for relief. Was it time? Was this child telling her to call for help, or was this a false distress like so many others that had plagued her on their flight through the wilderness? So many days had passed since she first remembered being with child, back when she got up in the middle of the night for a bottle of olives from the storehouse in the old orchard, only to find Lieutenant Daniel and his men burning the grove. The headaches were gone, the hair on the back of her head had grown back in, and the scars were hardly visible. Her spine ached with the same pain she suffered at the birth of her other children. She was having trouble with balance, and she craved olives and brown trout, the dish they served whenever the family celebrated the Feast of Trumpets on the first day of—

The unborn child kicked against her side and forced her to stand straight. That was odd. She'd not ever felt such power from an unborn.

Sariah slowly started across the tent toward the entrance. Oh, how she enjoyed preparing for the celebrations this time of year when they lived at their estate at Beit Zayit, but with the difficult conditions of living in this desert it wasn't possible to make preparations for *ha-Zikkaron.*

There it was again, the child kicking with enough force to take her breath. The day had arrived for her to be delivered, but was this child telling her the day of birth wasn't to come until the first day of the seventh month? Impossible. She was nothing if not foolish to consider such a notion, and she certainly wasn't going to carry the babe any longer than the day it was due to be delivered. She'd made all the preparations. A stack of clean towels sat in the corner of the tent next to a basin of water. There was a supply of oils in the satchel beside the bed, three jars of ointments, and sacks of every good herb lined the wall of the tent—some for sleeping, some for pains, and a sack filled with herbs to calm her spasms. That's what she needed most, herbs for the cramps that plagued her after giving birth. If this birth was anything like Nephi's, she was going to need every combination of herbs in this tent along with some she didn't have. The day had come, and she would not wait sixteen more until the Feast of Trumpets.

Not again. The moment she thought of the feast, the child kicked, and she let out a gasp that stirred Lehi from his sleeping. In the dimness she could see him sit up and rub his brow. He ran his hands through his hair and mumbled something about the danger of it all, but before Sariah could ask him to explain himself, the baby kicked again, and she let out a gasp and held her side.

"Sariah. It's time." Lehi hurried over and ushered her to the pillows stacked along the far wall. The touch of his hands assured her that she was to wait until *ha-Zikkaron* for this child to join them in life. It distilled over her like a warm blanket, entering her thinking like a calm shelter in the middle of a storm, assuring her of the delayed birth, and telling her that Nephi would return to them safely. She turned to see if Lehi was speaking, but he was busy arranging the pillows. And no matter how impossible it seemed, she could not deny the impression, and she asked Lehi for a drink of water to quench her mind of the fire of these revelations. No matter how much she hoped to get beyond the birth of this child and enjoy the company of a newborn, she could not deny the will of heaven. She'd not ever birthed a child this late. By her calculations, she was due any day, but her heart told her otherwise, assuring her that the days for this birth would not be accomplished until the first day of *Tishri*—the day Jews remembered their covenants with God.

Lehi said, "I'll call for Sophia and Rebekah."

"There's no need, dear." Sariah took a deep breath. "I would have this child today, but heaven will not cooperate."

"Quiet now. You're not making any sense." Lehi got a towel and a basin of water. "I don't want you getting dizzy, or you'll faint away and lose the child." He dipped a rag in the basin and placed it on her forehead before setting a pillow under each of Sariah's knees and propping her head on a third pillow. "Breath slow and deep. That's what midwives tell their patients."

How would he know what midwives advise their patients? Lehi may be a seasoned caravaneer, but after six children he had yet to endure the birth of any. He left the house when their daughters were born, stayed entirely away in the corrals when Laman and Lemuel came, and after she chastised him for his weak-heartedness, he made a feeble attempt to remain in the room when Sam and Nephi joined this family, but he ended up in the map room studying trade routes rather than endure Sariah's cries—and oh, how she could cry. It wasn't the most civil noise, but her screams tempered the pain and helped her children reach this world alive.

Sariah said, "This child isn't coming today, dear."

"Don't be afraid." Lehi tried to set her back down on the pillows, but she resisted his prodding. "You're healthy enough to survive this."

Of course she was, but it was difficult to know if Lehi would. He said, "You didn't carry this child halfway across the earth to leave me, woman."

"I'm not going anywhere."

"Lay back and be calm." Lehi dipped the cloth in the basin and pressed it to her brow, water dripping into her eyes and over her cheeks. "This will cool your head."

Cool her? He was going to drown her, and she pushed Lehi's hand aside and shook the drops off the end of her nose before propping herself against the pillow to watch her husband. He'd never remained with her while she gave birth, and though today was not to be the day this child joined their family, she humored Lehi with a long sigh followed by a quiet groan. "It isn't pretty, at least not until the child is here."

"I know that."

"I may cry out."

Lehi squeezed her hand. "I've endured much worse than your cries."

"It could be another false pain."

"I know a birth when I see it." Lehi prepared two more wet cloths and held them out to her. "I've been with you through six."

Sariah began to laugh.

Lehi said, "Calm yourself before you—"

"I'm going to get up off these pillows and go about my chores. There will be no birth today."

"What about the pain?"

"I've always wanted a child to come on a special day, and since there are so few special days in this wilderness I've decided to wait for the Feast of Trumpets."

"Can you do that?"

"It isn't up to me." Sariah stood and straightened the hem of her robe about her feet. "The first day of the seventh month is the day when the hearts of fathers turn to their children." She held Lehi's hand. "It's the day we remember the creation and the ties that bind our family together. What better day to bring a child into the world?"

"You're certain about this?"

"As certain as I know this boy will teach the covenants on the steps of the temple."

Lehi slowly shook his head. "We may never see the temple in Jerusalem again."

"If not there, then in another promised land."

Lehi smiled. "And if your son is a girl?"

"Then I'll name her after the wife of Abraham." Sariah nodded. "And she'll stand on the steps of the temple and teach her people that the marriage of her namesake to Abraham was a covenant that blessed all the nations of the earth."

Lehi pulled open the tent flap, and the first light of morning touched the tuft of beard at the end of his square chin with a golden light. His hands were calloused from working in the date palm groves, but he was no less handsome standing in the door of the tent than he was dressed in flowing robes trimmed in gold when they lived in the comfort of their estate at Beit Zayit.

Lehi said, "And what will you name the child if it's a boy?"

"Jacob, after the son of Abraham." Sariah walked a circle around Lehi, her hands raised like a maiden dancing a wedding dance, the hem of her blue robe slowly rising and falling about her ankles. She softly clapped her hands twice on one side, then three times on the other. "This birth will be a celebration of the promises given to Jacob of old." She slowly walked another circle around Lehi, clapping her hands and humming a melody. "And a celebration of Nephi's return to camp."

Lehi said, "I dreamed a dream."

"Not now, dear." Sariah clapped her hands again. "Celebrate for a moment."

Lehi said, "I must tell you of it."

Sariah took him by the hand and started him around in a circle with her. "Humor me."

Lehi leaned his head in. "There is little humor in sending our sons back to Jerusalem."

Sariah stopped. What sort of foolishness was this? She wouldn't let Lehi send their sons back to Jerusalem, not with Nephi still lost somewhere in the desert sands between here and Mount Horeb.

Lehi said, "We haven't a copy of the Law."

"We brought the writings of other prophets with us."

"I want your blessing to send our sons back."

Sariah didn't answer him, and he said, "I dreamed a dream that our sons were to go back to—"

"I heard you."

"Then you agree to send them?"

"It's far too dangerous to send them back for brass plates."

"I didn't say anything about brass plates."

Sariah took hold of the tent pole, the narrow timber bending under her but not breaking. "They're one of Captain Laban's relics, aren't they?" She slowly nodded as she spoke. "Laban keeps them in a treasury beneath his estate, locked away in some sort of vault—isn't that so? And he guards them with fifty soldiers."

"I don't know how many guards."

"There are fifty, and they keep watch at the front and back entrances day and night, armed with swords, and spears, and arrows, and slings, and every manner of weapon."

"Where did you learn that?"

Sariah slowly lowered herself to the ground, holding the center tent pole with one hand and Lehi helping her with the other. She pulled the lambskin blanket under her chin like a child hiding from the dangers of night. "Captain Laban keeps the record of the Jews and also a genealogy of your forefathers engraved on plates of brass." She glanced up at Lehi. "Why would the captain have your genealogy? There's no explanation for that, but for some reason he does."

Lehi said, "Where did you get such a notion?"

Sariah tightened her grip on the blanket, pulling it against her body. How could she agree to a journey that could take the lives of her sons? Nephi's trek into the desert was enough danger, and until the boy came through the door of this tent with his cheerful smile she could never give her blessing to such a foolish venture.

Sariah brushed a tear from her cheek before softly saying, "Last night I dreamed the same dream."

CHAPTER 16

—*Late Summer, 598* B.C.
Jerusalem

Elizabeth lifted a brass plate from the water-filled cooling vat, wiped it dry, and sprinkled a thin layer of lye salts to seal the finish. One plate done and one more to pull from the oven, and they were finished for the night. She helped Zoram organize Papa's hammers, chop wood to replace what they used, and sweep away the coal dust from in front of the oven door, both of them waiting for the simmering copper and silver to smelt to brass. Thankfully, Papa didn't douse the fires after he finished today. Zoram hardly had enough money to pay for the ore, let alone wood and coal for the smelting, but with the oven already fired and Papa agreeing not to let it go cold after he was done, they had enough money to purchase copper and silver for a few more plates.

Elizabeth wiped away the salts on the already-finished brass plate. It seemed an awful expense when they should be saving to purchase a small home. She worked a chamois over the brass. A home within the walls of the city was costly, but if they were frugal they could at least hope for a plot of ground in the Lower City near Mother and Father. And if not within the walls, then possibly on the flats south of the city, close enough that Zoram could finish his bonded years in Laban's treasury before he was released to pursue his own work.

Zoram took the mold from the oven. It was a shallow slip of clay with the edges fashioned to the precise measurements of the plates in Captain Laban's relic. He lowered it into the cooling vat, the steam streaming up around his dark cheeks like a gray beard before engulfing him in a cloud. Elizabeth reached for his hand, but couldn't find him in the thick mist. When all this was done and the debt for smithing these plates was repaid, they'd find a way to buy a home large enough for a quiver of children, with a writing room where Zoram could do his work and where she could sit beside a fire and read from a library of writings he was certain to accumulate. Elizabeth waved the steam from in front of her eyes. She was as sure of her vision of a future with Zoram as she was of . . .

Daniel? What was he doing standing in the steam-filled entrance of the shop dressed in a military tunic—the short gold-trimmed sleeves hardly covering his thick arms? A leather cord held a black patch against one eye, the strap disappearing into the thick black hair above the ears. He never explained how he lost his sight, and since it happened about the time Aaron was killed, she never bothered to inquire further. Blindness— even in a single eye—was a weakness for a soldier, but it didn't weaken Daniel. He was promoted to first lieutenant immediately after the accident, and the patch only added to the stories of his gift for warfare. However, the soldiers under Daniel's command didn't know him like she knew him. There was no question that he had a keen mind for knowing his adversary, and an aggressive manner that raised fears in the heart of his enemies. And he was strong to be sure. Why, he'd not ever lost a wrestling match since he was a young lad, except to the youngest son of Lehi. Daniel was a good man, but he was blinded to the rage that simmered just beneath the surface, and if she didn't find a way to temper his temperament, his soul may never warm to the message of the prophets that brought her and the rest of her siblings faith in the Anointed One.

Daniel rubbed the tanned leather of Elizabeth's smithing apron between his thumb and forefinger. "This is hardly a place for a woman."

Elizabeth turned away from his penetrating gaze. Papa's black-smithing business was nearly ruined when Daniel went off to the military to work for the man who killed their brother. She wiped mist from her cheeks. Daniel told her that Aaron stepped in front of an arrow meant for Lehi, but it was her brother's superior officer, Captain Laban, who was the instrument of Aaron's death, and she couldn't keep her hands from tying the knot in her apron tighter. The sound of Daniel's deep, penetrating voice and the image of his broad shoulders and expensive military clothing fired her soul with the memory of losing

Aaron to Captain Laban's vengeance. It was a flame that burned hotter than any in the smelting oven. And if Daniel didn't approve of her working in a blacksmith shop, he should blame Captain Laban.

Elizabeth threw her polishing cloth over the brass plate, the chamois hiding all but the bottom corner of the bright orange metal. "You didn't leave me much choice in the matter."

"Is that any way to greet your eldest brother?"

"You're not the eldest."

"Aaron's dead and that's the end of him." Daniel set his leather riding gloves on the forging table over top of the exposed portion of the brass plate, hiding the metal her polishing cloth didn't. He said, "Where's Papa?"

Elizabeth brushed her hair back off her brow. "He's gone home for the night."

"Papa left you on your own?" Daniel leaned past her and peered across the shop. Thankfully, Zoram was gone. He'd disappeared out the back door of the shop in a cloud of steam, but he'd left the clay mold on the table next to the cooling vat. Elizabeth reached for Daniel's arm and drew his gaze away from the brass-filled mold. "What message do you have for Papa?"

"There's to be a meeting of the Council the first of next week."

"Doesn't he already know that?"

"The king will be addressing the elders, and Papa's to invite his noblemen friends."

"He doesn't have any friends like that."

"Just see that you tell him." Daniel started for the shop door. "And tell Mama I'll stop by."

"When?"

"When I have reason."

"I'm getting married, Daniel." Elizabeth raised her head, and her long black curls fell over her shoulders. "Is that reason enough?"

"You?" Daniel marched back to her. "Married?"

"Didn't Zoram tell you?"

"The keeper of the treasury? You could do better than one of Laban's slaves."

"He isn't a slave. Five years more, and then he's a free man."

"A scribe then." Daniel waved his hand in the air. "Do you want to make a life with a man who spends his days writing on leather skins?"

"You have no idea what kind of work Zoram does." Elizabeth glanced at the brass-plate-filled mold. "Shall I tell Mama you'll be by the house for the wedding?"

"Tell her nothing."

"But . . . Daniel."

"I don't want to disappoint her."

Elizabeth lowered her head. Didn't he care about disappointing her? "Why won't you come and see us?"

"I don't come and go as I please."

"You're Laban's first lieutenant."

"The man requires my attention."

"And your soul."

"You've never liked him."

"What will it take to get you to come home? Another death in the family?"

"Aaron was a fool." Daniel tightened his hands into fists. "He trusted men he had no business trusting."

"It isn't good to hate the dead."

"It's no worse than siding with the foolish."

"Whatever anger you hold for Aaron is no reason to abandon the rest of us."

"I was the one who had to report to Captain Laban why our brother aided traitors, not you." Daniel adjusted the patch over his bad eye. "Aaron nearly cost me my commission."

"It cost Aaron his life."

"I haven't time for any more of this." Daniel snatched his riding gloves off the table, and his sudden movement knocked the chamois off the polished brass plate. Elizabeth reached to replace it, but not before Daniel saw the gleaming new brass—minted to the exact dimensions of the plates he was guarding in Captain Laban's treasury. He turned his lone eye toward the small stack of unused silver and cooper ingots on the table and then over to the cooling vat where the last wisps of steam rose off the newly smithed plate still resting in the clay mold. He didn't say anything, didn't ask why she was smithing brass plates, didn't mention the curiosity of their size.

Daniel said, "Don't let me keep you from your smithing."

Daniel sneaked across the street from the smithy and hid among the crumbling brick and splintered roof beams of ruined blacksmith shops. Elizabeth couldn't have anything to do with the curse on the relic he was guarding. No one beyond Zadock and Captain Laban knew that. Elizabeth wasn't a normal woman with her passion for reading and writing, but smithing brass plates was an odd thing even for her. It was far too costly an undertaking, and it couldn't be for her wedding. What man—even if he were a scribe—would accept such an odd gift from his bride?

The shop door creaked open, and Daniel ducked behind the remains of a chimney rising out of the ruins of an oven. Elizabeth stepped into the street, the light from inside silhouetting her frame. Her head was hidden beneath a hood and a small leather pouch hung from her shoulder like a courier carrying a satchel. She didn't appear to be in a rush, but curse her for leaving the shop doors open, the lamps burning, and the oven fired. Didn't she understand thieves roamed the night?

Daniel stepped into the street, his gaze shifting between Elizabeth disappearing up the street and the opened doors of the shop. If he locked up after her, he was certain not to find out where she was headed. The clinking of metal tongs turned his gaze back to the shop. Who was that? Papa was gone home for the night, and Mama wouldn't let Sarah or Joshua out this late in the evening. He glanced after Elizabeth. She was near the top of the street, and when he turned his gaze back to the shop he saw someone standing in the door watching him. He wore a white robe far too bold to be the costume of a thief. He was a thin, tall man, but before Daniel could focus on his shadow-covered face, he disappeared back inside and put out the lamp. Curse his sister. Why didn't Elizabeth have the sense to lock the shop?

Elizabeth knocked on the door to Baruch's home. His long, thin fingers came round the doorpost ahead of his graying head of hair and long beard. He was dressed in a sleeping robe, and he blinked twice before rubbing the sleep from his eyes. Elizabeth opened the satchel to let Baruch see the two brass plates. "These are for you."

"Not out here." Baruch ushered her inside and down a narrow hallway. A host of documents sat in open vessels on the shelves of his private study, and a tall stool stood beside his writing table. A single lamp flickered on the sill of the open window. Baruch set a leather parchment out and pinned back the ends of it with four stones. Next to the parchment, he placed the first plate, the reddish-orange metal gleaming in the lamplight. A small chisel and hammer sat in a box on the shelf above him, and he felt for them, his fingers coming alive the moment they touched the instruments.

Baruch's gaze shifted between Jeremiah's words written on the leather parchment and his nimble fingers manipulating the stylus over the metal plate, each hammer stroke giving up a soft ping and forcing the point into the metal. The cutting edge of the stylus angled up to chisel away the metal and then down to square the letters deep into the plate—deep enough that neither moth nor rust could ever corrupt the opening phrase announcing that Jeremiah was the son of Hilkiah of the priests that were in Anathoth in the land of Benjamin.

Elizabeth said softly, "You make it look so simple."

"Many years, my dear." Baruch blew away the metal fragments accumulating in the wake of his work. "After a time, the fingers come to know the pitch of an impurity in the metal and the depth of a well-crafted character."

"Is the brass to your liking?"

Baruch brushed away a shower of shavings, leaving a perfectly formed character, the newest phrase explaining that before Jeremiah came forth out of his mother's womb, God knew him and ordained him to be a prophet to the nations. "It's as perfect as any plate I've worked with."

Elizabeth stepped around to the other side of Baruch's stool. "How many will you require?"

"I won't know for some time yet." Baruch pointed the head of his small hammer toward the unopened scrolls at the far side of the table. "Not until I've gotten through the first of those."

"We only have—"

"Fifteen days, girl." Baruch rubbed the stiffness from his fingers. "I'll have these plates finished in three." He turned back to his writing table. "You'll have more plates for me by then, yes?"

Elizabeth glanced at the parchments before coming back to Baruch. How she had hoped he could transcribe everything on two plates and save Zoram the cost of the ore. They were going to need a good many more plates for all this, and the expense was certain to keep them from buying property—not to mention the dangers that came with delivering these plates under the cover of darkness. "I'll see you get whatever you need, sir."

Something moved outside the window. It wasn't the brush of olive branches against the outside wall. It was human—like the placement of footsteps coming near the estate, or the breaking of a twig underfoot, or possibly the kicking of a stone in the path. Baruch laid aside his tools and leaned out the window.

Elizabeth said, "What is it?"

"Did anyone follow you, girl?"

"I don't know. I was in a hurry."

"Did you see anything odd?"

What had she done? Elizabeth lowered herself onto a chair in the corner.

"What is it, girl?"

"Daniel. My brother. He saw the brass plates in the shop this evening. Could it be him?"

"It could be, or it could just as likely be a bird or creature of the night."

Elizabeth slowly shook her head. The only creature of the night she knew was her brother. "Could he have reasoned why we were smithing plates of brass?"

"He knows only what you've told him."

"I've not spoken a word to him."

Baruch took her by the hand. "Two brass plates may raise his curiosity, but it gives nothing away."

"He'll be watching us."

Baruch raised her out of the chair. "He'll be watching your smithy."

"We'll not lead him here."

"It's you I worry for." Baruch led her through the estate to the back entrance and unlatched the door.

Elizabeth said, "Shalom to you, sir."

"No, girl." Baruch let her out into the night. "There will be no peace for any of us until this is over."

CHAPTER 17

—Early Autumn, 598 B.C.
Valley of Lemuel (Wadi Tayyib al-Ism)

Laman pulled back the flaps of the main tent before entering the dimly lit compartment. Father sat on the far side next to a small lamp, the flickering flame hardly strong enough to chase away the shadows. A wooden lid taken from the chest of scrolls was a crude writing table set across his legs. His dark hair fell over his brow, and between the locks his gaze followed the movement of his pen.

Lehi didn't lift his head from his writing, didn't raise his hand or offer a word of thanks for coming on short notice to hear whatever it was Lehi had to tell him. It was just like Father to send word for Laman and his brothers to gather for an urgent matter and then lose himself in his scrolls. What could be so important that he couldn't put down the pen and speak to his eldest son?

Mother crossed the tent with the awkward stride of an expectant woman, her arms filled with pillows. She offered one to Laman, but he refused and sat near the entrance on the hard floor with nothing to soften the ground but his leather kilt. He didn't need her mothering—not after she slapped him in front of the entire family. Was that what this meeting was about—another lecture about Father's foolish plan to remain in this wilderness?

"For the love of Moses, what is it that couldn't wait?" Lemuel stepped through the entry, the smell of camels streaming in with him.

"Have some dates, dear." Sariah handed him a bowl, and the pain of carrying an unborn child flashed across her face. She pointed to a pillow beside Lehi. "Why don't you sit there?"

Laman said, "He can get his own dates."

Lemuel stayed just inside the entrance next to Laman, his thin body upright like the tent pole holding back the camel-hair wall. "I haven't time for sitting."

Sam turned in past the open flaps, and Sariah passed him a pillow. He squinted in the darkness, his eyes slowly adjusting from the bright light of morning.

Sariah said, "Any word of your brother?"

Lemuel said, "Nephi's dead."

"Son." Sariah raised her voice. "I'll not hear any of that talk."

"We haven't seen him for almost three days." Lemuel spoke between chewing on a handful of dates. "No one can survive in this wilderness without water."

Sariah said, "Aaron went after him with plenty to drink."

Laman said, "Then they're both lost."

"Is that why you called us here?" Sam spoke above the scratching of Lehi's pen. "Are we beginning a search?"

"Nephi's not coming back." Laman shook his head. "If he isn't dead, he's doing what the rest of us wish we had the courage to do."

Lemuel said, "He's going home?"

"That's ridiculous." Sam took the bowl of dates from Lemuel. "He hasn't a horse or any supplies."

Laman said, "Then where is he?"

"He told you before he left." Sam passed the bowl of dates to Laman before crossing the tent to sit next to Lehi, leaving Laman and Lemuel alone near the entrance. "He went to pray for you."

Laman said, "I don't need his prayers."

"Have something to drink." Sariah poured Laman a cup of tea, but he refused to take the drink. Mother was only begging forgiveness, but no matter how she asked he would not give it. She'd been deceived into following Lehi into this desert, and Laman didn't have the patience to forgive that depth of foolishness. Sariah wasn't bound to Father with such a powerful tie she couldn't break with this reckless venture and return to the comforts of their home at Jerusalem. Sariah retired to the far side of the tent, slowly lowering herself to the ground next to Lehi and arranging pillows beneath her legs. Not even a covenant of marriage should bind a woman to this hell.

Laman said, "Is there a reason for calling us here?"

"Of course there is." Sariah offered Lehi a cup of tea. "Tell them about your dream, dear."

Laman said, "Must we endure the retelling of a dream that brought us to this place?"

Lehi set aside his pen. "Will you suffer the telling of a dream that bids you return to Jerusalem?"

Lemuel said, "We are going home?"

Sariah said, "You're going after the record of our fathers. The one Captain Laban keeps in his treasury."

Tea sprayed from Lemuel's lips, and he set the cup aside.

"That's ridiculous." Laman slowly stood next to Lemuel. "What need have we of Captain Laban's record?" He stared at Lemuel, and he kept staring until his brother said, "That's right, it's nothing but a pile of brass."

Sariah leaned forward on her pillow. "Your father dreamed a dream that you're to bring the record down into this wilderness."

Laman said, "There are hundreds of soldiers guarding Laban's house."

Sariah said, "There are fifty."

Laman said, "How does she know that?"

Lehi said, "You'll have to negotiate with Captain Laban."

Laman said, "He'll put an arrow through us before he'll barter away his relic. Why do you ask such a foolish thing of us?"

"It isn't your father who is asking, son." Sariah lifted the parchment off the wooden writing board and handed it to Lehi. He blew the ink dry before reading from the parchment, the details of his dream filling the tent with the sing-song sound of his voice rising and falling with the retelling of his dream. He nodded when he described the brass record he'd seen in his vision, explaining that it contained a record of the covenants made with the House of Israel, and his voice slowed when he read that the plates contained an accounting of the genealogy of his fathers.

Laman stayed on the opposite side of the tent without interrupting Lehi's reading. Father knew the secret—that his genealogy was written on the brass plates. And if he knew about his genealogy, did he also know that the record named Lehi as the rightful heir to the royal relics passed down for generations since the days of Joseph, the patriarch of old who was sold into Egypt? And if he knew that, did he also know that Laman and Lemuel were in league with Captain Laban to keep the secret from him?

"It's royal blood you want. That's why you're sending us back." Laman raised his voice loud enough to speak above Lehi's reading. "You want the plates so you can start your own kingdom in this wilderness. You'll never be a king. You're nothing but a common olive oil merchant."

"Laman." Sariah pulled back the white linen hood from her head. "Don't speak to your father like that."

"This is madness, Mother. Our family hasn't any ties to the Northern Kingdom, and now Father thinks Laban's relic will make him our king." Laman turned to Lehi. "Isn't that so?"

"No, son." Lehi stood with the leather parchment hanging from his hand. "I've never been concerned with anything but your welfare."

Laman said, "Then why Laban's relic?"

"Once I have the record, I'll know more."

"We brought more than enough parchments and records into this wilderness to satisfy your fondness for reading. Why risk our lives for another?"

Lehi said, "God will bring you back safely."

Laman said, "If God cared about our safety, He'd not have let Nephi wander off and die."

"I'm not dead, brother." Nephi stood in the entrance. The boy's shirt was caked with mud from digging in the clay pit. Flecks of red earth dirtied his hair, and dust from wandering about the desert sands covered his nose and cheeks. His skin was a shade darker from wandering beneath the brutal sun, and his lips were parched from the wind. He pushed aside the flaps of stitched camel hair hanging free at the entrance and stepped inside. Since coming to this wilderness, the boy had grown level with Laman's stature, maybe a few fingers taller. His shoulders were as wide as Laman's, and his arms were as thick. A thin beard grew along the line of his jaw.

"You're back." Sariah shuffled across the tent and pressed her cheek against the boy's muddied sleeve. "How can I ever let you go back to Jerusalem after this?"

Nephi said, "Jerusalem?"

Laman said, "You heard her. Father wants us to fetch more reading for his pleasure."

Sariah said, "Captain Laban has a record of the Jews and a genealogy of our forefathers written on plates of brass."

Laman said, "That's a lie."

Lehi said, "Son, that is enough."

Laman said, "A mistake, then. Captain Laban's plates are a record of the kings of Ephraim and Manasseh. We're Jews from the south. We have no ties to the royals of the north."

Aaron stepped inside and stood next to Nephi. He nodded to Lehi, and when he smiled at Sariah she immediately took the blacksmith by the hand and thanked him for going after her youngest son and bringing him back safely.

"It's just as Nephi told me it would be." Aaron tightened his grip around Sariah's hand. "We're to go back for the record."

Laman came around in front of Aaron and Nephi. "You're willing to risk your life for a few pounds of brass?"

Aaron said, "We're not afraid of Captain Laban."

Laman forced his knee into Aaron's thigh where Captain Laban's arrow had wounded him eight months earlier, and the blacksmith recoiled back a step. "Now do you remember the fear?" He turned to Nephi. "You could be next, brother."

Lehi said, "Your older brothers believe it's a hard thing I've asked of them."

Nephi said, "There's nothing too hard for the Lord."

"Bless you, son." Lehi put his hand to Nephi's dust-covered cheek. "Bless you for not murmuring."

Nephi turned to Sam. "Can you have the animals ready?"

Sam nodded. "Two days."

Aaron said, "I'll mend the bridles."

Nephi offered his hand to Laman. "Come with us."

Laman said, "Where did you get your sudden passion for risking your life?"

"It was never sudden." Sariah reached for Nephi's hand. "God has been working on his heart since he was a boy."

Aaron said, "He heard a voice from heaven as clear as a man speaking to him face-to-face."

Laman spat on the ground. "A dreamer like father."

Nephi said, "Go with us to Jerusalem and see with your own eyes."

"What will we see?"

Aaron said, "The hand of God in our lives."

Laman said, "This is a journey for fools."

"Call it what you will, but I will go and do the things the Lord has commanded."

Laman said, "You have no idea what you're about to face. Captain Laban will crush you."

Aaron said, "We'll be protected."

Laman said, "You can't be sure of that."

"I am." Nephi stepped to the entrance of the tent. The morning sun filtered in around him and brightened the edges of his muddied tunic. He nodded as he spoke, the curls of hair falling into his eyes, his words barely audible above the breeze filtering in past the tent flaps. He said, "As certain as I know that God doesn't give a commandment without preparing a way to accomplish it." And then he was gone out into the morning with Aaron and Sam following him.

Laman nodded to his parents before taking Lemuel by the arm and escorting him outside, far enough away that Lehi couldn't hear. He said, "How is this happening?"

Lemuel said, "You heard Father. He had a dream."

"There's something he's not telling us."

"We can't go back for the plates."

Laman leaned forward. "You're willing to let Nephi go back without us?"

"Captain Laban will have their heads."

"This is our chance to go home."

"This is madness." Lemuel shook his head. "The captain will never give up his relic."

"We don't ask for it. We negotiate a return to our estate."

"The others will never let you do that."

"We send one of us to speak with Captain Laban."

"How do we keep the others away?"

Laman took out a leather pouch filled with lots—the same ones he used to cheat Lemuel out of gathering dung for the fires.

Laman said, "With these."

CHAPTER 18

—*Late Summer, 598* B.C.
Jerusalem

A single torch burned along the prison wall, casting a dim light over Baruch's writings. He adjusted the parchment on the small wooden table and held his pen to the leather. The prophecies spilled from Jeremiah's mouth like water cascading over a fall, though there was little refreshment in the telling of so much destruction. In two weeks' time, Baruch had filled ten leather hides to overflowing, and there didn't seem to be any end to Jeremiah's predictions of doom.

The prophet sat on a small stool in the center of the chamber, his words echoing off the walls. His gray beard rose and fell with each phrase, and he raised his hands as if he were speaking to a large crowd, though Baruch was the lone listener to the starkness of his foretelling. Jeremiah's tattered brown robe hung on his gaunt frame like flesh on a skeleton, but his speech did not lack for power, prophesying that the Jews were bruised with an incurable wound and there was no healing medicine that could cure them.

Jeremiah paused and turned on his stool. "They'll be coming for you."

Baruch began to write the words, but Jeremiah took the pen from his hand and said, "Your parchments are like honey drawing the hornet from its nest."

Hornet?

"I see a man dressed in a dark cape with only a loincloth to cover his nakedness."

"No one followed me here. I made certain of it."

"He comes to stop my words from the ears of the Jews at the temple."

Baruch turned back to the parchment laid over the writing table. Why was Jeremiah telling him this? He said, "Shouldn't we continue?"

"We're finished." Jeremiah set the pen on the table. "What I say now is for you." He ran his hand over the parchment, the new ink passing under his fingers. "These words will save your life. They will be your only protection from—"

The doors leading from the palace burst open, and Ebed-Melech rushed in, the keys to the prison jangling in his hand. "Get your things." He held the prison doors open. "Soldiers are coming to inspect the prison."

Baruch rolled the scroll and gathered his pens and inks into the satchel. Jeremiah took Baruch by the arm and pulled him close, the man's beard brushing against his robe. "I am shut up here and cannot go into the house of the Lord, but you can." He pointed to the satchel. "You have the book God commanded to be written. Read it aloud in the temple and try once more to change the heart of this people."

"Quickly now." Ebed held the door wide open, the fresh air from the palace rushing into this musty place. "There's little time."

"I can't read this in public." Baruch tied his satchel with a cord and started for the door with Jeremiah hurrying alongside. "Your words accuse every prince and noble in the city, openly condemning their evil practices." He adjusted the satchel under his arm. "Powerful men don't take lightly a call to repentance. They're sure to destroy these parchments."

"You have the plates." Jeremiah came around in front of Baruch. "When you finish the last, then it matters not what becomes of these parchments."

"Baruch." Ebed pushed the prison door full open. "Now, sir."

"Keep the parchments with you." Jeremiah laid his hand on Baruch's satchel. "Take them wherever you go, and when the black-robed man comes for you, go to the temple and read my words aloud in the ears of all the people." The prophet followed Baruch to the prison door, the torchlight flickering over his long, gray beard and across his penetrating brown-eyed gaze. "The parchments are your only protection."

Baruch wrapped both arms around the satchel and held it to his chest. How could these writings be a protection? They were nothing more than words on leather. He hurried through the opened doorway into the narrow stone hall leading from the prison and turned back to see Jeremiah standing in the entry, framed by the thick doorposts. The prophet raised his hand, and the tattered brown cuffs of his robe slid back from his fingers. He said, "Farewell, my friend."

Ebed shut the door, and the image of Jeremiah disappeared behind the timbers. Baruch followed Ebed through a twisting maze of corridors and up a run of steps to a secluded door in the west wing of the palace. The Ethiopian unlocked the latch and led him past the base of a vacant watchtower to an unguarded gate.

Baruch said, "Jeremiah seems more desperate than before."

"Go on your way, sir." Ebed let Baruch into the side alley, but when he tried to shut the gate, Baruch stabbed his boot against the post, keeping it from closing. He said, "What is it that you're not telling me?"

"Do as Jeremiah says and keep the parchments with you."

"What power do these have?" Baruch lifted the satchel in the air. "You saved Jeremiah from the well. You live with him. You hear what he says. Tell me what you know."

"Time is running out." Ebed's gaze wandered to the catwalks above before coming back to Baruch and saying, "Finish the plates before it's too late."

"What will happen when I finish the last one?" Baruch reached through the gate and took Ebed by the leather straps running over his shoulder. "Tell me what I should expect."

"Be ready."

"Is that all?"

"The gates of hell, sir." Ebed pulled free of Baruch's grasp. "They stand ready to open wide after all of us." He pulled the gate shut, and before he turned back toward the prison he said, "Jeremiah's prayers are the only thing keeping them shut."

Baruch stood staring at the closed gate. He was carrying so much doom in these parchments; must he also carry his own fate with them? He started down along the wall of the palace and turned onto King Street. Throngs of priests, merchants, and accountants crossed between the temple gates and the Citadel Building in the early September sun. Baruch pushed his way through the crowd, skirted around a group of slow-walking priests, and bid good day to three scribes heading up the temple steps when a man dressed in a black robe stepped out of a narrow alleyway and into stride a few paces behind him. His head was shrouded by a hood, and it was impossible to see his face behind the thick cloth with so many passersby shuffling through the square in late afternoon. He held the robe tight against his body, and it was impossible to see if he wore a loincloth beneath the black cloak. Baruch turned off King Street and up a narrow path behind a run of estate homes, and the footsteps of the black-robed man followed. He was eight, maybe ten strides back, but when Baruch spun around he was gone, turned down a side street, his footsteps fading into the afternoon and mixing with the sound of a bird chirping from beneath the wooden eave of a two-story home. Why did he allow Jeremiah's warning to fill him with so much fear? Baruch hurried up the path. No one knew of his work inscribing plates.

The gate to Baruch's home stood ajar. He pushed it with his foot, and it swung around, banging full open against the inside wall. How did that get left open? He never left the house without latching it properly. Nothing in the courtyard was disturbed, but when a breeze lifted through the sycamore tree growing outside the window to his writing room, the open shutters thumped against the outside wall. The latch was broken, and a cracked wooden slat hung from a nail. Baruch hurried up the porch and unlocked the front door. The hall leading to the writing room stood quiet. None of the parchments hanging on the wall were missing, and when he turned into the writing room there was nothing disturbed but the open shutter banging against the stone. He let it swing on its hinges and reached onto the top shelf, feeling about until his hand found the repository jar. Thank heavens the brim was still sealed shut with beeswax. There was no sign that an intruder had disturbed anything on the shelf. The latch on the shutters could have given way on its own. That's what it was. This was all a terrible case of his fears getting the best of him, but just to be sure, he pulled up the lid on the repository jar and peered inside to see—

"Is that where you keep your finished plates?"

The voice came from behind him, over in the darkest corner of the room. Baruch turned from the shelves to find a black-robed figure stepping from the shadows. The intruder removed the hood and let her long, black curls cascade out from under the head covering.

"Elizabeth?" Baruch set the repository jar on the writing table. "You gave me a scare, girl. You shouldn't sneak through the window like that. The whole world is likely to have seen you." He pulled the shutters closed and tried to fix the broken latch, but when he couldn't repair it, he tied a cord around the frame and knotted it shut. "I'll have to get a carpenter to repair your impatience."

"I didn't come in that way."

Baruch let go of the cord, and the breeze blew the shutters out of his grasp, the slats banging against the outside wall.

"I came in the back entrance," Elizabeth said in answer to Baruch's staring. She held out a small key. "Don't you remember?"

Baruch lowered himself into his writing chair.

"What is it?" Elizabeth handed over two newly smithed plates. "What's wrong?"

"Nothing, girl." Baruch set the satchel of parchments on the writing table next to the repository jar and took out three transcribed plates. "These haven't any of the tarnish like the ones in Laban's record. See that Zoram places them at the base of the relic where they won't draw any notice." He brushed the sweat from his brow, bundled the finished plates in a brown cloth, and tied it with a cord before telling Elizabeth to follow him down the hallway, through the small kitchen to the back of the estate, and out the door. He guided her through the garden, beyond a tall gate and into the narrow alley, and when he was a good distance from the house, he stopped.

Elizabeth said, "What is it?"

"The parchments?" Baruch took Elizabeth by the shoulders. "My satchel. Where is my—"

Elizabeth stepped back from his outburst. "You left them on your writing table."

Baruch ran back through the gardens, threw open the door to the kitchen, and hurried to the writing room. Why did he leave the house without them? Baruch secured the satchel under his arm and returned to the shadows of the alley to find Elizabeth still standing against the stone wall where he left her.

"I'm sorry, girl. I haven't been myself this afternoon. Hold these, will you?" Baruch handed Elizabeth the satchel before prying loose a large stone from the wall and exposing a cavity inside. "Leave the newly smithed plates here. Make sure no one sees you. I'll inscribe them and return them to the wall for you to deliver to Zoram."

"Why not exchange them inside?"

"It isn't safe there anymore."

"What about you?"

"I have these." Baruch reached out and touched the parchment-filled satchel before replacing the stone in the wall, tamping it in place until the seams in the mortar disappeared without a trace. He handed her the bundle of three finished plates. "Go on." He checked the alley, and when he was certain it was clear, he started her toward the way out. "Get yourself home."

Elizabeth turned back to see Baruch one last time, and then she was gone out of sight beyond the high walls and onto the lane leading to the Lower City. Baruch watched the empty alley long after the sound of Elizabeth's footsteps fell silent. Was the intruder who broke the shutters the same evil Jeremiah warned him to flee? He clutched the satchel of parchments close to his side and offered the only prayer he could think to offer: that the gates of hell be sealed until this was finished.

CHAPTER 19

—*Late Summer, 598* B.C.
Jerusalem

"Hail, King of Judah."

Zadock stood at the first sound of the palace crier's call, the man's voice piercing the thick incense-filled air of the council chamber. He motioned for the other elders to follow his lead. The gold trader, silk merchant, money changer, and perfume vendor came out of their chairs together, the ends of their white and black head shawls trailing down from beneath their caps and about their shoulders. The caravan master, mill owner, and the other merchant-elders finished their wine and handed the empty cups to the maidservants before standing beside their high-backed chairs.

Jonathan the blacksmith was the last to stand, the man slowly rising from the twelfth chair at the far end of the table opposite Zadock. His wide shoulders were uncomfortable beneath the cover of a black council robe, and his square chin and robust stature were out of place among so many well-heeled elders. The blacksmith didn't speak a word among the gathering of the wealthy princes and nobles, and it was no wonder his son Daniel preferred the company of men with greater aspirations than working metal with their hands. The blacksmith may have been the father of Daniel's youth, but Captain Laban gave the boy hope for a life far greater than any Jonathan could hope to provide.

Zadock counted the men gathered in the council chambers, but lost track somewhere past one hundred. There had never been this large an assembly, the nobles filling every space between the hearth and balcony, but then there had never been a reason to invite so many until this evening. The palace crier repeated his royal introduction, and the men in the chamber quieted their conversations, all of them parting like a flock of finely clothed sheep to open a way from the council table to the main doors.

Miriam was the first royal to enter. She wore a white veil, and it was impossible to tell where she cast her gaze. Zadock never should have invited the woman. Ever since he requested her presence, she inquired not less than once a day about the nature of the meeting. Must he always remind the woman that this gathering was arranged at the insistence of her husband? What Zadock didn't tell her was that he, with the help of the white powders, inspired Zedekiah's resolve.

Captain Laban quietly moved down behind the council members and came in next to Zadock. The breastplates of his office shimmered in the lamplight, and the gold-trimmed ends of his short sleeves gave way to the thick arms of Judah's most powerful soldier. He leaned his head in next to Zadock and spoke softly enough not to draw the notice of elders around the council table. Laban said, "Did he have his tea?"

"Two cups early this morning."

"Will he make the demand?"

Before Zadock could answer, the palace crier stabbed his staff against the marble floor at the head of the chamber and announced the arrival of the king to the chambers, his voice turning the gaze of assembled noblemen toward the main doors. Zedekiah stood in the entry, balancing his weight against the doorpost before stepping inside. The palace guards raised their banners on the ends of poles, and he slowly made his entrance beneath the ensigns decorated with the bright gold and red colors of the royal house and embroidered with the image of a lion head. Zedekiah paused below the last one, his gaze turned up into the furls and his hand reaching for the ends of the cloth. It was like watching a kitten play with the end of a string, and when he stayed far too long amusing himself, Miriam came back, took him by the hand, and led him to the throne. His face was ashen, and his cheek sagged about his lips far too much for a man of thirty-four years.

Zedekiah said, "Is there a reason for this gathering?"

Muted laughter rose from the guests until Zadock said, "We gathered at your request, sire."

"My request?" Zedekiah fanned his face with his hand and slowly turned his gaze out over the assembly. "So it was."

Zadock found his way through the throng of nobles and stood beside the throne. "Are you well, sire?"

"He hasn't been well for weeks." Miriam stepped between Zadock and Zedekiah. "You know that."

Zedekiah pulled on his collar. "You wouldn't happen to have any tea?"

"There will be time for that later." Zadock took Zedekiah by the hand and raised him to his feet. "Elders, princes, nobles of Jerusalem, I beg you, give ear to your king. For he is your king, and he will remain your king as long as the right of kingship is with him."

Zedekiah pushed his crown back off his brow and squinted into the faces in the crowd until his gaze rested on Laban standing over near the council table. He pointed his scepter at the captain and said, "Am I your king, sir?"

Laban neared the throne, raised a wine glass in the air, and said, "May you live long and prosper, sire."

The silk merchant shouted, "Hear, hear," and muted words of agreement rose up from the elders at the council table.

Zedekiah said, "The sword of kingship. Do you have it in your treasury?"

"All Jerusalem knows of my royal relic." Laban faced the gathering, his hands stretched out to the nobles. "Smithed by Joseph of old, the first king of the Israelites."

"Then hear me now, men of Jerusalem." Zedekiah raised his scepter to the crowded chamber. "I am king, and I will have the sword of a king."

An awkward silence fell across the chamber, and Laban stepped closer to the throne, the sound of his boots on the marble floor cutting through the stillness. "The relic is my inheritance."

"On the coming feast, your sword will be my sword."

"You have plenty of blades." Miriam reached for her husband's hand, but Zadock stepped between the couple, brushing her reach aside.

Laban said, "You don't mean this."

"I will have your sword, Captain."

"You would strip me of what is mine?"

"I am your king." Zedekiah adjusted his crown forward. "Where is my tea?"

Laban said, "This is madness."

Miriam spoke quietly, softly enough that her voice didn't carry through the chamber. "You don't know what harm a weapon like this could bring you."

"The relic is a symbol of kingship, my lady." Zadock stood next to Zedekiah. "Not a weapon."

"It will be mine." Zedekiah set his scepter under his arm, the gold rod shaking with the same tremors that plagued his body, and the weight of it forcing him back a step. He lost his balance, but before he fell, Miriam helped him sit on his throne. She said, "Call for the doctor."

Zedekiah said, "I haven't need of one."

"Look what you've done to him." Miriam knelt beside the royal chair, her hand on her husband's brow, and her gaze turned up toward Zadock. "How did you get him to speak such madness?"

"I have nothing to do with your husband's insanity." Zadock raised his voice enough to reach the farthest corners of the hushed chamber. "Zedekiah has gone quite mad on his own."

"Mad?" Miriam rubbed Zedekiah's hands. "He may be ill. He doesn't feel well. But he certainly hasn't gone mad."

Laban said, "His demands for my sword are beyond madness."

Miriam fanned air across Zedekiah's perspiring face. "I'll not let you nor your sword bring harm to my—"

"Wine all around." Zadock clapped his hands for the maidservants to begin serving the guests, and the chamber erupted in a flurry of chatter over the king's folly, loud enough to drown Miriam's accusations. Curse the woman. Where did she come by her fool notions? A maidservant returned to the chamber with a cup of tea. Zadock took it from the tray and offered it to Miriam.

He said, "Something to drink, my lady?"

* * * * *

Daniel waved his hand to clear the air of the frankincense burning in the brass bowls near the council chamber doors. He stood on the threshold, wearing a plain black robe with a large hood, none of the markings of his office, and no weapons beyond the dagger in his boot. He removed the hood and stood square-shouldered until Zadock saw him and directed Laban's attention toward the chamber doors. They put down their wine, excused themselves from the company of nobles, and went out into the hallway.

Zadock said, "What is it?"

Daniel said, "The brass plates, sir."

Laban said, "Are they secure?"

"The relic is."

"Then why do you bother us, Lieutenant?" Zadock glanced back into the incense-filled chamber. "We have guests."

Daniel removed the hood from his head. "It's Baruch, sir."

Zadock said, "The old scribe?"

"He made a visit to Jeremiah today."

"You didn't stop him?"

"I thought it best to find out what the scribe was doing."

Laban said, "You did right, son."

Zadock began to pace. "What did you learn?"

"Jeremiah may have hired Baruch to assemble plates of brass the same size as the plates in the relic."

"He'll not fool anyone into thinking he has Laban's relic." Zadock stopped his pacing in front of Daniel. "Where are these plates?"

"I believe they're hidden in Baruch's home."

"You've not seen them?"

"There wasn't time to finish searching his property."

"Go to the hill country." Zadock walked over next to Daniel, the ends of his robe snapping about his feet. "Shechem will know what to do."

"I can watch the man."

"You haven't time for that. You're to keep watch over Laban."

Laban said, "I don't need an escort."

Zadock said, "That was before."

"Before what?"

"Before the threat of Jeremiah thieving your plates of brass and killing you was nothing more than a curse from a foolish old man sitting in prison."

Laban said, "Nothing's changed."

"Such a short memory, Captain. The last time Jeremiah recruited men outside the prison to do his work, Lieutenant Daniel found Hananiah dead in his house. Baruch changes everything."

Laban came around in front of Zadock. "Hananiah didn't know how to defend himself."

"How do you defend against a curse?" Zadock turned to Daniel. "Is Baruch working with anyone, Lieutenant?"

Daniel adjusted the black patch on his blind eye. Did the Chief Elder need to know that Elizabeth supplied the brass plate to Baruch? "I need more time."

Laban said, "I don't need the boy watching over me."

"You have no choice." Zadock turned back to Daniel. "See that he's watched every hour of every day until the feast."

"I won't hear any more of this." Laban started down the stairs, and Daniel followed him as far as the first step before pulling up and watching the captain turn out of sight to the lower floors. There was no use following him. He didn't listen to logic when he was upset. It wasn't that he didn't believe Daniel could protect him, but the possibility that he could end up like Hananiah stirred fear in him that no one but Daniel could see. He didn't eat as much as he should, he slept poorly, he reacted to the slightest sounds about the estate with a dagger in hand, and he changed his daily schedule, never riding the same route through the city and never eating at the same hour. He didn't even polish his saddle or practice his archery at the same time each day like he once did. As soon as he calmed down, Daniel would speak to the man, get him to take every precaution to ensure his safety. That's all any of them wanted. Captain Laban had to be kept safe from anyone who might dare to harm him or his relics.

Daniel turned back from the stairs. In the middle of the hall, down by the doors to the council chambers, stood Jonathan the blacksmith. He removed his hat and ran his hand through his head of thick, black hair. He said, "What's wrong, son?"

Daniel said, "Papa. Go back inside."

"What is it with Captain Laban?"

Zadock stepped between Daniel and Jonathan. "Exactly what do you mean by that, blacksmith?"

"I think you know, sir." Jonathan let the head shawls of his office fall down around his shoulders. "Men with enough foolhardy passion to risk their good sense for a sword and some plates of brass." He glanced back inside the council chamber. "My son's life is worth more than a few pounds of metal."

"Papa, you're out of line." Daniel took Jonathan by the arm.

"I won't lose another son." Jonathan pulled free. "Not to some foolish war over possession of Laban's relics."

Zadock bowed his head. "A war Captain Laban gladly concedes."

"What about my son?"

"Daniel is responsible for Captain Laban's safety."

"And who will look after Daniel?"

"Enough, Papa."

"It isn't enough."

Zadock said, "Your son is an officer, and I expect him to live up to his obligation."

"When did looking after relics fulfill any military obligation?"

"I'll expect you to finish the iron door for the vault in Captain Laban's treasury." Zadock turned to Daniel. "And I'll expect you to do your duty."

Daniel stood at attention, his shoulders back and his jaw set.

"Good evening." Zadock tipped his head to Jonathan and started back inside the council chambers, but Jonathan called after him loudly enough to turn the Chief Elder around in the entrance. He said, "What's to become of my son?"

Zadock shifted his gaze from Jonathan to Daniel, still standing at attention, and then back to the blacksmith. "It appears he's made that decision for himself."

CHAPTER 20

—Early Autumn, 598 B.C.
Valley of Lemuel (Wadi Tayyib al-Ism)

Oh, bother. The pestle slipped out of Rebekah's grasp and knocked a handful of wild grain off the grinding stone. She salvaged what she could and tossed what was left into the air, the breeze blowing the chaff back into her face and coloring her cheeks with flecks of brown. Why did she ever hope to find a better life in this wilderness? She could make do without bakeries selling flat bread in this secluded mountain valley. She made her own perfumes, though they were nothing like the fragrances she purchased from merchants offering sweet-smelling aromas. There were no cobblers to craft her shoes and no tailors to sew her robes, but that wasn't the burden that turned life in this desert to drudgery—a drudgery that would not change until Aaron proposed marriage. Rebekah worked the pestle harder, wearing the grinding stone smooth with her disappointment. Whenever she asked him about their future, he said there were important arrangements to consider. What sort of twisted logic was that? They had a good water supply, figs beyond number, and there was enough wheat, barley, and oats growing wild along the banks of the river to support a young family. The grain didn't taste as sweet as what they grew at Jerusalem, but it had the power to stave off hunger, and she'd grown accustomed to the savor of these wild oats.

Rebekah leaned up on her knees to see across the river to the corral where Aaron packed two saddlebags and a water skin on Beuntahyu's backside. That was odd. He never let the Arabian out to others, but he had a good heart, and if Sam or his brothers asked for Beuntahyu to accompany them to Jerusalem, Aaron would no doubt allow it. He was a kind soul, and she prayed his heart was large enough to find room for both of them. Aaron was industrious, and she was hard working. He had a fine upbringing in the art of blacksmithing, and she had an education fit to raise their children after the manner of the finest teachers. He was patient; she was determined. He worried over the future, and she worked endlessly to fill the present with a touch of joy, though there was little happiness in the prospect of waiting for Aaron to propose marriage. They were a perfect match waiting for the matchmaker to lead them beyond this crossroads. Rebekah tossed the grain into the air and winnowed out more chaff onto her cheeks. What could possibly be keeping Aaron from asking for her hand in marriage?

Sariah stepped out of her tent. She was past the day she should be delivered, and she walked with a slow gait.

"I'll have the bread ready before your sons leave this morning," Rebekah said, brushing a strand of hair out of her eyes before gripping the pestle with both hands and working it over the hard grains.

"Careful, dear. Grinding wheat doesn't require such fury." Sariah stepped around in front of her. "You'll not rid yourself of your troubles with a pestle."

"This isn't any trouble at all."

"This desert has a way of hardening the spirit."

Rebekah wiped her chaff-laden face clean on the sleeve of her robe. "Do I look hardened?"

"Like a stone, dear." Sariah took the pestle from her and ran her hand over the surface, the rock worn smooth from the crush of the grinding stone. "I don't know if the worst is yet to come or if we're right now passing through our last crucible, but I can tell you that when I married Lehi we had few of the possessions of this world. There was no olive orchard, no estate to call home, no servants, nothing but a deed to some barren land in the hills west of Jerusalem. It was a difficult time for us, but they were happy times."

"Why are you telling me this?"

Sariah helped Rebekah to her feet and led her to sit on a ledge of rocks overlooking the narrow river running below camp. "I want you to be happy."

"I am." Rebekah nodded, but when Sariah raised her eyebrows, her nodding slowed, and her voice softened. "Fairly happy."

"Tell me about Aaron. Has he proposed marriage? He's a special boy, you know. Very special."

"He has a good heart, but—"

"But nothing, girl. He's worth waiting on a while longer." Sariah turned the stone pestle over in her hands. "The boy has the power to soften the stoniest heart."

"Do you think I'm in need of that sort of softening?"

"Why don't you speak to Aaron about that?" Sariah turned her gaze toward the corral. Aaron was bringing Beuntahyu around, and when he saw Sariah and Rebekah watching him from camp, he steered the animal out of the corral, through the river, and up the rise. Sariah offered Aaron a pleasant greeting and before leaving him to speak with Rebekah, she handed him the stone pestle and said, "Be gentle when you tell her."

Gentle? Rebekah stood and arranged the pleats in her robe. What sort of unpleasant news required a gentle touch? Aaron steadied Beuntahyu next to him, the morning light reflecting off the animal's groomed coat of white and over Aaron's sandy brown hair. Beuntahyu was a regal-looking beast, and with Aaron's tall frame standing beside her, they were like royal rider and mount from the palace stables.

Rebekah took the stone pestle from Aaron and waited for Sariah to walk down the incline and cross the river, carefully picking her way over to check on the preparations for her sons' departure. There was no doubt why she told Aaron to be gentle. For whatever reason, he was going to tell her that a marriage proposal wasn't to be. She said, "There aren't words gentle enough."

Aaron let go of the reins, and Beuntahyu rested her muzzle on his shoulder. "You were blessed with far too good of hearing."

"What is it that you're not telling me?"

Aaron said, "Do you remember the day we first met? It was morning on a firing day. I ordered two molds for my father's ovens."

Rebekah said, "Is that all you remember?"

"You were hiding from me in the smoke of the selling table."

"It was you doing the hiding."

"You were dressed in a white robe." Aaron's voice softened, and Beuntahyu grunted her approval. "Your hair was tied with white ribbons, and when the smoke cleared, I thought I was in heaven watching an angel gathering the cups and saucers and plates onto the selling table."

"I won't let you evade me like this." Rebekah folded her arms to keep from remembering the day she first met the recently arrived young blacksmith from Sidon. There was a more important matter to discuss, but with Aaron reminding her of the morning when he stood outside the gate of her father's pottery yard, half hidden in the billowing smoke from the kiln chimney, she couldn't keep back the flood of memories. The smoke blew into Aaron's eyes that morning, and while he was rubbing them clear, she set her pots out on the selling table and studied him without Aaron knowing she was watching. He thought he had crossed the street under the cover of the swirling smoke, but she saw him in the gaps that opened in the blackness, the flashes and glimpses of him still fresh in her memory. He was halfway across the street when she saw him pull up in pain from the tearing of the scars on the undersides of his feet. Tears stained his cheeks, and a quick hand brushed them away. He bent over at the waist, bowing his cane to near breaking before falling to his knees like a man in prayer, the blood oozing from his scars.

Rebekah would have left the selling tables and hurried to his side, but something told her to look away and permit him his privacy in a very public street. And when the smoke cleared and he was left without any cover to hide him from her gaze, he struggled to his feet, hid his cane behind him, and stared at her just like he was staring at her now.

Rebekah offered a slight smile. "I said, 'Good morning.'"

"And I said, 'Fine pottery you have there.'"

"I didn't understand a word. You were too far away to hear."

"You thought I was asking to see your father."

Rebekah pushed against his side. "You refused to come any closer."

"I didn't want you to see me limping. What woman would have a crippled suitor?"

"I would have. How could I not? You told me I was an angel."

"Daniel told you that. I didn't have the courage to say it aloud."

"He was flattering me."

"He wasn't buying pots for Mother. He's never purchased a pot in his life."

Rebekah nodded. "I knew that."

Aaron held her hands in his. "You saved me that day."

"God healed you."

"He cured my feet, but you healed my heart. I was less of a cripple that day because my burned feet didn't matter to you."

"You gave me a single yellow rose, do you remember?"

"I gave you my heart."

The sound of Lehi's voice calling for his sons to gather in the corral echoed across the river, and Aaron waved to him, telling him he'd be along soon. His words died on the morning breeze before Rebekah said, "It's their journey. Let them prepare for it."

Beuntahyu whinnied and pawed at the ground next to Rebekah. What a fool she was not to notice. The Arabian was lashed with Aaron's saddle, and Aaron was dressed in his riding robe. The stirring in the corral drew her gaze over across the river. Laman and Lemuel rigged their horses while Sam tended to four camels, placing large leather straps over their backs and readying them to take on the large water cisterns that Nephi, Setti, Hagoth, Moriah, and Yaush filled down along the river banks with enough water to carry five travelers to Jerusalem.

Rebekah said, "Why didn't you tell me before now?"

"I didn't want you to worry."

"Laban tried to kill you once." Rebekah stepped back from Aaron and slowly shook her head. "He won't stop trying if he finds you've returned."

Aaron took Rebekah by the shoulders. "I have to go back."

Rebekah said, "Why?"

"I must speak with Jonathan."

"Of all men, why him?"

"He's my father."

"He lied to you once, told you I was dead. There's no reason to believe he won't do you evil again."

"He isn't an evil man."

Rebekah turned away. "And if he forbids you to come back?"

Aaron laid his hand on her shoulder. "I belong here with you."

"We have no covenant of marriage." Rebekah stepped out from under the press of his hand, her head down and her face hidden from his view. "We haven't even a promise for that."

"That's the reason I must return to the house of my father." Aaron stepped closer, pulling Beuntahyu with him. He reached his long, calloused fingers around Rebekah's hand and turned her around to face him. "I'm going back for his blessing to marry you."

Rebekah peered up into the seriousness of his eyes before pulling free of Aaron's grasp and leaving him standing with Beuntahyu. She ducked inside Lehi's tent and quickly rummaged through the saddle-bags, leaving Aaron outside calling her name and asking her to come outside and speak about this with the sensibility their discussion deserved. Rebekah found Lehi's writing box hidden under a stack of pillows and took out the stylus and ink bottle. She carried it back outside, brushed past Aaron with hardly a glance, and stepped next to a stack of newly fired pots.

Aaron said, "Rebekah?"

She warned him off with a wave of her hand and smashed the pot over a rock, the largest potsherd falling in the dust near her feet. She fished out the long, smooth piece of clay from among the other frag-ments and started the stylus over the surface with a brusque greeting directed to Aaron's father. No, that's not how she should address this letter, and she struck out the word blacksmith and replaced it with the phrase: *to the esteemed father of my dearest Aaron.*

"What are you writing?"

"Stand over there with Beuntahyu until I'm finished."

"What sort of childish request are you—?"

"Over there." Rebekah dipped the tip of the pen in the bottle before writing her plea for understanding over the matter of Aaron's disappearance. With each phrase, the enmity drained from her heart like black ink sucked from the tip of the pen, the sweet light of forgive-ness filling the empty vial of her soul.

The sound of horses and camels stirred in the corral across the river, and she hurried her pen faster, telling Jonathan of the miracle of finding this valley. Lehi hadn't disclosed exactly how he knew to lead them up off the coastal plain south of Aqaba, through a narrow gorge, and down through a long, sandy wadi to this valley with a river running through it. He said it was a dream that brought them to this camp deep in the Borders nearer the Red Sea, seventy-five miles south of Aqaba along the mountainous coast. She was miles apart from Jonathan, but with this potsherd, her heart crossed the sands to the house of the blacksmith, thanking him for raising a noble son, and telling him that she hoped one day God would bring them together so she could speak her words of thanks without having to use this broken clay to convey the wholeness of her love for Aaron.

Aaron stepped closer. "Let me see that."

"Not a step closer, do you hear me?"

"I hear you losing your mind."

"Back you go." Rebekah waited for him to step back before skipping the tip of her pen past a rough spot on the potsherd and writing that God had protected Aaron from death at the hands of Laban, and though he suffered a terrible arrow wound in his leg, he was healed. She went on about how Captain Laban had threatened to kill Aaron for information about Lehi's escape, and when he refused, the man threw him down on the stone porch in front of the olive oil merchant's estate, stood over him no more than a few hands away, and sent an arrow into the flesh of Aaron's thigh. Rebekah slowed her pen, her mind racing back to the story of Aaron's miraculous escape. That's what it was, a *miracle,* and she wrote the word in bold Hebrew script, telling Jonathan that it was only by the grace of heaven that Aaron had the strength to run into the trees bordering Lehi's estate, tie off his leg to stop the bleeding, and then have the sense to follow Laban through the night and stop the man from killing Lehi. It was a heroic act, nobler than any she'd ever known, and in the quiet reflection of this letter, she could not contain her love for the son of the blacksmith spilling out through her pen and onto the clay.

Aaron had a slight limp in his right leg that may never go away—Jonathan deserved to know that. He tried to hide it, but she knew him well enough that she could see the limp others missed. She'd seen him wince whenever he didn't think anyone was watching. The nagging pain haunted him with the awful memory of Captain Laban inflicting the terrible wound. Rebekah quickly dipped her pen in the ink bottle before continuing with her letter, explaining in as few words as she could that though she didn't know the kind of pain Aaron suffered, she'd endured a different kind of hurt—not knowing if she'd ever see Aaron alive again—the same sort of pain Jonathan must have endured wondering if his son would ever return to them. She thanked heaven she was near Aaron now. No longer did she close her eyes and search her memory to see his sandy brown hair, hear the soft timbre of his gentle voice, or bask in the kindness of his blue eyes. He was here in this valley with her, far away from the threat of Captain Laban, and now that he was returning to Jerusalem she added her plea to this letter that Jonathan understand the nobleness of Aaron's return to ask his blessing on their marriage at the risk of his own life. Rebekah reached the bottom of the potsherd and added one last line, begging Jonathan to not let any harm come to Aaron while he tarried in Jerusalem, and more than that, did he have it in his heart to give his blessing to their marriage?

Rebekah lowered the pen from the potsherd. "Promise me you'll deliver this to your father."

Aaron reached to take the potsherd. "Why must I make such a—"

"Without reading it." Rebekah stepped back from his reaching.

"It's just like a woman to keep secrets."

"It isn't a secret."

"And neither should this be." Aaron took her by the hand and looked into her eyes, and for a moment she sensed he was seeing deep into her soul. He said, "Will you be my wife?"

Rebekah pressed her hand against Aaron's chest. She'd only ever wanted one thing since the day she saw him hiding in the smoke outside the pottery yard—to be the wife of Aaron the blacksmith.

Rebekah leaned over and kissed him, and Beuntahyu stuck her muzzle between them. The animal blew Aaron's hair off his brow with short bursts from his nostrils and whinnied before pushing her nose closer, the cold, wet flesh of the animal's nose forcing Rebekah back. Beuntahyu stomped her hooves and whinnied again. She was rigged with a worn leather saddle tied with two wide straps around her belly. The saddlebags on her haunches were packed for a long journey, and the water skins hanging down her side were freshly filled to over-flowing, the water collecting at the bottom and dripping into the dust at Rebekah's feet—reminding her that this journey would separate her from the man she loved. Aaron steadied Beuntahyu and told her to calm down; they'd be away soon enough. His voice soothed the powerful animal, and she quieted under his hand, her gaze shifting between Aaron and Rebekah. Aaron was dressed in a brown riding robe with a water skin strapped over his shoulder. Was this how she was to remember him—dressed for another journey that would take him far away from her again?

The memory of the pain Aaron suffered with his burned feet and again when Laban shot an arrow into his thigh flooded over her. He could have died twice before, and she shuddered at the thought of losing him forever. Good fortune did not come in threes, and she was about to try one more time to convince him not to return to Jerusalem, but her heart told her otherwise, the words whispering from deep in her soul that Aaron was going to suffer pain worse than the flesh-burning heat of the smelting oven or the sharpness of Captain Laban's arrow—pain that would somehow bind him to his father and bring all of them together into a family circle that could not be broken.

Lehi called from the corral asking Aaron to join them, and he adjusted his riding robe on his shoulders and took the reins in his hand. "Does that mean yes?"

Rebekah pressed the rough clay potsherd against Aaron's calloused palm. She shouldn't trust the welfare of the man she loved into the hands of Jonathan the blacksmith, but she felt the promise of heaven guiding him in this journey. She kissed him on the cheek, and through tears welling up in her eyes she softly said, "Come back to me."

Lehi hefted a water cistern onto a camel and tied the cords while Nephi held the vessel in place. His sons needed eight cisterns to get them through the driest parts of the journey, and with soldiers patrolling the King's Highway the only route left to them was the less-traveled Way of the Red Sea. The heat of summer was gone, and the cooler days of early autumn made passage possible.

"Sariah, you shouldn't be out like this." Lehi tied off the cistern and hurried down along the river to help her over the sand. What was she thinking? He left her in the shade of a date palm with instructions to stay there until their sons were ready to leave.

Sariah held out a small basket. "I brought dates for the journey."

Nephi said, "We have plenty."

"You haven't any picked by your mother."

Lehi said, "You should be resting, dear."

"Nonsense. Not when there's work to be done."

Nephi said, "We're packed. We have everything we need."

"You haven't everything, son." Sariah turned to Lehi. "Did you tell him?"

Lehi said, "I was waiting for the proper moment."

"This is as proper as any." Sariah took Lehi by one arm, Nephi by the other, and insisted they escort her down along the bank, leaving the work of loading the cisterns to the others. She tugged on Lehi's arm the way she did whenever she was bursting to tell something that wasn't her place to tell. She said, "One of the boys must know, dear."

Nephi said, "Papa, what is it?"

"Our land at Beit Zayit." Lehi stopped them near a bend in the river. "It wasn't the only thing Great-Grandfather left us." He spoke slowly, his voice hardly audible above the babbling water running beside them. "I would have brought our inheritance with us, but I left it under Ishmael's care. I was not certain why until now."

Nephi said, "The olive oil stores would have gone bad in this desert."

"God told me to leave your inheritance." Lehi wrung his hands together. "Before your great-grandfather passed from this life he told us it was set aside to preserve the covenants. He was very sick with fever. He could hardly speak. I did what he asked and used only a small portion of it to plant the vineyards and purchase the camels in our herd, but I never put any stock in Great-Grandfather's story."

Nephi said, "What story?"

"You may need the inheritance to bargain for the brass plates."

"Captain Laban doesn't trade in olive oil."

"It isn't the oil, son." Sariah spoke quickly, her voice rising as she explained that there was an inheritance of gold and silver left behind at the estate.

Lehi said, "I didn't know why God told me to leave the inheritance. Not until . . ."

Nephi said, "Until what?"

"His dream." Sariah patted Lehi on the arm. "Isn't that right, dear?"

"Go to Ishmael. He'll know what to do." Lehi took Nephi by the arm. "Repeat to him what Great-Grandfather told us many years ago. Tell him the day has come for God to begin remembering His covenants with Israel."

CHAPTER 21

—September 16, 1826
Palmyra Township, State of New York

Lucy Smith sat in the rocker near the cold hearth and worked two long wooden knitting needles around the beginnings of a sock. It was a skill her mother taught her when she was a little girl, but to this day, none of her daughters had taken a liking to the art—preferring to sew and stitch but not knit. The small boot was for her youngest—little Lucy. It wasn't the finest stocking she'd ever fashioned for the five-year-old, but it had enough thickness to keep the girl's feet warm come winter.

Five piles of yarn sat around her feet, none of them wound around spools or threaded to a bauble. The yarn was a gift from a seamstress in Palmyra—remnants from the discarded spools the woman couldn't sell, and Lucy collected the odds and ends to make winter clothes for the children. If there was enough left after she finished these boots for little Lucy, she'd knit each of her five sons a cap or at least an ear warmer, and she'd do her best to save back enough for a scarf for Sophronia and mittens for Catherine. The fear of not having enough money to clothe her children come winter festered in her soul, and there was no better medicine to ward off the dread of poverty than knitting. Somehow the good Lord would bless them.

The string ended halfway up the leg of the stocking, and Lucy reached for yarn of a different color. It didn't matter that they weren't the same. A matched pair was for the wealthy, and the only wealth she needed was the blessing of a roof over the head of a happy family. Mercy, how the good Lord had showered her with blessings—a fine husband, obedient children, and a warm cabin on one hundred acres of land. And as soon as Joseph Sr. returned from working in Pennsylvania they'd have enough money to pay the land agent the final hundred-dollar installment and make this farm their own. Lucy finished the stocking and started the next one, knitting a loop and hooking the yarn to start the toe. Once the burden of the mortgage was gone, they could afford to pay Mr. Stoddard for his carpentry work on the white frame house and, after three years of waiting, move into the comfort of a larger home with three fireplaces. Lucy finished knitting the toes and started up along the foot, her needles pulling the yarn from the pile of remnants. What would it be like to pass a winter in a home with three hearths? It was an impossible blessing, and as soon as Joseph Sr. and Joseph Jr. arrived home from working in Pennsylvania she was going to ask them how much longer until they could move out of this cabin and into their new home across Stratford Road.

Joseph Sr. spent a good portion of the year gleaning whatever work he could find to raise the money to finalize the land purchase. The first of the month he was off again in company with Joseph Jr. to find more work in South Bainbridge, thinking they might be able to hire on again with the wealthy lumber miller and farmer Josiah Stoal, the same man who hired him earlier in the year. It was a three-day journey on horse to South Bainbridge, but Stoal paid well—nearly fourteen dollars a month plus room and board. Last winter when they worked for the man, Joseph Sr. and Joseph Jr. brought home eight months' worth of wages between them, though this time her husband promised they'd only be gone three weeks at most. It was harvest time, and Joseph Sr. couldn't be away for much longer than that. Hyrum was running the farm with the help of eighteen-year-old Samuel Harrison, fifteen-year-old William, and ten-year-old Don Carlos, but the boys couldn't finish the work on their own.

If only Mr. Stoal and Mr. Knight weren't so insistent on having her two Josephs work for them. Her husband and son were both hard-working men, honest to a fault—Mr. Stoal said so himself last time he was through Palmyra Township. It was a map to a Spanish silver mine that first interested Mr. Stoal in Joseph Jr. He was certain there was silver hidden somewhere on his property of hundreds of wooded acres lining the Susquehanna River, and when he heard rumors about Joseph Jr. and gold plates and such, he came calling, thinking to convince the boy to join his search for the silver mine. It wasn't long before Joseph Jr. refused to help Stoal, but thankfully the man allowed him to spend his time working at the lumber mill or at the gristmill owned by his partner, Mr. Knight, in Colesville. Joseph Jr. wanted nothing to do with digging for treasure, not after his visits from the angel the boy called Moroni.

Had it been three years now since the first visit? Lucy slowly rocked back and forth. That it was—three years come next Friday, September twenty-second. She finished knitting the foot and started up along the leg of the second stocking. Besides all the digging and lumbering and milling, Joseph Jr. had another reason to find work around Harmony. A certain Emma Hale, the daughter of the man who owned the boarding house where her husband and Joseph Jr. stayed last winter, had captured his fancy. Joseph said the woman would be his choice for marriage in preference to any other woman he'd ever seen. He said she was tall, with long, black hair, and when they spoke at length in the evenings after work was done, she understood his heart like no other.

A knock sounded at the door, and Lucy walked over with her knitting needles and undid the latch. The cabin door creaked open, and Mr. Stoddard stood in the entrance, flanked by two of his neighbors. They were dressed in dark pants with white, go-to-meeting shirts buttoned up to the collars and tied with bowties. What sort of serious business brought them here dressed all proper? They owed Mr. Stoddard for his carpentry work on the nearly finished white frame house, but there was no need for him to dress so fine to deliver a bill on the note of credit issued for his efforts. Work pants and shirt would do just fine to discuss the payment of their debt. She invited him and his neighbors to sit down, but none of them took a seat, and Lucy returned to her rocking chair and took up the knitting needles. "What business brings you here, gentlemen?"

Mr. Stoddard held out a notarized bill of some sort with signatures and seals affixed to the bottom. He shook it at Lucy as he spoke. "Where's your husband?"

"He's been away these past few weeks with Joseph Jr."

"Away on business in the middle of the harvest?" Stoddard's taller neighbor leaned forward and told the carpenter it was just as he'd said it was. Mr. Smith and his son had run off and left their farm to escape paying their debts and earning a living.

Lucy said, "I'd hardly call milling lumber and working a gristmill running off."

The second neighbor folded his arms across his chest. "We hear he's been gone since last November, run off to dig for silver on the promise of an old abandoned Spanish mine."

"He and Joseph Jr. were gone four months last winter working for Mr. Stoal of South Bainbridge, and they went again this month for a short time." Lucy missed a stitch and had to undo it before she could go on. "He's a wealthy Pennsylvania businessman. Do you know the gentleman?"

"That wouldn't be Josiah Stoal, now would it, Mrs. Smith?" A smile pulled at Mr. Stoddard's lips. "The businessman who came through here last year hiring men to dig a silver mine he said was left there by the Spanish armies?"

"Mr. Stoal owns more wooded land along the Susquehanna River than any in South Bainbridge, and he pays a good wage for men who work in his sawmill. And the good Mr. Knight operates three milling machines out of his gristmill and pays my husband enough to make our last payment on this land. But I'm sure you didn't come to discuss our mortgage, now did you, Mr. Stoddard." Lucy put away her knitting needles. "What brings you here today, sir?"

"Actually, Mrs. Smith, your mortgage is the reason we stopped by."

"Mother?" The cabin door swung open, and Hyrum stepped inside. His shirt was wet with sweat from working the harvest, the cloth clinging to his chest and gathered about his suspenders. "William said we had visitors."

"Mr. Stoddard was just telling me the reason for their visit." Lucy took Hyrum by the hand. "Go on, sir."

Mr. Stoddard held up the signed document. "This here's a deed to your property—all hundred acres. The maples groves, the wheat fields, this here log cabin, and the home I worked on across the street." He nodded to his companions. "We three own it now, and we come to tell you that you best be moving off our land so the rightful owners can take possession of it."

"That can't be." Lucy turned in the rocker to look at Hyrum. "You went and asked the land agent to extend the due date three months until Christmas day, didn't you, son?"

"I did, and he'd not ever agree to sell the farm out from under us." Hyrum took the deed from Stoddard and quickly read through it. "We have only one more payment to make."

Stoddard said, "You were late."

"We had an agreement with the agent."

"He changed his mind once he heard your father and brother were run off, and that you was burning the sugar maples, and wrecking the homes."

Lucy said, "That's a lie."

Mr. Stoddard said, "I offered your husband fifteen hundred dollars last year for this place, but he turned me down flat out. When you folks didn't make your yearly payment last week, the land agent got real nervous, and I paid him cash on a delinquent note."

Lucy said, "You deceived him."

"Your men ran off to dig for gold and silver. That sort of thing the land agent ain't so willing to take a chance on."

Hyrum stepped up to Mr. Stoddard. "You lying—"

"Hyrum." Lucy stepped between the men. "What does this mean, Mr. Stoddard?"

"It means you're on my land, woman." Stoddard took the deed from Hyrum and started out the door. "I'll expect you to be gone by the end of the week."

The three men marched down the front porch toward the street. Lucy went after them. She had to convince them to give back the deed. This was their last home, the property where they could finally get ahead before they retired. Alvin was buried on this land, and she was going to grow old here, see her children buy farms in the township, and watch her grandchildren play in the yard in front of the frame house. Lucy hurried after Mr. Stoddard. Was it possible? Had this carpenter dashed all of her hopes?

Lucy's head went light, her knees gave out, but before she collapsed on the porch, Hyrum caught her and carried her back inside. He laid her shaking frame in the rocker, poured her a drink of water, and knelt beside her. "I'll fetch Dr. Robinson."

"I don't need a doctor, dear." Lucy fanned her face.

"He can sign an affidavit and accompany me to every farmer in the township for signatures attesting to Papa's character."

Lucy reached for his arm. "Stoddard has the deed, son."

"The land agent will get it back from him once he sees the carpenter is a cheat." Hyrum hovered over her rocker. "Do we know where Papa and Joseph are?"

"They weren't certain if they'd find work with Mr. Stoal on this trip. They could be anywhere between here and Harmony."

"Have the girls prepare handbills announcing our trouble and urging father's immediate return." Hyrum went to the door and called for Samuel Harrison, William, and Don Carlos to come in from the field. He turned back to Lucy and said, "Have the boys deliver them to the inns and boarding houses along the road to Pennsylvania."

"What else can we do?"

"Pray, Mother." Hyrum put on his wide-brimmed hat and started for the door. "Pray we don't lose this farm."

Lucy rubbed the small, half-finished stocking between her fingers, the untied ends of second-hand yarn hanging down over her hand. How much longer must they endure the insecurity of their poverty? She softly said, "I've never stopped praying for that, son."

—Three Days Later, September 19, 1826
Hale Inn and Boarding House
Town of Harmony, State of Pennsylvania

Emma carried a stack of clean towels to the top of the stairs and left one at the door of the overnight boarders from New York. She hurried down the hall, setting a towel at the door of an itinerant preacher, another at the door of a farm machine salesman, and one more in front of the door of a traveler from Ohio. There was little time to change the sheets, clean the vacated rooms, and still get to school on time. Her older students were recessed for the harvest, but the younger ones—the children too young to help on the family farms—continued their studies during the last weeks of September, and she was off to open the school as soon as she finished helping her father with work around the boardinghouse. With fourteen rooms, it was the largest and finest anywhere in the Susquehanna River Valley.

Emma walked up to the room that belonged to Joseph and his father. The door stood ajar, and she could hear them inside. The Smiths had never been anything but genteel, but this morning there was a certain sternness in their speech that spilled out into the hallway, betraying the trouble that stirred within.

"You can't go." Joseph Sr.'s low voice shot past the doorpost. "Is it the digging for the silver mine?"

Joseph Jr. said, "I never should have helped Mr. Stoal with that."

"He pays us well, son. You've worked hard clearing Stoal's land of trees. You spent a good many days in his lumber mill and working the machines in the gristmill. And there's no shame in helping the man dig on his property. He has a map to a silver mine, and if he wants your help from time to time, I say you give it to him."

"I can't. Not anymore."

Emma stepped closer to the door and peered in past the post. She could see Joseph standing beside his bed, organizing his things into a pack. He never said anything about leaving this morning.

Joseph Sr. said, "Why so sudden?"

"The days got away from me, Papa. I lost track. The twenty-second of September is three days from now."

Joseph Sr. sat on the bed next to his son's packing. "Will you get the plates this time?"

"I don't know."

Joseph Sr. rested his hand on his son's shoulder. "How many more years and how many more visits, son?"

Emma leaned against the doorpost, the stack of towels set on her hip. Her poor Joseph. Didn't anyone understand the difficulties he labored under? Last year in November when Josiah Stoal brought the Smiths over and asked Father Hale to take them on, she didn't think anything of the brown-haired son of Mr. Smith. He was handsome to be sure, but Mr. Stoal's two daughters were bent on gaining his affection, and she let the matter go until Joseph began taking an interest in her. They spent the evenings chatting in the parlor of the boarding-house—sometimes well past a proper courting hour—but it wasn't until they started talking religion that she knew she shared a kindred spirit with the man from Palmyra. He didn't profess any affiliation with any of the organized churches, but his heart was good, he read his Bible more than most men, and the story of his visions penetrated to the very depths of her soul. Papa said the boy was nothing but a charmer, but Emma knew otherwise. It was six years ago last spring that Joseph had his first vision. He didn't call it that, but it most certainly was, what with him having three angelic visits since then from a resurrected soul he called Moroni. Emma placed the stack of towels on her other hip and turned her head to hear the conversation inside. It wasn't in her nature to eavesdrop, but she had to know if Joseph was leaving Harmony to return to—

"Emma." Isaac Hale stood at the top of the stairs. "What are you doing, daughter?"

Emma dropped two towels at the threshold of Joseph's door and started down the hall toward her father. "I've a few more guests in need of a towel before I start on the bedding."

"I don't approve of this." Isaac Hale met her halfway. "Not one bit."

Didn't approve? Emma set down another towel at the door of a traveling salesman. He approved of Joseph when he first boarded here during the winter, but as her heart grew more attached to the young man from Palmyra, her father's heart became more indignant. "I don't want you spending your evenings in Joseph's company."

"Father, I'm twenty years old. I think I can—"

"I would rather follow you to the grave than see your head turned by that man."

Emma pulled up in the middle of the hall. "And I prefer my head turned by Joseph over any other man I know."

"He's a money digger and a glass looker."

"It's been more than three years since he had anything to do with that sort of company."

"What about Mr. Stoal?"

"Papa, how can you say such a thing? Mr. Stoal has been nothing but a good customer. He sends all his men to board here, and he pays on time."

"He employs his men in search of a silver mine."

"Is that such a bad thing?" Emma unfolded a towel and refolded it into a smaller bundle. "It wasn't but a year ago you witnessed the contract for the digging expedition at his property. I saw you sign the papers myself. If Mr. Stoal thinks there's a silver mine on his property, then let him dig it up."

"It isn't honest work what this Joe Smith does."

"He's tired at the end of the day. When I find him sitting in the parlor in the evenings he can hardly stay awake. If that isn't hard work, then what is?"

"I don't like what he does."

"You mean you don't like what he believes."

"The boy doesn't have religion, daughter. We're Methodists. We have a pew at the chapel in South Bainbridge. Where is Joseph's pew?"

"I never should have told you about his visions." Emma lowered her head. "They only make you angry."

"They cause me to worry."

"Over what?"

"That my wise, intelligent, well-educated daughter may have lost the sense to know when she's been duped by a—

"Papa." Emma held up her hand. "Your anger is sure to wake the guests."

"I'm not angry with you, girl." Isaac lowered his voice to a whisper. "I simply don't want you married to a, a . . ."

"A prophet?"

"Don't speak such blasphemy, young lady." Isaac stepped in next to Emma. "Do you remember when you were a little girl, only seven years old, back before I started attending meetings with you and your mother?"

"It's been far too many years."

"I ran across you out in the trees behind the house. You were praying back in the little grove of maples, asking God to give me enough faith to believe in Jesus." Isaac took Emma by the hand. "You were the reason I started attending with the Methodists."

"Then why is it you don't think better of Joseph? He did as I. When he yearned for something deep in his soul, he went out into the trees behind his home and asked God for wisdom."

"All he has is foolishness."

"I wish your heart could be touched." Emma pressed the towels to her breast. "The same way I'm touched when I hear Joseph speak of his visions."

The door to the Smith room swung open, and Joseph Jr. stepped into the hall, his leather satchel draped over his shoulder. He slowed his stride, offered a good morning to Isaac, and stopped before coming too close.

Emma said, "The time has come, hasn't it? You're going to the hill."

Joseph confirmed her inquiry with a nod, his deep-blue eyes penetrating to the very center of her heart. He had sandy brown hair, long eyelashes, and he stood a little over six feet tall, his broad shoulders commandeering the hallway. And when he spoke it was like the rush of a river over a fall.

Emma said, "You'll be coming back as soon as the harvest is over, won't you?"

"I'll work the winter for Stoal."

"And you'll board here?"

Joseph turned to Isaac. "If you'll have me, sir."

The hall fell silent, and when Papa didn't answer, Joseph tipped his hat to the man and said, "Good day, sir."

Emma stepped back against the wall to let him pass, the thin cloth of the towels as thick as a brick wall separating her from him. She said, "Until winter?"

"Until then, yes, Emma." Joseph turned down the hallway with hardly any of the limp he said he tried to hide from others—the limp he said only she and his parents were able to detect from the surgery in his left leg. She followed him to the top of the stairs and watched him descend to the landing when a traveler pushed through the doors. Joseph greeted the man, and then he was away, headed down the porch and up road running alongside the Susquehanna River toward the state line separating Pennsylvania from New York.

The traveler waited for the door to shut behind him before he turned in the entryway and glanced up at Emma. "Is there a Mr. Smith boarding here?" He looked down at three handbills balanced in his palm. "A Mr. Joseph Smith Senior."

Emma said, "Who shall I say is calling, sir?"

"Tell him two young boys—a William and Don Carlos—from across the state line up in New York are looking for him." The traveler stepped to the base of the stairs and held up the handbills. "You'll save me the trouble of posting these at the inns between South Bainbridge and Harmony if the man's boarding here."

"I'll see that he gets them."

"Much obliged, ma'am." He walked the handbills up the stairs. "Seems there's some need of him at the Smith farm in New York."

—Three Days Later, September 22, 1826
Palmyra Township, State of New York

Lucy Smith paced the main room of the cabin, careful not to wake the girls asleep in the bedroom just off the kitchen. Don Carlos was asleep in the loft, but the rest of the men of the family were out, and it was getting close to midnight. Lucy stopped pacing long enough to stir the fire with a poker and add another log to the hearth, the warmth dispelling the cool of an early-fall night, but it had little power to rid her of the chilling events of the past three days. Joseph Sr. returned from Harmony in time to request a meeting between the land agent and Mr. Stoddard, and he along with Hyrum, Samuel Harrison, and William had gone to Canandaigua. Lucy stirred the embers in the hearth and teased out a bit more flame to brighten the cabin, but there was little cheer to be had this evening. If the trouble with Mr. Stoddard didn't cause her enough agony, there was Joseph Jr. to worry over. He had headed home from Harmony well before Joseph Sr., but there was still no sign of the boy.

Footsteps sounded on the porch, and Lucy rushed to undo the latch and let William step inside ahead of Samuel, Hyrum, and Joseph Sr. Thank the good Lord they were back. Lucy rushed to her husband's side, holding her shawl on her shoulders with one hand and wrapping her free arm around him. She wasn't given to public displays of affection, but with her mind reeling over Mr. Stoddard's claim to their farm, her husband's steady hand and firm resolve was all she had left to calm her soul. She held him close for a moment, then stepped back and adjusted her shawl. "Did the agent give back the deed?"

"No, Mother." Joseph Sr. slowly shook his head. "No amount of persuading could convince Stoddard to give it up."

William said, "You should've heard the slander Stoddard spewed out about Papa right there in front of the land agent. Said he was a good-for-nothing drunk. A lazy indolent. Said he was—"

Samuel Harrison took William by the arm. "Mother doesn't need to hear that."

William pulled free and said, "Stoddard said it don't matter about Smith—he's got gold plates, a gold Bible, he's rich, he don't want for nothin'."

"Doesn't want for anything, son." Lucy patted William on the shoulder. The boy lost his good sense and his diction when he was upset.

"Yes, Mama."

Samuel Harrison said, "How does Stoddard know about the gold plates?"

"I never told no one."

"Never told *anyone,* son."

"Yes, Mother." William shook his head, and his dark brown hair fell into his eyes. "I never said nothin' to nobody."

Lucy drew her shawl over her shoulders. She and Joseph Sr. were still young when they lost the farm in Vermont, but now, with Hyrum ready to marry and Joseph Jr. wanting to save money for a marriage proposal, they couldn't count on the help they'd need to carve another farm out of this unforgiving land. She said, "What's to become of us?"

Samuel Harrison removed his wide-brimmed hat and stood beside Lucy. "We got help from Mr. Durfee and his son, the sheriff."

Hyrum said, "The affidavit from Dr. Robinson shamed Carpenter Stoddard into listening to them."

William said, "And we got Mr. Durfee to put up the money to buy the deed from Stoddard. Nearly fourteen hundred dollars."

Hyrum said, "Stoddard never would have given up the deed to Mr. Durfee if the sheriff wasn't there with him, looking over Stoddard's shoulder."

Lucy started the rocker moving and stared into the hearth, the dying embers of the fire gone a deep red. Joseph Sr. took her by the hand. "Durfee will let us stay on and pay rent."

"For how long?" Lucy stopped rocking, her foot wedged against the planks in the floor. "Until we're old and weak and can't work enough to pay the rent?"

"It's my fault." Joseph Sr. knelt beside the rocker with his head down. "If I'd only found a way to get more money. If I'd only had the luck to find—"

The cabin door swung open, and Joseph Jr. stood in the entry. His face was drawn out and pale. He stuffed his hat under his arm and stepped inside. There was a long silence, and when no one asked Joseph the reason he'd been so long returning from Harmony, Lucy finally said, "We missed you, son."

Joseph Jr. sat on the bench pushed up against the front wall of the cabin, his legs stretched out in front of him, his head leaned back against the rough-hewn logs. He closed his eyes and ran his hand through his hair.

"Joseph?" Lucy stepped closer. "What is it?"

Joseph Jr. lowered his head into his hands. He sat there a good while without speaking a word, not looking up at anyone. Samuel Harrison and William gathered around the bench, and Joseph Sr. stood next to Lucy, all of them silent and staring down at the poor form of Joseph Jr. huddled on the bench. He finally raised his head from his hands and said, "I never solicited the business of digging for money. I declined it at every turn." It was an odd thing to say, especially after what the rest of the family had endured these past three days, but she'd learned to be patient with Joseph Jr. His shirt was open three buttons down from his neck, he was sweating something fierce, and he had a faraway look in his eyes and a silent, contemplative mood that occupied his mind with such completeness that he didn't bother to ask the reason why they were up at such a late hour, with all of them gathered here in the main room of the cabin.

"If not for our poverty and the pleading of neighbors and Josiah Stoal and . . ." Joseph Jr. glanced at his father. "I never would have come near such business."

"What is it, Joseph?" Lucy stood from the rocker and stepped to the bench seat, close enough to lay her hand on his shoulder. "What happened tonight?"

Joseph Sr. said, "Did you get the plates?"

Joseph Jr. said, "I have taken the severest chastisement that I have ever had in my life."

Lucy said, "From whom, son?"

"The angel. I met him at the hill this evening, and he warned me that I'd not been engaged enough in the work of the Lord. He said the time for the record to come forth had arrived and that I must be up and doing, and set myself about the things that God had commanded me to do. The angel was troubled, Mother. More troubled than I've ever seen him. And he reminded me of what he told me on his first visit. He warned me against the spirit of treasure hunting. Said that because of our poverty, Satan would try to tempt me to get the plates for the purpose of getting rich. I remember his words exactly and how he said them that very first day—that I should have no other object in view in getting the plates but to glorify God." Joseph straightened against the wall of the cabin. "I now know the course I'm to pursue, so all will be well."

"The plates, son." Joseph Sr. leaned his head in. "Did you get them?"

"One more year."

"It's been three already."

"I don't know why, but this is God's timing, not mine. One more year, Papa, and the time will have arrived."

"The time for what?"

"These past three years were not the right time to get the plates. Maybe I wasn't ready, or possibly I had things to learn, or it could be that there was some heavenly timing beyond my understanding that needed fulfilling." Joseph scratched the back of his head. "Maybe it was all those reasons. All I know is that Moroni said that one year from today the time for God to begin remembering His covenants with Israel and for me to get the plates will have arrived." He leaned forward on the bench, his gaze slowly moving to Hyrum, then to Samuel, and finally to William before coming back to his parents. None of them smiled at the news. They didn't pull up chairs and gather around to hear him tell his stories. There were no questions about gold plates or Nephites or the coming of Christ to America like years past. No words about salvation and none of the enthusiasm that filled the house with so much joy these past three years. The boy simply didn't know how difficult it was for any of them to find any delight in his announcement after enduring the trouble Mr. Stoddard had brought upon them.

Joseph Jr. stood from the bench. He turned his gaze over his brothers and then back to Lucy. "Mother, what is it?"

"Oh, Joseph." Lucy wrapped her arms around him. "We lost the farm."

—Ten Days Later
Old City of Jerusalem

Reuben Kessler stood beneath the arching, vine-covered poles of the large wedding canopy. It stood in the gardens behind the synagogue high on the hill with a majestic view overlooking Jerusalem. Where was Avram? Katerina's father had threatened to not come to the wedding, but he couldn't be serious, no matter that he didn't approve. He wouldn't stay away from the wedding of his only family left on earth simply because the Kesslers were Sephardic Jews and the Weiss family was Hassidic. It wasn't right. No matter how strong Avram's reservations, the love for his daughter had to be stronger than tradition, didn't it?

Reuben held two wine glasses in his hands, one for him and the other for Avram. Hopefully he would arrive in time to participate in the glass-throwing ceremony after the nuptials. The glasses were blown in the shop of the finest glassmaker in the city. They had a wide base, a narrow neck, and a cup large enough to hold a shot of wine for the ceremony. Reuben stood up on his toes and searched the gardens for Avram's round, bearded face and red cheeks among the gathering guests, but he was nowhere to be found.

The shade of thick green vines clinging to the iron canopy shielded Reuben from the heat of the midday sun. The tendrils wound through the intricate latticework, decorating the metal arching over this blessed place in the gardens. A good many guests gathered along the path leading from the sanctuary to the canopy—twice what Reuben expected, what with no one attending from Katerina's family. It must be the holiday. The lunch hour on a Monday was not normally a good time to host a wedding, but with all the shops closed to celebrate the first day of the seventh Jewish month, many family friends gathered for the nuptials. Danny and Katerina insisted the wedding be today. They first met on *Rosh Hashannah* three years ago, and no other day than this Day of Remembrance would do for their wedding.

The garden doors to the synagogue opened, and the rabbi emerged with the prayer book under his arm, followed by the bride and groom. Danny looked ten years older than his twenty years, dressed in a new dark gray suit Reuben ordered from Paris eight months before the wedding, and it was a good thing he had acted early—it took twice as long to ship the suit from France than it did to get clock springs and gear wheels from Switzerland. He was a handsome son, with dark brown hair, strong hands, and a heart more than able to put the hopes and fears of his lovely bride ahead of his own. They were to live at the Kessler estate until Danny saved enough money to purchase the small home next door to the clock shop. Reuben tried to fight back a smile, but he couldn't keep his pride from pulling at his lips. What a magnificent scene—his son marrying the elegant Katerina Weiss. She wore a beautiful white gown. The poor girl couldn't afford such a lovely thing, so Reuben had hired her the past two months to sweep out the clock shop, and he paid her many times the wage of any maid he'd ever employed—just enough so that she could buy the dress for her wedding. It was embroidered with white lilac flowers, and not even the lace veil over her face could hide the beauty of her wide, brown eyes and long, black hair that spilled down over her shoulders. She was an angel, and there was no doubt she had power to lift Danny's spirits to new heights and begin a wonderful family.

The gardener's gate along the back wall creaked open, and Avram Weiss hurried down past the spruce trees and around a low hedge, pulling his black *caftan* down over his long earlocks to hide them from the stares of the guests. The white fringes of 613 knots hedged out from under his coattails and hung about his hip. He swore he wouldn't attend the wedding, said he was going to celebrate the Day of Remembrance alone at his small apartment in the Lower City, but here he was in his Hassidic dress—black coat buttoned up the front, and the tail of his undershirt showing beneath the hem of his coat.

Avram sidled in next to Reuben. "I come a moment late, and the good rabbi starts without me?"

"He didn't think you were coming."

"Who told him such nonsense?"

"I let him know there was a chance you wouldn't be attending."

"Then why two wine cups?" Avram took one from Reuben, filled it with red wine, swirled the liquid about the cup, and took a sip before turning his gaze toward Katerina. The girl was holding Danny's arm, the two of them greeting the guests lining the path leading to the canopy. "She's the only family I have left on earth."

Reuben held his glass in the air and offered a traditional toast to life. He said, "Mazel Tov, my dear friend."

"Today we are family." Before joining the toast, Avram directed his wine glass toward the approaching couple working their way down through the gardens. He said, "To life."

Reuben reached into his coat pocket and took out a roll of papers sealed with a single red bow. It was a calendar for the coming year prepared by his son. "Danny wanted you to have this. All the feasts are listed, and today's New Year is marked for September thirtieth. It's Danny's wedding gift to his new father-in-law. He asked me to wish you a happy New Year and tell you he hoped there would be many more."

"Must I remind the boy every year it is the Day of Remembrance?"

"He hasn't forgotten."

"Very well, then." Avram stuffed the calendar under his arm and leaned his head in. "Happy New Year to you, Reuben."

"Good Day of Remembrance, Avram."

The bride and groom reached the canopy, and the rabbi asked Danny to sign the *ketubah*—the marriage contract sitting on a small table set near the entrance to the canopy. Danny wrote his name below the words of the contract, stipulating the bride's rights under Jewish law and making Danny responsible for her well-being and comfort and promising to care for her in sickness and in health. He passed the pen to Reuben to sign on the line as the first witness and then to Avram as the second. And when the rabbi carried the contract over to Katerina telling her that the document was her personal property attesting to Danny's willingness to honor and cherish her, she ran to her father, kissed Avram on the cheek, and thanked him for permitting her this happiness.

The rabbi blessed a glass of wine and asked the bride and groom to each take a sip before instructing Danny to place the ring on Katerina's finger, the carefully crafted gold band sparkling in the midday sunlight, the single diamond in the center reflecting the light back onto her face. Danny fitted it onto her forefinger while the rabbi told her that this finger was best suited to carry a wedding band because the nerves and sinew connected directly to her heart. Reuben and Avram wrapped the couple in a large prayer shawl, the white cloth with wide blue stripes knitting them together as one. The rabbi pronounced the *Sheva Brachot*—the seven blessings of the marriage ceremony—intoning the approval of heaven for the couple, reminding them of the story of the Creation and their first parents, Adam and Eve, and asking for peace in Jerusalem and in their new family. He told them it was fitting they decided to marry on this day when all Jews ask God to remember the covenants promised to Israel. His voice slowed and took on a somber tone. The poor man couldn't sing, but he could recite with a steady voice. He said, "It was on Mount Sinai where the Lord God restored to Moses the covenants of the fathers, the same covenant given to Abraham when he married Sariah, promising the couple that through their seed all the earth would be blessed." The rabbi nodded to Danny and then to Katerina. "May the blessings promised our fathers be yours, and may this Day of Remembrance be doubly blessed to you forever." The rabbi turned his gaze up through the canopy, to the sky beyond. "And may the trumpets heralded on this Feast of Trumpets awaken God to a remembrance of His covenants with Israel, that you and your children may be blessed forever."

Avram Weiss raised his glass in the air, cried *Mazel Tov—to life—* and threw the glass crashing to the ground. The guests erupted in applause and rushed to greet the newlywed couple. They escorted the couple to the terrace above the gardens, sat them down in two chairs, and the dancing began, the guests circling them and singing the wedding song while Danny and Katerina clapped to the rhythm of the music.

It was a God-blessed scene, and Reuben was so taken by it he kept hold of his wine glass. He should have thrown it to the ground with Avram, but the moment to cry Mazel Tov had passed, and he tucked the wine glass in his coat pocket to keep in remembrance of this day when their friends gathered to see his son Danny marry the beautiful girl from Russia—the newlywed Mrs. Katerina Kessler.

The sun faded on the horizon, and the dancing drew to a close, but where was the carriage? The driver hadn't reported to Reuben, and he hurried through the synagogue to the street. He had paid the livery to send their largest carriage and two strong steeds, but the cobblestone lane in front of the synagogue stood vacant. What a disappointing end to a wonderful ceremony. There was no transport to deliver the couple home—at least not until the clap of horse hooves carried on the early evening breeze and the driver turned the black carriage past the sharp bend at the bottom of the steep hill and up the incline toward the sanctuary. He was dressed with a tall black hat and a matching coat with a bow tie and long tails—clothing Reuben loaned him for the occasion. It was the finest transport for hire in the city, and it didn't matter that it cost him a week's earnings. The driver snapped his whip near the ears of the two steeds, the animals straining against the pull of the carriage and grunting their way up the narrow street.

"Apologies for the late arrival." The driver tipped his hat. "I had trouble hitching the animals." He got down from the stoop and kicked at the pin latching the carriage to the harness. "Takes a strong hitch for these animals to make a show up this hill—steepest one in the city it is."

Thankfully he arrived in time for the wedding guests to file out the main doors and watch the bride and groom's departure. The street erupted in cheers and well-wishing as Danny and Katerina emerged from the synagogue. The driver brought the carriage around, and Reuben helped them up the stoop. The guests waved their last good-byes, and the steeds whisked the couple away, the pull of the steep incline lurching the carriage forward. It teetered on the poorly moored hitch, but the driver kept going, steering down the narrow lane with towering, stone-walled buildings rising up either side.

Reuben stepped into the street with the wine glass raised in one hand and a white handkerchief in the other, but before he could wish them well one last time, the carriage began to reel. The bed lagged hard to one side, and Reuben lowered the wine glass and pressed it between his fingers. They were to the steepest part of the hill when a mule-drawn cart turned out of a side alley, its sudden appearance spooking the horses. The animals reared back onto their hind legs, the force of their movement dislodging the hitching pin, breaking the carriage away from the horses and throwing the driver to the ground.

Reuben started after them, his hurried stride turning to a full sprint, his bow tie slapping at his neck, and his hand gripping the empty wine glass. He could see Danny helping Katerina to the door, but the carriage accelerated too quickly to jump to safety. The wild reeling of the carriage threw them back onto the bench seat. Reuben's prayer shawl fell from his shoulders, but he kept running after the carriage. He cried, "Jump, Danny! Get yourself and Katerina out!"

The carriage raced toward the sharp turn at the bottom of the hill, and Danny fell over his bride, protecting Katerina from the impact. The broken hitch hit the curbing, catapulting the large back wheels up off the ground and throwing the bride and groom against the stone wall while the metal frame twisted around their fallen forms.

Reuben reached the upended carriage and ducked beneath the still-spinning wheels. Their lifeless figures lay in a heap. He pried back the broken cart and slipped into the wreckage to kneel next to their bruised bodies. There was no breath in their lungs and only a faint beat in their breasts. He held Danny's head in one hand and Katerina's in the other, pressing their bloodied faces against his coat and staining the cloth with the horror of life slipping unmercifully away. Dear God, this couldn't be. Not his children, not Danny and Katerina. Not on their wedding day. Was there no blessing to stop the river of their lives from going over the falls?

The empty wine glass fell from Reuben's hand. It crashed on the cobblestones, and he softly spoke the only phrase he had strength to utter, the words rising from deep in his aching soul and slowly falling from his trembling lips.

"*Mazel Tov.*" Reuben slowly rocked back and forth to the rhythm of his prayer, his children nestled against his side. "To life, my dearest."

CHAPTER 22

─Early Autumn, 598 B.C.
Jerusalem

Baruch set aside the stylus and rubbed the pain from his fingers after so many hours of holding the etching tool. If only there was a simpler way to write on metal plates. A few lines he could manage, but a full plate in a matter of days strained his fingers beyond their limits.

Two finished plates sat near the edge of the writing table beneath the oil lamp, waiting for him to finish his work and get them to Elizabeth. How the women ever found the means to smelt enough brass for this many plates was a miracle, and they were going to need at least three more miracles if he hoped to finish before the Feast of Trumpets.

Baruch passed his fingers line-by-line over the etching. That last run of characters was too shallow, and he cut them deeper into the brass before blowing the metal shavings out of the carefully quarried channels. He was never this vigilant with other documents, but something deep inside urged him to be precise. Jeremiah's words were to be a marvelous work and a wonder, and he had to be certain every phrase was transcribed without error. He wasn't simply copying words; he was preserving them for something great.

What was that? Baruch raised his head from the plates. There was someone outside his window. The subtle sound of footsteps on the stone path and the catching of a leather sole on the uneven ground beside the cypress tree carried on the evening breeze. It couldn't be Elizabeth. She wasn't to come to the house. They agreed to exchange plates in the hole in the wall down the alley.

Baruch polished the surface of the plate with a chamois and set it in a satchel with the others before taking the plates out of the writing room. He fumbled with the latch on the back door and stepped into the moonlit courtyard. Jeremiah told him not to leave his house without taking the parchments with him, said he'd need them to protect his life, but that wasn't until after he'd finished transcribing all the plates, and there were still more left to engrave. He pushed through the back gate and hurried down the alley to the place in the wall where he and Elizabeth agreed to make the exchange. Five stones up from the corner and three stones to the right. He removed the cover stone and reached his hand in to feel for the newly delivered plates, but there was nothing beyond the coarse rub of rough-cut limestone against his skin.

"Is this what you're looking for?"

Baruch spun around.

"Elizabeth? We're not to meet like this, girl." Baruch checked the alley before coming back to her. She stood in the shadows of night, a hood pulled tight around her face. She held out three brass plates and said, "You will finish in time won't you?"

Baruch handed over the finished plates in exchange for the newly smithed ones. "I should have these for you by the feast day."

"That's too late."

"Zoram said I had until then."

"They're hanging the vault door any day. My father's nearly finished with it."

"Slow him down. Douse the fires."

"The steel's already smithed."

"Hide his tools."

"All that remains is the curing."

Elizabeth tucked the finished plates under her robe. "Once the vault door is fitted in place, Zoram won't have access to the plates."

"Dear girl. Why didn't you tell me sooner?" Baruch scratched the back of his head. "Check here twice each week. I'll put the plates out as soon as I've finished. Now go on. Get yourself to the safety of your home."

Baruch waited for her to disappear around the corner before returning to the back gate of his home. He reached for the latch and noticed the pin was pried up and the nails pulled away. Was someone trying to loosen the latch enough to break into his home? Baruch scanned the gardens. There was no sign of anyone hiding among the ivy. He unlocked what was left of the latch, stepped into the kitchen, and sealed himself inside before leaning against the planks in the door. Who could be trying to steal into his home? Jeremiah had warned him that his life stood in the balance. Baruch felt along the wall of the kitchen, down the hall, and back into the flickering light of his writing room. The leather parchments he copied from the lips of Jeremiah were stacked along the far edge of the table, and he gathered them into his satchel and set them on the shelf next to the entryway. He would never leave home without them.

Not ever again.

CHAPTER 23

▼▼▼▼▼▼▼▼▼▼▼▼▼▼▼▼▼▼▼▼▼▼▼▼▼▼▼▼▼▼▼▼▼▼▼▼▼▼

—Early Autumn, 598 B.C.
Judean Hill Country

Aaron spurred out of the hills south of Bethlehem ahead of Laman, Lemuel, Sam, and Nephi and down onto the first stretch of flat land since entering the Judean hill country. It took them a day to ride out of the Border Mountains near their camp along the Red Sea, another to travel up the coastal plane to Aqaba and across the southern extremes of the Arabah Valley, and one more to traverse the Judean wilderness and find their way through the hill country. Aaron slapped Beuntahyu on the backside, the two of them racing toward the setting sun.

Jerusalem sat on the far north end of the valley, its towering limestone walls reflecting the orange-yellow glow of late afternoon. Aaron leaned forward and pressed Beuntahyu through a stand of scrub oak and onto the trail skirting around Bethlehem. Just then, Laman spurred past and came around. He reared his animal on its hind legs before veering off the main road and back toward Bethlehem. Where was he going? He never said anything about stopping here.

Bethlehem sat nestled in a low stretch of land along the south end of the valley. The city walls were built of smooth creek stones pieced together without mortar, and in the dying light of late afternoon, yellow shafts of sunlight filtered through the holes in the city's wall. A double gate stood near the middle of the east wall where soldiers inspected the farmers and merchants passing inside to the kingdom's largest grain markets.

Aaron spurred Beuntahyu alongside Laman. "We can make it as far as Jerusalem before nightfall."

Laman said, "We're spending the night here."

Nephi reined in next to Aaron. His black hair hedged out from beneath the brim of his turban and over his brow. "We agreed to ride to Beit Zayit tonight."

Laman said, "It's too late for that."

"There's a full moon rising." Sam guided the camels near. "We can travel the last stretch after sunset."

The captain of the watch started down the incline from Bethlehem's gate in company with five soldiers. They gathered around Nephi's horse, examining the empty saddlebags, the animal's dirty coat, and mentioning Captain Laban's name more than once in their conversation. Nephi lowered his chin into the loose ends of his turban. Both Nephi and Laman possessed features similar to those of Captain Laban, but in the year since fleeing Jerusalem, Nephi had grown to have more of the captain's wide-shouldered stature, straight nose, and powerful jaw line. It was such a striking likeness that these soldiers recognized Nephi's resemblance to Captain Laban more than they had ever noticed Laman's likeness to Laban.

"We've come to trade in the markets." Lemuel nodded. "Spent three days on the King's Highway to reach Bethlehem."

The watchman said, "Your saddlebags are empty."

Laman said, "He told you we came to buy."

"You're not really a merchant, boy." The watchman slapped the saddlebags. "No one rides three days on the King's Highway without hiring out their saddlebags."

Laman tossed the watchman three pieces of silver.

The watchman said, "What's this?"

"Tax."

"You haven't any goods."

"And you have nothing to report." Laman tipped his head to the man and reined inside the main gate with the rest of them following his lead. A small inn stood down a side street. Laman paid the innkeeper for the largest room on the main floor and three extra shekels to stable their animals. The sleeping chamber was large enough to require two lamps. A small vent high on the wall let air pass inside. A single chair stood in the corner, and two water basins with a full pitcher sat atop the small wooden table. Aaron was the last to enter, and when he came inside, Laman locked the door behind him and pointed the double-toothed key at Lemuel.

Laman said, "King's Highway?"

Sam said, "Leave him be."

Laman said, "Every soldier in the city knows where we came from."

Sam said, "We traveled the Way of the Red Sea."

"They all lead to the coastal mountains." Laman turned the tip of the key to Nephi. "The same place where Captain Laban chased a rider who looked like him."

Nephi said, "We should have gone on to Beit Zayit."

Laman said, "We came for the plates."

Nephi said, "There's an inheritance at the plantation, enough to barter for the relic."

"Inheritance?" Lemuel grinned. "Captain Laban, sir, won't you please sell your relic for a cistern of our best olive oil?"

Sam said, "That's enough."

Laman said, "Father took his gold and silver with him into the wilderness."

Lemuel nodded, his thin shoulders moving in rhythm with his head. "He counts it in his tent when no else is watching."

Sam said, "If no one's watching, how do you know he's counting it?"

"He has it." Lemuel nodded. "A bag of gold, and more hidden away somewhere."

Nephi said, "He hasn't anything hidden but what he left behind with Ishmael."

Laman said, "Olive oil is our only inheritance, and if we offer Captain Laban some of it for his relic, he'll give us nothing less than a shallow grave for each of us."

Sam said, "There could be more than oil at Beit Zayit."

"Don't be a fool. What does Nephi know? We're olive oil merchants." Laman ran his hand through his straight, black hair. "And there isn't enough land in our estate to convince Captain Laban to part with his relic."

"There is one thing." Lemuel sat on the edge of the bed, removed his riding boots, and set his feet into the cold water of a washing basin, stirring them in the soothing salt waters before slowly running his gaze over the faces staring back at him, all of them waiting in silence for him to say what he had to say.

"For the love of Moses." Sam leaned forward on the bed. "Tell us what you were going to tell us."

Lemuel added a piece of salt to the basin of water and stirred it with his feet. "Captain Laban wants to know where father's hiding."

Aaron said, "He's your father."

Sam said, "We can't negotiate with his life."

Lemuel said, "I never said anything about giving him over to Captain Laban. I was thinking of something more like . . ." He glanced over at Laman.

Laman said, "What he means is the captain agrees to give us the plates, and we agree to keep Lehi in the desert—exiled from the land of his inheritance."

Lemuel nodded. "There, you see? It could work."

Nephi said, "You're willing to forfeit ever returning to the estate?"

"We came to get the plates, didn't we?"

Sam said, "That's honorable of you."

Nephi fitted his turban over his head and started for the door, but Laman took him by the arm and said, "Where do you think you're going?"

Nephi said, "To speak with Captain Laban."

"I negotiate with the man."

Sam said, "We should all go."

Laman said, "No more than one. We don't want to attract attention. It's too dangerous."

Nephi reached for the latch. "I'm going with you."

"I said only one goes." Laman pushed Nephi's hand aside. "And that one will be—"

Lemuel said, "We should cast lots."

Sam said, "There's some sticks in the firebox behind the inn."

"We use these." Laman retrieved four creek stones from his saddlebag, each one the size of a hen's egg, flat like bread, rounded at the ends, and each with an X etched into one side. He shook the stones in his hand and told them that if all four fell with the x showing, the blacksmith would go to Jerusalem. Three stones with the x showing and Lemuel would go, two for Sam, one for Nephi, and if all four stones came up blank, Laman would go.

Laman tossed the stones on the floor, and they clattered in every direction, the first rolling against the far wall, the second landing on the open floor, and the third coming to rest in the corner—all three blank. The fourth lot spun on end before rolling beneath the bed. Nephi fell to his knees to gather it up, but Laman pushed him aside hard enough to send the boy sprawling over the floor. He lifted the bed frame aside and there, lying on the floor, sat the last stone, the blank side facing up.

Aaron lowered himself into the solitary chair next to the blank lot in the corner. What poor luck. Bartering with Captain Laban wasn't a task he sought, but he would have gone for the chance to deliver Rebekah's potsherd letter to his father and ask his blessing to marry the girl.

Laman gathered the stones off the floor, but before he came for the lot in the corner, Aaron turned it over with his foot. That was odd. The lot was blank on both sides. And if the other stones were like this one, then the only possible result was four blank lots. Why would Laman cheat them to win a chance to speak with Captain Laban . . . alone?

CHAPTER 24

—*Early Autumn, 598 B.C.*
Jerusalem

Lieutenant Daniel left the door to Captain Laban's third-floor chambers ajar and marched across the bedroom. The open window presented far too large a target, and he pulled the shutters closed. There was no one hiding among the cloaks hanging in the captain's dressing area, and the space behind the bench along the far wall was clear. A full pitcher stood on a table near the window, and Daniel slowly emptied the cool spring water into the basin and checked for any yellow. It didn't appear the maidservants had tampered with it, but to be sure he touched a drop of water to the tip of his tongue.

"It isn't poisoned, son."

"Captain?" Daniel spun around and adjusted the black patch over his bad eye. "I was preparing your chamber, sir."

"I didn't hire you to be my maidservant." Laban stood by the basin and pushed open the shutters to let a breeze filter inside. "You're my next-in-command."

"Not there, sir." Daniel ushered Laban from in front of the window.

"What harm is there in a bit of fresh air?"

"An archer could—"

"Must you worry over me like a hen for her chickens?"

"Hananiah didn't have anyone to worry over him."

"And you think I'll suffer the same fate?"

"They say Jeremiah sent an angel of death."

"Angels make poor archers." Laban pushed the shutters open wider.

"Shall I search the dining room before you go down for evening meal?"

Laban ran his hand through his long, black hair, which had gone nearly three months without being cut. "How much longer will you torment me with these precautions?"

"There's still—"

"One week before Jeremiah's threat is past, and that's why you're going to attend to your father's visit." Laban pushed the shutters full open and let Daniel see Jonathan the blacksmith waiting at the front gate for admittance into the estate. "He's come to install the vault door."

"He doesn't need my help for that."

"The watch won't let him inside without your word." Captain Laban pulled an evening cloak on over his tunic. "You can search the dining hall when you're finished with the blacksmith."

"I'm not to leave you alone."

"You're to secure the plates—and that's an order."

"But sir . . ."

"That will be all, Lieutenant."

The smoke from two cauldrons burning outside the gate to Captain Laban's estate stung Elizabeth's nose and forced a muffled cough. She wrapped one hand around the basket of measuring cords—the ones from Mama's weaving basket that Papa insisted she bring to make one final measurement before hanging the vault door in Laban's treasury. She kept the other hand pressed against three inscribed brass plates hidden away in a pocket beneath the pleats in her robe. She would have carried them with the measuring cords, but something told her to hide them among her skirts, and with five soldiers marching through the gate of Captain Laban's estate and ordering them to stand aside while they searched the mule cart there was wisdom in the whispering. Elizabeth stood behind Papa and let him shield her from the threatening gaze of the soldiers. The captain of the watch examined the vault door lying inside the mule cart before turning his gaze to Elizabeth and demanding she show him the contents of her basket. She hesitated, and he took it from her with such force that the cords fell to the ground.

"That's enough, soldier." Daniel ordered his men to back away. He was dressed in a black tunic with gold stripes. He said, "This is a bad time, Papa."

Jonathan gathered the measuring cords off the ground. "You hired me to do this."

"Come back in the morning, and I'll show you to the treasury."

"I don't plan to cart this door about the city again."

Daniel leaned over the cart and ran his hand across the metal slab. "What does this weigh?"

"Enough that it may fall from the hinges."

"Recess it, then."

Jonathan sidled in next to Daniel. "And if it fails?"

"Set the door back far enough so that it rests on the ledge."

"I don't do shoddy work."

"There's nothing shoddy about recessing a door this heavy."

Jonathan offered a weak smile. "You haven't lost your touch for smithing, son."

"I'm not a blacksmith."

"You can always come back."

"Not here." Daniel glanced back to the gate. "Not in front of my men."

"I have a right to worry over my children."

"What's to worry about?"

"The relics are no good, son." Jonathan lowered his voice. "They say they're cursed."

"You should lecture Elizabeth about that."

Elizabeth felt for the plates hidden beneath her robe. "Whatever makes you say such a thing?"

Daniel said, "I don't know what you're doing, but I want you to stay away from Captain Laban's relic."

Jonathan said, "She's your sister."

"She doesn't go near the relics."

Jonathan said, "She's my assistant."

"Find another."

"You were the other."

Elizabeth followed the company of men to the back of the estate where Zoram stood in the opened door of the outside treasury entrance. He was dressed in his long-sleeved white coat and matching turban. He escorted her inside behind Jonathan, Daniel, and the treasury guards carrying the steel door—the damp air from the underground corridors rising past Elizabeth's cheeks. She stopped at the base of the stairs, out of sight of the guards, and waited for Daniel and the others to disappear past a turn in the corridor before whispering, "I have them." She reached beneath the pleats in her robe and presented Zoram with Baruch's masterful cutting and etching of brass plates. The metal caught the light of the lamp and reflected it over the precise letters in a rainbow of red, yellow, and green. These were the prophecies of Zoram's father, preserved in these plates forever. It was just as Zoram said it would be the first time she came to this treasury two years ago, and now she had part in adding Jeremiah's words to the words of all the holy prophets since the world began. Elizabeth said, "Aren't they beautiful?"

"Just in time."

"Baruch has three to finish yet."

"The vault will be sealed today." Zoram removed his white turban and ran his fingers through his thick, black curls. "Place what you have with the relic."

"Daniel won't let me near the plates."

"You can do this." Zoram held her face in his hands. "Remove the three metal rings, place the new plates at the base of the record, and then reconnect the rings."

"And if I fail?"

"Daniel won't harm you. You're family." Zoram leaned in close, but before he could say another word Daniel appeared around the turn in the corridor and ordered him to open the treasury.

The entry door was made of thick timbers framed by a metal casing and recessed into the limestone three fingers deep. It was hinged in place with thick crosspieces and nailed together with iron rivets. Papa and Daniel stepped aside, revealing three wide bands of iron protecting the wood and painted with a coat of fire-resistant glue from boiled ox bones. Zoram unlocked the door, and a gasp of air shot around the post. Shelves filled with sealed repository jars lined the vast chamber from floor to ceiling. Persian rugs covered the stone floor, and deep red tapestries decorated the walls. The ceiling lamps flickered with the last of the day's oil supply, but Zoram didn't bother to fill the cisterns and cast a stronger light over the rows of accounting documents lining the aisles. He steered past the shelves of silver locked in wooden boxes, past a shelf filled with gold vessels, and another brimming with brass medallions.

High-backed reading chairs stood at the head of every aisle, and when Elizabeth came in past the last run of shelves, she found a domed ceiling embedded with crushed abalone shells that cast a shimmering glow over a long table. Zoram caught Elizabeth's gaze and nodded toward the purple curtain draped between two pillars, his eyes telling her to do as he'd asked. Papa reached for the basket of measuring cords, but before he took it from her, something deep in her soul whispered to remove the chisel. Why such a foolish thing? Papa needed the tool to prepare the stone to fit the steel door, but she lifted it out without anyone seeing and hid it in the sleeve of her robe. She was about to hand it back when a voice deep in her soul told her no—she was to keep the chisel a while longer—and she let Papa start his work without a full complement of tools.

The space behind the purple curtain was the only forbidden place in the estate. Zoram told her once that he suspected Captain Laban was hiding more than the relics from him, but he never told her what. Nothing in this treasury was barred from Zoram's view except what lay behind the curtain, and now she was charged with doing the forbidden. Captain Laban said it was out of respect for the holy words of God written by the hand of Moses when he was at Mount Sinai, but the captain wasn't a God-fearing man, and it wasn't like him to revere the words of Moses unless there was something in the relics the man desperately desired to keep from the eyes of men. Elizabeth held tight to the plates hidden beneath her robe. How could she sneak behind the curtain without Daniel noticing she was gone?

Elizabeth found the seam in the curtains, drew back the purple cloth, and stepped out of sight of the others. The yellow light from the treasury cast its beam over a three-legged pedestal with a cushioned top supporting an opened sword case. The blade lay in an ivory case-ment wrapped in red silk, the hilt hedging out from under the end of the cloth. Emeralds and jade decorated the solid gold handle, and a large diamond lay embedded in the end. The steel had kept its polish since last it was bathed in resin oils. The blade was as wide as a man's hand, and inscribed along its length were the words Joseph of old spoke when he anointed the weapon with olive oil, declaring that this sword was not to be sheathed again until the kingdoms of this world became the kingdom of the God of Heaven and His Anointed One.

Papa's voice echoed through the chamber telling the others he'd need to hammer away the edges of the vault to recess the door properly and make a tight fit and could Daniel hand him the hammer from the basket. Thankfully he didn't ask for the chisel, and the sound of Papa's tamping assured her she hadn't been found out. She lifted away the red silk and exposed the tarnished metal of the brass record. A cobweb hung from the three rings holding together the codex of plates, and she brushed the silky strands aside and blew away a coating of dust. What an odd thing for the most prized treasure in this vault to be left unattended for such a long time. Laban valued it more highly than his gold and silver, but for some reason it lay neglected in this remote corner, never to enjoy the redeeming sheen of resin oils or the luster-giving burnish of a good polishing cloth.

The metal rings binding the plates together were sealed into the codex with metal clasps, and Elizabeth quickly pried them loose, unbinding the plates from their ancient mooring. She removed plate after plate, pulling each one clear of the rings and stacking them on the pedestal. She was to the last plate when Papa's voice echoed through the chamber. He said, "Elizabeth. Hand me the chisel from the basket, would you, girl?"

Elizabeth threaded the new plates onto the rings followed by the tarnished ones, but there were too many to fit in place at once.

"Elizabeth. A chisel, girl."

What was she to do? There wasn't time to thread these plates one by one back into place with Papa calling her name.

The sound of Daniel's boots running over the stone floor grew closer. He said, "Elizabeth? Curse you, sister, where are you?"

Two cooks stood at the entrance of the dining room, and Captain Laban informed them he would take his dinner across the hall in the solitary confines of the ready room. It was without the many oil lamps that lit the other chamber, with only the dimness of dusk casting a gray shadow through the shuttered windows. Two high-backed chairs stood facing the cold hearth with a small wooden table set between them. One cook arranged a plate of lamb and cucumbers next to Laban's chair, while the other woman lit a lamp above the meal. They scurried about the ready room, dusting the furniture with scented oils, but when they went to open the shutters, Laban informed them to keep them closed. And could they please leave him alone and in peace while he ate?

Laban latched the door behind their departure, and the scent of basted lamb cooked with chopped onions and a hint of basil drew him to his high-backed chair. He had just lowered himself into the comfort of the cushioned seat when the shutter behind him creaked open on the breeze, revealing three stable boys drawing horses past the open window. The frame slapped against the inside wall, and the brass latch came off its nails and crashed to the floor.

"Good evening, Captain."

The deep, resonating voice came from the shadows on the far side of the room. There was no one standing below the repository shelves. The hanging tapestries lining the wall hung still, and not a soul stood before the cluster of giant Philistine urns.

Captain Laban crossed to the window and picked up the latch before spinning around with the brass in hand. "How did you get past my men?"

"Close the shutters."

"No one steals into my estate." He slashed the air with the latch. "Who are you?"

"The window, Captain."

"I don't obey the orders of a—"

"The window. Or would you prefer an arrow?" The form of a man stirred from behind the giant Philistine urns. He didn't move out from the cover of the shadows to show his face, but the outline of a drawn bow was clear. Was it possible? Could Jeremiah have escaped the prison? Captain Laban removed his cloak and wedged the cloth into the frame to keep the shutters from swinging open. He said, "So you've come to steal my plates of brass, have you?"

"I don't share your obsession for the relic."

"Revenge, then? You want me to suffer like you suffered."

"I want my freedom."

"You didn't have any trouble getting free of the prison."

The intruder stepped from the cover of the urns. His robe was dirtied by the dust of a hard ride. His hair was long, the ends of it reaching to his shoulders, and his beard was full, without any trimming to mark him a member of the wealthy class he once enjoyed in this city.

"Laman?" Captain Laban took a step closer. "Put the bow down."

"Not until you agree to let me go home in peace."

"Where's your father?"

"You'll not have trouble with him."

"He's dead?"

Laman stared down the length of the arrow. "Swear you'll let me return to my estate in peace."

"I don't negotiate with traitors."

"Don't you mean family?"

Captain Laban worked the brass latch between his fingers. "Are your brothers still alive?"

"They're my security."

"You'll never be secure."

"I have claim to the throne."

"Your kind could never make such a claim." Captain Laban rubbed the latch on his sleeve and stared at his reflection in the metal like a judge reading from a scroll. He spoke slowly, his voice rising from deep in his chest. "If only you worked your craft among your neighbors, stealing bread from the baker, sheep from the farmer, and coins from a blind man's purse, you could make a sin offering at the temple and be done with your crimes."

Laman lowered his aim. "What have I ever stolen from you?"

"You're worse than a thief." Captain Laban moved toward the ready room door, slowly enough not to incite Laman to redraw his bow. "You and your brothers are the kind of men who burn farms and besiege villages, plunder the trade route from your mountain hideouts, and coerce men in government, or worse, assassinate them to get what you want." Captain Laban stopped at the entrance, his hand on the latch. "The law allows for the slaying of your kind without trial and without mercy."

"I don't need your mercy. I'm offering you a deal. We get our lives back; you keep your secret."

"You were never smart enough for any of this." Captain Laban unbolted the door and burst from the ready room and into the hallway.

He cried, "Robber!"

Daniel marched toward the purple curtain.

"Elizabeth's not back there." Zoram left the vault door half hinged and resting on the recessed ledge.

Daniel said, "Then where is she?"

"Looking for your father's chisel."

"Chisel?"

"It's a draft," Zoram said in answer to Daniel staring at the hem of the curtain swaying over the stone floor as if parted by someone sneaking in behind.

"A draft down here?"

"Mostly in the evenings." Zoram pointed out the vents in the ceiling where fresh air from outside filtered down into the chamber. "The hot air rises out of the treasury and the cool night air finds its way down through the—"

"Enough." Daniel reached for the seam in the cloth, but before he pulled it aside Zoram said, "Are you sure you want to do that? Captain Laban isn't a forgiving man."

"I look after his relics."

"You're wrong. I'm the one who looks after them, and I'm telling you it's forbidden to go back there."

"The captain will understand."

"The last scribe to disobey him lays in an unmarked grave on the flats south of the city."

"I'm no scribe." Daniel yanked the curtain hard enough that it pulled free of the rods. The drape fell to the floor, revealing a sword case perched on a cushioned pedestal inside an opened casement, but thankfully there was no sign of Elizabeth. The red cloth hiding the brass plates bulged with the awkwardness of three unhinged rings and a stack of unthreaded plates beneath the covering that begged Zoram to put them back together before Daniel noticed their altered state.

Daniel said, "Where did she go?"

Zoram gathered the purple curtain from the floor. "She was never here."

"She's got to be—"

"Is this what you're looking for, Papa?" Elizabeth stepped from around the last repository shelf holding a long chisel.

Zoram tried to hang the purple curtain when the treasury door swung open and Captain Laban marched inside. Sweat streamed off his brow. He took the curtain from Zoram and threw it at Daniel's feet. "Curse him."

Daniel said, "I can explain, sir."

"There's only one explanation for this."

"I was protecting the plates."

Captain Laban slowly turned his gaze over the fallen curtain and the exposed relics before coming back to Daniel. "Did Laman do this?"

Daniel said, "The son of the olive oil merchant?"

"He tried to kill me for the relics. Forced his way out a window. The guards are chasing him now."

Daniel said, "It's still a week before the feast."

"He wasn't sent by Jeremiah, but he'll be back. Laman has his reasons to want my relics as much as Jeremiah." Captain Laban marched to the vault. "Bring them here."

Zoram said, "The door isn't hung."

"Then hang it." Laban slapped his hand to the wall above the opening. "I want my relics sealed away now. I won't wait for the first day of the seventh month, do you understand? No one will rob me of my inheritance."

"Come here with it, son." Captain Laban motioned for Zoram to walk the brass-plate record around the writing table and hold it out for inspection. He took the corner of the silk cloth covering the brass plates between his thumb and forefinger. The man's eyes were dark, without any of the nuances that usually reflected his fierce temperament. He was lost within himself, and Zoram turned his gaze to the floor, away from Laban's penetrating stare.

"Seal it away."

Zoram said, "Don't you want to inspect the record, sir?"

"I don't ever want to see it." Captain Laban left the red silk in place. "It's brought me nothing but trouble."

Zoram brushed the sweat from his brow before carrying the record to the vault. His hands trembled slightly, but not enough to give away the mixture of fear and relief that rushed through his soul. If Captain Laban had found the plates disassembled, it was certain that Zoram was a dead man. Zoram set the plates into the vault, and Daniel eased the sword casement in next to it. How would they add the rest of Jeremiah's prophecies with the record sealed away? And if, by some heavenly miracle, they were able to add the last plates before the feast, how could any man hope to take them from this treasury when they were locked away in here with so many soldiers guarding the estate? It was like staring into a deep cave, the dark opening warning that once the relics were locked away, his father's prophecy of the brass-plate record would never be fulfilled.

Jonathan finished hammering the pins in place before handing Captain Laban a long key on the end of a leather cord.

"This will bring Laman and his brothers to me." Captain Laban sealed the vault, pushing the door into place and latching it shut. "Like bees to honey." He glanced at Daniel. "And when they come, I want you to treat them like we treat all their kind."

Daniel said, "Exactly how is that, sir?"

Captain Laban hung the brass key around his neck. "Behead them all."

CHAPTER 25

—*Early Autumn, 598 B.C.*
Bethlehem

The poorly carpentered chair wasn't large enough for Aaron's long frame. He stretched his legs out into the small room and leaned his head back. How much longer would they have to wait for Laman? Nephi and Sam busied themselves polishing the leather in the saddlebags, and Lemuel had fallen asleep on the lambskin bedcovers. They hadn't gone out of the room since they arrived except to purchase food in Bethlehem's market, and if he had to endure another day cooped up in this place, Aaron was sure to go mad.

Laman should have been back last night, and if he didn't return by midday, Aaron was going to tell the others they should ride to Jerusalem. He reached into the leather pouch at his waist and took out the potsherd letter written by Rebekah. Her careful handwriting covered the surface with her heartfelt plea for Jonathan to understand the details of Aaron's disappearance. He turned away from reading more. He'd promised her he wouldn't, but his passing glance captured that much. The letter began with the phrase: *to the esteemed father of my dearest Aaron,* and he would have read another line if not for the stir at the door. The latch turned, the leather hinges creaked, and Laman stood in the entry. His face was covered with dust, and when Sam told him to come inside, he didn't move. He checked the main hall of the inn before turning back and saying, "Pack your things."

"We're not going anywhere." Sam held up a stone lot without any marks etched into either side. "Not until you tell me why you cheated us."

Aaron said, "You should be more careful to pick up after yourself."

Nephi set aside the saddlebag. "What about the plates?"

"Tell them." Lemuel walked to the entry and pulled the door closed. "We can't keep it from them any longer."

Laman said, "Either you leave with me now, or you're dead men."

"What are you hiding from us?" Sam tossed the stone lot to Laman, but before he caught it, Lemuel's long-armed reach snatched it out of the air. He said, "Enough of this. Sam's our brother. He deserves to know. They all deserve to know."

"You're fools if you don't come with me now. I trusted Captain Laban, and he—"

"Trusted him?" Sam stood in front of Laman. "You don't trust a man like that."

"I spent the night hiding in dust-filled wadis and riding about the countryside until Captain Laban's men lost my trail."

Sam said, "What did you do to anger the man?"

"It isn't anything we've done." Lemuel rubbed the stone lot between his fingers. "It's who we are."

Laman took the lot from Lemuel. "Not another word. Do you hear? I won't let you—"

"Tell them who we are, who our father really is." Lemuel backed into the corner of the room. "Tell them the brass plates belong to—"

Laman jumped at Lemuel, his hands clutching the boy's neck and strangling his speech.

"Stop this." Sam pulled Laman back. "What is it about Laban's relic that turns you into a madman?"

Laman said, "We're going back to the deserts where it's safe."

"When did you ever want to go back there?" Lemuel coughed. "All you've ever wanted is to return to our estate."

"That was before."

Sam said, "Before what?"

"Before Captain Laban accused me of being a robber."

Nephi swung his saddlebag over his shoulder and started for the door.

Laman said, "If you go, you go with us."

"I'm not returning to the deserts until we have the plates."

Laman said, "Ten pounds of brass isn't worth your life."

"We can't leave without trying once more." Nephi adjusted the saddlebag on his shoulders. "Every covenant delivered to the prophets is written in Laban's record."

Laman said, "I did what father asked, but Captain Laban refused. That's enough."

"Father didn't ask us to do this. He dreamed a dream." Nephi turned his gaze to his brothers. "Do any of you doubt God commanded Father to send us after the plates?"

Laman said, "His dreams won't save us from Captain Laban and his men."

"Let them come." Nephi stepped to the center of the room, the glow of the lamps flickering across his face. "As the Lord lives and as we live, we'll not go down to our father in the wilderness until we've accomplished the thing which the Lord commanded us."

Nephi's words brought Aaron out of his chair. They were the words of an ancient oath calling men to be courageous in defending their inheritance. Aaron crossed to the door and pulled it open, the rush of outside air filtering into the room. He had a letter to deliver to his father, but for the first time since leaving Midian, he felt the urgency of Lehi's dream sending them back for the brass plates, and if that meant he waited a while longer to deliver Rebekah's letter, then he'd wait. He said, "I'll get the horses and bring them around front."

Laman said, "You'll be dead before you speak a word to Captain Laban about your precious plates of brass."

Nephi turned to his brothers. "Are you with me?"

CHAPTER 26

—Early Autumn, 598 B.C.
Beit Zayit

Ishmael spurred his steed through the middle groves, telling the gangs of Ethiopian pickers to be gentle with the harvest sticks. If they didn't knock the fruit from the branches with a tender stroke they'd ruin the shoots for next year's harvest. He reached the end of the row, jumped his steed over the cobblestone wall and onto the road leading down through the canopy of olive trees toward the pressing yard. He couldn't let the servants go too long without him. Yesterday he found them mixing sweet olives with wild ones, and they ruined an entire vat of the highest-grade oil.

Sixteen carts waited at the gate of the pressing yard, and he ordered the men with sweet yellow and light-green olives to the near press, the darker green olives to the middle press and the sour olives to the back press. The pressing mule was hitched wrong, and Ishmael slid from the saddle to fix it when he found oil spilling from the drain. Mercy—would he ever find a press master to replace Laman? He dropped the hitch, crawled beneath the large stone bowl, and cleaned away the pulp from the strainer. He never should have helped the sons of Lehi escape into the wilderness—at least not with the harvest coming on. Laman knew the difference between an olive fit for oil and one suited for camel feed. Lemuel's mules were always hitched properly, and Nephi's storage vats were clean and flowed without a clog to waste even a cup's worth of oil.

"You see this?" Ishmael held the two ends of the unlashed hitching rope up to the manservant and spoke loud enough to be heard over the braying of mules and stir of carts moving about the yard. He said, "You tie them in a double pin knot through the harness just like . . ."

Laman? Five men on horseback passed the entrance to the pressing yard on their way toward the estate homes. The lead rider had the same stature as the former press master. Ishmael blinked in the sunlight. Was it possible that heaven sent these angels to help with the harvest? That was most certainly Laman riding point on a brown steed, and the thin boy at his flank had to be Lemuel. Sam and Nephi followed on sleek, black-coated Arabians. And in the full light of day, the white coat of the last horse in the troop reflected the brightness of afternoon, the animal's appearance turning the heads of every servant in the pressing yard, all of them murmuring the names *Aaron* and *Beuntahyu.*

The riders tied their horses and started inside, and Ishmael hurried up the rise after them. He was nearing the fountains when Mary, his youngest daughter, ran from the gardens to greet them. Nora, Abigail, and Hannah followed, their robes swirling about their feet, flower baskets in their arms, and the sound of their calls filling the afternoon with a gleeful welcome.

Mary reached them first, her long, black hair streaming out behind her, and the blue Egyptian robe Ishmael purchased for her on his last trip to that part of the world pulling against her stride. Her basket was filled with red, white, and purple pansies picked from the garden, and she threw them on the path like a maidservant before a royal procession. Ishmael stopped just inside the gate, careful not to disturb the reunion. The grounds were kept in perfect order for their return. The hedges were groomed, the paths swept clean, and the ivy trimmed from the balcony windows. And over in the gardens running alongside the estate he caught a glimpse of his two daughters-in-law, Rachel and Leah, both of them gathering potatoes for the evening meal. He nodded to them, and they stayed in the gardens as he patiently allowed these unmarried girls a private reunion. Rachel and Leah no doubt wanted to see their younger brothers and get word of Lehi and Sariah, but they had the sensitivity to wait a while longer.

"Welcome home!" Mary ran to Nephi.

Nora, Ishmael's eldest daughter, was the tallest of the sisters, and she walked behind Mary, the ends of her straight black hair dancing at her shoulders. She had a steady manner, and her voice didn't betray the excitement that filled her eyes. She wasn't the sort to let on about anything—especially matters of the heart. She said, "Come inside and see what we've done." She took Laman by the hand and led him down along the porch toward the main doors of the abandoned estate, telling him that the window shutters were repaired and there wasn't a single broken pot or wooden molding inside.

Abigail walked next to Lemuel, insisting that his mother was sure to love the kitchen. Her voice rose and fell like a song, telling him that Sariah always wanted larger hampers for her flour and grains, and now she had them along with more shelves in the pantry to store her olives. She'd not ever have to go hunting through the storage barns for pickled ones again.

"You must be hungry." Hannah lifted the hem of her robe and stepped into stride next to Sam. "We'll start dinner right away."

Ishmael followed them inside and stood in the doorway. Sam inspected the new Egyptian urns fashioned of blue porcelain; they were even larger than the ones that once graced the entry. Lemuel sat on a small bench feeling the fringe of the new wall tapestries. Laman took a seat on a new, cushioned chair beneath the hanging oil lamps, and Nephi stood with Aaron in the center of the anteroom, the two of them speaking quietly in the stillness of the abandoned estate and turning around to see the new plaster fixed to the walls. The carpenter had repaired the banisters on the stairs. The broken doors leading to the bedrooms were replaced with newly hewn woods and set in place only last month. The mason had finished replacing the stone in the damaged walls, but he still had work to do in the kitchens.

The reading room down the hall where these boys studied under their Egyptian tutor stood quiet without the droning sound of his thick accent filtering into the hallway. The high-backed chairs in the dining hall across from the map room circled the table with just the right number for every member of the family to sit and eat together and speak of the events of the day. And for a moment, the muffled sound of his daughter's excited welcome of these sons of Lehi mixed with Ishmael's memory of faint whispers of many happy meals passed together on these precincts. These were the haunts where these boys ate and slept and learned at their parents' feet. This was their home—an estate they abandoned to escape with their lives into the wilderness. Ishmael had watched these boys grow to men in this house. They were the ones he'd promised his daughters to in marriage, and he waited in silence until enough time had passed for them to enjoy the sight of their repaired home before he asked, "Does Captain Laban know you've returned?"

"Uncle." Laman stood from the cushioned chair. "You've watched over things nicely."

Ishmael said, "What about Captain Laban, son?"

"He didn't follow us from Jerusalem."

"Then he knows?" Ishmael turned back to the door and scanned the road leading through the vineyards. There were no soldiers approaching and no one riding along the ridges above the groves.

Laman said, "Captain Laban's men think I've headed back into the Judean wilderness."

"The last time Captain Laban thought anything about any of us, he sent his men to burn our vineyard." Ishmael turned back through the opened doors to the burned trees in the old vineyard bordering the estate homes. The servants had cleared a section of the land to plant new trees, but the rest of the vineyard was a mass of charred stumps and blackened trees. "They chased your mother in the middle of the night and nearly killed the poor woman."

Lemuel said, "It isn't Mother he's after."

Sam said, "The captain accused Laman of being a robber."

Ishmael stepped to the center of the anteroom and lowered his voice to a whisper. "You never should have come here."

Laman said, "This is our home."

"What's to stop Captain Laban from ordering his soldiers to kill every one on the plantation and claim we're all part of your band?"

Laman said, "He's already said as much."

"Dear boy." Ishmael took Laman by the arm. "What have you done to anger the captain so?"

"We won't be staying long." Nephi crossed the anteroom and stood next to Mary. He took her by the hand before telling Ishmael, "The time has come for God to remember His covenants with Israel, sir."

Ishmael quickly turned his head, his white hair falling down in front of his eyes. "What did you say?"

"Lehi told me to warn you the time has arrived."

"Were those his words? Did he actually tell you the time had come for God to remember His covenant with Israel?"

Nephi nodded. "Father said you'd know what to do."

Ishmael ran his hand through his white hair, combing it back off his brow in wide furrows. Great-Grandfather left them this land, but it wasn't an inheritance. They were to inherit something far more valuable, but they were going to have to purchase it back, redeem it from its present owner, and he left them enough wealth to do it. He never told them exactly what it was they were to buy back, only that one day God would set His hand again to remember His covenants with Israel. When that day arrived, they were to use the riches he left them to redeem their inheritance. He called it a royal birthright.

Ishmael said, "You've come to buy back our inheritance."

"No, sir." Sam came around in front of Ishmael. "Father sent us back for the brass-plate record."

Ishmael worked his white beard between his thumb and forefinger. Was it possible? Could the brass plates from the Northern Kingdom have once been the possession of their family? He'd always believed they were Jews with ties to the south, while Captain Laban was descended of the royal family of the Northern Kingdom. Ishmael said, "Captain Laban's relic?"

Sam nodded. "That's right."

"Come with me." Ishmael sent his daughters to return to their duties in the garden before leading this band of brothers and a blacksmith across the anteroom and down the hall. They were to the door of the map room when Ishmael turned back to find Nephi still standing in the anteroom speaking with Mary. He waited a moment, but when Nephi didn't come, he left the others and retraced his steps back down the hall. He halted a few strides away and allowed his daughter a moment longer in the company of Lehi's youngest son.

Mary said, "When you're finished speaking with Papa, come to the house and I'll see there's a table set for you and your brothers." She adjusted the blue bandana on his brow. "We've never had a robber to dinner before."

Nephi said, "I don't know what's to become of us."

"We'll defend ourselves against Captain Laban." Mary took hold of the boy's hand. "We'll make a stand right here if we must."

Nephi touched the back of his hand to her cheek. "You're worried."

"It isn't worry. It's—"

"Daughter." Ishmael cleared his throat. "Let the boy alone. He has business to attend to."

"Go." Mary pushed Nephi away, but he refused to leave. He took both her hands in his and said, "No matter what happens, no matter what you hear or however long it takes, you must believe that I'll come for you."

"Things will never be the same, will they?" A tear rolled down Mary's cheek, and she quickly brushed it away. "Everything we thought to enjoy in this land will never be."

"There will be better times in a far better place."

"All I know is Beit Zayit." Mary turned her gaze out through the opened doorway to the endless acres of olive trees gracing the estate. "All I've ever wanted to know was this valley away from the stir of Jerusalem's society."

"Mary." Ishmael tipped his head toward the map room. "They're waiting."

Mary said, "He's coming, Papa."

Nephi turned back to her. "Promise me that whatever happens, you'll never stop believing that I'll come for you."

"You're not leaving again."

"Promise me."

"We'll speak at dinner, won't we?" Mary let go of his hands.

"I'll come for you."

Ishmael led Nephi down the hall to where his brothers waited. They turned into the map room, and Ishmael asked the two maidservants dusting the shelves to leave the chamber. He locked the door behind them before leading the boys down past the rows of accounting documents to the reading area. Laman fit himself into Lehi's chair along the far side of the chamber. How many times did Lehi sit where Laman sat preparing for their travels across the world? There were maps of the countries along the north shores of the Great Sea, maps of Egypt along the south shores, and there were even maps of the Dark Continent beyond the kingdom of the Pharaohs. The shelves were filled with detailed maps of Babylon and the Orient farther east. There were sea maps purchased from sailing captains, expedition maps bartered from caravaneers, and trade maps gotten from merchants—all of them stored here in what was surely one of the finest collections on earth. And then there were the maps of places they never traveled. There was no reason for Lehi to keep them on the middle shelf. They were better suited out of the way at the bottom, but Lehi insisted they remain untouched in that place, and no maidservant was ever allowed to dust beneath them. The unused maps were sealed away in large urns just as Lehi left them. The clay jars were set one after the other along the middle shelf, not for convenience, but because of what they concealed from view.

"Your father was a fine caravaneer and an even better merchant trader." Ishmael stood in front of the map shelves. "But not even he was capable of this." He removed the two large cisterns from the middle shelf, and behind the vessels was a long brass latch chiseled into the wall. Ishmael turned it open, and the center portion of the shelf—about the size of a door—dislodged from the wall, the wooden frame coming open like the door to a giant vault hinged on large pivot stones inlaid deep into the foundation. Nephi took hold of the other side, and together they pulled open the stubborn doorway, the musty scent of stale air filtering out of the hidden chamber.

Laman took down a lamp from the wall and walked it to the entrance. The vault was the size of a small linen room, and the light cast its glow over a table in the center covered with precisely stacked gold and silver coins. Amulets hung from hooks along the back wall. Bracelets decorated with emeralds sat in small wooden cases. The shelves down both sides were stocked with gold cups and vessels. Intricate works of silver and sapphire from Egypt and Phoenicia graced the walls like great tapestries of wealth. Laman stepped past Ishmael and pushed inside the vault, the lamplight flickering on his quick movement and dancing over the gems, bracelets, silver coffers, and gold incense burners. The boy had helped build a thriving merchant olive oil trade, and he no doubt expected to inherit this land passed down from his great-grandfather, but there was more treasure in this vault than Laman and his brothers could amass in five lifetimes of selling olive oil to the Egyptians.

Laman said, "Where did this come from?"

Ishmael said, "Your ancestors left it to you."

Laman slowly turned back to Ishmael. "You know the secret, don't you?"

The vault fell quiet until Lemuel turned his penetrating gaze onto Laman and said, "Are you going to tell them, or shall I?"

Ishmael looked deep into Laman's dark eyes, searching the boy's soul for what he kept hidden inside. Whatever conspiracy his deception inspired, it was still down there, festering inside of Laman. He could see it in the boy's blank stare and lifeless spirit.

"They deserve to know what inspires our enemies." Lemuel turned to his brothers. "It's the relic. The plates are our inheritance, not Laban's. And as long as we're alive, we're a threat to Captain Laban's claim to the throne."

Nephi said, "We'd know if we were heirs. Father would have told us."

"He doesn't know." Laman leaned close to Ishmael. "Isn't that right, Uncle? None of you knew we were descended of the royals of the Northern Kingdom."

Sam said, "This is impossible. We didn't inherit anything. We built this estate with our own hands."

Laman said, "Beit Zayit was given to Great-Grandfather in exchange for his silence. He took the land and never told his family they were of the tribe of Manasseh. Lehi never knew we were descendants of the sons of Joseph who was sold into Egypt."

Lemuel lowered his head and stared at the floor. "Father thinks we're all Jews."

Sam said, "This can't be."

"Look at him." Laman took Nephi by the jaw and turned his face to the daylight streaming through the vault door. "Why do you think our youngest brother looks more and more like Captain Laban with every passing month? He has the man's blood flowing in his veins—we all have the blood of Joseph in our veins. Captain Laban is our closest kin."

Sam said, "All this time you knew the reason for Laban's hatred, and you never told us."

Laman said, "What does it matter that we're of the house of Manasseh and each of us cousins to Captain Laban?"

"It matters, son. More than any of us may ever know." Ishmael reminded the boy that 120 years earlier Hoshea, the last king of the North, along with his sons, fled to Jerusalem when their kingdom fell to the Assyrians. They brought with them the royal relics—the sword and brass plates Laban kept in his treasury—along with all the wealth they could carry. The king of the Southern Kingdom granted Hoshea a residence in the Upper City and deeded him a thousand acres of land. Ishmael braced both hands against the edge of the table. It wasn't until today that he understood that Beit Zayit was the tract of uncultivated land given to the deposed king, and this wealth was the treasury they brought from the North Country. Ishmael turned his gaze over the interior of the hidden vault. It must have been an easy bargain for Great-Grandfather; with no kingdom left to rule, he would have gladly taken the tract of land that was to become Beit Zayit and agreed to his younger brother's conditions, covenanting for full title to the land and these riches in exchange for the promise that his claim to the national treasures would forever remain their secret. Ishmael picked up a handful of gold and held it out to the brothers. "This was the price for Great-Grandfather's silence."

Laman said, "Why didn't you tell us we were rich as kings?"

"You're the sons of a king." Ishmael turned his gaze over the boys gathered around the table. "The brass plates are your rightful inheritance, and with this wealth you can purchase back your birthright from Captain Laban."

Sam took the handful of gold from Ishmael and held it out to Laman. "This is why we were driven from our lands."

"Not the treasure." Laman shook his head. "I never knew anything about this wealth."

Nephi said, "You knew we were heirs to the plates."

Laman said, "Enough about the relic. This is our wealth now."

Nephi came around the table. "Great-Grandfather intended for us to buy back the record with it."

"How do you know his intentions? He's been dead for more than two generations." Laman walked a circle around the table. "Think of what we can do with this wealth."

Ishmael said, "You'll not enjoy these riches with Captain Laban hunting you."

"We can buy an army to protect the plantation." Laman spoke quickly, the words spilling out of him like a man possessed. "We'll hire mercenaries and build a wall about the estate and—"

Ishmael said, "You'll only buy yourself a hopeless war."

Laman said, "There's nothing hopeless about wealth."

"Since the day your father inherited this treasure, he knew it was to be used for our birthright, and now the Lord has made known to

Lehi exactly what our inheritance is. Get the plates, son." Ishmael laid his hand on Nephi's shoulder. "Preserve the covenants so our children and our children's children are not cast off forever."

CHAPTER 27

—Early Autumn, 598 B.C.
Jerusalem

"Not too high, son."

Ruth stood near the trunk of the largest olive tree in the courtyard watching Joshua climb among the branches. It was a sight to frighten her heart, but the boy was determined to hear every trumpet blast leading up to the Feast of Trumpets, and he spent every morning and evening in the branches of the courtyard waiting for the temple priests to sound the *shofar* horns.

"Mama." Joshua's head poked out from behind a cluster of leaves. "Do you think they forgot?"

"It's doesn't matter, son." Ruth stepped around the trunk until she found the shadowy outline of his slight frame perched among the highest branches. "As long as you never forget."

"Never forget what?"

The doors to the house swung open, and Sarah hurried across the courtyard begging for help with the ribbons in her hair and complaining she didn't know where to find a brush. She was dressed in a sleeping robe, her bright red braids falling down around her shoulders, complementing the freckles dotting her face.

"Quiet." Joshua waved his hand at her. "I can't hear the—"

"Boys." Sarah set her hands on her hip. "Why do they think they have to climb a tree or a roof or a wall to hear something they can hear perfectly well standing on the ground?"

Joshua said, "Mama, tell her to stop."

Sarah said, "Boys never make any sense."

Ruth said, "There they are now. Do you hear them?"

Joshua slid down the trunk of the olive tree and landed on the ground in front of Sarah. "How can I hear anything with her chirping like a bird?"

"I don't chirp." Sarah turned to Ruth. "Mama, make him stop."

"Listen, both of you." Ruth took Sarah by one hand and Joshua by the other. "Do you hear the trumpets?"

The faint blasts of the *shofar* horns filtered over the rooftops and into the courtyard, echoing off the front wall of the house and coming back to them. It wasn't the rhythmic trumpeting of high- and low-pitched blasts that would sound across the city on the day of the Feast of Trumpets. Tonight it was a simple, long blast on the horn, and Ruth walked them over to the bench near the water cistern and sat Joshua and Sarah down next to her. "Do you know what the sounding of the trumpet means?"

Joshua nodded. "Two days until the feast."

Ruth ran her hand over Joshua's cap of straight brown hair. "That's right, but—"

"To keep us up at night." Sarah spoke between yawns and stretched her hands overhead before laying her head on Ruth's shoulder.

"The trumpeting reminds us of the forty days Moses spent atop Mount Sinai speaking with God before coming down the mountain with the Law on the Day of Remembrance."

Joshua said, "Did Moses really speak with God?"

"What do you think?"

Sarah said, "I don't know anyone who speaks with God."

Ruth said, "Do you remember when we first moved to Jerusalem?"

Sarah pointed at Joshua. "He collected every odd-colored rock, stick, and insect he found on the journey from Sidon."

Joshua said, "I didn't keep all of them."

Ruth wrapped her arms around both of them, pulling them close enough to quiet their wrangling. "Since the day we arrived, I've come to know that God speaks to His prophets just as He did to Moses."

The sound of the long trumpet blasts died against the far wall, and Sarah said, "God never speaks to me."

"He does, dear." Ruth glanced up into the starlit sky. "When God speaks, you listen with your . . ."

Sarah said, "What is it, Mama?"

Ruth had felt the inspiration of heaven before, but never with as much force as she felt it now. It entered into every part of her being, and she hurried across the yard to the stables where Jonathan kept Queen Miriam's horse—the same animal he rode to Sidon a few months back. He finished putting on new shoes but didn't return the horse. He was waiting for an opportunity when he was certain he could get the animal to the palace stables without raising suspicions.

"Up you go." Ruth helped her children onto the horse and led it out the gate and into the street.

Joshua said, "Where are we going?"

Ruth led the mare into the darkness of evening. "We have a horse to return."

Queen Miriam combed her long black hair over her shoulders.

"What are you doing?" Zedekiah sat in a chair on the far side of the chamber, his body slouched over the armrest and his hand clutched around a cup of tea.

"I always comb my hair before retiring."

"Don't speak to me when I'm taking tea." Zedekiah opened a leather pouch, poured some powdered herbs into the brew, and took a long drink before crossing the room to her side. His eyes were red, his speech slurred, and when he spoke, a line of drool fell from his lips. What was she to do with a husband she hardly recognized? She'd already lost her eldest son to whatever terrible fate awaited him on the seas west of Sidon, and now she was losing her husband to insanity over Captain Laban's sword. Was misery to follow her all the days of her life?

Miriam said, "Why do you insist on acting so horribly?"

"I told you not to speak to me." Zedekiah threw his teacup on the floor, the clay crashing into pieces and forcing Miriam to sit upright. He leaned his head in next to her ear and whispered, "I need Laban's sword."

"You have a hundred weapons at your disposal." Miriam set the comb down. "What need have you of another?"

"Laban's sword is the sword of kings, and I am king." Zedekiah turned back across the room to the teapot steaming on the table next to his chair. He poured another cup and added more powders. "If you won't help me get the weapon, then I'll find another to help me."

"Don't you think you've had enough to drink?"

"They warned me you'd want my tea."

"Who warned you?"

Zedekiah fell silent, and Miriam said, "I don't drink tea, dear." She pulled her black outer robe on over her shoulders and started for the bedroom door.

"Where are you going?"

"I need some air."

"At this hour?"

"If you need me, I'll be in the gardens."

"I want your company."

"You have your tea."

Zedekiah took hold of her arm. "I'm your king."

"You were my husband before you were ever my king." Miriam pulled free, the cloth in her robe tearing along the seam. She hurried down the stairs and through the main palace doors into the dark courtyard. What was she to do? Ebed, the palace jailer, hadn't come with more news about the brass plates or the sword, and there was no telling if he ever would. She turned beneath the stone archway and found a narrow entrance at the back of the livery. She unlatched the gate, and when the thick, wood frame came open she found Ruth standing in the entrance, holding the reins to a horse from the royal herd. Her two youngest children sat atop the animal's polished saddle, and the new metal shoes pinged against the cobblestone. "What in the name of heaven are you doing out at this hour?"

Ruth stepped the horse closer to the gate. "This belongs to you."

"Oh, Ruth." Miriam took her by the hand. "How did you know to come?"

Joshua leaned over the saddle and said, "God told her."

Miriam came down alongside the boy. He was younger than Mulek, but Sarah was nearly the same age as her lost son. The girl sat behind Joshua, her red hair shimmering in the moonlight. Miriam took both children by the hand and said, "You have a fine mother."

Ruth said, "What is it that troubles you so?"

"I lost my son to the sea, and now I'm losing . . ." Miriam held her hand to her mouth, and her fingers began to tremble. "Mulek doesn't even like the sea." She laughed between her tears. "He can hardly swim, and now I'm afraid my husband may drown in a sea of insanity."

"I was afraid this was about Zedekiah."

Miriam closed the gate behind her, shutting out the torch lights that burned in the palace grounds and leaving them in shadows. "He's going mad, and I don't know what to do about it. I asked the palace jailer to seek Zoram's help, but I've not gotten word from Ebed, and I fear I may lose my husband to this insanity before . . ."

"Before what?"

"There are only two days left."

"Until what?"

"The Day of Remembrance." Joshua sat up in the saddle, and his voice rushed out of him. "Did you hear the trumpets tonight? I thought they'd forgotten until I—"

Sarah said, "There you go, chirping like a bird."

"Children." Ruth held up her hand, and they fell silent.

"My husband's possessed by Laban's sword." Miriam came around in front of Ruth. "He thinks he must have it to preserve the kingdom as his, and if there were any way for Zoram to prevent my husband from having the sword, maybe I could save him from the curse."

Ruth said, "Curse?"

"Zoram's father pronounced a curse of death on any man who stops the brass plates from leaving the city." Miriam removed her hood and let her ribbon-tied hair fall down past her shoulders. "The sword my husband desires carries the same terrible promise—whoever sheaths it at their side is certain to die a terrible death."

Ruth said, "Then we'll not let Laban's sword come into your house."

"How?"

"With the help of heaven, we'll find a way."

"Do you hear that?" Joshua stood in the saddle, his ears turned toward the wall separating them from the temple grounds.

Miriam said, "Hear what?"

"Wait for it." Joshua held both hands out for balance until a round of trumpeting heralded over the temple walls. "See there. You can believe Mother." He jumped from the saddle and landed on the ground next to Miriam. "She speaks with God."

Miriam patted Joshua on the head. "She does indeed, my boy."

CHAPTER 28

—*Early Autumn, 598 B.C.*
Jerusalem

The watchman guarding the back entrance to Captain Laban's estate stopped Elizabeth at the gate. She held out a basket—a large wicker affair filled with fresh-baked bread and roasted lamb that scented the air with the sweet smell of her cooking. A sack of dates reached above the brim next to a jar of fresh water. The watchman insisted it was too late to be bringing Zoram his dinner, but when she offered him a round of bread, he waved her inside.

The path led through a winding labyrinth of shrubs before ending near the back entrance to the treasury. A lamp burned above the sealed door and cast a dim light over the iron crosspieces that held the thick timbers in place.

Elizabeth knocked until an eye appeared in the hole near the center of the timbers. Not again. Must she endure Zoram's watchful eye every time she came to the treasury? If Zoram knew the fears she'd endured to make late-evening deliveries from Baruch these many weeks, he'd not play the jester. She didn't primp her hair and didn't bother to adjust her robe over her shoulders. And when he didn't open the door immediately, she shook her finger at the eyeball and said, "I haven't time for your teasing."

The door swung open, and a guard stood in the rush of damp air streaming up from the underground corridors. He smiled a toothless grin and said, "You'll do what, princess?"

Elizabeth straightened her robe on her shoulders. Why did she always manage to embarrass herself?

"Elizabeth, is that you?"

Zoram stepped from his quarters a few strides beyond the reach of the lamplight. A late September breeze blew across the grounds, and he pulled the collar of his coat up around his neck. His turban was missing from his head, and thick locks of black, curly hair hung down about his ears and across his brow like the tendrils of a canopy of vines. His dark features were darker in the dimness of the yard, but when he stepped into the lamplight she could see . . .

Dear no, not again. It was the same look she'd seen in her dreams every night for that past week. He was leaving her. Not by any choice of his, but for these plates of brass. She could see it in the nuances of his smile, the way he turned his head and returned her stare. It was the same Zoram she'd seen in her nightmare, and she could hear him telling her that for some reason these plates would take him from her. Elizabeth lowered her head. If not for the curse of death to any man who stopped the brass plates from leaving the city, she would keep them locked away in Captain Laban's vault and make certain this nightmare never came to pass.

"I waited for you in the treasury most of the evening." Zoram took the basket from her, ushered her inside his quarters, and locked the door behind them. The fresh bread and roasted lamb came out onto the table first, then the dates and the bottle of fresh spring water. He felt along the bottom, his fingers pressing against the wicker.

"You won't find them there," Elizabeth said in answer to his searching. "Baruch is working as fast as he can."

"He isn't finished?"

"It's difficult work."

Zoram set aside the basket. "The feast comes the day after tomorrow."

Elizabeth touched Zoram on the arm. "We've done all we can do."

Zoram paced in front of the table. "We'll be cursed for this."

"The brass plates aren't the only cursed relic."

"What do you mean?"

"Laban's sword."

"The weapon doesn't concern us."

"It does if it carries the same curse as the brass plates."

"Jeremiah didn't say anything about the sword. It's always been about the plates."

"If not for Queen Miriam, you would never have had the ore to finish your work."

"What has she to do with this?"

Elizabeth stepped closer. "You must keep the weapon from falling into the king's hands."

"Zedekiah requested the sword. Captain Laban plans to deliver it to the palace on the eve of the feast."

"Deliver it the next day. Do anything to keep the king from having it that night."

"Why do you make such a request?"

"It isn't a request. Queen Miriam is certain the weapon will do harm to her husband and her sons."

"We have the plates to worry over."

"What if something happens to the royal family? Something you could have prevented but failed to do so simply because you refused to believe me?" Elizabeth spoke quickly, her fears spilling out of her in a rush. "What if Baruch doesn't finish the plates in time? What if I can't find you so you can deliver the plates? What if . . . ?"

Zoram took her by her hand. "You'll always find me here."

Elizabeth lowered her head. She desperately wanted to believe he would always be here for her, but she couldn't rid herself of the apprehension that clouded his words with a dark future. She said, "Promise me you'll help Miriam."

"I'll do what I can."

"Tell me I won't lose you to these plates of brass."

"You're a nervous bride." Zoram kissed her hand.

"Promise me."

"Very well." Zoram took Elizabeth by both hands and spoke slowly, the sound of his firm voice reaching deep into her soul. He said, "I will always be yours."

Aaron reined Beuntahyu behind his brothers Laman, Lemuel, and Nephi down a narrow traverse and into the cheese maker's valley.

And that's exactly what the sons of Lehi were—brothers. Aaron slept in the same tent with them, ate around the same fire with them, fled into the same desert under their name, and now he was riding in their company back to the estate of the man who tried to kill them. What else could he call these friends but brothers?

Sam was the last one down off the plateau, leading three camels over the crumbling shale traverse. Two animals carried gold and silver, and the last one was packed with amulets, jewels, and gold vessels. The treasure was disguised in large grain sacks, and what didn't fit onto the camels was hidden in saddlebags, the treasury of ancient kings divided among their five horses.

They reached the west gate, and the watchman let them through without asking anything beyond the nature of their merchant trade— Laman told them they were vineyard owners. Aaron spurred Beuntahyu onto the deserted Main Street ahead of the others. The city didn't appear any different than when they left. Mule carts stood covered and tethered in place with rocks chocked below the wheels. It was a calm scene, but there was tension in the air. This was a city ruled by Captain Laban, and coming here was like returning to a nightmare. Aaron tightened his grip on the reins and glanced into the dark alleyways emptying onto Main Street. He could still remember the image of the man hovering over him on the porch at Lehi's estate, shooting an arrow into his thigh and threatening him with certain death unless he revealed where Lehi had fled.

Aaron led their band past the entrance to Hezekiah's water tunnel. Moonlight outlined the circular stairs trailing off into the darkness, but there were no women balancing jars on their heads and waiting to descend to the waters below. All that remained was the bittersweet memory of the night Aaron negotiated the well-worn steps with nothing but moonbeams to guide his crutches. That was the night Rebekah first saw the burned flesh that reached from his ankles, ran along both arches and disappeared into the hollow spaces where there should have been muscle and sinew. She didn't call him a cripple or ridicule his hideous feet. She knelt beside him and lightly touched the wounds as if her caressing could make the pain disappear. It was down there, below ground, where Aaron told Rebekah of the day when Jeremiah the prophet found him half-conscious and lying in a pool of molten ore. The man pulled him to safety, laid his hands on Aaron's head and promised him by the power of heaven that his feet would be made whole to save the life of a prophet in order to preserve the covenants for a remnant of the House of Israel. Aaron spurred back into line and sidled in next to Nephi, the two of them riding side-by-side through the dark city streets with only the clap of hooves and the grunting of horses and camels to fill the silence. Tonight the promised healing of his feet came full circle.

The company of riders reached Milo Hill, but before turning into the Upper City, Aaron caught a glimpse of the pottery yard that belonged to Josiah the potter. There didn't seem to be anyone living at the property. The gate was boarded shut, and the burned remains of the home rose above the outside wall, reminding him of the potsherd letter he promised Rebekah he would deliver to his father. The rough-edged clay pressed through the leather satchel and rubbed against his ribs. He wasn't to read it, but the few glances he did get revealed that it was addressed to Papa, telling him of the route they followed in the Border Mountains to their camp along the shores of the Red Sea and asking Jonathan to accept Rebekah as his daughter-in-law. It was a noble thing for Rebekah to write when she preferred that Jonathan suffer the same curse Aaron suffered and let Papa believe he was dead, just as Papa let Aaron believe Rebekah had died in the charred remains of the pottery yard.

They cleared the rise at the top of Milo Hill, and Laman pulled up behind the cover of three olive trees a hundred cubits from Captain Laban's estate. The front gate was lined with double the number of soldiers usually stationed at the entrance. Orange flames burned in the cauldron lamps on the main porches, and thick plumes of black smoke lingered on the air about the upper floors.

Laman slid out of the saddle and peered around the trunk of the olive tree. "Captain Laban will cut our throats before he'll hear us out."

"Not if he knows there's more than this." Sam handed Laman a grain sack filled with gold. "Arrange an exchange outside the walls of the city, down in the flatlands on the way to Bethlehem. Captain Laban comes alone with the plates, or we ride into the desert with our wealth."

Laman handed the sack back to Sam. "You barter with the man and see how well a sack of gold protects you from the swords of fifty soldiers."

Nephi said, "I'll do it."

Laman said, "You know nothing about bartering."

"Let him go if he likes." Sam came around in front of Nephi. "If they come at you, stand your ground, but don't provoke them."

Laman said, "He'll get us all killed."

Sam said, "Show them the sack of gold, tell them there are three camels laden with a fortune a hundred times greater than this, and give them the terms for an exchange—the lost treasury of the Northern Kingdom for the brass plates."

Laman took back the sack of gold. "I decide who barters for the plates."

"Open the treasury!"

Elizabeth let go of Zoram's hand. Who was that calling in the night? She opened the door to Zoram's quarters and peered across the dark grounds until she found her brother Daniel marching at them with his sword drawn. He was dressed for battle, and his hurried march was like the front line of an advancing army. A black officer's tunic matched the darkness of the patch over his left eye. His polished boots reflected the lamplight streaming from the treasury entrance, and his silver-studded leather kilt slapped against his powerful legs. He cleared the trunk of the last cypress tree, adjusted the patch on his eye, and said, "Bring me the plates."

Zoram said, "They stay in the treasury. Captain Laban's orders."

"His orders have changed."

"I haven't the key for the vault."

"I said unlock the treasury. That's an order." Daniel reached for the treasury keys around Zoram's neck, but he pulled free and said, "No one goes into the treasury without Captain Laban's approval."

Daniel pushed Zoram hard enough to send him to the ground. "You'll do as I say."

"Stop this." Elizabeth pulled on Daniel's arm. "What's gotten into you?"

"At ease, men." Captain Laban appeared in the yard. He strapped on his breastplate and tucked the ends of his tunic under his belt before handing Zoram the only key to the vault. "Do as Daniel says."

Zoram brushed the dirt from his white coat. "But sir, is it safe to bring them out two nights before the feast?"

"Get me the plates, boy."

Zoram disappeared past two watchmen into the depths of the treasury. Elizabeth waited in the quiet behind the estate with Captain Laban and Daniel. Why did they want the plates? The relic never left the confines of the treasury, and if the time had come for the plates to leave the city, had they failed in their quest to include all of Jeremiah's prophecies?

Laban said, "How long has he been at the gate?"

Daniel said, "I'm not certain. I woke you when I got word from the gatekeeper."

Elizabeth stepped closer. Who were they talking about?

Laban said, "Are you sure he came alone?"

"He's the only one at the gate."

"Curse him. I was certain we'd draw all of the sons of Lehi here. Is he dangerous?"

Daniel said, "There's no report of a weapon."

Zoram returned from the underground vaults carrying the brass codex on his palms like a priest in a procession. A red silk cloth covered the plates, but it wasn't long enough to reach down along the sides, and Elizabeth could see the ones she added to the base of the record. In the short time Zoram was gone, he threaded the plates she had left unattached and set the metal rings in place against the record's spine. Elizabeth stepped into stride with Zoram, and together they followed Captain Laban and Daniel through the darkness of the yard to the small kitchen door near the back of the estate. If tonight was the night the record left the city, then at least most of the prophecies of Jeremiah were preserved. They turned through the empty kitchen and into the hall filled with soldiers hurrying out onto the porch. The gatekeeper met them by the front door, and Laban said, "What was his offer?"

"I'm not certain it can be believed." The gatekeeper cleared his throat. "He claims to have the treasury of the Northern Kingdom."

"So much for so little." Laban smiled at the brass plates in Zoram's hands. "Did you see the treasury?"

"Only a single sack of gold. The man says you must claim the rest outside the city gates."

Laban pulled on his riding gloves. "Is my horse saddled?"

Daniel said, "I won't let you do this. It's too dangerous."

Laban said, "You've never learned to barter with your life, have you, boy?"

Daniel came around in front of Laban. "It's two days before the feast."

"This man wasn't sent by Jeremiah."

"Who else would lure you away from the estate?"

"The treasury he offers is my inheritance, and I will have it. All of it."

The gatekeeper unlatched the anteroom door and stepped aside to let them onto the porch. Elizabeth hurried out behind Laban and Daniel to gain a glimpse of a lone man holding a grain sack and facing a wall of soldiers standing shoulder-to-shoulder in the gate entrance. It wasn't Lehi; the outline of his stature against the orange flicker of the cauldron lamps was too tall. It wasn't Ishmael; the man didn't have a beard like the vineyard keeper, and it didn't appear to be any of the sons of Lehi, though it was impossible to see the man's face in the dim glow. He stood like the rail of a fence leaning into the wind, the same way she remembered . . .

Aaron? Could it be him? His hair was longer than she remembered. His skin was darker, and his shoulders more broad, but he had the same calm manner that infused his being right down to the careful way he held the sack of gold.

Elizabeth started down the porch, but Zoram held her arm and pulled her back. He said, "Don't say a word."

"But it's—"

"I see him."

Elizabeth struggled against his grip. "I want to be certain."

"There'll be time for that later."

Elizabeth turned her gaze across the courtyard and beyond the gates to the ghost of a man standing in the street. Was it possible? Was her eldest brother still alive? He raised the sack of gold like a shield with power to protect him from Laban, but his offering of riches didn't slow the captain. He pushed through the line of soldiers, marched at the man, and kicked him in the stomach before swinging his fist across the man's jaw, sending him reeling to the ground in a deluge of falling gold pieces. "Hear me, sons of Lehi." Laban placed the tip of his sword to the man's neck. "Come barter with me, all of you, or I kill your friend."

Elizabeth escaped Zoram's grasp and tried to get past the soldiers, but the men held their line, blocking the way into the street, and all she could do was press her face to the iron bars in the fence and watch Captain Laban raise his sword in the air over the man.

"Let him go."

Nephi stepped into the dim light outside the gates with two more bags of treasure. He tossed one toward Captain Laban, the silver spilling over the ground and mixing with the spilled gold. He'd grown a good deal since Elizabeth last saw him. He stood nearly a hand taller—the same height as Captain Laban—and in the flickering orange light it was like looking on the face of Captain Laban's twin.

Nephi said, "I bring you the treasure of the Northern Kingdom."

Laban lowered his sword. "That's hardly enough to fill a royal treasury."

"There's more."

Laban called for Zoram to come into the street. He pulled the red silk off the brass plates and let the cloth fall to the ground, the record rising a full two fists above Zoram's palms. "Is this what you came for?"

"I have five more bags of gold like that one." Nephi helped his companion to his feet. "And just as many of silver, and three times as many of precious stones and amulets."

"The life of a robber suits you well."

"You know how we came by our wealth. All we want is for you to return the plates to us and we'll leave you to your secrets and this treasure."

"He wants me to return them to him?" Captain Laban turned a circle in the street, his sword raised to his men. "How can I return what was never his?"

A cheer rose up from the soldiers at the gate.

Nephi said, "Do we have an agreement?"

Captain Laban snapped his fingers, and a stable boy hurried through the line of soldiers, pulling the captain's white Arabian in tow, the ornate saddle strapped in place, the animal grunting its arrival.

Nephi said, "Come on foot or we keep the treasure."

"I'll need my scribe to carry the plates out of the city."

"I said alone."

"You don't really have the royal treasury, do you, boy?" Captain Laban worked the toe of his boot through the gold and silver spilled over the cobblestones. "Your father used it to build an olive plantation and a merchant trade, and now you're bartering with nothing more than a legend of the great treasury of the kings of the Northern Kingdom." He picked up a piece of gold. "Tell me. What sort of fool would give away so much for a few pounds of brass?"

"What sort of fool wouldn't take it?"

"I'm no fool." Captain Laban put the tip of his sword to Nephi's chest. "Curse you for trying to steal my—"

"Let him go!" Sam ran out of the darkness with two treasure-laden camels galloping behind him. Lemuel followed with another camel, and behind them, standing just beyond the strength of the cauldron lights, was the thick-shouldered frame of Laman holding the reins to five horses.

Sam untied a sack and threw it on the ground, spilling amulets and rubies. "Our wealth for their lives."

"Come here, boy." Laban lowered his sword. "Bring your camels inside with you."

Sam said, "Agree to the terms."

"I'll see your treasure before I make any oath."

Sam said, "Shut the gate or we ride away with this."

"Do as he says."

Daniel said, "But, sir."

"Back inside the gate with your men, Lieutenant." Captain Laban pointed his sword at Sam. "You were never anything more than a foolish vineyard keeper."

"I'm no vineyard keeper." Sam sounded a high-pitched whistle that pierced the night air like the hiss of a mighty arrow. The deafening sound spooked Laban's Arabian to rear on its hind legs, the animal striking the captain in the shoulder, knocking him to the ground and sending his sword skidding beyond the reach of the lamplight.

Sam said, "I'm a caravan master."

Captain Laban shouted for Zoram to save the relic, and he slipped back through the gate to the safety of Elizabeth's company.

Sam slapped the camels and sent them galloping at the entrance, the animals blocking the gatekeeper from the opening. Sacks of gold and silver ripped loose in a shower of riches, and in the confusion, Laman brought around the five horses, and the sons of Lehi rode into the darkness.

"After them." Captain Laban struggled to his feet, holding his shoulder. "Kill them all."

Daniel marched toward the livery, ordering his men to their horses, and Elizabeth ran after him. "You're not really going to—"

"They're robbers."

"Aaron's with them. Didn't you see him?"

"I saw a fool threatening Captain Laban."

Elizabeth came around in front of Daniel. "It wasn't a threat."

"And I suppose this wasn't either." Daniel lifted the patch exposing his blind eye, his vision clouded by scarred flesh. "I'm blind because of Aaron."

"Then you did see him? There's no mistake."

"The only mistake was letting Aaron learn the faith of Lehi and his sons."

"What faith would you have him learn?"

"Blacksmithing." Daniel took the reins from the stable boy and jumped into the saddle. "That would have made him something in this world instead of chasing after the foolish imaginations of an olive oil merchant."

"Promise me you won't harm him."

"I don't know what you think you saw tonight." Daniel came around, waiting for the other soldiers to gather. "Aaron is dead."

Elizabeth stood watching long after Laban and Daniel disappeared into the night, the clatter of hooves dying in the shadows. What was she to do? Aaron was alive. She was certain the man who stood in the gate was her dead brother, but there was no telling how much longer Daniel would allow him breath.

Why must a sacred relic cause so much trouble?

CHAPTER 29

—Early Autumn, 598 B.C.
Jerusalem

Ruth sat in the darkest corner of the main room. Where was Elizabeth? The girl had never been out after sundown; however, through the entire month of Elul she was nothing but a night owl. The rest of the family ate a late-evening meal and went to bed a good while ago, but Ruth couldn't sleep until she was certain her eldest was home safe. She pulled a blanket over her knees and slowly rocked in the chair.

A dim light flickered from a lamp in the kitchen windowsill—the one Ruth had left burning there since the day Aaron went missing. Even after word came that he was gone, shot dead by Captain Laban's arrow, she couldn't bring herself to put it away. Nearly nine months the lamp had burned on the kitchen windowsill and never once had she let the oil go dry. The lamp was without the strength to reach the far corner of the main room and chase away the shadows, and Ruth rocked in her chair in darkness.

The latch clicked, the front door pushed open, and Elizabeth stood in the entry, her narrow frame silhouetted by the moonlight. She squinted into the darkness before stepping inside and feeling her way across the main room to the stairs leading to her bedroom. She hurried up four steps and paused before saying, "Mama?"

Ruth stayed in her chair. How did the girl know she was there? Ruth sat where Elizabeth couldn't see her, especially with the girl's eyes accustomed to the brightness of moonlight.

Elizabeth leaned over the handrailing. "Is that you?"

"I'm here, girl." Ruth walked into the dim light of the oil lamp streaming in from the kitchen. "You're late."

Elizabeth came back down the steps and held out the wicker basket. Cold rounds of bread lay wrapped in a cloth, the bowl of figs sat untouched, and the water pitcher was full to the brim. Ruth said, "Zoram wasn't hungry tonight?"

"It's the brass plates, Mother, the ones Zoram looks after in his treasury."

"He lost his appetite over a relic?"

"I'm losing Zoram over it."

"Zoram adores you, daughter." Ruth took the basket from her. "You're nothing but a nervous bride-to-be."

"That's what Zoram said, but—"

"What?"

"I have this awful sense that the plates will take him from me."

"How could you think such a thing?"

"Every day the thought grows stronger. I can hardly speak of it without weeping." Elizabeth held the back of her hand to her mouth, and the tears streamed down her face. Ruth pulled her close and held her until the sobbing ended. She ran her hand over the girl's long black hair. "I don't know everything, but I can promise you Zoram will be your husband. He's a man of his word, and I know he'll keep his. I feel it deep in my heart. You must be strong in all of this."

"Oh, Mama." A tear dropped from the end of her nose. "How can I be strong when Captain Laban sent his men to kill Aaron?"

"Stop that, girl." Ruth held her by the shoulders. "I won't have you open old wounds."

"It isn't an old wound." Elizabeth got the lamp from the kitchen windowsill. "Aaron's alive. I saw him standing outside Captain Laban's estate tonight."

"It's late, daughter. You need your rest."

"I know what I saw."

"You've mistaken someone for your brother."

"It was him."

"It's dark outside. Your eyes were playing tricks."

"Why won't you believe me? You've kept your lamp alive all this time hoping he wasn't dead and praying he'd come back to us, and now I tell you he's alive and you say he isn't."

Ruth took the lamp from Elizabeth and held it with both hands. She told her children she kept the flame alive all these months in hopes that Aaron would return, but the constant warmth of this light was really meant to heal her soul, and she couldn't bear Elizabeth picking at the scabs that sealed the wounds of his death without good reason. The rough clay surface of the lamp was warm, but it didn't have power to cheer her soul, no matter how much Elizabeth's words were meant to cheer her. "I've lost one child." She returned the lamp to the windowsill. "I won't lose another. Not with all this talk about the curse of Captain Laban's relics. Did you tell Zoram about the sword?"

"He knows of the king's madness for it."

"And?"

"Mama, he's a scribe, not the king's physician."

"He can stop the weapon from going to the palace."

"He could lose his post for interfering."

"What am I to tell Miriam?"

"If Zoram hears of anything that could harm the king or the princes, he'll stop it."

"And if he's not able?"

"He's watchful, Mother."

Ruth reached for Elizabeth's hands. The girl's fingers were cold, and there was a slight trembling in her bones. "What is it, dear?"

Elizabeth took back her hands and wrapped them around herself. "Daniel went after Aaron to kill him."

"He would never do such a thing."

"He's changed, Mama." Elizabeth slowly shook her head. "He isn't the brother I once knew."

"Enough." Jonathan stood in the shadows at the top of the stairs. He gripped the railing with both hands. "You'll not speak of Daniel like that without him here to defend his good name."

"Jonathan." Ruth stepped to the base of the stairs. "Did we wake you?"

"I couldn't sleep."

"Another nightmare?"

"The same one." Jonathan lumbered down the steps and turned past Ruth. He poured a cup of water from the clay pitcher and sat at the table. "Is it possible Captain Laban could be wrong?"

Elizabeth said, "I've never thought he was right about much of anything, Papa."

"No more, girl."

Ruth stood beside his chair and laid her hand on his shoulder. "Wrong about what?"

"For days now, I can't sleep. I close my eyes, and the vision is there. And every night it gets closer, as if I could reach out and touch it, like a picture from an unseen world, but the picture is alive. It moves and breathes and . . ." Jonathan rubbed the sides of his head with both hands. "Look at me; I'm a babbling fool."

Ruth said, "There's nothing foolish about your dreams."

"Why now? I've not been troubled with thoughts like this since I made peace with my eldest son and laid his memory to rest." Jonathan drank the water cup dry in one long swallow and set the empty vessel on the table. "Is it possible Aaron isn't dead?"

"It most certainly is, Papa." Elizabeth took the lamp from the windowsill, set it on the table in front of Jonathan, and filled the vessel with oil. "Aaron's alive."

Aaron spurred Beuntahyu at full gallop with Laman, Lemuel, Sam, and Nephi riding with him. They headed south until they were beyond sight of Jerusalem's gate before Aaron turned up into the thick cover of brush on the Mount of Olives. He led the fast-riding band over a low-lying wall of loose stones and through a hillside vineyard before pulling up alongside an abandoned olive press and coming around to listen to the commotion in the valley below. The sound of Laban's men filled the night with the thunder of horses' hooves and the resonating voice of Daniel ordering his men to split up, the largest troop to head south along the road to Bethlehem, a smaller band north to Anathoth, and the last detail was to scour the hillsides.

Sam sidled in next to Aaron. "What do we do?"

Laman said, "We hide among the trees until they're gone."

Lemuel turned his mount in a circle. "They'll find us here."

Laman said, "Then we fight."

"There's a narrow valley down the other side of this ridge." Aaron leaned forward in the saddle. "I can lead you to an abandoned cave."

The sound of soldiers starting up through the brush along the base of the Mount of Olives brought Aaron around. "Follow me." He led them along the rockiest part of the hillside to hide their trail, spurring over the limestone ridge and down a steep descent. The moon plunged out of sight beyond the valley walls of the narrow canyon, and Aaron leaned back in the saddle to keep from going over Beuntahyu's neck.

The slope eased into a gentle decline, and Aaron kept Beuntahyu running through three mountain gorges, across a long ridge, and over two hills. They rode through a creek bed and past an abandoned collection of stone dwellings before the trail turned up a short rise and then down a steep three-mile run, coming onto level ground and forcing them into a single-file column. Sam called from the back asking how much farther, but Aaron didn't answer. They couldn't stop with the light of morning turning the eastern horizon from black to gray and giving away their position to riders on the cliffs above.

A familiar run of scrub oak ran along the valley floor, and Aaron spurred off the trail at full gallop, cutting through brush and over to a cliff where the low-growing trees hid a wide cleft worn deep into the limestone wall. A canopy of rock hung over the entrance, and there was enough room among the thick bushes to tie the horses out of sight. There were no signs of a recent campfire in this secluded cave since the last time Aaron and his father harvested coal from the mines in this canyon. Aaron came around in the cavern entrance. There was no sound of riders following them, and he swung down from the saddle and tied Beuntahyu to the scrub oak.

Laman said, "We sleep out the day and head for the desert tonight."

Nephi said, "What about the plates?"

"Forget them." Lemuel carried his saddlebag inside the cavern and threw it against the far wall before lying down on the uneven leather, his long legs spread out in front of him, his hands behind his head. "We gave Captain Laban enough gold to smith a thousand plates, and instead of a little brass in return, he tries to kill us."

"It isn't the brass." Nephi stood in the entrance of the cavern, the gray light of morning outlining his form. "It's the Law of Moses and the words of the prophets."

Laman said, "Captain Laban doesn't care about any of that."

Nephi said, "We have to try again."

Laman said, "We go back to Jerusalem, and we'll never come out alive."

Sam said, "You survived the first attempt."

Laman said, "That was a different matter."

"And we all survived the second, didn't we?"

Laman marched over to Sam. "We lost our fortune."

Nephi said, "It wasn't ours to lose."

Laman turned on Nephi. "If you weren't such a fool, we could have lured Captain Laban onto the flats outside the city and gotten the plates and kept our treasure." He pushed Nephi back, forcing him against the wall. "Why did you show yourself?"

Nephi said, "I couldn't let him hurt Aaron."

"It was your doing." Lemuel stood next to Sam. "You sent the camels at the gates. You gave the captain our treasure."

Sam said, "I had to stop the soldiers from taking us all."

"It was all a ruse." Laman closed in on Sam. "Captain Laban fooled you into giving away our wealth."

Sam backed away from Laman's powerful body, but Lemuel was standing behind him, trapping him between them. Sam said, "Laban was going to kill them."

Nephi said, "Harsh words won't get our riches back."

"You've never seen harsh." Laman swung at Nephi, landing a blow across the boy's jaw and sending him back against the cavern wall. "You lost our fortune." He found a fallen branch among the trees lining the cavern opening. It was thick like a rod, with a rough surface and knotted ends. Sam tried to stop him from going after Nephi, but Lemuel wrapped his arms around him and pulled him to the ground, telling him to let Laman alone.

"We have nothing, thanks to you." Laman held the rod with both hands and whipped the thick end across Nephi's stomach, doubling him over and sending him to the ground. He swung the rod at Nephi's head, but the boy ducked out of the way, the branch hitting the ground and cracking the wood but not breaking it.

"Stop this!" Aaron grabbed the rod, but Laman pushed him away. He pointed the rod at Aaron, then at Sam, and finally at Nephi. "I should have killed all of you and taken our wealth." He widened his stance, held the rod with both hands and swung the knotted branch at Nephi's head, the thick, crooked end coming down with the speed of—

Light? Aaron rubbed his eyes until he made out the form of a man in the middle of the brightness holding the end of the rod, stopping it from smashing Nephi's skull. They were a half day's ride from any town or city, down a narrow run of canyons along the western edges of the Judean wilderness, and this man appeared out of nowhere without a sound. He wore a white robe, and the longer he stood there the whiter it grew until the cloth had the brightness of the sun at midday, the light from the man's countenance filling the entire cavern beyond the brightness of the morning sunrise that filtered beneath the cleft in the rock.

Was it possible? Aaron leaned against the cavern wall. Was this an angel come to save Nephi? The man stood in the air a little above the ground, his robe open at the cuffs and about the neck. His hair was as white as his robe, his whole form glowing with a radiance brighter than any earthly light. It was as if he'd been there all along, protecting Nephi from a blow that was certain to end his life, and Aaron was just now permitted to see this spirit from the unseen world. There was no doubt Sam and Lemuel were seeing what he was seeing, their gaze fixed on the same being standing in the air over Nephi. The angel lifted the rod out of Laman's hands, the powerful movement throwing him to the ground. And when the angel spoke, his words burst from his mouth like the rushing of a strong wind, filling the cavern with his unearthly presence. He pointed the rod at Laman and said, "Why do you smite your brother?"

Laman shielded his eyes from the brightness.

The angel moved closer to Laman. "Know ye not that the Lord hath chosen Nephi to be a ruler over you? And this because of your iniquities?" The angel threw the rod at Laman's feet, the branch splintering into hundreds of pieces. He said, "You will go up to Jerusalem again."

Lemuel said, "We can't go back. Captain Laban will—"

"Silence." The angel raised his hand to Lemuel. "You will go back for the plates, and the Lord will deliver Laban into your hands." The light began to gather around the angel, and with his words still ringing in the rocky chamber, he was gone as quickly as he'd appeared. Aaron searched for him about the cavern entrance, but he found nothing beyond the dim light of morning sunrise.

Laman said, "How is it possible that Captain Laban will be delivered into our hands?"

Aaron said, "You saw what I saw, didn't you?"

"Laban's a mighty man." Lemuel rubbed his hands together, and his thin frame rocked back and forth as he spoke. "He commands fifty men."

Aaron said, "Tell me you saw heavens open."

Laman said, "We can't stand against an army."

"All of you heard what I heard." Aaron helped Nephi to his feet and pressed a cloth to the bleeding along his jaw. "You saw what I saw." He gathered the splintered pieces of the rod, walked them over to Laman and let them slowly fall through his fingers, the shattered wood landing at Laman's feet. He said, "No mortal has the strength to do this."

CHAPTER 30

—Early Autumn, 598 B.C.
Beit Zayit

Ishmael led a mule from the stall inside the main stables and hitched the animal to a cart.

"Papa." Mary, his youngest daughter, ran through the opened door. Her faced was flushed, her long black hair hung loose around a ribbon, and her white shawl had fallen off her shoulders and tangled in her arms. "Come quickly."

Mary led him back to the livery entrance. The evergreen canopy of leaf-laden branches hung on the hillsides above the stables like an overcast sky, and through the foliage a cloud of dust swirled among the branches. The thunder of horses' hooves broke the morning quiet, and Lieutenant Daniel appeared on the road leading down through the vineyards. He sent a company into the pressing yard, and his men dispersed, opening the gates to the corrals, letting loose the camels and horses. They scared off the menservants before tearing loose the doors on the storage barns, the sound of breaking olive oil vessels echoing out of the building.

Daniel continued on to the estate home with the rest of his men, and Ishmael chased after him, running out of the pressing yard and up the rise to his home with Mary following him. The soldiers pushed down the gate and forced their way inside, and when Ishmael entered the house he found soldiers turning over chairs in the anteroom and tearing the tapestries from the wall. His wife, Isabel, stood on the second-floor mezzanine, overlooking the intrusion with their three other daughters—Norah, Abigail, and Hannah—huddled around, and their two daughters-in-law, Rachel and Leah, standing by. Mary ran up the main stairs to join them.

"What's the meaning of this?" Ishmael took Daniel by the arm, but the Lieutenant pushed him away, throwing him back against the timbers of the front door.

Nathan and Seth—Ishmael's eldest sons—bolted through the back door of the estate and down the hallway. Daniel drew his sword and met them at the entry of the anteroom. He stopped them at the point of his blade and said, "Turn the robbers over to us or you'll lose more than a tapestry."

Ishmael said, "Leave them alone. They have nothing to do with this."

Daniel spun around. "Then you lead me to the robbers."

Ishmael said, "You're the robber, sir. You've sold your soul to the vilest of men."

"Curse you, vineyard keeper. You'll not speak of the captain like that." Daniel came around in front of Ishmael, his eyes filled with an intensity he'd never seen in the boy. It wasn't the sternness of a commander leading his men or the rage of a warring soldier headed to battle. It was hatred that seethed in Daniel's eyes—a look of loathing that infused the boy with a spirit of contention powerful enough that Ishmael could see it in his pushed-forward shoulders, his tight fists, and the veins in his neck that pulsed like a raging torrent overflowing its banks. He said, "Where are you hiding Nephi and his brothers?"

Mary leaned over the railing, "You've seen them?"

"Don't play me for a fool, girl. Where else would they take refuge but here?"

Ishmael slowly backed up the stairs to his wife and daughters. He should have known the coming of the sons of Lehi would haunt them like this. "They aren't here. They left with their family last spring."

Daniel said, "Your nephew tried to kill Captain Laban, and last night the band of them tried again to steal his brass relic."

"You can look for yourself if you like, but do your searching in peace." Ishmael raised his hand to the hallways of his estate. "You'll find none of them here."

"If you're lying, I'll not spare anyone at this estate." Daniel's words fell from his lips in a fierce cadence. He ordered his men back to their horses, but before going out the front door and leaving them amid the torn tapestries and broken chairs, Daniel said, "I'll be watching."

Jonathan filled a crucible with silver ore, clamped tongs around the vessel, and walked it over to the forging oven. The high priest had ordered a new silver bowl for the temple altar to celebrate the Feast of Trumpets at the end of the week, and Jonathan had come to the shop early this morning to purify the precious metal. He set the crucible in the hot coals and tilted the brim back to keep watch on the silver. What a temperamental ore this was. He couldn't smelt it in the oven like he did iron. Fire silver too long or too hot, and it cracked into pieces when it cooled. And if he didn't fire it long enough, it gathered into clumps, and the impurities ruined the finish. Jonathan slowly rocked the crucible over the coals like a mother rocks a newborn. There was only one way to know when the silver was purified—as soon as he saw his reflection in the surface, it was done. Jonathan stared down at the molten mass, the impurities slowly bubbling out in short puffs of hot steam. It was like looking at the surface of a muddy pond and waiting for some miracle to change the clouded ore to a clear, shiny finish. The change only lasted a moment, hardly long enough to pull the crucible from the refiner's fire and cool it in a spring-water bath. And if he waited too long, the silver was sure to cloud again, the reflection of his image lost and the silver ruined. Jonathan leaned in closer, watching for the reflection of his eyes, the length of his narrow nose, and the end of his chin to appear in the silver.

"Good morning, blacksmith." A man entered the shop from the street, but Jonathan kept his gaze on the ore. Couldn't the customer see he was busy? He leaned over the forging oven, the heat from the coals flashing across his face, but not hot enough to singe the straight, black hair that hung down over his brow. "What work do you bring me, sir?"

"It's about your son."

"You can find him at Captain Laban's estate in the Upper City."

The visitor set the broken remnants of a metal latch on the forging table next to Jonathan. "He paid a visit to our estate this morning and broke this."

The news turned Jonathan's gaze up for a moment, long enough to find Ishmael the vineyard keeper standing across the forging table. Hadn't he told Ishmael he wasn't welcome here? Jonathan turned his gaze back into his silversmithing. If he wasn't trapped here holding the crucible he'd throw Ishmael into the street. More than nine months had passed since Aaron died, but the memory of it still stung his soul, and with Elizabeth opening old wounds with her claims of seeing Aaron's ghost last evening, Ishmael's coming to the shop only fanned the embers of his grief. Jonathan forced the crucible deeper into the bed of coals, the silver sloshing against the sides but not spilling over the top. "I told you never to come here."

"What do you see in your silver, sir?" Ishmael pointed to the crucible set in the coals beneath Jonathan's watchful gaze.

"It isn't purified."

"When I was a boy, I used to wait beside my grandfather for the chance to see my reflection in the metal." Ishmael reached for the tongs. "Do you mind?"

Of course he did. How could he work next to a man who brought him so much pain?

Ishmael took hold of the tongs, adjusted the crucible in the coals, and stared down at the simmering molten silver. "Raising children is much like refining silver. Do you know when the refining is finished?"

"Of course I do. I'm a blacksmith."

"I was talking about raising sons."

"Give me that." Jonathan took back the tongs and pushed the crucible deeper into the coals. What did Ishmael know about the refiner's fire? He didn't have to endure the pain of losing a child. The cloudiness in the silver was beginning to fade, and the hint of a shine formed across the surface.

"My grandfather used to sit for hours refining and purifying silver over hot coals." Ishmael leaned his head in. "He used to tell me that God sits as the refiner and purifier of a man's soul. And if you live a God-fearing life, the impurities will melt away, and you can look into the crucible of life and see the reflection of God on your countenance."

"And if God doesn't sit as the refiner and purifier of your soul?"

Ishmael set two more broken latches on the table. "Daniel broke these as well."

"Don't you think you've caused my family enough pain?"

"Daniel's done the same for mine."

"You don't know pain, sir."

"I'm sorry your son abandoned this shop to follow Captain Laban."

"He joined the military."

"He burned our olive groves to the ground."

"That's a lie!" Jonathan flinched hard enough that the molten silver spilled over the edge of the crucible. "My son would never do such a thing."

"You may not have raised your son to dreadful deeds, but Captain Laban turned his heart after evil."

Jonathan gripped the tongs with both hands. How could this vineyard owner stand here and accuse Daniel of wicked deeds when it was Ishmael and his cousin who were responsible for the evil that had come to Jonathan's house? He said, "Get out of my shop."

"Don't you see the change in the boy?" Ishmael moved down along the side of the forging oven. "Look into his eye and you can see—"

"The only thing wrong with my son's eye is the blindness in the left side, and I have you and your kin to thank for that."

"The first time I came to your shop, Daniel had a passion for forging. There was a brightness about him, a light in his eyes, and a love for his family." Ishmael lowered his voice. "Do you see any of that in him now?"

"Why must you torment me?"

The silver gave up a final burst of steam, and immediately the surface changed into a shiny shell. Jonathan could see a figure peering back from the refined metal, but it looked nothing like his reflection. The hair was too short, the cheeks too flushed with youth, the chin too narrow, and the eyes too dark to be his.

"Cursed silver!" Jonathan yanked the crucible from the coals but lost the grip, and it fell from the tongs, the molten silver spilling over the floor.

Ishmael reached for a scoop, but Jonathan told him to back away. He didn't want to save the silver—not from that batch. He ushered Ishmael to the door, pushed him out into the street, and locked the latch. What did all this mean? He looked up into the rafters. Did Jonathan sit as the refiner and purifier of his son's evil deeds? Is that what God was telling him? Aaron sided with zealots, while Daniel joined the ranks of Judah's military. Aaron was a rebel. Daniel was an officer doing an honorable work in the house of Captain Laban. None of this made sense, but he couldn't rid himself of the impression. Was Daniel guilty of burning Ishmael's vineyards? And if he'd done that, was he guilty of other evils?

Jonathan picked the empty crucible off the floor and stared into the emptiness. It wasn't his reflection he saw in the silver. It was the angry, hardened face of Daniel, and he had no one to blame but himself for sacrificing the boy's soul for a command in Captain Laban's military. He held the crucible closer. Was this a reflection of the past?

Or a likeness of things to come?

CHAPTER 31

—Early Autumn, 598 B.C.
Valley of Lemuel (Wadi Tayyib al-Ism)

Sariah sat up in bed, the lambskin blanket falling down around her waist. A stack of towels and a large basin of water sat near the bed next to bottles of ointment and incense she laid out before retiring. She brushed her long black hair back from her eyes and peered across the tent. She'd hardly slept, but the feast day was nearing, she was certain of it. There were no long, low blasts on a *shofar* horn in this desert, no priests standing at the entrance of this tent like they did at the gates of the temple in Jerusalem reciting prayers and thanking God for the Creation, begging forgiveness for the sins of Israel, and petitioning heaven to remember the covenants made with their fathers at Sinai. There was nothing to remind her that the day to make a memorial of blowing of trumpets had arrived except the sharp contraction that shot through her. She grabbed Lehi by the arm. "It's time, dear. The feast is come."

"It's the middle of the night." Lehi adjusted his pillow beneath his head and turned on his side. "Sleep a while longer, dear."

Sariah said, "Did you hear me? I said it's time."

"I haven't a horn to blow in this desert." Lehi pulled the lambskin over his head and mumbled something about not having anyone in their camp skilled enough with a *shofar* even if they had one.

"Not the trumpet, dear. The child." Sariah held her breath against another contraction, her silence raising Lehi off his pillow. He pulled the blanket from in front of his face and stared at her, not saying a word, his eyes wide and his body stiff.

Lehi said, "What do we do?"

"Call for the women in camp." Sariah threw off the lambskin blanket. "The Day of Remembrance is come."

The pain of a bruised arm wrenched Nephi from his dream. The cavern was filled with the deep breathing of his brothers, and there was no telling how long they'd sleep. He pulled the blanket up around his neck and let his weariness overcome his bruised body. His eyes slowly fell shut, and in the fading moments of his dreams, his mind wandered back to the image of the brass plates in Captain Laban's courtyard the night before. The relic was engraved with the words of prophets from centuries gone by, their voices rising up from the dust, warning him not to leave the covenants locked away in Captain Laban's possession.

Nephi sat up and threw off the blanket. The evening air was as still and untroubled as the surface of the Galilee before a storm, but the tempest raging in his soul would not be still. He wasn't going back without the plates, and he placed the bridle into the black Arabian's mouth and strapped the saddlebag into place. If he left now, he could reach Jerusalem before the feast dawned.

"You'll never make it alive." Sam stepped around the horse, his light brown hair matted against the side of his head, his eyes red from tossing and turning on a bed of cold rock. "Captain Laban's men will be watching for you."

"We never should have done what we did alone." Nephi cinched the saddle down and tied the cords under the horse's belly. "We never asked God's help." The horse sidestepped against the pull on the cords, and Nephi steadied her with a stroke of his hand on her mane. "We were proud enough to think we could do this on our own. We never asked heaven to guide us, never prayed for safe passage, never thought to seek the blessings of heaven in getting the plates."

Sam said, "What more could we have done?"

"God didn't send us here to fail." Nephi tied the saddlebag shut. "I'll barter differently this time."

"Captain Laban doesn't want anything we have." Laman stepped out of the shadows of the cavern. "You're not going back."

"I promised Father we'd return with the plates." Nephi picked the burrs out of the horse's mane and rubbed down her coat. "I plan on keeping my word."

Laman took the reins of Nephi's horse. "You go back to Jerusalem, and Captain Laban will put a knife in your heart if his men don't cut off your head first."

Nephi said, "The Lord is mightier than all the men on earth."

"Then let God get the plates." Laman threw the reins on the ground hard enough to stir Lemuel from his bed. He leaned up on his elbow and said, "You saw how many soldiers there were."

"God is mightier than Laban and his fifty." Nephi retied the saddle-bag and brought his horse around in the cavern entrance. "Then why not mightier than Laban's tens of thousands?"

Lemuel said, "You're not God, brother. You're one man."

"Moses was a man, but he spoke by the power of God, and the waters of the Red Sea divided, and our fathers came through out of captivity on dry ground, while the armies of Pharaoh were drowned in the depths of the Red Sea."

Laman said, "You're living in the past."

"What about our past?" Aaron sat up and walked over to stand between Laman and Lemuel. "Captain Laban burned your vineyards, his men injured your mother, he tried to kill your father, he forced all of us to flee into the desert and abandon our homes, and now he's stolen your inheritance."

"Stay out of this, blacksmith."

"Aaron's right." Nephi swung up into the saddle. "Captain Laban has been no better to us than Pharaoh was to our fathers in Egypt."

"Do you see any shackles?" Laman raised his arms. "We're not slaves. We're free to head back into the desert."

"We'll never be free of Captain Laban." Nephi leaned over the saddle. "Not until we get what belongs to us."

Laman held Nephi's horse by the bridle. "You take his plates, and you'll never be free of him."

"An angel told us to go back for the plates." Nephi reined his horse out of Laman's grasp, the animal's hooves kicking through the broken pieces of the wooden rod left shattered on the ground. "Go with me one more time up to Jerusalem." He reined across the cavern entrance. "The

Lord is able to deliver us, just as he delivered our fathers out of the hands of the Egyptians."

"Deliver us from what?" Lemuel stood next to Nephi's horse. "We're alive, we're free, what more deliverance do we need?"

Nephi said, "We'll never be free until we settle this with Captain Laban."

Lemuel said, "You'll never get the plates from him."

"God drowned the armies of Pharaoh in the sea." Nephi came around to the entrance. "The Lord is able to deliver us even as our fathers, and destroy Laban even as the Egyptians."

CHAPTER 32

—Early Autumn, 598 B.C.
Jerusalem

What was that? Baruch raised his head off the writing table, rubbed the sleep from his eyes, and turned his ear to the door of the writing room. Was there someone inside, or was he dreaming again? The fruit bowl stood empty, and when he reached for a drink of water from the narrow-necked jar it was dry. And if not for the mournful sounds of the *shofar* horns heralding through the open window reminding Jews that tonight the Feast of Trumpets was come, he'd have slept through the night and never finished the plates.

Baruch leaned over the windowsill to check the hour, but thick gray clouds and patchy mists from an evening storm masked the evening sky, and there was no way to know how long he'd been sleeping. He pulled back inside, picked up the fallen writing stylus, found the place where he left off, and started the hammer and chisel over the metal. The soft, animal-hide scroll filled with Jeremiah's words sat next to the brass plate, and he turned his gaze between the documents, transcribing the text from leather to metal. Of all the prophecies, these of the last days of the earth were the ones that cried out to be included in Laban's brass record, and he hurried the stylus faster, copying the words of Jeremiah's prophecy. *Behold the days come, saith the Lord, that I will make a new covenant with the house of Israel and with the house of Judah. Not according to the covenant I made with their fathers in the day that I took them by the hand to bring them out of the land of Egypt; which my covenant they brake . . . I will put my law in their inward parts, and write it in their hearts; and I will be their God, and they shall be my people.*

Baruch carved the characters slightly smaller to make certain he got all of Jeremiah's words onto the last plate. Every prophecy had to be here. Men in the last days of the earth had to know that God would work a mighty miracle among them, gathering together Israel for the last time. He tapped the head of the hammer, imprinting the metal with the promise that the miracles attending the final gathering would be so astonishing that men would proclaim, *The Lord liveth that brought up the children of Israel from all the lands whither he had driven them.*

Baruch kept the stylus moving over the metal, the words proclaiming that in the last days the Lord would call *fishers* to cast their nets wide in nations where there were many seeking the blessing of the covenants, and He would call *hunters* to hunt one of a city and two of a country in nations where there were but few searching to abide by the covenant, until every ear had heard and every heart was touched by the knowledge of what was preserved in these brass plates. The tailings of the soft metal flew from before the point of Baruch's stylus and scattered about the surface of the plate. He blew them away, his gaze shifting between the plate and the last lines on the leather scroll to make sure he transcribed the words correctly. His fingers ached with a numbing pain, but he kept them wrapped around the etching instrument and added the final characters to the thousands he'd carved the past few weeks, the work crippling his fingers beyond feeling, but filling his heart with the spirit of Jeremiah's prophecies: *Behold I will send for many fishers saith the Lord, and they shall fish them; and many hunters shall hunt them from every mountain and from every hill and out of the holes in the rocks.*

Baruch etched his mark in the bottom corner, attesting to the accuracy of his transcription, and he was finished. He set aside the stylus when the sound of someone breaking down the kitchen door brought Baruch into the hall. A man dressed in a long black cape rushed at him, the cloth lifting away from his body enough to expose the loincloth about his waist, the red bandana tied around his neck, and the glint of a dagger in his hand. It was no dream. Shechem King of Robbers was inside his house.

Baruch slammed the door to the writing room and set the latch as Shechem ran up against the wooden slats. He placed the metal plates and the leather scrolls inside a satchel and climbed out the window to the pounding of Shechem on the writing room door.

There were no mule carts clattering past his home, and when he turned onto the darkened Main Street there were no cries of farmers selling their crops from beneath canopied pushcarts, and thankfully no sign of Shechem following him in the shadows of the gates and walls along the street. He reached the vacant government district on a dead run. There were no priests, lawyers, accountants, or moneychangers in the square, and he was left without the cover of a crowded street to hide his flight, but the temple on the far side offered safety. He climbed the steps through the New Gate, pushed past a group of temple priests, up a narrow run of steps, and out into the chamber of Gemhariah. The white, marbled walls rose up on either side of this gathering place for scribes—some seated at a long table at the far end arguing points of law from a stack of scrolls, and others gathered in small groups, the murmur of their conversation filling the chamber with a low rumble. Baruch knew these men well enough to merit a greeting. He returned their welcome with a nod and walked to the obscure corner where he could wait for—

Shechem? How did he follow him here? The robber stood in the stairwell. There was no place to run. Baruch couldn't climb out the narrow windows to deliver these plates to Zoram, and there was no back way out to save his own life. He was trapped in the corner of this chamber with the king of robbers pushing toward him through the crowd of scribes.

Zoram hurried up the steps from the treasury and asked the chief watchman to let him out into the evening.

The watchman said, "Do you know what day it is?"

Of course he did. Every servant, soldier, and cook was on alert, and anything suspicious was to be reported to Lieutenant Daniel. "I won't be long."

Zoram scanned the yard. Where was Elizabeth? He'd waited most of the day in the basement vaults, and still no word of her arrival. The low-lying clouds and patchy fog from the early-evening storms were beginning to lift, but there was no sign of her speaking with the guards at the back gate on Market Street. What could be keeping her?

The watchman said, "I've got to close, sir."

Zoram came back inside. "Send me word the moment she arrives."

"Will she be bringing you your dinner again tonight?"

"Dinner, yes. Have her bring me my dinner."

The watchman nodded, and Zoram scaled down the steps to the treasury. He turned the corner into the main run of the underground passage to find Daniel inspecting ten soldiers assigned to escort Captain Laban to the palace. Captain Laban joined them from the stairwell leading from the upper floors, and Zoram slipped behind a stone column to wait for these men to finish their dealings so he could pass without drawing the Captain's attention. It was the least he could do to keep from being asked to remove the sword from the vault without having the last plates to slip into place with the brass record.

Captain Laban was dressed in full regalia for this evening's celebrations—polished brass breastplates strapped to his thick shoulders, the gold-trimmed sleeves of his black tunic hedging out from beneath the shimmering metal. A black cloak hung from his shoulder, and he carried a red-plumed helmet in his arms. He never wore it anywhere— said he'd rather drown in the depths of the Galilee than suffocate under the constricting confines of a headpiece. He carried it about for show on occasions like this, but it didn't sit well on his head, and the sidepieces protecting his cheeks hid his finely trimmed beard. He peered back up the run of steps until Chief Elder Zadock descended from the upper floor of the estate. He was dressed in his customary black robe with the black and white shawls of an official visit streaming out from under his pointed headdress and falling down over his shoulders.

Daniel said, "The men are ready, sir."

"Wait for us in the yard."

Daniel took his leave with the soldiers, and when they had gone up the steps he turned to Zadock and said, "Did the king take his tea?"

"He can hardly remember his name." Zadock's high-pitched words echoed in the passageway.

Captain Laban said, "Will the nobles think he's fool enough to kill himself?"

Zoram leaned forward against the rough stone column. What did he mean by that? Did Captain Laban know about some harm coming to the king and his family? Zedekiah may have suffered a good deal of mindlessness these past few weeks, but he certainly wasn't mad enough to kill anyone, least of all himself.

Zoram waited until Laban knocked on the treasury door and called his name before leaving his hiding place and coming down the corridor. He excused himself for not being at the door when they arrived and let them inside. Laban handed over the vault key and ordered Zoram to dress him with the sword. He removed the weapon from the casement and turned it over, exposing the words inscribed in the finely polished steel—the ones Jeremiah etched into the blade the day Captain Laban brought it to the family vineyard at Anathoth. It was a little more than a year ago that Zoram hid in a basket when Captain Laban stormed inside his father's house and threatened to cut off Jeremiah's head. He watched through the wicker as his prophet-father wrote what the Captain was unable to write—that this sword would never be sheathed again until the kingdoms of the world became the kingdoms of God and His Anointed One. That was the day Jeremiah warned Laban that he had uttered his own fate.

"Go on, son." Laban raised his arms for Zoram to see the empty sheath at his side. "Place the sword."

Zoram balanced the blade between both hands, the words turned for Captain Laban to read. He said, "Wouldn't you rather carry the weapon in its casement, sir?"

"I don't have time for foolish curses."

"But sir?"

"Give me that." Laban snatched the sword from Zoram and threaded it into the sheath, the polished blade disappearing beneath the brim of the leather slip. "How do I look?"

Zoram said, "Regal, sir."

Nephi cleared the summit atop the Mount of Olives, leading his brothers through a thicket and out into a meadow overlooking Jerusalem. Moonlight showered the endless rows of square rooftops, spreading out below them in a winding path of faint yellow lamplight flickering in the windows of thirty thousand Jews preparing to celebrate the Feast of Trumpets. The sound of the *shofar* horns at the temple filled the evening, heralding the arrival of the feast, and from this height the faint light of the menorah cast a yellow glow across the temple entrance.

The East Gate stood open well past the usual hour with holiday travelers entering the city. Nephi spurred his mount across the meadow, through a stand of olive trees, and down a steep, rocky incline to the road running through the Kidron Valley. He pulled into a steady stride with the other travelers, slowing enough for his brothers to ride down the last slope. They rode past the entrance of the East Gate to get a good look at the night watch. Four soldiers stood in the entrance, stopping travelers entering the city. Another four soldiers stood atop the wall.

Nephi kept them riding down past the towering height of the south wall built on a high ridge above the valley floor, and then around to the west side along the new wall to the middle gate. This was the best place to enter the city, and he reined into a thicket a good hundred cubits shy of the entrance and down a rocky ravine where the watch couldn't see them nestled in behind a run of scrub oak.

Sam sidled in next to Nephi. "Stay to the side streets, and don't stop if any soldiers hail you. There's a good light from the moon. You don't want any of Laban's men to get a look at you."

"You're a fool for trying this." Laman spurred down into the ravine with Lemuel. "You'll not get past the gate."

Sam said, "Don't scare him like that."

Nephi said, "I don't fear this."

"You should." Laman came around. "What will you do once you're inside?"

Nephi lowered his head. God sent him to get the plates, but how was he to do it?

Sam said, "Leave him alone."

"At least he has the courage to try." Aaron got down from the saddle, and Beuntahyu forced her muzzle over his shoulder, blowing a burst of air past her lips and shaking her head. Aaron said, "I'm going with you."

Sam said, "You're not going anywhere."

Aaron handed Nephi a potsherd with writing on one side. "I need to speak with my father about this."

"You'll get us all killed, boy." Laman came around in front of Aaron. "Your father is one of *them*."

"He wouldn't do anything to bring us harm."

Laman said, "You don't know that."

"Stay here until I return." Nephi handed the letter back to Aaron, wrapped his friend's long, thin fingers around the potsherd, and said, "If there isn't a stir in the city, you can deliver this letter and see your father."

Aaron said, "And if there is a stir?"

"Wait for me." Nephi reined out of the ravine, but Sam ran alongside him, telling him to leave the horse. Soldiers wouldn't be watching for a man on foot.

Nephi slid out of the saddle, and Sam took him by one arm and Aaron by the other. They lowered their heads, and Sam offered a prayer, petitioning heaven to fulfill the promise delivered by the angel last night—that God would deliver the plates into their hands.

Sam said, "If you're not back before the moon sets in the west, I'm coming after you. Now go on. God be with you."

Elizabeth pried away the stone in the alley behind Baruch's home and reached inside. Where were the plates? She felt about the hole in the wall, her fingers running over the coarse limestone, but there were no smooth metal sheets hidden there. She quietly picked her way down toward the back entrance of the scribe's home.

The latch was broken, and the breeze blew the gate ajar. Elizabeth stepped into the courtyard and found the kitchen door left open. She called Baruch's name, but there was no answer. The parchments gracing the wall in the corridors were torn down, the pedestal holding a leather copy of the Law was pushed over, and when she turned into the writing room the timbers in the door were broken down, and the repository jars on the shelf holding a lifetime of Baruch's work were thrown to the ground, the clay vessels broken to pieces and the potsherds strewn across the floor. She fell to her knees and searched through the records, but there were no metal plates among the parchments.

Where was Baruch?

Baruch took a parchment from his satchel and held it up. "Fellow scribes, I bring you the words of the prophet on the eve of this holy feast day." He repeated his greeting until the chamber quieted.

"I've known all of you most of your lives." Baruch nodded to Elishama the scribe, and Delaiah, and Gemariah. "I have here the words of Jeremiah." The scribes gathered close enough to close Shechem off from coming closer.

Baruch read from Jeremiah's writings beginning with the account of the prophet's posterity, followed by a retelling of his youth in Anathoth and his call as a prophet. He glanced up from his reading to find Shechem waiting in the shadows. He read through the first leather scroll and took out another describing the destruction of the Northern Kingdom. It wasn't a flattering thing to read, but what else could he do to save himself from Shechem? He read a third scroll detailing Jeremiah's prophecies of the destruction of Jerusalem, telling the scribes gathered around him that not one stone would remain upon the other—not of the walls of the city, nor the dwellings, nor any of the stones of this temple where they stood. The king of Babylon would bring them down like a farmer's furrow in a field. He went on about the fate of the king of Judah, reading Jeremiah's prophecies of the man's loss of his throne. He said, "The Lord will bring upon the king of Judah and the inhabitants of Jerusalem and all the men of Judah the evil that all the holy prophets have pronounced."

The scribes gathered closer, and a defiant murmur rumbled through their number. He couldn't stop reading, no matter how many scribes he offended. Baruch started on another scroll.

Captain Laban stood behind a tall pillar near the front of the royal chamber and downed a bottle of wine. The palace was filled with nobles and princes standing along the edges of the marble floor watching a troop of dancers prance about to the beat of a drummer and a host of trumpeters. A maidservant stepped through the throng, headed to the kitchens, and Laban took the last bottle of wine from her tray and told her he didn't need a glass. He pulled the cork, took a drink, and stepped to the other side of the tall column away from the group of noblemen and in next to Zadock, the two of them staring across the expanse of the chamber to Zedekiah sitting on his throne, eating from a plate of lamb.

Laban said, "He hasn't said a word about the sword."

"It's still early."

Laban took another drink and wiped his lips on the back of his sleeve before glancing out the large window looking out over Jerusalem. The flickering lamp lights in the windows of a thousand homes spread out below the palace. "We've been here half the night."

"Make yourself seen."

"I stood near the throne until those fools came along." Laban pointed the neck of his wine bottle at a troop of jugglers. "Did you give him enough of the white powders?"

Zadock said, "He's taking more now."

Zedekiah sipped from a cup of tea. He raised his hand to stop the dancers and leaned forward in his throne, his gaze set on Laban's sword.

"It's time." Zadock leaned his head in next to Laban. "When he retires with the weapon, go straight to the royal quarters on the fourth floor. I'll see that the palace guards are elsewhere."

The doors of the royal chamber pushed open, and a temple scribe hurried inside. He pushed through a crowd of nobles at the back of the court, hurried down the run of steps to the main floor, and came around past the troop of dancers near the base of the throne. He bowed, and when he didn't get up off his knees, Zedekiah said, "What is it?"

"Baruch, sire." The scribe stood, his gaze hurrying over the faces of the noblemen in the court. "He's in the temple reading a scroll."

"Isn't that what scribes do on the eve of a feast day?"

"He's reading the words of Jeremiah in the ears of all the people gathered in the court of scribes."

Zedekiah came out of his throne. "Did he speak a curse?"

"He did indeed, sire. He said the Lord would bring upon the king of Judah the evil that all the holy prophets have spoken."

"Curse him for cursing me." Zedekiah dropped his scepter on the floor, and the sound of it echoed up into the vaulted ceiling. He ordered Jehudi—a nobleman from the wealthy Nethaniah family—to bring Baruch to him.

Captain Laban started out of the chamber, but Zadock took him by the arm.

"Where do you think you're going?"

"To finish what Shechem failed to do."

"This is much better." Zadock took the wine bottle from Laban. "You have the blessing of heaven to kill the royal family."

"I must be certain Baruch brings Jeremiah's curse with him." Laban took back the wine bottle and raised it to Zadock. "To Jeremiah's curse."

"Give me that." Zadock reached for the wine bottle, but Laban kept him from taking it.

"Tonight is the last night I enjoy the king's wine." Laban downed the rest of the bottle, but before he slipped out the door near the back of the chamber he said, "Tomorrow the palace wine stores will be mine."

Baruch reached the final phrases near the bottom of the parchment when he noticed Shechem move from the shadows and come down through the circle of scribes. He slowed the pace of his reading, his gaze shifting between the words and the robber coming toward him. Was he to end up like so many others? Murdered in a public square at the hands of a robber? How many men of government and scribes of court had been killed in the light of day by Shechem and his band? The robber pushed his way to the front of the crowd, and all Baruch could do was pray that Jeremiah was right, that by reading the words on these parchments God would save him from—

"Baruch." Jehudi, the wealthy nobleman, accompanied by an escort of soldiers, cleared the steps at the far end of the chamber. "By order of the king of Judah, you're to come with me."

The soldiers took Baruch under guard and escorted him out of the chamber, their metal-plated armor protecting him from Shechem, standing not ten paces away. Baruch held the scrolls against his chest while the soldiers marched him out of the temple gates and up the rise toward the palace. The prophet was right. Baruch had read the scrolls in the temple, and he was delivered. He felt for the brass plates in his satchel. Now all that remained was to fulfill Jeremiah's other prophecy— prepare the records for the last days of the earth.

CHAPTER 33

The Jewish Sabbath
Saturday, September 22, 1827
Mount of Olives, Jerusalem

Avram Weiss held a bouquet of white roses in one hand and pushed open the gate to the cemetery with the other. A narrow lane led past the gravestones that cluttered the ground on this hillside with the haunting memory of his loss. A heavy fog gathered in the early morning after a night of rain, and Avram pulled his collar tight around his neck to keep the cool breeze from chilling him to the bones. It was a Saturday morning—a Sabbath Day that transformed this Feast of Trumpets into a much holier Day of Remembrance than any of the four years since Avram emigrated from Russia. For the first time in a long while, the first day of the seventh month fell on *Shabbat*, but there was nothing holy about remembering his daughter one year after the terrible accident that took her life. Today should be a day for celebrating Katerina's first year of marriage to Danny Kessler, delivering a gift to their home and wishing the couple well, not trudging through this fog to a secluded corner of a graveyard. There should be the joyful cries of a new baby, not the mournful sound of a lone trumpet echoing across the valley from the Sephardic synagogue on the highest hill in the Old City, announcing the arrival of this Day of Remembrance.

Tradition required that Avram visit the grave of deceased family on the first day of the seventh month. But that was a remembrance better suited to ancestors long since dead—not his youngest daughter. Avram lost his wife and children in the uprising against the Jews in Russia, and he came to Jerusalem with Katerina to forget the loss, not bring it with him to these haunts on the hills east of the city. A father should never have to look on the grave of his last child. Katerina was the end of his posterity. He had no more children, no one left on this earth to call his own. He would never again hear anyone call him Papa, never know the sweetness of looking into the faces of his family and see his reflection in their eyes. The memory of Avram Weiss would not live on in anyone when he died. This was the end of generations. The last hope for his family was snuffed out last year on the day when he should have been celebrating the beginning of a new generation.

The lane turned down a rise near the back of the graveyard, and Avram followed it along the ridge of the hill over beside two small stones. He had trimmed the grasses earlier in the week and straightened the border of white limestone setting off both graves. He bent over and adjusted two of the stones to make a perfect line around the burial site. The gravestones named Katerina and Danny as husband and wife, born in the same year, 1805, married in 1826, and died on the same day. Thankfully Danny's father had the money to hire a stonecutter to add the inscription that they were bound together in life and they were not separated in death.

Avram stood between the gravestones, raised his hands out in front of him, and slowly rocked back and forth, offering a prayer of remembrance for his departed daughter and son-in-law. And if it were possible to turn the hearts of children to their fathers, then please turn Katerina's heart back to him. Let her remember that he loved her, that he knew deep in his heart that she and Danny were a good match, far finer than any he could have made for her.

The mournful blasts of the trumpet sounded across the valley from the synagogue in the Old City, cutting through the mist that blanketed the graveyard and calling the faithful to offer prayers asking God to remember His covenants with Israel. Avram turned his gaze up into the mist, his prayer directed to heaven, begging the Almighty to remember the law given to Moses on Sinai and His covenant with Israel.

"Avram?" Reuben Kessler walked through the mists. He was dressed for his cantor duties at synagogue, the fringe-ends of his blue and white prayer shawl dancing about his knees. He stepped off the path and came in next to the gravestones. "I thought you might be here this morning."

"A year it has been, my friend. A year ago today."

Reuben nodded. "Are you well?"

"The silent moments when the house is still I find most difficult." Avram breathed in the wet air and let it soothe his lungs. "There isn't any hope that a child or a grandchild will ever break the quiet of my loneliness."

"Danny would have wanted you to have this today." Reuben reached beneath the lapel of his coat, pulled out a calendar, and handed it to Avram. The Gregorian calendar was done in Reuben's flowing pen strokes. All the feast days for the coming year were marked, and the words *ha-Zikkaron* were written in bright-red ink below today's date, September 22, 1827.

Avram thanked him for the calendar and said, "Happy New Year, my friend."

"You were always quick to lecture my Danny that it was to be called a Day of Remembrance."

Avram folded the calendar, hiding the date for today's celebration. "Today is a day I would remove from the calendar if I had the power."

Reuben laid his hand on Avram's shoulder. "Why don't you come celebrate the feast in my house?"

"You would have an old Hassid as your guest?"

"I would have you as my own flesh and blood."

Avram turned his gaze back to the gravestones. "There's a grave site not too far south from here in Bethlehem where they buried Abraham and Sariah." He spread his hands out to Katerina and Danny's graves. "Just like this, husband and wife, side-by-side." He began to rock again, his body slowly swaying forward and then back like a man in prayer, but he didn't fall into a chant or sing a verse from the Torah. He said, "My wife I left in an unmarked grave near Minsk. Every day I called her my Russian princess, and then one day she is gone."

"I'm sorry, Avram." Reuben pulled out the gold pocket watch that belonged to his son and clicked open the cover protecting the precision-balanced arms. "Danny used to stand outside the synagogue on this feast day with this watch in one hand and his trumpet in the other. He'd look across the city into the western sky and tell me what time it was in Moscow,

Rome, Madrid, Paris, London, New York, and every city in between, and he'd go on reciting which cities across the earth were already celebrating the Day of Remembrance, and which ones were still waiting for the midnight hour to arrive when Jews began to remember their covenants with God." He reached for Avram's arm. "Come with me to synagogue, and we'll talk of our family and celebrate the day with a fine meal."

"What is left to celebrate?" Avram held up his hand to keep Reuben from escorting him off. "Can I ever hope to have the same blessings promised to Abraham?" The long, low blasts of the trumpeters rose up from the synagogue across the valley, their solemn tone faint but certain. Avram turned his ear and waited for another round of trumpeting before he said, "God told Malachi to remember the covenants given to Moses at Sinai. Do you know the verse?"

Reuben nodded slowly.

Avram tightened his grip on Reuben's wrist. "Sing it for me?"

Reuben straightened his prayer shawl over his shoulders. He cleared his throat and in a clear, deep baritone softly sang the rising and falling melody of the last words of Malachi, his rich voice telling of the return of Elijah to the earth before the great and dreadful day of the Lord to turn the hearts of the children to the fathers and the hearts of the fathers to the children. He repeated the verse three times, each time with a softer melody until his voice faded into the mists lingering about the graveyard.

Avram lowered his head, the tears rolling off the end of his nose, and his body shaking with grief, waiting for the pain of losing Katerina to pass, but it would never be gone, not until he knew deep in his heart that he would see her again—that he would see all his children again and stand beside his Russian princess and know that he was blessed like Abraham with the promise of eternal life for all his family. He waited until the tears slowed before raising his head and drying his cheeks with the back of his hand. This was the Feast of Trumpets, the feast when Jews were to awaken to a remembrance of their covenants with God—a day Avram prayed with all his soul would come quickly and take away this curse that left him without the promise of family.

Avram raised his tear-stained face to the gray sky and said, "When will God begin to remember His covenants with Israel?"

—That Same Day
Palmyra Township, State of New York

Where was Father?

Joseph Smith Jr. pulled the curtains back from the window of the main room of the family's nearly finished white frame house and peered into the dark of night. There was no sign of him coming down the moonlit road from the Samuel Lawrence farm, and he let the curtains fall back into place, the ends of the thick linen playing in the cool evening breeze. The old spring clock on the mantle above the fireplace, the one Mother inherited when Grandma passed, was edging toward midnight and the arrival of Saturday, September 22. He'd not wait until morning and risk interference from the neighbors watching the house, but he couldn't start for the hill until Father brought word that farmer Lawrence wasn't gathering a rabble to follow him. Word of his visits to a hill in the county had gotten out over the past four years, but thankfully no one knew which of the many drumlins he visited. He didn't tell anyone it was located about three miles southeast of the family farm. Not even Mother and Father knew where he went every September twenty-second. He told his family bits and pieces of what he learned on each visit, but nothing about where the plates lay buried. Joseph ran both hands through his hair, the light brown strands poking between his fingers. Four years he'd waited, and now the clock was ticking down to the appointed hour, and if Moroni permitted him this time, he'd bring the plates home and do what he could to see the ancient record translated.

Joseph held his fist to his lips, tapping his tightly held fingers to his mouth. If Mr. Lawrence knew the exact date of Joseph's yearly visits—something he could have discovered innocently from young Don Carlos or little Lucy—he was certain to gather Willard Chase, the Stafford clan, Mr. Stoddard, and every money digger this side of the Finger Lakes District to watch the house tonight and all day tomorrow, to say nothing of the local clergy and newspaper men who spoke ill of him and his family, and all because he would have no part in either of their causes. Joseph was neither a superstitious money digger nor a preacher. He was doing what was asked of him. He knew it, and he knew that God knew it, and he prayed for the blessing of heaven to allow him safe passage this evening.

A weak spot in the new wood floor creaked beneath Joseph's pacing, and he stayed on the edge of the rug to keep from waking the family. Mother had pieced the rug together from tattered and worn bits of old clothing. It was Lucy's house-warming gift to celebrate their move across Stratford Road from the cabin to their newly finished frame house, but they didn't really own this dwelling, and it certainly wasn't finished. There were still walls to plaster, boards to paint, furniture to build, a chimney to finish on the north wall, and a flu to brick and mortar on the south. More than half the windows were without panes, and they'd remain that way until they could afford to buy poured glass—an expense that didn't seem worth the cost now that they'd lost the house. They were reduced to the station of renters since the day Mr. Stoddard lied to the land agent and took possession of the deed to their property. And the cruelty of Mr. Stoddard would have had them evicted last year if not for the kindness of Constable Durfee, who threatened to throw the man in jail if he didn't confess to his lies and agree to sell the deed to Mr. Durfee's father—a Quaker in town and a much more suitable landlord. For a hundred dollars a year they were allowed to farm the land and live in the house, but they would never own this property, and the new landlord certainly wasn't inclined to let them stay here forever. A few years was all Mother and Father could hope for before the holder of the deed, Mr. Lemuel Durfee, asked them to move so that he could take full possession.

A stiff breeze drew Joseph back to the window. He pushed the curtains aside and leaned over the sill far enough to see around the line of trees along the north edge of the property. There was still no sign of Father, and if he didn't get back soon, Joseph was going to have to venture off without knowing the risks. There were too many neighbors and town folk watching the house to consider venturing out in the light of morning. He was caught here, trapped inside this house with unseen enemies waiting to do him harm—the same money diggers and clergymen who made Joseph the focus of their own confusion over religion. They begged Joseph to join their money digging with as much fury as the clergymen and newspaper editors who railed against Joseph's claims to visions from heaven, denouncing his good name and the good name of his family, telling all who would listen to their sermons and read their editorials that grace was the only divine intervention and all else was ungodly, unchristian, and unreasonable. So many people in this township clung to myths of water witching and treasure hunting. They yearned for the powers beyond this world to raise them out of their poverty—unwilling to reason that heavenly gifts were not meant to bless idle hands. Had they forgotten the divine decree that a man made his way in this world by the sweat of his brow? The curtains flapped on the breeze, and he held them still. The clergymen hated Joseph because he would not deny his visions, and the money diggers hated him because he would not employ his gift to make them rich.

Joseph pulled back inside the window and turned to the hearth, stirring a metal poker through the dying embers. He kindled it to take the chill out of the fall evening, but the warmth did little to comfort his soul, and he turned away from the red-orange glow, took the lamp from the table, and walked it across the hall to the kitchen. He stepped up on a stool to search the top shelf above the cast-iron stove. A few years back, Mother had a wooden chest with a lock, and it had to be here somewhere. He moved to the next shelf and felt around the sack of wheat and behind the bottles of oil and—

"Joseph, is that you, dear?" Lucy stepped into the kitchen, dressed in her sleeping gown. Her hair was tied back under a small white bonnet, and the ends of a long braid trailed out beneath it and down the back of her neck. She rubbed the sleep from her eyes. "It's late, son. You should be sleeping."

"Mother." Joseph got down from the stool. "The wooden chest with a key; do you know where it is?"

"Dear, I haven't a chest like that."

"I've seen you with it. Do you remember a few years back?"

"That wasn't a chest of mine. I kept it for a friend in town while she moved her family to . . ."

The spring clock in the main room stroked the hour of midnight, and Lucy fell silent, the sleep draining from her eyes. She stepped closer to Joseph, her hand reaching for his. "Mercy, Joseph, you're going to the hill, aren't you?" She started about the kitchen, searching for a pine box or a barrel, anything that might serve in place of a wooden chest. "Dear me, Joseph, I've failed you. Surely there's something here you can use. A bread box or possibly one of your father's crates for hauling chickens, or what about—?"

"Never mind, Mother." Joseph took her by the hand and pulled her back from her searching. "I'm well enough off."

"You say that whenever you're most troubled about your visions. I know that now. You're not well enough off, not by any measure."

"I can do very well for the present without a chest. Be calm. All is right."

"Does Mr. Knight know you're leaving?"

"I suspected as much." Mr. Knight stepped into the kitchen from the hall. "Is there so much need for secrecy?"

Joseph Knight had boarded these past two days in the room off the hall. He came here in company with Mr. Josiah Stoal, the two of them traveling as they did to Palmyra on business every few months, but that wasn't the reason they planned their arrival for the weekend of September twenty-second. Joseph had confided in them during his winter work trips to Colesville, and they had come to see this event with their own eyes.

Mr. Knight said, "Will you get them tonight, son?"

"I believe so, sir."

"You believe so? That isn't what you told me, boy. You said if you did right according to the will of God, you'd have the plates, and if not, you never would have them." Mr. Knight leaned against the doorpost. "I didn't ride here from Pennsylvania for you to make another visit to the hill without bringing home the plates. I want you to tell me, have you done right, son?"

"Of course he has." Lucy took Joseph by the arm. "He's a good son and a loyal husband to Emma."

Mr. Knight leaned forward, his arms folded across his chest. "Have you, son?"

Before Joseph could answer, the front door swung open, and Joseph Sr. stood in the entry, the cool night blowing in with his arrival.

Joseph Jr. said, "Did you see anything, Papa?"

"Nothing." Joseph Sr. slowly shook his head. "I waited until Mr. Lawrence retired for the night. I didn't see any neighbors gathering, and there was no sign of the Stafford clan. If they're expecting anything, they're thinking it will come tomorrow. You can go without any worries, son."

Mr. Knight pulled on his coat and buttoned it to the collar. "I'll hitch the surrey."

"Wait there, sir." Joseph Jr. took Mr. Knight by the arm.

"You need a companion, someone to stand watch. I heard you say so myself."

"The relics hidden in the hillside are filled with ancient covenants."

Lucy said, "You've told us that already, son."

"My companion tonight should fully represent those covenants."

Mr. Knight said, "I drove more than a hundred miles to see this thing. Certainly my pains, not to mention my interest in this venture, qualify by whatever standard you have in mind. I'm a religious man. I've lived a reputable life. What greater embodiment of heavenly covenants is there?" Mr. Knight placed a top hat on his head and fished his cane out of the tube near the door. "What better watchman could you want, son?"

"Joseph, are you ready, dear?" Emma scaled down the stairs from the upper rooms. She had on her bonnet and a gray riding dress with black trim and a matching cape draped over her shoulders and tied with a large bow at the neck. Her long, black hair was done in large ringlets over her ears, the same way she did it for their wedding at the home of Squire Tarbill, Justice of the Peace, in South Bainbridge eight months ago. Her lips were painted a deep shade of red, and she'd touched her cheeks with a thin layer of pale, white powder. She was one of the finest ladies to grace the township. Emma was educated far beyond Joseph's learning—a school teacher, no less—but her education and her upbringing in the Methodist sect didn't keep her from believing the reports of his visions—and that's what they were to her, nothing more than a report. She'd not ever seen an angel, and none of her prayers were answered with a glorious manifestation from heaven, but she never doubted Joseph. She led an ordinary life with extraordinary faith, and that's what drew Joseph to her when he first met her two years ago at her father's boardinghouse. She was an elect lady with a refined faith that buoyed her up and filled her with peace when there was good reason to fear. She fixed her bonnet like a woman preparing to go to church, and when she reached the last step in the stairs and turned into the kitchen, she nodded to Lucy, then offered a "good evening" to Mr. Knight and Father Smith.

"With all due respect, Mr. Knight, my wife is the only embodiment of those ancient covenants." Joseph Jr. took Emma by the arm. "Don't wait up for us. It may be a good while before we're back."

Joseph escorted Emma around behind the house where he already had Mr. Knight's horses hitched to the surrey with a canopy on top. He helped Emma up onto the stoop and laid a quilt around her legs to keep her warm against the chill of early autumn. They drove down Stratford Road a mile, then east on a narrow dirt road that cut through flat farmland and a thick stand of maple and oak. The night sky was clear without a cloud to obscure the canopy of stars leading them to the crossroads at Canandaigua Highway and then south three-quarters of a mile to the hill. The moon shone on the west-facing slope, and Joseph turned the surrey off the main road and through an open pasture, driving to a secluded spot behind a ridge near the base of the drumlin. He pulled up beneath a stand of maples and tied the horses to the trunk of the nearest tree.

Joseph said, "You're certain you'll be safe here alone?"

Emma smiled down at him from the stoop. "I have nothing better to do at this hour."

"If you see anything, if you're frightened, if anyone approaches, call out, and I'll come quickly."

"What is it you always say?" Emma took his hand. "I'm well enough off?"

"I should take you home this instant."

"You asked me to come, and I happily agreed."

"Mr. Knight would have been a wiser choice for keeping watch." Joseph tightened his grip on her hand. "But I brought you here because you're my wife, and the record in this hill contains the same covenants given to Abraham and Moses and all the ancient prophets— covenants that have power to preserve our family and all the families of the earth forever." He leaned against the sideboard. "You'll call at the first sign of trouble, won't you?"

"There isn't going to be any." Emma leaned over and kissed him on the cheek. "Tonight God stands watch with us."

Joseph climbed the north face of the drumlin until he was level with the tree line before traversing across the western slope. A little way down from the top of the hill he found the grove of trees where he'd come every year for the last four. There was no sign of Moroni, no white-robed man waiting among the trees, and Joseph found his way among the oaks and juniper by the light of the moon filtering through the branches. He found the cover stone, pried it up with the end of a dead branch, lifted it onto its edge, and let it fall into the tall grasses with a soft thud. He knelt beside the edge of the stone box, felt along the side of it, the thick walls cemented in place with ancient mortar.

The golden-plate record assembled by Moroni and his father—a prophet named Mormon—sat in the center of the stone box next to a record of similar construction, except that it was fashioned of brass and tarnished a black-green color from a millennium of sitting here in the ground. Both records were engraved with beautiful characters well beyond the penmanship skills of any modern scribe. And near the two metal-plate records sat a brass ball of curious workmanship with spindles like the arms of a compass or the hands of a clock. Along the length of the stone box lay the Urim and Thummim—a half-moon-shaped silver bow with two clear stones—and an armored plate molded to conform to a man's chest. Along the other side of the box lay an unsheathed sword, its double-edged blade as sharp and polished as the day it was smithed. The relics were difficult to see clearly in the moonlight, their outline hidden in the darkness of night until a bright light chased away the shadows and Moroni stood beside Joseph, bathed in the same light that accompanied his other visits. He spoke in a firm, steady voice like the sounding of a trumpet. He rehearsed everything he'd taught Joseph on his previous visits to the hill, heralding the same prophecies he spoke of on their first visit four years earlier, but instead of repeating them as they were written in the Bible, he spoke of their fulfillment, promising Joseph that tonight God would begin to fulfill His promises to Israel and remember the covenants made to all the prophets since the world began. He went on to tell Joseph that with the reception of these golden plates, the fullness of times was coming to the earth when every promise made to every prophet since the beginning of the world was to be restored. He repeated the instructions given to Joseph at each of his interviews, reminding him what the Lord was going to do, and how and in what manner His kingdom was to be conducted in the last days.

Moroni directed Joseph to lift the gold record out of the stone box and turn each plate until he reached the end. They had the appearance of gold. Each one was the same size, about six inches wide and eight inches long and not quite as thick as common tin. They were filled with engravings in what appeared to be Egyptian or Hebrew characters and bound together in a volume, as the leaves of a book, with three rings running through the whole. The volume was something near six inches in thickness, a part of which was sealed. The characters on the unsealed part were small and beautifully engraved. The whole book exhibited many marks of antiquity in its construction and much skill in the art of engraving. The ancient characters shimmered in the brightness of Moroni's presence, and when Joseph reached the last plate in the unsealed portion, Moroni told him that this was the beginning of the codex—that his ancient people placed the beginning of their metal records at the bottom—and he was to begin translating the last plate first. He instructed Joseph to rest the silver bow of the Urim and Thummim over the bottom plate. They were like large spectacles, too large to wear over the eyes, but when he attached them to the breastplate, he could look through these miraculous eyepieces with his hands free to handle the writings on the codex. He adjusted the last plate beneath the Urim and Thummim, and immediately the translation appeared in the lens. Joseph leaned away from peering through the stones to see if the characters on the gold plate had been altered or if Moroni had placed some English words beneath the spectacles. He hadn't. The characters weren't changed; the ancient writings were as undecipherable as they were before he looked through the lenses, but when he brought his gaze back to the Urim and Thummim the English translation was there, fixed into the iridescent glass of these stones.

Moroni said, "The translation is given by the gift and power of God, and as long as you're faithful, the ability to translate will be yours."

Joseph read the translation that appeared in the stones. The bottom plate in the record contained some sort of preface written by the hand of Moroni—the very angel standing next to him—fourteen hundred years earlier when he was mortal and before he deposited the plates in this stone box during his mortality. The introduction explained that these gold plates were an abridgment of the record of the people of Nephi, and also of the Lamanites, written by the spirit of prophecy and of revelation. Joseph adjusted the breastplate down to the next run of characters and waited for the translation to appear in the clear stones, the words stating that this record was sealed by the hand of Moroni, and hid up unto the Lord to come forth in due time by way of the Gentile—the interpretation thereof by the gift and power of God.

Moroni said, "Whoever brings this record to light, him will the Lord bless." He went on, instructing Joseph that he was to show them to no one but the men God would send to him as witnesses. And he was to use all his endeavors to preserve the plates until Moroni should call for them back.

Joseph held the plates with both hands. They were heavy—nearly thirty pounds of gold by his guessing, but they were a far greater burden than their weight. Joseph was charged like Moses of ancient days with a record of a new covenant, and this stone box where they lay for fourteen hundred years was the ark of this new covenant—a receptacle that had sealed for centuries a record preserved to come forth out of the dust. This small drumlin didn't rise to near the altitude of Sinai's summit, there were no trumpets sounding his ascent to the top, and there were no Israelites gathered at the base of this hill waiting to receive the record—only his dear wife, Emma, waited below in a surrey—but Moroni promised Joseph that one day the writings on these plates would go to all nations to bless all the families of the earth.

Moroni said, "Read the last words on the first plate—the ones I wrote many years ago before I hid this record here."

Joseph adjusted the plates beneath the double lens of the Urim and Thummim, and Moroni read the translation as it appeared on the surface of the clear stones. His voice was like the sound of a trumpet blast rising up through the trees and proclaiming that the day had arrived for God to remember His covenants with Israel.

Moroni said, "This record will show unto the House of Israel what great things the Lord hath done for their fathers; and that they may know the covenants of the Lord, that they are not cast off forever—and also to the convincing of the Jew and Gentile that Jesus is the Christ, the Eternal God, manifesting himself unto all nations."

A conduit of light opened around Moroni, and he walked up into it until the brightness gathered around his form and Joseph was left alone on the hill in the darkness of night. He set the golden-plate record on the ground next to the edge of the box and lifted the stone lid into place, but before he fitted it shut he caught a glimpse of the brass-plate record that lay in the shadows with the other relics. It was a record much like the Old Testament—at least that's what he understood from his many visits with Moroni—and its writings were copied into the golden-plate record entrusted to Joseph. He let the stone lid fall into place and seal the brass plates back into the ground, arranged the long grass around the edges, and spread a thin layer of dirt over the top to hide his coming to this place. He wrapped the gold plates in a cloth, but before hefting them down the hill to join Emma, he stood for a long moment beside the stone box, the brass record sealed under his feet. He knew the story of the coming forth of the golden-plate record. He'd lived it for the past four years, but he couldn't help but let his mind wander to the other record that lay in this stone box, hidden for centuries in the dust of the earth. Joseph and his family had suffered years of poverty and a good many other hardships, all the while knowing the precious metal in this hill could remedy their ills. Over the past four years, he had rid himself of the greed of wanting these metal plates for any other purpose than the work of God. Joseph ran the toe of his boot along the seam where the stone lid met the ground. Did the brass record beneath his feet share a story similar to his? Were there other men who suffered like he suffered to preserve ancient covenants for future generations? Joseph tucked the golden plates under his arm and started down the hill.

Would he ever know the story of the brass plates he left behind and how this night was unlike any other night in the calendar of events in the history of men?

CHAPTER 34

—*Early Autumn, 598 B.C.*
Jerusalem

Nephi walked behind two travelers entering the city through the middle gate. The watchman started over, but with three travelers already waiting to pass inside and another company wanting to leave by the same gate, the soldier waved them through without inspection. There was enough moonlight for Nephi to find his way to the steps leading up Milo Hill and to approach Laban's home by the back gate. He wasn't certain how he'd get past the guards. He could climb the wall, but there were watchmen posted along every cubit of the property. And if by some miracle he got into the grounds, how would he ever get to the treasury? It seemed like such an impossible venture, but he had to try one more time, and he prayed God would lead him. That was all he could hope for. Left to his own designs, he didn't know beforehand what he should do.

The homes at the top of Milo Hill stood far enough back from the street to allow moonlight to filter down onto Market Street. Nephi started toward the captain's estate, but pulled up when a man stirred in the shadows next to a mule cart. He cursed the cart for getting in his way and cursed himself for getting lost. He swung a wine bottle in one hand and a gleaming metal sword in the other and called for the palace guards to let him inside to finish his work. He said, "Fools. Open for your king." He spun around, and Nephi backed away from the swing of his sword. The force of his movement and the weight of the wine that filled his head sent the man to the ground, the sword clanging over the cobblestones and the wine bottle crashing into pieces around his fallen form.

Nephi hurried over to help the poor drunk, and in the dim light of the moon he found Captain Laban delivered into his hands. His breast-plates rose and fell with his heavy breathing. The hilt of his sword shimmered in the moonlight. It was forged without any unsightly hammer or chisel marks, and when Nephi hefted it in his hand, the double-edged blade was perfectly balanced on both sides from point to hilt. What was Laban doing in the street with this? He never took the relic out of his treasury, but here he was, flaunting one of his two most valuable possessions.

What good fortune. With Captain Laban and his sword as hostage, Nephi could barter for the brass plates. He lifted Laban back to his feet and started walking him up the rise toward his estate, but the captain was without any strength in his legs, and it was impossible to carry his drunken body farther than the alleyway leading in behind the first estate, away from the view of thieves who were certain to rob a drunken man lying out in the open. Nephi couldn't wait until Laban wakened from his stupor, but he could dress like the captain. He had Laban's thick shoulders, the same straight nose and strong chin. He took the key from around Laban's neck and put it around his own. He placed the captain's helmet over his head, the brass headpiece hiding his long black curls that matched Captain Laban's longer-than-usual hair. The helmet fit perfectly over his brow, and Nephi used the strap to hide as much of his face as he could. He was reaching to untie the captain's breastplate when he heard a voice—the words coming to his mind as clear and certain as if God were standing beside him, speaking with him face-to-face and telling him that he should kill Laban.

Nephi let go of the captain's breastplate and gently lowered the man's body back to the cobblestones. How could he kill him? It wasn't his disposition to harm anyone, even a bitter enemy. Never at any time had he shed the blood of a man, and Nephi lowered his helmet-covered head into his hands, begging heaven not to ask him.

Kill Laban. The voice penetrated into the depths of his soul, telling him that the Lord had delivered Laban into his hands. This man was no better than a robber. He had tried to murder Nephi and his brothers, he had stolen their gold and silver, and he had made oaths to kill men for gain. And the only way to protect his family and keep the captain from chasing them into the wilderness was to—

No. Nephi let go of the sword, and it fell to the ground, clanging on the cobblestones next to the captain's drunken form. He couldn't kill a man—not even this man. Couldn't he get the plates by disguise and not suffer the blood of this man on his hands? Nephi finished dressing in Laban's clothes and started out of the alley when the Spirit spoke to him more powerfully than before, declaring that it was better that Captain Laban perish than an entire nation dwindle in unbelief.

Nephi stood over Laban's drunken body. He slowly pulled the captain's head back by the hair, exposing his neck to the moonlight. There was only one awful course he could follow to secure the brass plates and end the captain's senseless pursuit of his family.

Nephi brought the sword down across Laban's neck.

Zoram was sitting at the writing table in the stillness of the treasury, staring at the sealed vault, when Elizabeth pounded on the door. She had a basket filled with evening meal. She said, "Is it too late?"

Zoram took Elizabeth by the hand. "Do you have the plates?"

"The palace guards took Baruch prisoner."

"What?"

"I saw them march him to the palace gates." Elizabeth nodded. "It was terrible."

"Then we've failed."

"We haven't." Elizabeth fished a leather satchel from her basket with three brass plates concealed inside. "Baruch dropped this at my feet as he passed in the street."

"It isn't safe for you here." Zoram took Elizabeth by the hand and led her to the treasury entrance. Her long black hair fell in front of her face, and Zoram lifted the strands back to see into her eyes. "I want you to go home and stay there until I come for you."

"Add the plates to the record, and then you can come with me."

"You know Laban has the key."

"Then ask him for it." Elizabeth turned Zoram around by the shoulders to see the dark outline of Captain Laban walking through the shadows of the passageway. He was wearing his helmet, the brass vents along the sides covering his cheeks, the strap hiding his thin line of beard, and the brim pulled down over his head. His breastplates and armor had lost their shine, dirtied by . . .

He was covered with blood. A spray of red fanned across his breastplate and over his face, and a line of blood dripped off the end of his tunic and onto his thigh. He carried his sword in his hand, the polished metal smeared red from a hasty attempt to wipe away the blood. He'd done it. He'd killed the royal family. Zoram took Elizabeth by the arm and said, "Go home now."

"But . . ."

"Whatever happens tonight, know that I will come for you." Zoram pushed her away. "Go on, before anything happens to you."

Elizabeth nodded, a tear slowly running down her cheek, and then she was away, lifting the skirts of her robe. She paused when she passed Captain Laban, her hand over her mouth and her eyes wide with the horror of his appearance, and then she was gone, the soft fall of her footsteps fading into the passageway.

"Captain, sir. You're hurt." Zoram picked up the leather satchel with the last plates in it. "They're searching the city for you."

Laban stopped five paces from Zoram, and when he spoke he held his fist to his mouth. He said, "Bring me the plates, please."

Please? When did Laban ever use that word? It bordered on begging, and Laban was no beggar.

Zoram turned his head to keep from staring at Laban's bloodied clothing. "Did you meet with the Elders?"

"The food was very good."

"And the wine?"

"I didn't drink."

That was odd. His clothes smelled of wine.

"Get the plates and follow me." There was a slight trembling in Laban's voice. He said, "Do as I say, would you?"

Zoram walked down between the shelves to the vault and waited beside the sealed door for Laban to get out his key and unlock the vault door. Zoram said, "Do you have the key, sir?"

"Key?"

"Around your neck."

The chain wasn't long enough to fit over Laban's helmet, and he said, "Haven't you another?"

What a strange question. "That's the only one."

Laban searched for a latch in the chain, but there was no other way to remove the key other than take off his helmet. He slowly removed the headpiece, the dim light of the treasury lamps casting a soft orange glow over his face. There was something different about his appearance, but beyond the blood sprayed across his high cheeks, it was impossible to tell exactly what. His long hair fell down past his ears, and he pulled it back before nestling the helmet beneath his arm and slowly removing the key.

"Is there something wrong, sir?" Zoram said in answer to Laban's staring.

"Nothing's wrong." The captain blinked twice and placed the helmet under his other arm. He wiped his sleeve across his mouth, smearing the blood over his lips. "Nothing at all, thank you."

It was an oddly cordial exchange from a man he'd come to expect as nothing short of ill-tempered. It wasn't until Laban handed over the blood-stained vault key that Zoram spotted the difference in Laban's look. It was his eyes—they were clear and bright, and they responded to every word Zoram spoke.

Zoram unlocked the vault, leaned inside and slipped the final brass plates into place without Laban seeing, and then he was done. His part in preparing the record was complete, and he could leave whatever happened to the plates to the will of God.

They left the vault door open and climbed the steps to the back entrance of the treasury. The door was sealed, but the guards were gone—all of them pressed into the search for Laban.

Zoram said, "They're off looking for you, sir."

"Let them look." Laban stepped out into the night. "And leave the treasury unlocked."

It was an odd request, with so much wealth besides the relics still guarded below. Zoram covered the brass relic with a red cloth and carried it as he'd been taught—stretched out in front of him on both hands. He followed Laban out the abandoned back gate and down Milo Hill, then west across the city toward the middle gate. Torches moved about the streets, and the call of soldiers searching for Captain Laban filled the night.

Laban avoided the patrols, stepping into an alleyway to let two soldiers pass. There were the actions of a guilty man, and Zoram should have called to the soldiers to come take his master, but he held his tongue. How could he betray Laban? He was sworn to obey the man, not pass judgment on him.

Zoram followed close behind Laban, and when they reached the middle gate, the solitary soldier standing guard jumped from his stoop. There were no torches burning at the entrance, and in the pale light of the moon, the man couldn't see the blood that covered Laban's hands and stained his clothes. He turned his gaze over the cloth-covered relic in Zoram's hands before coming back to Laban. He said, "Captain, sir."

Laban said, "I have a meeting with the Elders."

"Tonight?" The watchman's glance flitted between Laban and the city gate. "Out there?"

"Let us pass, soldier."

The watchman stepped aside, and Zoram followed the captain outside the walls of the city.

Daniel left his men searching the streets and turned up Milo Hill toward the estate. There was a chance Laban had returned home and they could end their searching. Of all the nights to let the captain out of his sight, why tonight? Daniel had taken every precaution these past four weeks. There wasn't a door or gate at the estate he hadn't secured, a maidservant he hadn't interrogated, or a watch he hadn't doubled. No one could get near Laban without first surrendering their weapons to Daniel, and as soon as he found the captain he was going to insist he return to the estate and wait out the entire feast day under close watch. Daniel was to the top steps when the light of his torch played across the cobblestones. There was a trace of blood on the path, and the stains led down a narrow alley and up a rise. Daniel turned past the first gate and found a naked beggar lying against the wall. Blood pooled on the ground around him, and Daniel walked the torch closer to see—

Laban? Daniel dropped the torch in a spray of sparks. The captain lay in his own blood. His chest was without breath, and when Daniel took the captain by the shoulder to lift him from the cobblestone, his head fell back, half severed and hanging by the thick skin of his neck. Daniel let go, and Laban's body fell limp on the stones. He'd failed to protect the man who'd given him everything. Curse whoever did this! Daniel removed his cape and laid it over Laban's body.

Curse him to death!

Jeremiah lay on a bed of straw in the corner of the upper prison below a small air vent in the ceiling, waiting for the sound of the morning *shofar* horns to announce the arrival of the feast. The guards assigned to him stood a few paces off, leaning against the wall and waiting for the night to pass and their watch to end.

The prison doors pushed open, and Daniel stepped inside ahead of Ebed-Melech.

Daniel said, "Did he speak to anyone?"

The first guard said, "He hasn't moved from this spot all day, Lieutenant. Says he's waiting for the judgments of God to come."

Daniel walked a slow circle around Jeremiah. "Did he have contact with anyone?"

"No one."

"Laban's dead and his relics stolen." Daniel spit on the ground next to Jeremiah. "You cursed him to this."

Jeremiah stared up into the ceiling like a man searching the sky. He said, "Men reap what they sow."

"You have yet to see the whirlwind." Daniel marched from the prison, and when he was gone, Jeremiah slowly stood. He said, "I must see the sky."

"It's late." Ebed took him by the arm. "Why don't you sleep?"

"I won't sleep." Jeremiah pulled free of Ebed's grasp. "Not until I see the sky tonight."

"You can't leave the prison. Not tonight. Not after this. Daniel already suspects you in Captain Laban's death."

"Look at me." Jeremiah stood in his tattered robes, his thin legs barely able to support his frail frame. "Could I ever hope to escape?"

"If they catch you outside the prison, they'll likely kill you."

"For one brief moment, I beg of you, let me look into the sky."

"The sky will be there another day."

Jeremiah started for the prison door, but Ebed wrapped his powerful arms around him and held him back. "I can't let you."

Jeremiah struggled to get free. "I will see the heavens."

"Why must you be so difficult?"

Jeremiah stopped struggling, and Ebed released his hold on the prophet. He said, "The heavens with all their planets and stars and the revolutions of this earth are a great timepiece. I must look into the sky and know for myself that the time appointed to preserve the records of the covenant is come."

Where was Nephi?

Aaron stood on the sloping bank of the ravine just off the road, watching for any sign of his return. He'd been gone nearly an hour and still no sign of him. The potsherd letter written by Rebekah hung from his hand, and he angled it to the moonlight, the ink outlining her reconciliation to Jonathan. Aaron ran his fingers over the rough surface. He didn't come all this way only to fail to get his father's blessing in the matter of his proposal of marriage to Rebekah, but he couldn't go inside the city without word of the outcome of Nephi's desperate final attempt to get the plates.

"Get down, someone's coming." Sam pulled on Aaron's arm. The outline of a shadowy figured appeared on the road. He carried a sword in one hand; the plume of a feather rose up from the helmet on his head, and a second man walked a few paces behind.

Aaron and Sam quietly retreated down the ravine to where Laman and Lemuel stood with the horses, but when the soldier started down the slope after them, Sam ordered them to ride away. Aaron jumped onto Beuntahyu's back and reined about to see the soldier quickly descending the slope with his companion kicking up the loose dirt behind him. He reined Beuntahyu through a stand of scrub oak. Sam followed, pulling Nephi's horse with him, and Laman and Lemuel reined in behind him. They cleared the ravine and came onto the road when the soldier's voice pierced the night, telling them it was Nephi, their brother. Aaron came around to see him remove his helmet and wave it in the air, and immediately his companion turned and ran for the city gate.

Nephi threw down his helmet and sword and ran after him, diving to catch him, the two of them rolling on the dusty road. Aaron galloped over with Sam, Laman, and Lemuel, reining into a circle around them.

Nephi pinned the man to the ground and said, "As the Lord lives and as I live, if you'll listen to me, I'll spare your life."

There was no reason for Nephi to utter such a binding oath. The man couldn't escape with Nephi's powerful arms wrapped around him like a tight cord. He could have sworn an oath on the moon shining overhead, or on the stones in the road, or on the strength of his arm. That's what he should have said—by the strength of his hand if the man would listen, his life would be spared. But Nephi swore the most sacred oath of all, a covenant that could never be broken even on the pain of death. There was no oath more holy to a faithful Jew than *ha Elohim*— an oath sworn before God—and the man immediately stopped his struggle against Nephi's hold, stood under his own power and turned around, and in the faint light of the moon, Aaron could see the white-turbaned head, the straight white teeth, and the uncertain gaze of . . ."

"Zoram?" Aaron got down from the saddle. "Is it really you?

Zoram's gaze flitted between the men surrounding him before coming back to Nephi and saying, "As the Lord liveth?"

"I gave you my solemn word. You have no reason to fear us." Nephi reached for the brass record, but Zoram curled his body around the codex. He said, "Are you the ones? The ones my father said would come tonight?"

Aaron said, "Your father knew about us?"

Nephi said, "You can be a free man like us. Free of Captain Laban and his—"

"What did you do to the royal family?" Zoram pressed the plates to his chest. "Where's Captain Laban?"

"Your master is dead."

"Dead?"

Nephi picked the blood-soaked helmet out of the dust. "I killed him."

"You did what?" Laman reined around in front of Nephi. "You'll bring the wrath of the entire army down on us. Did you ever think of that?"

"I wasn't seen by anyone."

A legion of torch-bearing soldiers poured out of the city on foot, running down the rampart toward them. Laman said, "No one?"

"My father said you'd come for this tonight on the holiest feast day of the year." Zoram handed the brass relic to Nephi. "The feast when all Jews beg God to awaken to a remembrance of His covenants with Israel, and when Israel awakens to a remembrance of their covenants with God."

Nephi said, "Then you'll come with us into the wilderness and be a free man and have place with us there?"

The cry of soldiers filled the night. Zoram said, "I have few other choices."

"Mount up." Laman came around in the road. "We ride into the desert."

Zoram said, "What about Elizabeth?"

Aaron swung down from Beuntahyu and handed the reins to Zoram. "I'll speak with her."

The soldiers were halfway down the road, their cries growing louder with each passing moment, the light of their torches penetrating the shadows around them.

"Go with them in peace." Aaron helped Zoram up into the saddle. "They'll watch over you."

Nephi sidled in next to Aaron. "What are you doing?"

"I have a letter to deliver. I'll join you as soon as I can."

Zoram said, "Tell Elizabeth I'll come for her."

"I will." Aaron slapped Beuntahyu on the flank and sent her and Zoram galloping into the night, but before they were out of earshot he said, "Tell Rebekah I love her."

Daniel knelt on the dusty road with his men gathered around him. He held a torch over the place where a single set of footprints diverged from the tracks of four horses. The animals were headed out into the flats south of Jerusalem, and he said, "I want these riders followed. They're likely accomplices." He started down the narrow road into the cheese maker's valley, and one of the soldiers said, "Where are you going, sir?"

"Whoever killed Captain Laban knew him well enough to find him on a dark street." Daniel pulled up on the side of the ridge, and before descending to the valley floor he said, "I'm going after Laban's murderer."

Aaron circled the city to the east gate. It stood open without any watchmen standing guard and no soldiers walking along the catwalks above the entrance—all of them gone searching for the man who killed Captain Laban and stole his relics. There was no one to see him enter the city, and he sprinted up the rise out of the ravine and ducked inside the gate. A troop of soldiers were searching the plaza, and Aaron slipped past them in the shadows and ran down Water Street to his home in the Lower City. The gate was locked, and he climbed over the wall and lowered himself into the courtyard of his home. He was safe here, and he wrapped his fingers around the potsherd letter. Finally he could present to his father what he came back to the city to deliver.

The windows on the first floor were shuttered with only the light of a solitary lamp shining through the wooden slats of the kitchen window. Aaron tried the latch on the front door, but it was locked, and he stepped back to call to the windows on the second floor. But before he could raise his voice, a man leaped over the wall and ran at him, tackling him to the ground, the two of them rolling across the courtyard stones and up against the large water cistern. The attacker came over on top, his body pinning Aaron down. His good eye was filled with a wild light, and immediately Aaron recognized the fierce manner and powerful frame of his brother.

"Murderer!" Daniel swung his fist, the pain shooting through Aaron's jaw and the blow smashing his head against the stones. Daniel cursed him for letting him believe he was dead, cursed him for coming back to take revenge on Captain Laban, and told him he'd rot in the depths of hell for stealing the man's relics. He swung his fist again, landing the blow across Aaron's nose. He cursed him for blinding him in his left eye and causing him to wear a black patch, and then he swung his fist again, this time landing three blows over Aaron's left eye.

Blood clouded Aaron's vision, and he tried to fend off Daniel's blows with his arms, but he couldn't see the blur of fists coming at him, pummeling his face with painful blows and crushing his skull. Two more hit his chin, and another slammed across his cheekbone, shattering it with stinging pain. Aaron felt his body go limp, but before his mind fell into unconsciousness he could see the outline of Daniel standing above him, the moonlight silhouetting his frame. He spit on Aaron, kicked his side and said he was going to fetch the elders of the Jews to come see Captain Laban's murderer before they beheaded him, and then he disappeared out the gate. Aaron tried to lean up on his elbow, but the crushed bones and the loss of blood unbalanced him, and he fell back against the courtyard stones.

The starry sky went dark.

Jonathan the blacksmith sat up in bed, and the blanket fell from his chest. He peered across the darkness of the second-floor bedroom, his ear turned to the distant cry filtering up from the main floor of the house.

Ruth stirred next to him and softly said, "What is it, dear?"

"Go back to sleep." Jonathan pulled back the blanket and set his bare feet onto the clay floor, his toes feeling for the sandals next to his bed. "I'll be back in a moment."

Jonathan draped a cloak over his shoulders and turned down the hall to Elizabeth and Sarah's room. The girls were sleeping soundly, and when he checked the next room the steady sound of little Joshua's breathing filled the darkness. He'd heard an agonizing cry—like a ghost calling in the night—but the children were fine, and he walked to the end of the hall and leaned over the railing at the top of the stairs. There was nothing stirring in the kitchen below. The embers in the hearth were burned down, the front door was locked, and the lamp Ruth left burning day and night on the kitchen windowsill was still flickering in front of the wood shutters, casting a dim glow over the kitchen table. There was no reason to be up and about checking the house. He'd gotten out of bed over nothing more than—

A muffled groan filled the night air. It streamed inside from the courtyard, and Jonathan slowly descended the stairs to the kitchen, pushed open the shutters, and leaned out. There was no movement among the olive trees growing up in the yard, there was no thief stealing fruit from the grape arbors along the far wall, and when the milking goat bawled from inside the small animal stable on the other side of the yard there was no doubt about the source of the odd cry. The poor goat was ready to be milked well before morning.

Jonathan pulled the shutters closed and started back to bed when he heard another low, rasping groan coming from the other side of the yard, opposite the manger. It was not the cry of a goat, and he snatched the lamp from the sill and walked it out into the courtyard. The light rested on the form of a man lying on the ground. His face was bloodied, and his left was eye swollen shut. It was like the pool of blood on that smelting day three years earlier when Jonathan had returned to the shop to find Aaron.

Jonathan fell to his knees beside the fallen form. He had the same long-legged, thin stature as his dead son, the same straight, brown hair, and when he held the lamp closer, he could see the swollen face of Aaron. Jonathan lifted the boy's shoulders off the ground, cradling him in his arms. "Son, is it you?"

Aaron opened his mouth and tried to speak, but he didn't have the strength to form the words, and Jonathan brushed back the bloody strands of hair from Aaron's eyes and ran his fingers lightly over the brow of the boy's fractured skull.

"For you." A fresh line of blood streamed from the gash above Aaron's eyes. He held a potsherd in his trembling hands, and Jonathan carefully took it from his grip. The words were inked in a dark flowing script. It was addressed to him, written by Rebekah, the daughter of Josiah the potter. The greeting was respectful, the words carefully chosen, telling Jonathan of her love for Aaron and begging him to arrange their marriage.

Jonathan said, "You suffered all this to ask my blessing?"

Aaron wrapped his bloodied fingers around the potsherd and managed to say, "Please, Father?"

"Who did this to you?"

Aaron's face twisted with pain, and he clenched his teeth before taking a deep breath and softly whispering, "Daniel."

"No." Jonathan began rocking back and forth, gently holding Aaron's body close to him, the blood of his eldest son staining his robe. This wasn't Daniel's doing; it couldn't be. Daniel was an honorable soldier, the second in command of Captain Laban's military, and he wouldn't dishonor his station by harming his brother, no matter how much they disagreed on the matter of Lehi the prophet.

The door to the house swung open, and Ruth hurried out, wrapping a shawl over her shoulders. "Jonathan?"

"Stay back."

"What is it?"

"Go inside and get a clean cloth." Jonathan put out the lamp to keep it from lighting Aaron's face and allowing Ruth to see the horrible wounds. He lifted Aaron from the stones, the boy's limp body hanging from his arms. "I'm going to need a pot of warm water and ointments for this man."

"For whom?"

"Get the bandages."

Ruth stepped close enough to see the hideousness of Aaron's bloodied face, and immediately she went still, her hand over her mouth and her head slowly shaking. "Tell me it isn't . . ."

"I told you to heat some water."

"Dear God of heaven, not like this." Ruth fell to her knees, her hand reaching out for Aaron's limp body. "Don't bring him back to us like this."

"Papa?" Elizabeth ran out the door, tying the sash around her sleeping robe. Her voice stirred Aaron to lift his head off Jonathan's arms enough to say, "Elizabeth. I'm sorry. Zoram is gone."

"No." Elizabeth ran to his side. "Oh, Aaron."

The sound of a crowd gathering at the top of the street echoed down past their home. Torches lighted the sky, the orange glow moving quickly from the Upper City toward their gate. And above the din, they could hear Daniel's voice telling his men that Captain Laban's murderer lay in the courtyard of the blacksmith's property.

Murderer? Jonathan's arms strained under the weight of Aaron's limp body. It wasn't possible. He didn't have the disposition to harm anyone. This had to be an awful mistake. The boy may have sided with Lehi when he shouldn't have, but he was no murderer.

The orange light of the torches turned down the last run toward their gate, the windows of the homes across the street brightened with lamps, and the neighbors next door leaned out their windows to see the coming of the soldiers to the blacksmith's home.

Ruth laid her trembling hands on Aaron's chest. "What has become of my sons?"

"Oh, Mama." Elizabeth held Ruth close.

Jonathan said, "Get the children, both of you."

"Not out here." Ruth raised her tear-streaked face. "I won't bring them out to hear this."

"Do as I say."

Elizabeth said, "What about Aaron?"

"You never saw him, do you hear? Aaron is dead."

Jonathan carried Aaron's unconscious body to the stable near the back of the courtyard and laid him in the dark enclosure. He covered the boy with a thick layer of hay and set the goat in among the freshly placed straw before hurrying back across the courtyard. He tipped over the cistern and let the rush of water clean away the blood, carrying it between the cracks in the stones, leaving the courtyard wet, but clear of any sign of Aaron's brutal beating.

Daniel rattled the gate on the pivot stones and pounded on the planks, announcing that the Chief Elder had arrived. He said, "Open this gate or I'll tear it down."

Jonathan lifted the latch, and Daniel burst past, leading Zadock and a troop of torch-bearing soldiers inside. The Chief Elder was dressed in the formal black vestments of a feast-day celebration with the white and black shawls of his office streaming down over his shoulders and the gold amulet hanging at his chest.

Daniel searched the wet stones of the courtyard with his torch. "Where is he?"

Jonathan said, "Where is who, son?"

Daniel paced the length of the courtyard. "I left him right here."

The door to the house creaked open, and Ruth appeared holding Sarah and Joshua by the hand, with Elizabeth following behind. Her gaze shifted quickly between Jonathan and the soldiers before she said, "What's going on here?"

Jonathan said, "These men are searching for an intruder."

Daniel said, "We're looking for Aaron."

Little Joshua spoke in a thin, young voice. "Aaron's dead."

"You know that." Ruth stepped her children closer to Daniel. "He's been gone for a good many months."

"I followed him to this courtyard." Daniel raised his bloody fist. "I beat him with my own hands."

Zadock spoke in a rasping voice. "You won't mind if we search your home?"

Ruth said, "And why would you want to do such a thing?"

"Captain Laban was murdered tonight, and the robber who killed him stole his royal relics."

Ruth let out a forced gasp, and Elizabeth lowered her head.

Daniel said, "That's right. Aaron's a robber. He was biding his time, hiding in the hill country or in the deserts, waiting to come back to the city and avenge Captain Laban's arrow."

Zadock motioned toward the house. "Do you mind, blacksmith?"

"Aaron and Captain Laban's relics aren't inside. There isn't anyone in the house."

"We should hope not." Zadock motioned for the soldiers to draw their swords and go inside. "Aiding a robber is a crime worthy of death."

Ebed allowed Jeremiah to lead him out of the prison and into the cool breezes of early morning before dawn. A loud flurry of trumpets filled the sky over Jerusalem announcing the arrival of the Day of Remembrance and calling Jews to petition God to remember His covenants made with Israel. The palace gardens were quiet, but Jeremiah insisted they go into the streets beyond the gates.

Ebed said, "They're filled with soldiers."

"I must see the sky."

Ebed peered up past the palace walls rising five stories above them. "Can't you see it from here?"

"Not that sky." Jeremiah started toward the side gates along the far side of the palace grounds, his weak stride growing stronger with each step. "The skies over the southern deserts."

Lamps lighted the windows of every home in the city, the stir from last night's deeds still spreading through Jerusalem. They stayed in the less-traveled walkways and narrow stone alleys to avoid the soldiers dispatched along the main thoroughfares, but when they started onto a secluded path in the Lower City, a troop of men turned the corner, and Ebed pulled Jeremiah back into the deeply recessed doorway of a bakery. Military orders echoed off the stone facades and over the cobblestones, all of it focused on Captain Laban's murder and the theft of his royal brass-plate relic and his ancient sword. The national treasures were gone, and the murderer who stole them was still hiding somewhere in the city. The soldiers passed the darkened stoop where Ebed and Jeremiah hid, their leader rattling off a description of the perpetrator of the crime. The guilty man had sandy brown hair grown well past his ears. He was thin of girth, tall in stature, and was likely suffering bouts of confusion from a crushed skull. He was last seen with a bloodied face and open wounds above both eyes and across his jaw. The murderer answered to the name of Aaron the blacksmith, and if they found him they were to kill him on sight. The soldier raised his voice and said, "Long live the memory of Captain Laban."

Ebed waited until the soldiers turned out of sight before leaving the safety of the doorway. Impossible. The son of the blacksmith was dead, and these men were fooling themselves if they thought Aaron's ghost had power to—

"It isn't impossible, my friend." Jeremiah laid his hand on Ebed's shoulder. "Nothing is impossible when God sets about to do His work."

They doubled back three times across Water Street until Ebed was certain they weren't followed, then turned down toward the south wall in the farthest reaches of the city. Of all the watchtowers protecting Jerusalem, none rose as high or provided as expansive a view as the south wall. It reached more than a hundred cubits above the valley floor. The high stoops and narrow catwalks stood abandoned without any guards watching from the parapets—all of them pressed into service hunting for the man with the stolen brass-plate relic. Jeremiah scaled the worn steps to the top, and Ebed followed. It was far too early for the sun to light the sky, but an unearthly glow moved across the southern horizon, and inside the eerie cloud of light Ebed thought he could see a heavenly army. He rubbed his eyes and squinted up into the night, but he couldn't rid himself of the image. It grew larger and brighter and then faded back into the horizon before returning brighter than before, the vision of legions of angels moving across the sky like a royal army headed south into the deserts across the borders of Israel, then on to the Red Sea and points beyond.

"What is this?" Ebed leaned over the edge of the stone railing. "What is it I'm seeing?"

Jeremiah's gaze slowly moved across the horizon. "Isn't it marvelous?"

"What's the meaning of this?"

"A marvelous work is about to come forth. Even a marvelous work and a wonder."

"A work?"

"When you pulled me from the well of the prison, I told you God gave Moses a vision of the great time-keeping orbits and revolutions of the planets in the heavens. Do you remember?"

Ebed nodded. "I thought you had lost your mind."

Jeremiah stood next to Ebed, both of them peering up at the scene in the skies over the southern deserts—the endless heavenly legions marching into the wilderness. He began to speak in a low voice with the same steady cadence Ebed remembered hearing on that night twenty-eight days earlier when Jeremiah insisted the brass-plate record was to be taken from the city and copied by another prophet into a record fashioned on plates of gold.

Jeremiah said, "In the last days, the covenant will be read upon the housetops, and all things shall be revealed unto the children of men that ever have been among them and that ever will be, even unto the end of the earth."

Another round of trumpeting heralded over the city, rising up from the temple grounds, but it didn't slow Jeremiah's words. His voice grew stronger, and he lifted his hands from the stone railing as he spoke, telling Ebed that the heavens with all their planets and stars and the revolutions of this earth were a great timepiece, more accurate than the most precise water clock. And hidden in the calendar revealed to Moses was the appointed day for the record of the covenants to come forth in the fullness of times.

Jeremiah pointed to the skies over the southern deserts. "Tonight God begins to remember His covenants with Israel."

CHAPTER 35

Ten Days Later
Valley of Lemuel (Wadi Tayyib al-Ism)

Sariah's sons were dead. That's why they hadn't returned. Sariah nestled her newborn Jacob against her side and slowly scaled the narrow trail winding up the side of the red rock canyon from camp to the ledge overlooking the wadi. Lehi was up there preparing the altar to make an offering and pass the Day of Atonement in a proper way. She could hear him replacing fallen stones, the sound of rock on rock breaking the morning stillness. The sun wasn't high enough to warm the canyon, and the deep shadows darkened the trail. She pulled the blanket tight around the head of her newborn son. He nestled his head against her side, pursed his lips, and then faded back to sleep. Oh how she loved this boy—she loved all her boys—and losing any of them had power to wound her soul beyond healing.

It wasn't weakness from fasting that filled her with a lingering fear. This new babe needed nourishment from a strong mother, and going without food was not something she dared risk. Ten days had passed since they celebrated the birth of this child—more than enough time for her sons to return, and there was simply no room in her heart for making penance on this Day of Atonement and renewing her covenant to live free of sin. How could she when she was filled with so much doom? Sariah reached the last turn in the trail and came around onto the ledge above camp. The wadi below stood quiet—there was no sound of horses galloping into the camp or the call of her boys hailing their return.

Nothing but a gentle breeze filtered through the fronds of the date palms along the banks of the river below.

"Are the men awake? Moriah? Hagoth? Setti? Yaush?" Lehi stepped in next to her. "I'm going to need two goats from the herd."

Lehi was dressed in a white linen, ready to perform the day's ceremonies just as he did on every Day of Atonement at Beit Zayit. He always selected the finest two goats—one for a sin offering on the altar and the other for a scapegoat to release into the desert to carry away their sins. But that was when they lived in a fine house with servants to help with the meals, when there was a herd as large as any at Jerusalem, and their family was safely gathered around to enjoy the breaking of a fast with wine and fresh breads and basted lamb from the altar. Sariah brushed another tear from her cheek. Would she ever celebrate another Day of Atonement together with her family, or were they doomed to be separated for the rest of their lives? Her two oldest daughters, Rachel and Leah, were living safely with their husbands, Nathan and Seth— the oldest sons of Ishmael—at Beit Zayit, and for that she was mildly grateful. But what of Laman, Lemuel, Sam, and Nephi? The pain of losing any of them was too much to bear, and losing all of them had power to still her heart. She lowered her face into the infant's blanket.

"Sariah?" Lehi touched her shoulder. "You need more rest."

She didn't. What she needed was her family. All of them safely gathered in and celebrating this High Holy Day together. Instead they were dying in a forsaken wilderness, or hunted by a madman, or . . .

She couldn't bring herself to think it. How could she ever imagine her sons murdered?

"Jacob kept you up during the night again." Lehi reached for the infant. She resisted at first, but finally relented and let him take the boy in his arms. He said, "I'll watch him for a time."

"Who's going to watch over our other children?"

Lehi slowly rocked Jacob. "They're on God's errand."

Sariah pressed her hand to her mouth to hold back her swirling emotions. The dream of her sons returning to fetch Captain Laban's brass plates was a distant memory, pushed to the side by a rush of fears. Had she lost her sons? Could she endure the weariness of mothering a newborn in this wilderness? And what of the constant worry of their fate in this unforgiving desert? The dream she shared with Lehi was faint enough that the vividness of the vision was gone. She'd forgotten the warmth of the spirit that accompanied it, and lost to her memory was the sound of the still, small voice of heaven whispering that her sons would be protected by the hand of God.

Sariah said, "They've perished because of your dream."

Lehi said, "You dreamed the same dream."

"I wish I never had."

"Sariah." Lehi reached for her hand. "If I'd not seen the things of God in a vision I would never have known the goodness of God. I know that the Lord will deliver my sons out of the hands of Laban and bring them down again unto us in the wilderness."

"Is there no room for reason in your thinking?" Sariah's shoulders rose and fell to the rhythm of a quiet sob, and between her tears she said, "Must you always be a visionary man?"

Lehi reached for her, but she turned down the path, leaving him to tend Jacob. She hurried over the winding trail to the valley floor, through the cool waters of the river to the corral, and herded a goat out the gate. Her harshness wasn't meant for Lehi, but somehow the frustration of so many fears spilled out of her in a rush of terrible words. She shooed the goat higher up the valley towards the open sands of the main wadi and let it find its way among the sagebrush— the animal bearing away the sin of her indiscretion. She never should have used Lehi as her scapegoat, blaming her fears and faithlessness on him. She'd seen a vision. The same vision Lehi saw in his dream. Did not God speak to her soul, telling her to have her sons bring the covenant-laden brass plates down into this wilderness? Sariah chased the goat out onto the main run of the wadi and stood on the rocky entrance to their secluded valley, the same outcrop where she watched Nephi disappear on his quest to find the mountain of the Lord where Moses received the covenants. The goat ran off into sands, but before it disappeared in the distance, she offered the only prayer of penance that came to her heart on this Day of Atonement.

Dear Lord, forgive my unbelief.

Five Days Later
Valley of Lemuel (Wadi Tayyib al-Ism)

Lehi stood in the door of his tent, the flaps tied back and the door facing east in preparation for celebrating the first day of the week-long Feast of Tabernacles. He held little Jacob in his arms and let the infant reach for his fingers. It was the boy's first celebration of this ingathering feast, but how could they celebrate without the rest of the family? This should be a festive day at the end of the harvest. They'd gathered a good supply of wild wheat and oats from the grains growing up along the river bed. They had more than enough dates and figs sealed away in pots fired by Josiah the potter with help from his daughter Rebekah. The river had never stopped flowing even in the hottest, driest months of the year, but Lehi still insisted they collect a good supply of fresh water in cisterns, in case of drought. They had stored tubers and roots in burlap sacks, and Lehi had speared a good many freshwater fish in the large pools at the bottom of the river where it emptied into the fountain of the Red Sea, and these too were dried and stored away. This was the season of ingathering, and this Feast of Tabernacles marked the end of the harvest, but all was not safely gathered in.

Sariah sat on an outcrop of rocks just outside the tent, preparing the dough for flat bread. She caught Lehi's gaze and offered a resolute smile before turning back to her breadmaking, slowly pressing the dough with a rolling stone. In the five days since telling Lehi of her sorrow, she'd gone from distress to grief, and had finally surrendered to the possibility that their sons might never return. They didn't speak of it again, but their mutual sadness filled the camp with heaviness that would not disperse, and if not for their willingness to submit to the will of heaven, it would have been impossible to consider celebrating the feast with any sort of muted joy. If only his sons had returned.

"They're home!" Rebekah ran through the date palms and pushed through the river without lifting the skirts of her robe out of the water. She came up the rise to camp at full sprint and jumped over the outcrops, taking Sariah by both hands and standing her on her feet. She faced her toward the mouth of the canyon and said, "See there." Through the date palms, the distant movement of horses descended into the valley. "The white horse must be Beuntahyu. And there's Nephi and the others." She held Sariah close. "They've come home to us."

Lehi joined them, and they stood arm-in-arm waiting for the riders to come into camp. Laman was first up the rise, followed by Lemuel, Sam, and then Nephi. Zoram sidled in next to them, riding on the back of Beuntahyu.

"Aaron?" Rebekah leaned forward. "Where's Aaron?"

"He didn't come back." Nephi slowly slid out of the saddle and stood next to her. "He had to deliver a letter to his father."

"No." Rebekah lowered her head into Sariah's shoulder. "I never should have asked him to do it."

"Not to worry, dear." Sariah stroked her head. "He'll come back to us."

Zoram retrieved a bundle wrapped in a red silk cloth from his saddlebags and walked it over to Lehi, holding it out like a priest making an offering. He said, "This is for you, sir."

Laman, Lemuel, Sam, and Nephi got down from their horses, and Setti, Moriah, Yaush, Josiah, Hagoth, and Sophia gathered from across the camp to listen to them recount the miracle of getting the brass plates. The fires for making an offering for the Feast of Tabernacles were already kindled, and Lehi placed an offering on the altar, letting the smoke rise up into the heavens. And with his family gathered around, he offered a prayer for the Feast of Tabernacles, thanking God for bringing their sons safely home. Sariah stood beside him with little Jacob in her arms. She wiped a tear from her eyes before saying, "Now I know that the Lord has commanded my husband to flee into the wilderness." She smiled at Lehi, and he nodded back. "And I also know that the Lord has protected my sons." She placed her hand on Nephi's shoulder. "And delivered them out of the hands of Laban, and given them power to accomplish the thing which the Lord commanded them."

Lehi left the family celebration. He sat down inside the entrance of his open tent and slowly removed the silk covering from the brass plates. They were strung together on three metal rings, and he ran his fingers over the name Joseph, Viceroy of Egypt—the man who began this codex of plates. The first four plates detailed Joseph's life in Egypt and his prophecies of the last days when another Joseph would rise up to bring to light this ancient history. There was an accounting of the allegory of the olive tree by the ancient prophet Zenos, something written by Enoch, a few more plates written by Noah and Abraham, and then an account written by . . .

Moses? Lehi leaned over the record. The name was inscribed in the square, rigid characters of the ancient prophet's hand, declaring that this portion of the record was made in the deserts of Midian at the base of Mount Horeb—the same deserts where Lehi sat reading from this brass record. It began with an account of what was revealed to Moses atop Sinai, and it reminded Israel that this earth was a secluded planet in the far reaches of heaven, far removed from the presence of God, designed by the Creator as a place for proving the faith of His children. Lehi held his finger on the phrase. That was the purpose of this earth, it said so here near the end of the thirteenth plate. Moses wrote that it was the work and glory of God to bring to pass the immortality and eternal life of man.

The next plate was aged more than the others, the years of neglect collecting on the metal surface in a black, tarnished hue, and when the sunlight angled over the carefully etched Hebrew it revealed the genealogy of Captain Laban's family, beginning with Joseph who was sold into Egypt, followed by his sons Ephraim and Manasseh, then to their sons and on through the kings of Israel down to Captain Laban's great-grandfather, Hoshea, the last king of the Northern Kingdom, who escaped the fall of Samaria and brought his sons to Jerusalem, where they were granted asylum and property in the Upper City— property that was to be left to the oldest son of . . .

This couldn't be right. Lehi ran his finger down through the list of names until he came to the last one in the genealogy. Laban wasn't listed as the last living descendant of the eldest son of the king of the Northern Kingdom, and in the bright light of day Lehi slowly read the name of the man who was heir to the throne with an inheritance that included the brass plates. Could it be? Were Lehi's fathers the keepers of this record since the days of Joseph who was sold into Egypt?

"What is it, dear?" Sariah stepped into the tent and touched his shoulder.

"These plates." Lehi reached for her hand. "I never presumed such a thing."

"What thing?"

"These words will never perish, neither will they be dimmed by time." Lehi stood next to her and with a rush of inspiration flowing into his mind he said, "They'll go to all nations, kindreds, tongues, and people."

Sariah reached down and turned the record to the last plate. It was newer than most of the others, the metal bright like copper, without tarnish, and the letters sharp, without any of the smooth edges that come with the wearing of time. They were the words of Jeremiah the prophet quoting Isaiah, and together they silently read the last line in the record: *For behold, a marvelous work is about to come forth among the children of men.*

Even a marvelous work and a wonder.

HISTORICAL NOTES

Author's Note: *Day of Remembrance* is a split novel based on two major historical events. The first follows the events leading up to the return of Nephi and his brothers to Jerusalem in search of the brass-plate record as recorded in the opening chapters of the Book of Mormon. The second follows the events surrounding the coming forth of the Book of Mormon as recorded by the Prophet Joseph Smith in his history found in the Pearl of Great Price. These two stories are tied together by the historical and religious significance of the Feast of Trumpets celebrated on the Jewish holy day known as the Day of Remembrance. The story, settings, and, in some instances, the plot lines were developed from historical research of the period. Though it is impossible to review all the sources that contributed to the preparation of this novel, the following notes summarize the historical basis for elements in these stories.

CHAPTER ONE

Both Ebed-Melech and Jeremiah are historical characters mentioned in the Old Testament. The old jailer is a secondary fictional character who remains unnamed. Ebed was of Ethiopian descent. The Old Testament records that he had close contact with the prophet Jeremiah while in prison and may have been assigned to look after or even guard the prophet while he was imprisoned. We do know that he assisted in Jeremiah's removal from the well of the prison, defended him before the king, and succeeded in finding him more hospitable living conditions in the upper court of the prison, where he had access to his scribe, Baruch, and was able to continue recording his prophecies (see Jer. 38). Because of Ebed's role in the prison, he is characterized in this novel as the Chief Jailer.

* * * * *

The characterization of the prophet Jeremiah and the dialogue attributed to him was taken from his writings in the Old Testament. Jeremiah's dialogue regarding the revolution of the planets is based on the revelations found in Jeremiah's Old Testament writings (see Jer. 31: 35–37) combined with statements on lunar, solar, and planetary observations revealed to Abraham (see Abr. 3:4–10) and Moses (see Moses 1:29–38) as recorded in the Pearl of Great Price, and also from Joseph Smith's revelations recorded in the Doctrine and Covenants. Jeremiah made important connections between the new covenant revealed in the last days, which Joseph Smith Jr. indicated was the Book of Mormon, and the Hebrew calendar, which is based on the yearly revolutions of the sun and the monthly phases of the moon (see Jer. 31:33–37). The Babylonians and other Gentile neighbor nations observed their own holy days and calculated their dating based on a solar calendar much different than that used by the Israelites of Lehi's day.

* * * * *

The calendar used in most modern societies today is solar-oriented, based on the observable yearly revolutions of the earth around the sun and the daily twenty-four-hour rotations of the earth on its axis. The Hebrew calendar adopted by Moses for use by ancient Israel (see Ex. 12:2; Rom. 3:2) is a solilunar calendar where the years are based on the movements of the earth around the sun and the length of each of its thirteen months, dictated by the phases of the moon. It functioned within ancient Israelite society, as it does today, as a means for calculating the dates on which sacred Israelite feasts were celebrated. Many Israelite feast dates appear to come from an era that predates Moses, and these dates were already in full use during the times of the patriarchs. The prescribed dates were likely passed on to Moses through the Enoch calendar. Jewish scholars, concerned about the accuracy of celebrating the sacred feasts on the proper date, use the Enoch calendar as a collaborative dating instrument to ensure precision. The Book of Enoch, an ancient text not included in the King James version of the Bible but believed to be an authentic ancient record, indicates that the Enoch calendar was given to the prophet Enoch by the angel Uriel. Astronomer John P. Pratt suggests that both the Enoch and Hebrew calendars provide correct dating, but they were intended for different purposes, and they work together as independent witnesses of God's divine timing of important religious and historical events (John P. Pratt, "Enoch Calendar: Another Witness of the Restoration," *Meridian Magazine,* August 5, 2002, 1). Dr. Pratt points out that God may be using the Enoch and Hebrew calendars as instruments for the dating of important religious occasions through timing events in ancient times with similarly themed modern events. Feast dates on the Hebrew calendar and sacred themes associated with specific dates on the Enoch calendar accurately predict events like the birth of Christ, important events during His life, His crucifixion, and the Resurrection. Restoration events in the history of The Church of Jesus Christ of Latter-day Saints are also predicted, including Joseph Smith's First Vision, the coming forth of the Book of Mormon, and the birth and death of the Prophet Joseph Smith. Pratt writes that, "Joseph Smith was born on Monday, 23 December 1805, which coincides with the Hebrew day marking the winter solstice, leading to the suggestion that it symbolized the return of the light of the gospel to a dark world. Thursday, 27 June 1844, the day on which the Prophet went 'like a lamb to the slaughter' (D&C 135:4), was one of four Hebrew days of atonement" (ibid.). The Law of Moses required priests to sacrifice two lambs every day, one in the morning and one in the afternoon (Num. 28:3–8). Because the Hebrew day begins around sunset, the morning sacrifice was near the meridian of the twenty-four-hour Hebrew day, and the afternoon sacrifice was near the end of the day. The morning sacrifice appears to have represented Jesus Christ, who would come in the meridian of time, and the afternoon lamb might well have symbolized the Prophet Joseph Smith, who came in the latter days and did "more, save Jesus only, for the salvation of men in this world, than any other man that ever lived in it" (D&C 135:3).

* * * * *

The Feast of Trumpets celebrated on the first day of the seventh month of the Hebrew calendar (1 Autumn on the Enoch Calendar) is not only a religiously themed day for repentance and redemption, but also a day for the making and renewing of covenants with God (Lenet

Hadley Read, "Joseph Smith's Receipt of the Plates and the Israelite Feast of Trumpets," *Journal of Book of Mormon Studies,* vol. 2, no. 2, Fall 1993, 110–20). This same covenant-making purpose for the feast is also one of the main purposes of the Book of Mormon, and in this chapter the prophet Jeremiah alludes to the important covenant-making purposes of the record when he quotes Isaiah (see Isa. 29:14), and also when he states that the covenant will be read upon the house-tops by the children of men (see 2 Ne. 27:11, 22). The ancient prophet Moroni wrote on the last metal plate of the ancient Book of Mormon record that its purpose was to bring modern peoples to a remembrance of the covenants made by their ancient ancestors in order to assist them in understanding the importance of making and keeping covenants with God.

* * * * *

The many calendars that grew out of ancient societies, and the emergence of the twenty-four-hour clock with its divisions of sixty one-minute periods have their beginnings in antiquity so ancient that there are few records of origin. The clock, as did most calendars, emerged over time from observations of planetary orbits by ancient astronomers, and, in the case of the Enoch and Hebrew calendars, by revelation given to ancient prophets. Priests in antiquity were often trained in astronomy to help them develop the skills of making precise dating measurements in order to declare when religious feasts were to be observed. The measuring of the passage of time may have originally developed out of the dating of prophesied events including the birth, mission, and ministry of Jesus Christ, the Fall of Adam, Noah's proph-esied flood, and numerous events in the Restoration of The Church of Jesus Christ of Latter-day Saints in the 1800s. Astronomer John Pratt writes, "It appears the Lord's signs and wonders were designed in detail to display in the heavens what men would chronicle on earth" ("Enoch Calendar: Another Witness of the Restoration," 1). In order for the movements of planets and other celestial bodies to be used as dating instruments for important future events, the precise dates of those events would have to have been known before the creation of the earth, and the orbits of other celestial bodies within view of earth would have to have been set at the time of their creation (see Abr. 3: 4–10). For example, the appearance of a new star at Christ's birth as prophesied in the Old Testament (Num. 24:17) is a celestial event that was likely calculated into the movement of a celestial body before the world was created. The use of planets, moons, stars, and other celestial bodies as instruments for dating and specifically calendaring important sacred events may be, in part, what God revealed to Abraham when He stated that "it is given unto thee to know the times of reckoning, and . . . the set time of the earth upon which thou standest, and the set time of the greater light which is set to rule the day, and the set time of the lesser light which is set to rule the night" (Abr. 3:6) (Pratt, "Enoch Calendar: Another Witness of the Restoration," 1).

CHAPTER TWO

The members of the Kessler and Weiss families are fictional characters, but the conditions under which they lived and the history of their lives was drawn from historical information of the time. Uprisings of Russian citizens disgruntled over taxation by the royal family often attacked and many times killed Jews hired to collect taxes and act as caretakers for government buildings in far-flung villages across the Russian empire. Prior to the opening of this novel, the Weiss family survivors fled to Jerusalem after an uprising killed the other members of the family. Hassidic males follow the Old Testament proscription against shaving the hair near the ears. Faithful Hassidic men wear an undergarment with the fringe ends of the shirt showing at the hip and tied with 613 knots as a reminder of the covenants recorded in Jewish religious texts. Moses commanded Israel that, "Ye shall not round the corners of your heads, neither shalt thou mar the corners of thy beard" (Lev. 19:27). Orthodox Jews today interpret that injunction as a command for men not to cut their sideburns, and modern Hassidic Jews often wear curling locks of hair that fall from beneath their skullcaps and down over their ears. In the days of Moses, however, the prohibition against shaving the head along the side and back of the skull—a practice known as "rounding" among ancient peoples—was part of a greater prohibition against following the customs and practices of Israel's heathen neighbors.

* * * * *

The name most often used for the day on which the Feast of Trumpets is celebrated today is *Rosh Hashannah,* which means "New Year." But that was not its original name, and the significance of the day is really a new beginning rather than the start of a new calendar year. On this day, the Lord is said to move from His seat of judgment to His mercy seat by mercifully providing a new beginning through gathering Israel out of exile, remembering His covenants with their fathers, and restoring them as His covenant people. This new beginning was to be initiated by the sounding of the trumpet (Max Artz, *Justice and Mercy: Commentary on the Liturgy of the New Year and the Day of Atonement* [San Francisco: Holt, Rinehart and Winston, 1963], 36, 146). The night Moroni visited Joseph Smith Jr. for the first time, he quoted, among other things, the eleventh chapter of Isaiah. Dr. Terryl Givens notes that this particular scripture refers to a millennialist prophecy regarding the second gathering of Israel (*By the Hand of Mormon* [Oxford University Press, 2002], 64). Without referring to the ancient Israelite Feast of Trumpets or the Day of Remembrance, Moroni identifies themes of gathering associated with those holy days when he tells Joseph Smith that God "will set up an ensign for the nations . . . and shall assemble the outcasts of Israel, and gather together the dispersed of Judah from the four corners of the earth" (Isa. 11:12).

* * * * *

Though the Feast of Trumpets is celebrated on the first day of the seventh month of the Hebrew calendar as prescribed by the Old Testament, that day does not fall on the same day each year on the solar calendar used in Western societies. The Hebrew calendared date for the feast (see Lev. 23:24) falls anywhere between the first days of September to as late as the first days of October on the Western solar calendar. The two scenes in this chapter as well as subsequent chapters dramatize, among other things, the difference in dating of these two calendars as it relates to the Feast of Trumpets, and correlates them to the visits made by Moroni to Joseph Smith, which occurred each September between 1823 and 1827. The Feast of Trumpets was celebrated on September 5, 1823—sixteen days before Moroni first visited Joseph Smith Jr. during the late evening hours in the bedroom loft of his family's small cabin on September 21, 1823, and seventeen days before Joseph went to a hill three miles southeast of his home on September 22, 1823, where he unearthed the golden-plate record buried in the ground and had his first viewing of this ancient record. Moroni did not allow Joseph Smith to remove the record from the subterranean stone box. Religious scholars have suggested numerous possible reasons why he was instructed by Moroni that the time had not yet come for him to receive the plates and wouldn't arrive for four more years. Among the reasons suggested were his youth and inexperience, his need to be tutored and prepared by the angel Moroni for his calling as a prophet, the need to prove his willingness to keep the commandments of God—something his mother Lucy mentions in connection with his desire to use the precious metal in the plates to relieve the oppressive financial burdens of the family—and possibly his unmarried status. This chapter begins a sequence of chapters in this split novel that explore those possible reasons, but focuses mainly on the coming forth of the Book of Mormon as it relates to the divine timing of the celebration of the Feast of Trumpets.

* * * * *

The economic misfortunes of the Smith family compelled their move to New York and required the efforts of every family member over many years to pay the debt on their new farm near Palmyra. Lucy Smith wrote about the untimely frost in 1816. On June 8, several inches of snow fell across New England, and ice formed on the ponds. Two seasons of wheat crop failures in 1814 and 1815 followed by what was later called the year without a summer in 1816 forced the Smith family to move from Vermont and settle in upstate New York on the promise of good soil, a more temperate growing season, and a larger harvest. Lucy recorded that she had only nine cents left when she arrived there with her eight children. A few years after their arrival, in 1818 or 1819, the family purchased, on credit, wooded land south of town straddling Stratford Road. In order to make the writing in this novel more efficient, the yearly $100 land payment is dramatized as

coming due each year in September; however, the actual payment was
due each December. Meeting this yearly financial obligation loomed
over their heads and was the main reason the older boys, Joseph Sr., and
even Lucy worked outside the farm. Lucy sold painted oilcloth table-
cloths, and the children began a candy and cookie confection business,
selling their products from an open cart in Palmyra. Historian Richard
Bushman indicates that formal education was likely out of the question
as long as paying the debt on the farm required the family's complete
attention (Richard L. Bushman, *Joseph Smith and the Beginnings of
Mormonism* [University of Illinois Press, 1984], 49). John Stafford
remembered the Smith family holding home school from time to time.
Clearing ten acres of land a year was considered a very difficult task.
The Smith family cleared thirty acres in the first year after taking
possession of the property, an accomplishment that left the family
feeling good about their prospects of success. Alvin convinced Joseph
Sr. that they could purchase materials for the construction of a frame
house, hire a carpenter by the name of Stoddard to do some of the
work, and move the ten-member family from the small, two-room
cabin to a larger dwelling. Alvin took the lead in supervising the
building of the frame house beginning in November 1823 after the
harvest ended.

* * * * *

The religious revivals of the late 1700s and early 1800s had the effect
of increasing a congregation's size for the Methodists, Presbyterians, and
Baptists in Palmyra. This extended period of revivalism bridging two
centuries earned the area the distinction as the "burned over district."
Many revivalists claimed to see visions. Though the congregants of the
various sects were encouraged to seek a personal conversion, the contrary
doctrine that came from some visionary experiences and the claims that
these visions gave heavenly permission to breech the moral code were too
much for the clergy. During the 1817 and 1818 revivals, two years before
Joseph Smith's First Vision, the clergy of various Palmyra Christian sects
taught that the only orthodox experience of a spiritual nature was related
to forgiveness of sin and acceptance of Jesus Christ as Savior. All other
visions, manifestations, or revelations were suspect. The *Connecticut*

Evangelical Magazine printed an article in 1805, which included the pronouncement that "no person is warranted from the word of God to publish to the world the discoveries of heaven or hell which he supposes he has had in a dream, or trance, or vision. Were anything of this kind to be made known to men, we may be assured it would have been done by the apostles, when they were penning the gospel history." It was in this religious climate that Joseph Smith Jr. received what he later called his First Vision and shared it with his Methodist minister.

Reverend George Lane is the only clergy Joseph Smith mentions by name in his personal history in conjunction with the "severe persecution at the hands of all classes of men, both religious and irreligious" (JS–H 1:21–26). Author Terryl Givens suggests that it was primarily Reverend George Lane who reviled the prophet Joseph Smith over the telling of his vision (*By the Hand of Mormon,* 249, n. 4). Historian Richard Bushman indicates that the fierce rebuke Joseph received from Reverend Lane and other clergy still riled him twelve years later when he wrote the first of three accounts of his First Vision—the fourth account was written by a Chicago reporter after interviewing Joseph Smith in Nauvoo (see next note below in this section). "I had actually seen a light," Joseph wrote in 1832, "and in the midst of that light I saw two Personages, and they did in reality speak unto me, or one of them did. And though I was hated and persecuted for saying that I had seen a vision, yet it was true." According to Richard Bushman, Joseph's first account of his vision indicates that he still understood it as a personal conversion rather than the opening of a new gospel dispensation. Joseph wrote that a pillar of light rested on him and he was filled with the Spirit, which lasted for several days. In the first account he mentions inadvertently that one personage, Jesus Christ, gave him instructions. "I saw the Lord and he spake unto me saying Joseph my son thy sins are forgiven thee, go thy way, walk in my statutes and keep my commandments." Bushman concludes that this was the message of forgiveness and redemption that Joseph longed to hear. "Behold, I am the Lord of glory, I was crucified for the world that all those who believe on my name may have Eternal Life" (*Joseph Smith and the Beginnings of Mormonism,* 56, 57).

In later accounts of his vision written in 1835 and again in 1838 and 1842, Joseph began to understand the significance of God the

Father appearing to introduce His Son Jesus Christ and to open a new dispensation, and he includes a description of both Personages and quotes God the Father's introduction before giving details of what Christ taught him during his visionary experience. By this time, the importance of his personal conversion and forgiveness is overshadowed by the important question of which church he should join—the pivotal question that initiated the restoration of the gospel of Jesus Christ. He was told, "I must join none of them, for they were all wrong, and the Personage who addressed me said that all their creeds were an abomination in His sight; that those professors were all corrupt; that: 'they draw near to me with their lips, but their hearts are far from me, they teach for doctrines the commandments of men, having a form of godliness, but they deny the power thereof'" (JS–H: 1:19).

Though Joseph Smith only recorded that it was on a beautiful, clear day early in the spring of 1820 when he had his First Vision, some LDS scholars believe that the precise date provides additional evidence that God has calendared important events into the Hebrew, Enoch, and other revealed or inspired calendars. Examination of sacred ancient calendars and also the temperature-dependent nature of the maple harvest of 1820 add important understanding to the significance of the First Vision. Dr. John P. Pratt points out that Sunday, March 26, 1820, is what is called a New Year's Day of a New Year's Year on the Enoch calendar, an event that happens only once every 364 years ("Enoch Calendar: Another Witness of the Restoration," 2). In another part of these chapter notes there is a more detailed explanation that the Hebrew celebration of *Rosh Hashannah* is a day of new beginnings, sometimes referred to as a New Year when God begins to gather Israel out of exile, remembers His covenants with their fathers, and restores them as His covenant people. It is likely that Dr. Pratt noticed the prophetic themes of covenant restoration connecting Joseph Smith's First Vision with the Enoch calendar pointing to Sunday, March 26, 1820, as a type of new beginning. He also notes that four other sacred calendars point to the day before Joseph Smith's First Vision as a sacred day set aside for selecting a new prophet. The Hebrew calendar designates 10 Nisan (beginning after sunset on Friday, March 24, 1820, and continuing through sunset on Saturday, March 25, 1820) as the day of consecration when Israel chooses a new lamb (see Ex. 12:2–3). It was also the day 1 Wind on the Native American calendar—the day of the spirit—and it was day 1 Prime on the Mercury calendar, a holy day symbolic of the prime of life. Finally it was the day 0 Spring on the Enoch calendar, which began the spring equinox. Dr. Pratt indicates that the day preceding Joseph Smith's First Vision, if that vision actually occurred on the morning of Sunday, March 26, 1820, clearly indicates that these calendars act as four additional witnesses to the correct dating of the vision on a New Year Day of a New Year Year and suggest a precise interpretation as "a day for the Spirit to choose a new prophet who has just come of age" (ibid.).

Independent of Dr. Pratt's observations of these sacred calendars, Dr. John Lefgren compared temperature readings from the 1820 weather diary of Dr. Wheaton to the 1820 maple sugar production in an effort to pinpoint a possible date for Joseph Smith's First Vision (John C. Lefgren, "Oh How Lovely Was the Morning," *Meridian Magazine,* November 10, 2001, 1). There were five snow days during the first two weeks of March 1820 with twenty-three inches of accumulated snow. Only three of forty-two temperature readings in Dr. Wheaton's diary reached above freezing. During the third week of March 1820, there were no morning temperature readings above freezing. By Friday, March 24, 1820, the weather had cleared, and the morning temperature reached above forty degrees, the first day in early spring that meets Joseph Smith's description of a beautiful, clear morning for the First Vision. Saturday, March 25, and Sunday, March 26 were also clear and warm with a morning temperature reading of fifty-six degrees. The 2:00 P.M. temperature for both these days was sixty-four degrees, and Dr. Lefgren indicates that they were both beautiful days that "might stand out in young Joseph's memory as having been unusually pleasant." Beginning Monday, March 27, the weather became cloudy, and the temperature dropped through the end of March. During the first week of April there was snow, sleet, and rain. It wasn't until April 13, 1820, that the ice on Lake Ontario broke, and by Saturday, April 15, the weather was clear with morning readings above forty degrees. Taking these weather reports and comparing them to the maple harvest of 1820 supports Dr. Pratt's conclusion from the sacred calendars that Sunday, March 26, is the likely day for the First Vision.

Lucy Smith recorded that in the spring of 1820 the Smith family tapped more than 500 maple trees on their property, collected 60,000 pounds of sap, and boiled off water by burning 10,000 pounds of wood. According to Lucy, they "Commenced making maple sugar of which we averaged one thousand pounds per year" (ibid.). When temperatures rise above freezing, positive pressure in the maple tree forces water into the root system and pushes sap up the trunk. If the temperature remains warm for more than thirty hours, the pump effect dissipates and the sap production slows, allowing farmers to take a break from the maple harvest. Based on the recorded temperature readings in Palmyra during March 1820, this warming and cooling pump effect likely began on the Smith farm around March 18 and would not have slowed until late in the day on Saturday, March 25.

It is interesting to note that one of the four accounts Joseph Smith wrote regarding his First Vision implies that he had been cutting timber on the day prior. When the editor of the *Pittsburg Gazette* visited Nauvoo in 1843 and interviewed the Prophet, he quoted Joseph Smith as saying, "I immediately went out into the woods where my father had a clearing, and went to the stump where I had stuck my axe when I had quit work, and I kneeled down, and prayed, saying, O Lord, what Church shall I join?" It is likely that the Smith family rested on Sunday, March 26, from nine days of intensive wood cutting, water boiling, and sap collecting—a labor-intensive, twenty-four-hour-a-day process known as sugaring—allowing Joseph Smith his first respite from the maple harvest in more than a week and allowing him the opportunity to fulfill the prophetic dating indicated on five sacred calendars where the Spirit chose a new prophet who had come of age on a beautiful, clear morning early in the spring of 1820.

Joseph didn't tell his family about his First Vision. He spoke to his mother immediately after he returned home, and when she inquired about his evident weakness (he was leaning against the fireplace) he said, "Never mind all is well—I am well enough off." The only information he shared with his mother was that he knew her Presbyterianism was not true. Not until three years later during the 1823 angelic visits of Moroni where Joseph was commanded to tell his father did the family start to become aware of Joseph's visions. In the preliminary manuscript of Lucy's personal memoirs—what she later titled *Biographical Sketches* in its final edition—she wrote that Joseph took his questions over which church to join to Moroni in 1823, when in reality it was Jesus Christ three years earlier in the maple groves behind their Palmyra cabin who answered those questions for Joseph Smith (Lucy Mack Smith, *Preliminary Manuscript,* LDS Church Archives and BYU Special Collections). Lucy described a family conversation where she mistakenly confused Joseph's First Vision with Moroni's appearance and connected it with the statement that there was not a true church upon the earth (ibid., 40). Lucy also wrote that it was Moroni who told him that the churches on the earth were all "man made churches." In the final draft of her personal history, Lucy abandoned her account of Joseph's visions and instead quoted directly from her son's account (Lucy Mack Smith, *Biographical Sketches,* LDS Church Archives and BYU Special Collections, 80–86). Joseph's brother, William Smith, was likely repeating the account he heard from Lucy when he made the same mistake. Richard Bushman suggests that Joseph's silence about his First Vision in 1820 followed three years later by the sharing of his visionary encounters with the angel Moroni prevented Lucy and William from "getting the story right."

* * * * *

The golden-plate record was buried in the top of a hillside about three miles southeast of the Smith farm. Neither Joseph Smith nor the angel Moroni gave the hill a name except to call it the "place where the record lay buried" and the "highest drumlin in the county," and in this novel, the hill is never referred to as the Hill Cumorah. Associates of Joseph Smith, beginning with Oliver Cowdery, likely named it Cumorah after a hill mentioned in the Book of Mormon text where the prophet Mormon anciently buried numerous records that had been entrusted to him before he turned the golden-plate record, which contained the text of the Book of Mormon (a record called the Plates of Mormon and also the Small Plates of Nephi) over to his son Moroni prior to one of the final battles in Nephite history (see Morm. 6:6). The hill where the prophet Mormon buried numerous Nephite records is likely not the same location where thirty-six years later his son, Moroni, buried the golden-plate record (see Moro. 10:1–2). The prophet Moroni indicates that 900 years earlier the Jaredites gathered for battle at this same hill, which they called "the hill Ramah" (Ether 15:11). The Hill Cumorah was near where the Mulekites landed (Alma 22:30), and it was in the area the Nephites referred to as the narrow neck of land (Alma 22:32). When Joseph Smith didn't correct his associates with regard to the name of the hill where he unearthed the golden-plate record containing the text of the Book of Mormon, the folk name Cumorah gained popularity, and its use persists among Latter-day Saints to this day. David Palmer indicates that the yearly pageant entitled *America's Witness for Christ* performed on the hill where Joseph Smith recovered the golden plate record is commonly referred to by Latter-day Saints as the *Hill Cumorah Pageant*, further blurring the distinction between the ancient hill mentioned in the Book of Mormon (Morm. 6:6) and the hill where Joseph Smith unearthed an ancient record written on golden plates.

The golden-plate record was buried in a stone box, held together by cement and covered by a rounded capstone, among trees along the western slope near the top of a hill three miles south of the Smith farm in Palmyra. In addition to the golden-plate record, the box contained an instrument used for translation, which Joseph referred to as an interpreter, Urim and Thummim, or seer stone—two crystal-like stones that Joseph Smith showed to his family and which Lucy Smith described as similar to spectacles. A similar instrument is mentioned in the Old Testament, but its purpose is not explained, and many scholars believe the lack of explanation indicates that it was a common enough instrument that it did not warrant explanation. The Urim and Thummim were attached to a breastplate, which likely functioned to support the interpreters and allow the operator to work with his hands free. Other accounts by Joseph's associates and his mother Lucy indicate that an ancient brass-metal compass called the Liahona and the ancient Sword of Laban were also included in the box. It is uncertain whether the brass-plate record was present in the cement box or was later shown to Joseph Smith and other witnesses, but the influence of the brass plates in establishing the Hebrew law among the ancient inhabitants of the Book of Mormon and also transcribing the prophecies of ancient prophets like Zenos, Isaiah, and Jeremiah into the golden-plate record is obvious. LDS researcher David Palmer explains that "Alma, the son of Alma, prophesied to his son Helaman that the brass plates of Laban (the Nephites' version of the Old Testament) would be 'kept and preserved by the hand of the Lord until they should go forth unto every nation'" (Alma 37:4; 1 Ne. 5:17–19; see also David Palmer, *Encyclopedia of Mormonism,* ed. Daniel H. Ludlow [New York: Macmillan, 1992]).

On his first trip to the hill on the morning of September 22, 1823, Joseph may have forgotten the angel's prohibition that "he should have no other object in view in getting the plates but to glorify God." Not twelve hours before arriving at the designated site, Joseph was warned by Moroni that because of the difficult financial situation of his family he was to avoid the temptation to "get the plates for the purpose of getting rich." Dr. Terryl Givens suggests that Joseph may have forgotten the instructions (*By the Hand of Mormon,* 15), but historian Richard Bushman indicates that the sight of golden metal plates and other valuable objects buried in the stone box was likely too great of a temptation for young Joseph to resist (*Joseph Smith and the Beginnings of Mormonism,* 63, 73). Lucy Smith wrote that Joseph removed the plates from the hill and was then curious if other treasures remaining inside the stone box could be used to help alleviate the financial burdens of the Smith family. Her account may be somewhat unreliable in that she attributes this event to Joseph's second visit to the hill one year later in 1824, and she also mentions that he took the plates from the hill after which Moroni returned them to the stone box and then Joseph was thrown back by a powerful shock and prevented from taking the plates (*Preliminary Manuscript,* 83). An account written by Oliver Cowdery supports Bushman's observations. Oliver Cowdery as well as Joseph's mother Lucy write that Joseph told them that he reached for the plates three times and each time received a severe shock that threw him back into the grass. When he cried out, "Why can I not obtain this book?" Moroni appeared and said, "Because you have not kept the commandments of the Lord." Oliver Cowdery records that Joseph was then given a vision of the "prince of darkness" dressed in flowing black robes and was told by the angel that "all this is shown, the good and the evil, that ye may know hereafter the two powers and never be influenced or overcome by that wicked one." Dr. Bushman points out that the angel's instructions took the greed of money diggers out of the realm of curious adventure and placed it squarely in the realm of evil. Oliver

Cowdery recorded that Moroni said, "You now see why you could not obtain this record. The commandment was strict, and if ever these sacred things are obtained they must be by prayer and faithfulness in obeying the Lord" (Joseph Smith, *History of the Church,* 1:14; *Messenger and Advocate,* Oct., 1835; see also *Preliminary Manuscript,* 41–42).

CHAPTER THREE

Joseph Zias, an anthropologist at Jerusalem's Hebrew University, indicates that the drug trade, which included opium and hashish, thrived in ancient Jerusalem and supplied narcotics to cultures throughout the eastern Mediterranean as a balm for the pain of childbirth and disease. Ancient ceramic pots, most of them nearly identical in shape and about five inches long, have been found in tombs and settlements throughout the Middle East, dating as far back as 1400 B.C. The drugs were probably used as medicine, and the finds are helping researchers better understand how ancient people treated illness and disease. When turned upside down, the thin-necked vessels with round bases resemble opium poppy pods. If there was any doubt about what was inside, the round bases have white markings, designs that symbolized knife cuts made on poppy bulbs so the white opium base can ooze for harvesting.

CHAPTER FOUR

It is uncertain who accompanied Lehi and his family on their journey. The text of the Book of Mormon follows the ancient patriarchal tradition with the author writing almost exclusively about their own history and experience with little or no mention of even close relatives—often the women of the family—and even less about non-family members who may have traveled with them (John L. Sorenson, "The Book of Mormon as Lineage History" in *An Ancient American Setting for the Book of Mormon* [Provo: Neal A. Maxwell Institute for Religious Scholarship, 1996], 50–56). Zoram is referenced only in terms of his involvement in Nephi's introductory story about how they came to leave their home in Jerusalem; he subsequently fades into the background of Nephi's account. In this chapter we reintroduce characters from previous volumes in this series who fictionally accompany Lehi's family. It is not improbable to suggest that others beyond the immediate family traveled with Lehi through the wilderness despite not being named in Nephi's account.

* * * * *

This chapter dramatizes the events recorded in the Book of Mormon immediately following Laman's possible attempt on his father's life (see 1 Ne. 2:13). Nephi's prayer to know the mysteries of God and the subsequent confirmation from the Spirit that his father was led by God and could be trusted takes place off scene (see 1 Ne. 2:16). In this chapter, Nephi shares his spiritual confirmation with his brothers. Sam believes his account (see 1 Ne. 2:17), but Laman and Lemuel reject Nephi's words (see 1 Ne. 2:18). The Book of Mormon tells us that despite Laman and Lemuel's rejection of revelation in general and Lehi's leadership role specifically, Nephi wrote that "being grieved because of the hardness of their hearts I cried unto the Lord for them" (1 Ne. 2:18). This chapter concludes with Nephi telling Laman that he is going to pray for his eldest brother—a prayer that resulted in Nephi's vision of future generations of his descendants in the New World (see 1 Ne. 2:19–24). The details of this vision are covered in more detail in the historical notes for Chapter Twelve.

Scholar Hugh Nibley writes:

> When Father Lehi led his little clan into the wilderness in search for a promised land he was not engaging in a fantastic enterprise at all. He was only doing what hundreds of idealistic and courageous men had done before him. If he had visions of a bountiful land in some far place (1 Nephi 5:5), so did they. If his followers never forgot their homeland and wept to remember it in the desert places, so did theirs. And if he had to rebuke and encourage them with strong words, so did they. The Book of Mormon opens on a note of complete authenticity (Hugh Nibley, *An Approach to the Book of Mormon* [Salt Lake City: Deseret Book Co., 1988], 43–44).

Nibley explains that "small bands of people, usually friends and relatives," left the larger communities of the ancient Near East in search of other lands "under the direction of an able and daring leader." The term *patriarch* or "Father-leader" may have had its origin in these movements of bands of people during Lehi's day who left their "mother city" (a possible origin for the word *metropolis*), in search of a "promised land." As unsettled lands decreased, "explorations became more daring and settlement projects more ambitious. . . . In the year Lehi left Jerusalem, the Egyptian government sent an expedition . . . sailing clear around Africa from east to west. . . . The Phoenicians reacted . . . by sending Hanno on the same mission . . . in the opposite direction."

Nibley indicates that the ancients of Lehi's day believed they were limited by their knowledge of geography, but outside of our modern time there was never an era in human history when cartographic and geographic understanding was more prevalent, and in this novel Lehi is shown to have possessed numerous maps of the ancient world (ibid.).

It was likely while encamped at the Valley of Lemuel that Lehi spoke of his prophetic understanding of the life and mission of Jesus Christ, whom he referred to as the Messiah or the Savior of the World. In what is possibly his most prophetic recorded testimony, Lehi declared to his family that six hundred years after they left Jerusalem, God would raise up the Messiah among the Jews (see 1 Ne. 10:4). This prophecy aids in dating the exodus of Lehi and his family at approximately 600 B.C., around the time of the initial Babylonian conflicts and prior to the captivity.

CHAPTER FIVE

The actual location for Mount Horeb, more popularly known as Mount Sinai, is not known. Pilgrimages to the mountain were conducted in the years after the Israelites completed their Exodus from Egypt. Within two centuries, the pilgrimages ended, and the location was never recorded. The Talmud contains a map indicating eight possible locations, and Old Testament scholars, geographers, and cartographers have suggested more than thirty possible sites. Restoration scriptures indicate that the name of the mountain where God revealed His covenants to

Moses may never be known, and that may have implications for ever precisely locating the site where God spoke face-to-face with Moses, though it does not rule out the possibility (see Moses 1:42). The Apostle Paul indicated that the mountain was located somewhere in modern-day Saudi Arabia, and he may have actually visited the mountain himself (see Gal. 4:25). The maps in the Latter-day Saint publication of the King James Version of the Bible place Horeb (Sinai) on the Sinai Peninsula with a question mark listed in parentheses to indicate that this site is one of many proposed sites. This traditional site for Mount Sinai was selected by the mother of Constantine I at about A.D. 300, despite the many geographic problems it poses. Bible scholars indicate that this site is a poor candidate for the location where Moses led a large group of Israelites, possibly exceeding thirty thousand travelers, on their exodus from Egypt. There are no locations on the Sinai Peninsula with enough water or arable land to support a large group of Israelites for the time period (about one year) in which they made camp at Sinai, and climatic conditions have not changed dramatically since that time (see Ex. 15 and 16). In addition to the lack of water or grasslands to support a large population with large numbers of sheep, rams, goats, and cattle, the Bible account itself points to a location farther east across the Gulf of Aqaba, in Saudi Arabia, in a geographical region anciently known as Midian. The Bible names Midian as the location for Mount Horeb (see Ex. 3:1) and places the mountain in a range along the "back" or edge of a desert similar to the Jabal or Higaz mountains that Nephi calls the "borders" (see 1 Ne 2:5). LDS explorer George Potter indicates that a number of sensitive military radar installations are located in the peaks and ridges of these mountains today. Potter, as well as other explorers, secured permits to conduct explorations, and they report the discovery of compelling archaeological and geographic evidence for placing Mount Horeb in the mountains near where Nephi and his family likely made their base camp in the Valley of Lemuel (George Potter, "Where Is the Real Mount Sinai?" *Meridian Magazine,* November 10, 2001, 2).

* * * * *

The Jabal Mountains run parallel to the east shore of the Gulf of Aqaba and have been referred to for centuries as the Northern Hijaz or

Northern Borders. During the British occupation of these territories, military mapmakers used the name "Northern Hijaz" in their maps, journals, and geographic explorations as the proper name for the range (David George Hogarth, *Hejaz Before World War I, a Handbook*). Hugh Nibley indicates that Nephi's use of the word "borders" was a logical choice when he penned what to him were obvious directions detailing the route his family followed to the Valley of Lemuel. Somewhere between Joseph Smith's verbal translation of the word "borders" to his scribe Oliver Cowdery, and the printer's typeset version of the first printing of the Book of Mormon, the case-sensitive (capitalized) word "Borders"—a proper name for the Jabal Mountains—may have been lost and replaced by the lowercase word "borders." The uppercase usage of "Borders" implies the proper name for the mountain range running along the Gulf of Aqaba, while the lowercase usage connotes any geographic boundary (desert, plateau, wadi). In this chapter, as well as in subsequent chapters, the word "Borders" is printed in uppercase, suggesting the Jabal Mountains as the range Nephi and his family traversed in their journey. Hugh Nibley suggests that Joseph Smith and Oliver Cowdery may have left the word in lowercase, since neither of them was aware of the proper names in that region of the world ("Lehi in the Desert," in *Lehi in the Desert/The World of the Jaredites/There Were Jaredites,* ed. John W. Welch [Salt Lake City: Deseret Book Co. and Provo: F.A.R.M.S., 1998]). The Jabal Mountains are a split range with dual peak elevations running side-by-side and extending north-south through the region anciently known as Midian, parallel to the Gulf of Aqaba. The dual nature of this range is not immediately evident on examination of spatially flat, one-dimensional maps, but it is readily apparent to travelers making their way through these mountains. One array of summit peaks lies inland from the coast. The inland range shelters the second "split" chain of mountains that run directly along the coast. The inland chain extends north beyond the port city of Aqaba. The "sheltered" second chain of mountains begins about forty miles south of the port city of Aqaba along the coast. This second chain of mountains—the borders nearer the Red Sea—presents an imposing array of mountain peaks with two-thousand-foot elevations rising directly out of the sea in an impressive bulwark of sheer cliffs. These nearer-to-the-coast mountains block passage for about thirty miles, making it virtually impossible to travel uninterrupted along the shore-line by camel, horse, or mule. It is within these nearer-to-the-coast mountains where Lehi and his family likely made their camp in the valley of Lemuel.

CHAPTER SIX

Zoram is a historical character mentioned in the Book of Mormon. It is highly unlikely that he was related to or had significant contact with Jeremiah, but their relationship in this novel makes the story line more efficient. We do know that Zoram was employed in Laban's treasury and that Nephi recognized him as the keeper of the keys (see 1 Ne. 4:20). Sidney B. Sperry indicates the possibility that Zoram may have actually aided in the incorporation of Jeremiah's prophecies into the brass plates or at least assisted Nephi and his brothers in obtaining the plates:

> Many other interesting problems arise as a result of Nephi's words concerning the brass plates. One wonders how Jeremiah's prophecies found their place on the brass plates, since Laban, their former keeper, was a thor-oughly unrighteous man. How did Jeremiah, or his scribe Baruch (Jeremiah 36:4), or some other represen-tative of the prophet gain access to the plates in Laban's treasury, in view of the difficulties which Nephi and his brothers had in getting at them? Were they aided and abetted by Zoram, the servant of Laban? We shall have to wait for more light before these questions can be answered (Sidney B. Sperry, *Some Problems of Interest Relating to the Brass Plates* [Provo, Utah: F.A.R.M.S., 1995], 185–91).

CHAPTER SEVEN

Baruch is a historical character mentioned throughout the book of Jeremiah as the prophet's scribe. The opening of the book of Jeremiah begins with a revelation to Jeremiah that, "Before I formed thee in the belly I knew thee, and before thou camest out of the womb I sanctified thee, and I ordained thee; a prophet unto the nations" (Jer. 1:5). This chapter also includes the revelation from the prophet Moses that it is the work and glory of God to "bring to pass the immortality and eternal life of man" (Moses 1:39). These two passages indicate that ancient prophets had a deep understanding of the Plan of Salvation and the eternal nature of man, which began prior to life on earth and extends eternally into the future.

* * * * *

There are a number of dating errors in the Book of Jeremiah where the dynasty under which historical events occurred—Zedekiah or his nephew Jehoakim, who preceded him on the throne—remains in question. Hugh Nibley suggests that Baruch, acting as editor for Jeremiah, may have inadvertently dated the events incorrectly. Scholars originally believed that Uriah's escape to Egypt, detailed in the first volume of this series, *Pillar of Fire,* and Uriah's trial, detailed in the second volume of this series, *Power of Deliverance,* occurred much earlier, since the Old Testament names Jehoakim as the king of Israel, not Zedekiah, who later replaced him as king. The Lachish Letters, however, indicate that Zedekiah was actually on the throne at the time of Uriah's trial. Scholars now believe that the ancient scribe, Baruch, mistakenly wrote the former king's name in the Old Testament record when the intended king was actually Zedekiah ("Dark Days in Jerusalem: The Lachish Letters and the Book of Mormon" in *The Prophetic Book of Mormon* [Salt Lake City: Deseret Book Co., 1989], 380–406).

CHAPTER EIGHT

On November 1, 1823, five weeks after Joseph Smith's first visit to the hill where the golden-plate record lay buried, Alvin, Joseph's eldest brother, took ill. The family doctor was not available, and another doctor, Mr. Greenwood, diagnosed bilious colic and prescribed calomel oil to restore bowel function. Lucy recorded that Alvin protested, and when he finally relented, the calomel oil only served to further block his intestinal tract. Three days later, the work of four doctors could not dislodge the blockage, which ultimately led to the onset of gangrene and Alvin's death on November 19, 1823. His death was a terrible blow to the family, and it ended, for a time, the family gatherings to discuss the revelations given to Joseph. Historian Richard Bushman indicates that Alvin had taken a greater interest than any other family member (*Joseph Smith and the Beginnings of Mormonism*, 64–65). Before he died, Alvin told Joseph to "do everything that lies in your power to obtain the Record." Lucy Smith recorded that when they spoke of the record they thought of Alvin's zeal, and "when we looked to his place and realized that he was gone from it, to return no more in this life, we all with one accord wept over our irretrievable loss, and we could not be comforted, because he was not."

In her personal history, Lucy Smith wrote of the family gatherings "all seated in a circle, father, mother, sons and daughters," to hear Joseph Smith tell of his meetings with the angel Moroni and his visit to the hill where the plates were buried. "The whole family were melted to tears," she later recorded, "and believed all he said." To Lucy, the family gatherings "presented an aspect as singular as any that ever lived upon the face of the earth. The sweetest union and happiness pervaded our house and peace and tranquility reigned in our midst." At one family gathering, Joseph warned his family to keep to themselves what he told them because "the world was so wicked that when they came to a knowledge of these things they would try to take our lives." Despite the ominous nature of the warnings, Lucy wrote that they rejoiced at "a more perfect knowledge of the Plan of Salvation and the redemption of the human family. At last we had something upon which we could stay our minds."

CHAPTER ELEVEN

In this chapter, Queen Miriam remembers the events of the first Babylonian invasion of Israel. It was a short, three-month war ending with the fall and surrender of Jerusalem. Three days prior to the burning of the east gate with an oil fire, Israelite King Jehoiakim died of a heart attack. His seventeen-year-old son, Jehoiachin, was placed on the throne. As was the custom among conquering armies in antiquity, the Babylonians confiscated the spoils of war, which included the Ark of the Covenant, believed to have contained the tablets of stone given Moses on Mount Sinai, and other relics from the temple and transported them to Babylon (see Jer. 52). The invading armies took Jehoiachin and his immediate family and court back to Babylon as a symbol of their conquest, but the conquerors were not interested in ruling the kingdom. They appointed the boy-king's uncle (his father's brother), Zedekiah, as a vassal king with the stipulation that he pay a tribute tax each year of about one-quarter of the gross national product (The Reader's Digest, *Great People of the Bible and How They Lived* [Pleasantville, NY: The Reader's Digest Association, Inc., 1974]; see also Hugh W. Nibley, "Dark Days in Jerusalem: The Lachish Letters and the Book of Mormon," in *The Prophetic Book of Mormon* [Salt Lake City: Deseret Book Co. and Provo: F.A.R.M.S.,1989], 380–400). They also took captive all of Jerusalem's blacksmiths, uprooting whole families and leaving their property without a legal birthright heir. Blacksmiths were the foundation of a strong army, and no intelligent general went to war without a host of them to mend swords and breastplates. Before the Babylonian army left the city in April 601 B.C., they ran roughshod through Jerusalem's blacksmithing district to keep the Israelites from rebuilding their military might.

CHAPTER TWELVE

The sounding of the trumpet, the main ritual on the Feast of Trumpets, symbolizes both redemption and revelation (Leo Trepp, *The Complete Book of Jewish Observances* [New York: Jewish Publication Society, 1970], 95). The trumpet is associated with revelation, since the first mention of its use was at Mount Sinai, and the Feast of Trumpets is understood as a memorial of Sinai. Dr. Phillip Goodman notes that "the celebration of Passover was to be an annual reminder of the exodus. The ritual blast of the *shofar* would similarly recall by association the revelation on Mount Sinai" (Phillip Goodman, *The Rosh Hashanah Anthology* [Philadelphia: Jewish Publication Society, 1970], 42). The sounding of the trumpet appears not only as a remembrance of the revelation given at Sinai, but also as an indication of future events. Just as the trumpet preceded God's revelation of the law at Sinai (see Ex. 19:16), some scholars believe the trumpet sounding during *Rosh Hashannah* signals further revelation, including the establishment of the true law (ibid.,

42). Old Testament, Book of Mormon, and Doctrine and Covenants scriptures speak of the trumpet preceding the establishment of truth that leads to redemption (see Isa. 58:1; Alma 29:1; D&C 33:2). "And at all times, and in all places, he shall open his mouth and declare my gospel as with the voice of a trump" (D&C 24:12). The statue of the angel LDS atop Mormon temples is portrayed as blowing a trumpet, proclaiming the gospel to the world, and particularly to the house of Israel. A review of LDS history and scripture indicates that most of the restored truths in the gospel of Jesus Christ began with the coming forth of the Book of Mormon.

* * * * *

In this chapter, Nephi recalls what he knows of Moses' revelation and the covenants made at Sinai between God and the Israelites recorded in the Old Testament (see Ex. 19 and 20). The three-day, covenant-making experience for these ancient Israelites included a ceremonial washing in preparation for covenant-making and dressing in clean clothes (see Ex.19:10). A trumpet was used to call the Israelites to the foot of the mountain with their families and again to announce the covenant-making ceremony. The Israelites were forbidden to go beyond the foot of the mountain, and Moses was directed to set priests along the perimeter to keep the throngs back. Moses was then instructed to bring Aaron up into the mountain, where the details of the covenants were given, which include the Ten Commandments popularly associated with this covenant-making event. It is likely that God used Sinai as a temple in the absence of an edifice dedicated as a house of God. Moses later built a tabernacle that served as a transportable temple, where rites pertaining to the covenants given at Sinai were remembered. It is easy to relate the symbolism of the Day of Remembrance and the Feast of Trumpets to this experience, which acts as the nascent event of later religious and civil life in ancient Israel.

God made a covenant with Nephi that he would be a ruler over his people and that his descendants would prosper as long as they obeyed God's commandments (see 1 Ne. 2:19–24). In addition, Nephi was promised that the descendants of his older brothers would be a scourge against his descendants if they did not abide by God's commandments.

This covenant is referenced often by Book of Mormon writers throughout Nephite history. Many of the wars between Nephite and Lamanite peoples were attributed to this covenant. Scholar Hugh Nibley indicates that this covenant made with Nephi is the major theme from beginning to end of the Book of Mormon record.

CHAPTER THIRTEEN

When Lehi read the brass plates for the first time in the wilderness, Nephi recorded that his father found "many prophecies which have been spoken by the mouth of Jeremiah" (1 Ne. 5:13). Dr. Sidney B. Sperry indicates that Lehi's use of the idiomatic Hebrew phrase "spoken by the mouth of Jeremiah" was a direct translation by Joseph Smith and is in keeping with how ancient Hebrews expressed the manner in which prophets communicated their prophecies (*Some Problems of Interest Relating to the Brass Plates,* 185–91). In this and subsequent chapters, Jeremiah is shown reciting his prophecies to Baruch in keeping with this ancient expressive form, as well as portraying how ancient prophets like Jeremiah would have likely communicated their revelations.

In this chapter, Baruch records many of Jeremiah's prophecies found in the Old Testament, among which are his condemnation of idol worship and his testimony that the Messiah is the fountain of living waters and the only way to salvation (see Jer. 2:13; 17:13). The section of this chapter where Jeremiah quotes passages similar to what Book of Mormon prophet Moroni wrote in the title page of that scripture is fictional. It does not appear that Jeremiah was given any revelation specific to Moroni's later writings; however, it is clear that Jeremiah understood that his words would come forth in the latter days and stand alongside the words of prophets like Moroni.

CHAPTER FOURTEEN

Lucy Smith recorded that Mr. Stoddard, the man hired to help with carpentry work on the frame house begun by Alvin before his death, had designs on the property. She mentions that he offered $1,500 for the farm and improvements. Many holders of land contracts in western

New York during this time were unable to finish their payments. Historian Richard Bushman suggests that Mr. Stoddard may have believed the Smiths would end up negotiating with a second party (*Joseph Smith and the Beginnings of Mormonism*, 66–67).

About a year after the events dramatized in this chapter, Josiah Stoal's nephew, concerned over what he called "undue influence" over his uncle, entered a complaint in the South Bainbridge, Chenango County, New York district court citing Joseph Smith as a disorderly person. It is not certain if this trial actually occurred or if the trial record is authentic; however, in the court testimony in question, Josiah Stoal is recorded as saying, "He had the most implicit faith in the prisoner's skill." The trial centered on interest in treasure hunting, and some of the testimony included a stone Joseph Smith was believed to have used to help him find the location of treasure in the earth. Moroni warned Joseph Smith against participating in treasure-hunting activities, and in the trial records, witnesses testified that Joseph "did not solicit business of this kind, and had always rather declined having anything to do with this business." Scholar Richard Bushman notes that Joseph Smith was under pressure from neighbors, Josiah Stoal, and from his own father due to their impoverished conditions, to participate in the hunt for buried treasure (ibid.). The Stafford family was likely among the neighbors who pressured Joseph Smith to participate in money digging, and in this chapter they are the principal characters representing the money-digging interests in and around Palmyra. The Stafford family was known to be heavily involved in money digging and a few years earlier had hired Joseph Smith to dig for treasure on their property. Joseph Smith ended his association with money diggers well before the rest of his family did—likely due to Moroni's warnings. It wasn't until about a year after the account portrayed in this chapter that Joseph Smith Sr. began to demonstrate an observable change in perspective with regard to treasure hunting and the supernatural powers he believed were given to Joseph Smith to find treasure in the ground. In an account of the March 1826 South Bainbridge trial, W. D. Purple, though one of Joseph Smith's detractors, recorded that Joseph Smith Sr. said, "Both he and his son were mortified that this wonderful power which God had so miraculously given his son should be used only in search of filthy lucre, or its equivalent earthly treasures. His constant prayer to his Heavenly Father was to manifest His will concerning this marvelous power."

CHAPTER FIFTEEN

The marriage covenant and the perpetuation of eternal increase through childbearing is another important theme celebrated during the Feast of Trumpets, and in this chapter Sariah's pregnancy is a metaphor for this religiously important premise. Scriptures dealing with Sarah bearing Abraham a son in their old age (see Gen. 21) as well as the ending of Hannah's and Rachel's barrenness (see 1 Sam. 1–2:10) are read as part of the feast-day memorial. According to Jewish tradition, Sarah, Rachel, and Hannah are symbolic of all women and are remembered on the Feast of Trumpets as having their fruitfulness restored (Norman H. Snaith, *The Jewish Festival Year* [London: Society for Promoting Christian Knowledge, 1974], 168). The Talmud records that "on New Year Sarah, Rachel and Hannah were visited," meaning that their barrenness ended. Lenet Hadley Read points out that through these women, previously promised covenants are remembered ("Joseph Smith's Receipt of the Plates and the Israelite Feast of Trumpets," 110–20). After Rachel was remembered by the Lord she was blessed with Joseph, the father of Ephraim and Manasseh. With the end of Hannah's barrenness came the return of a righteous priesthood. The covenant of marriage, the promises of an eternal seed through the bearing of children, and the remembrance of covenants through the perpetuation of family are of significant importance to the celebration of the Feast of Trumpets (see Gen. 12:3). It is interesting to note that Moroni did not give Joseph Smith the golden-plate record until after his marriage to Emma Hale.

* * * * *

We do not know if Sariah was given any revelation or dream regarding sending her sons back to Jerusalem to retrieve the brass plates from Laban's treasury. In this novel she is portrayed as having had divine inspiration in the matter.

CHAPTER SEVENTEEN

Nephi recorded that immediately after he spoke with God and received a promise regarding a land of promise for his family and descendants—a revelation that likely polarized further his already-strained relationship with Laman and Lemuel—he returned to the tent of his father to find his older brothers rejecting his father's appeal that they return to Jerusalem to obtain the brass plates from Captain Laban's treasury (see 1 Ne. 3:1–8). This chapter dramatizes a fairly well-known verse of scripture (see 1 Ne. 3:7) where Nephi declares his faith that God will provide a way, regardless of the dangers of the God-given task.

CHAPTER EIGHTEEN

Baruch, whose full Hebrew name was Baruch ben Neriah, served as a scribe to the prophet Jeremiah (see Jer. 32:12–16). It is not clear if he was a childhood friend to Jeremiah or if his first contact was through employment established by Jeremiah's friends to assist the prophet with his record-keeping later in life. He became, nevertheless, a scribe, disciple, secretary, and devoted friend from the time they were first associated until the ends of their lives. Baruch wrote down the first and second editions of Jeremiah's prophecies as they were dictated to him by the prophet. Baruch remained true to Jeremiah, although, like his master, he was at times almost overwhelmed with despondency. Jeremiah commanded Baruch to read his prophecies of warning to the people gathered in the temple on a day of fasting (see Jer. 36). The task was difficult and dangerous, but Baruch performed it without flinching.

CHAPTER TWENTY-ONE

Due to the cash-poor conditions of most farmers in and around Palmyra, New York, and the decreasing prices for grain, cows, and butter that put many farmers in financial jeopardy, land agents were fairly lenient about late payments. By 1828, more than seven hundred debtors were in the Rochester prison. In 1825 the Smiths were uncertain about how the land agent, newly hired by the seller (the Evertsons of New York City), would deal with them. They sent Hyrum to make arrangements for paying their yearly land payment past the due date. Agents had the legal right to reclaim property and evict the occupants if they missed a payment without compensation for their improvements. Agents usually only invoked their powers when the tenants were known to be preparing to vacate without making payment. It was just such a claim made by Mr. Stoddard one year later—that Joseph Smith Sr. and Joseph Jr. had burned their wheat crop and run off—when actually they were in Harmony earning money for the land payment by working for Josiah Stoal. The story seemed plausible to the new land agent, and based on the false claims of Stoddard, he revoked the Smith's deed and negotiated a new contract with Stoddard for cash paid in full. Records indicate that the land agent was chagrined to find out later of his error, but there was little he could do beyond appeal to Stoddard's sense of fairness and decency, which ultimately proved ineffectual. The year previous to the loss of the property, records indicate that Hyrum was successful in nego-tiating a late payment, and the Smith family deposited their 1825 assess-ment about a month late on Christmas Day.

Sometime after Joseph Smith Sr. rejected Mr. Stoddard's offer as dramatized in Chapter Fourteen of this novel, the carpenter raised money from neighbors to purchase the Smith farm. Lucy recorded in her journal that the newly hired land agent panicked. With a question-ably negotiated deed in hand, Stoddard told Lucy Smith to get off his property. She recorded that she nearly fainted. The boys in the family prepared handbills, which they spread among travelers on the road leading to Pennsylvania since they were uncertain if Joseph Sr. and Joseph Jr. were working for Josiah Stoal or had found employment to earn money to make the land payment elsewhere. The handbills asked Joseph Sr. to return home to deal with what Lucy believed a most devastating circumstance. The battle to regain the property lasted three days, with at least two trips to the land agent. In this chapter, the events of the negotiation for the property are compressed into a single day and take place off scene. When Hyrum Smith provided the land agent with affidavits attesting to the Smith's ethical conduct, the agent was surprised to find out later that Stoddard had fooled him. Stoddard refused to return the deed. It wasn't until the Sheriff interceded that

Stoddard agreed to sell the deed for $1,000 and gave the Smiths a two-day deadline. The sheriff's son, Mr. Durfee, purchased the deed and allowed the Smiths to remain on the land as renters. They were never able to get back the deed to their farm, though they may have been paid as much as $700 for their improvements (Bushman, *Joseph Smith and the Beginnings of Mormonism,* 66–68).

* * * * *

Emma Hale was employed as a school teacher in the fall of 1826 as well as in her father's boarding house when she first met Joseph Smith Jr.—one of the many men hired by Josiah Stoal to work in a mining project. Joseph spent most of his time working in the gristmill and in other farming labors on Stoal's vast estate near Harmony, likely due to the warnings from the angel Moroni to distance himself from money diggers. Emma was immediately drawn to Joseph, and she spent many evenings in the parlor of the boarding house discussing Joseph's visions. She believed him completely and became one of his most trusted confidants—both of them sharing similar religious convictions and a spiritual temperament that drew them close at first meeting (Norma J. Fischer, *Portrait of a Prophet's Wife* [Silver Leaf Press, 1992], 10). Emma's father, Isaac Hale, was a staunch member of the Methodist congregation in Harmony. He had not always been a devout congregant. When Emma was about seven years old he happened across her out in the woods near their home praying that her father would develop similar faith in Christ as she had at that young age. The simple faith of young Emma inspired him to join the Methodist congregation, which membership continued until his death. He became a strong Methodist due, in part, to Emma's prayer as a young girl asking God to touch her father's heart (Buddy Youngreen, *Reflections of Emma* [Salt Lake City: Keepsake Paperbacks, 1982], 14).

* * * * *

The *Ketubah* first appeared in Jewish wedding ceremonies around the first century B.C. as a legal document outlining the rights and obligations of husband and wife to each other during marriage and in

the case of divorce. Though still signed before the ceremony, a
Ketubah is no longer a binding contract, but rather a spiritual decree
expressing a couple's commitment.

The *chuppah* or bridal canopy is one of the central traditions at
most Jewish weddings. It is usually made of ornamented satin or velvet
and supported by four poles. Marriage ceremonies in the Middle Ages
customarily took place outdoors, as an omen that the marriage should
be blessed with as many children as stars in the heavens. The original
meaning of the word was "room" or "covering" from the phrase in the
Bible: "Let the bridegroom go forth of his chamber, and the bride out
of her closet" (Joel 2:16). The *chuppah* symbolizes the new Jewish
home that the couple creates together.

The *Kiddush* or blessing over the wine is repeated twice during
the ceremony, once on its own, and then with the seven blessings.
Added to the ceremony in the sixth century, the two cups represented
the sanctification of the betrothal and the marriage. The cup of wine
is referred to as the cup of life. The sweetness of the wine symbolizes
the sweetness wished upon the couple, while sharing the cup of wine
represents sharing whatever the future holds, whether bitter or sweet.

For some Jews, the breaking of the glasses, the most familiar of all
Jewish customs, represents the destruction of the temple in 70 A.D.
Modern interpretations include the fragility of human relationships,
the beginning of a new life, and the dismissal of prejudice and igno-
rance.

CHAPTER TWENTY-THREE

The casting of lots is a system of divination practiced by throwing
black and white beans, little bones or dice, stones, or anything suitable
as an object of chance bearing particular marks or characters. The word
lot is used in the Old Testament in association with pagan magic and
also in association with the Urim and Thummim, which was likely
divinely sanctioned or inspired. The word *lot* influenced the modern
word for the game of chance known as a "lottery." When Matthias was
chosen by lot (see Acts 1), the type of lot used is uncertain, but the
common non-magical or non-pagan practice was to write the name or
symbol of your chosen candidate onto a potsherd (piece of broken

pottery) and place it into a basket. The potsherds were counted like ballots. The linguistic confusion of the use of the word *lot* in ancient scripture comes from trying to determine whether it is associated with paganism or divine inspiration (W. R. Halliday, *Greek Divination,* The Ancient Library, 1913). When we say that someone was "chosen by ballot" we don't speculate about whether the paper on which the ballot is recorded was a tarot card, with obvious pagan implications, or a paper ballot. The context of using the *lot* for the purpose, in this case, of balloting usually answers that question. *The Anchor Bible Commentary* indicates that:

> Since practices of superstition and magic were forbidden to Israel (Deut. 18:9–14), only the priestly Urim and Thummim could be used to ascertain an oracular decision (Ex. 28:30; Lev. 27:21; cf. 1 Sam. 14:41). The word "kléros," which has a broad basic meaning, "share, lot, portion," expresses a variety of nuances in the Greek OT. It can translate Hebrew "nahalah," "inheritance, heritage, possession" (Num. 16:14; 18:21; Isa. 57:6) or Hebrew "goral," "lot" (Lev. 16:8–10). It is being used here in the latter sense. Significantly, it is the means chosen by the early community to ascertain God's will in this matter, since not a democratic election but a divine choice is involved (1st ed., Vol. 20 [New York: Random House, January 1993]).

Historian Eric D. Huntsman ("And They Cast Lots: Divination, Democracy, and Josephus," *BYU Studies,* vol. 36, no. 3, 1996–97, 365–77) indicates that Yigael Yadin, the excavator of Masada, found ostracae (broken pieces of pottery with writing on them) in Room 113, each with a different name written on it, including the name of Eleazer ben Yair, the leader of a zealot group called the Sicarii. Josephus, a contemporary to Eleazer ben Yair, recorded, "After the men had chosen by lot ten of their number who would be their butchers, and when they had laid down beside and thrown their arms around their wives and children who lay waiting, they offered themselves up for the slaughter" (*Jewish War* 7.395). Excavator Yadin believed that these lots were the very ones used in that final desperate selection. Dr. Huntsman examined the evidence and concluded that there were suicides and that lots were used, but that Josephus had embellished the story. One of the problems is that Josephus had been involved in just such a situation himself. During the early stages of the Jewish War, Josephus and forty others found themselves holed up against the Romans at a cave near the fortress of Jotapata. They resolved that the only way out was mass suicide. They decided to draw lots to determine the order of their deaths: the one who drew the first lot was to be killed by the one who drew the second, who was to be killed by the one who drew the third, etc. In theory, the use of lots made the process fair and random. Josephus managed to draw the last lot, and when he and the second-to-last participant were left, they decided not to follow through on their suicide pact and surrendered to the Romans rather than die at their own hands. This, of course, led to the suspicion that Josephus had somehow "fixed" the lots, which was apparently also a common practice in ancient times. The lots used in this novel are made of stone with markings etched into the surface and are in keeping with the ancient use as a ballot of chance. This chapter dramatizes the fixing of the lots that was sometimes the case in the ancient world. The use of the lot in this novel does not imply divine inspiration as in the use of the Urim and Thummim as indicated in the Old Testament, nor does it suggest the use of magic by the sons of Lehi.

CHAPTER TWENTY-FOUR

Laman went alone without any witnesses on the first visit to the estate of Captain Laban. Though Nephi recorded the event, it is a second-hand account given to him by his brother Laman (see 1 Ne. 3:11–12). Nephi has no other source for the details of that first visit other than what Laman tells him on his return (see 1 Ne. 3:14). Nephi recorded that Laman went to Captain Laban's estate and requested the "plates of brass, which contained the genealogy of my father." Based on what we know of Laman, it is not impossible to suggest that he did not give Nephi a complete or accurate account of his first visit with Captain Laban. In this chapter, Laman does not request the plates as he later tells Nephi, but instead uses their father Lehi in his negotiation to return to the family's estate.

In Joseph Smith's day, the terms dealing with theft and robbery were synonymous, but law scholar John W. Welch notes that under ancient Near Eastern law, a thief was a local citizen of the community who was guilty of stealing from his neighbor, while a robber was something akin to our modern understanding of an enemy combatant or even comparable to a terrorist (John W. Welch, "A Steady Stream of Significant Recognitions" in *Echoes and Evidences of the Book of Mormon* [Neal A. Maxwell Insititute for Religious Scholarship, 2006], 331–87). The local elders usually dealt with thieves by judicial means of a trial, with a jury composed of fellow townspeople, and thieves were punished through civil means, which usually required repayment of stolen goods and the making of a sin offering at the temple. A robber was treated as an enemy combatant similar to how the Gadianton robbers in ancient America were likely viewed. Anciently, robbers were defined as outsiders, outcasts, or foreigners to the community. They were enemies of the state and were dealt with through military means. Soldiers were authorized by law to execute robbers on sight without a civil trial. The Book of Mormon account records that Captain Laban accused Laman of being a robber and may have attempted to kill him or at least ordered the men under his command to carry out the execution (see 1 Ne. 3:13).

English law professor Bernard S. Jackson points out that ancient Jewish robbers acted in organized groups with a complex hierarchy rivaling local governments and with the aim of attacking and sometimes usurping entire towns (Bernard S. Jackson, *Theft in Early Jewish Law* [Oxford: Oxford University Press, 1972], 13, 16). They swore oaths and extorted ransom and were considered a threat as great if not worse than war. Dr. Welch suggests that these same characteristics describe the Gadianton robbers of ancient America, and in his research details the legal and linguistic distinctions observable in both the robbers of the Book of Mormon and ancient Israel (John W. Welch, "Theft and Robbery in the Book of Mormon and in Ancient Near Eastern Law" [Provo, Utah: F.A.R.M.S., 1985); "Thieves and Robbers," *Insights* (July 1985), 2; and Welch, ed., *Reexploring the Book of Mormon: The F.A.R.M.S. Update* [Salt Lake City: Deseret Book Co. and Provo: F.A.R.M.S. 1992], 248–49. See also my "Legal and Social Perspectives on Robbers in First-Century Judea" in *Masada and the World of the New Testament,* ed. John F. Hall and John W. Welch [Provo, Utah: BYU Studies, 1997], 141–53). The distinction between robber and thief in ancient Israelite and Book of Mormon cultures explains how Laban could use the accusation against the sons of Lehi as an excuse to execute them without trial. It also explains why the Lamanites were, without exception, recorded as having robbed from the Nephites but never from their own people, which is something that would have been considered a theft. It also explains why the Gadiantons were consistently referred to by Book of Mormon authors as a society of robbers but never as thieves. It is interesting to note that the Hebrew word for band or bandit, *gedud,* has similar linguistic roots as the Book of Mormon's Gadianton band. Dr. Welch explains that the translators of the New Testament erred often in their use of the legal distinctions between robbers and thieves, while Joseph Smith remained consistent throughout his translation of the Book of Mormon. Dr. John Welch writes:

> Had Joseph Smith relied on the language of his King James Bible for legal definitions of these terms, he would have stumbled into error, for that translation uses the English words *thief* and *robber* indiscriminately. The same phrase is translated inconsistently from the Hebrew or Greek of Jeremiah 7:11 as "den of robbers" and yet from the identical Greek in Matthew 21:13 as "den of thieves," even though Jesus was quoting Jeremiah on that occasion, to say nothing of the fact that thieves do not have dens. In addition, the same word for robbers in the Greek New Testament *(lestai)* is sometimes translated as "thieves" (crucified next to Jesus in Matthew 27:38) and other times as "robber" (describing Barabbas in John 18:40). Nevertheless, there was indeed an important ancient distinction between thieves and robbers that no translator should neglect, and over which Joseph Smith did not blunder (*Re-exploring the Book of Mormon,* 248–49).

CHAPTER TWENTY-FIVE

Nephi indicates that the wealth left behind by Lehi was done by commandment from God for the purpose of getting the plates from Captain Laban (see 1 Ne. 3:16). It is not clear whether Lehi received by revelation the express purpose for leaving behind his gold and silver, but that he was commanded to do it is supported in scripture.

CHAPTER TWENTY-SIX

Nephi indicates that because of Captain Laban's bloodline as a descendant of Joseph he was entitled to keep the brass plates (see 1 Ne. 5:16). The record was likely begun many generations before Laban's day, and in this novel the sword of Laban, the brass plates, the land given to Nephi's family, and the treasures left behind at Lehi's estate are all consistent with tradition and historical evidence. Birthright treasures, or treasures of inheritance, were commonly passed from father to son in the royal families of both the Old Testament and Book of Mormon and usually included an inheritance of land as well as the authority to preside. Based on scripture and the diaries of early LDS Church members who were with the Prophet Joseph Smith when he discussed the sword of Laban and the brass plates, it is likely that Joseph who was sold into Egypt prepared these treasures for his sons before his death and that they served to designate Ephraim and Manasseh as his heirs, who were worthy of a royal birthright (Brett L. Holbrook, "The Sword of Laban as a Symbol of Divine Authority and Kingship," *Journal of Book of Mormon Studies*, vol. 2, no. 1, 39). Sidney B. Sperry indicates that the brass plates would have been kept by Ephraim, the senior tribe of Israel (see Gen. 48:5, 13–20; 1 Chron. 5:1–2). Laban was likely a descendant of Joseph through Ephraim. The tribes of Ephraim and Manasseh were allied for generations as part of the Northern Kingdom of Israel. Sperry also indicates that when the Northern Kingdom of Israel fell to the Assyrians and its capital of Samaria captured by Sargon II in 721 B.C., Captain Laban's forebears may well have fled to Jerusalem to prevent the sacred records from falling into alien hands. Dr. Sperry further suggests that Lehi's grandfather or great-grandfather may have left his northern home for Jerusalem in order to prevent his children from intermarrying or making religious compromises with the foreigners

brought into the land by the Assyrians. Such a course would not be unreasonable on the part of many devout families (*Some Problems of Interest
Relating to the Brass Plates,* 185–91).

Dr. Jeffrey R. Chadwick suggests that Lehi's great-grandparents,
before fleeing to Jerusalem to escape the advancing Assyrian army
sometime between 724 and 722 B.C., placed their gold and silver in
jars and buried their family's inheritance in the ground on property
on which they likely owned some sort of written deed and to which
Nephi later referred as their family's land of inheritance ("Lehi's
House at Jerusalem and the Land of His Inheritance," in *Glimpses of
Lehi's Jerusalem* [Provo, Utah: F.A.R.M.S., 2004], 81). Chadwick
further suggests that the property was likely very near the borders of
the northern and southern kingdoms of Israel under the tribal admin-
istration of Manasseh of the Northern Kingdom of Israel, about fifty
kilometers north of Jerusalem. Based on references in the Book of
Mormon text indicating that Lehi lived "at" Jerusalem—a reference
indicating the land outside the city's walls, as well as phrases like
"going down" to the land of their inheritance—scholar Hugh Nibley
suggests a location for Lehi's estate somewhere outside Jerusalem's
walls but in the vicinity of the city. Nibley does not give any more
details regarding his proposition for the location of Lehi's estate;
Chadwick, however, suggests that Lehi's great-grandparents, grandparents, and parents likely purchased a home inside the walled city of
Jerusalem on the west side of the city where King Hezekiah extended
a wall around the thousands of refugees building homes on the
unprotected western plateau known as the Mishneh refugee camp. He
points out that during the time when Lehi's great-grandparents and
grandparents lived in Jerusalem they would not have survived the
numerous Assyrian attacks and the decades-long Assyrian control of
the lands surrounding Jerusalem if they did not live within the walls
of the city. In this series of novels, Lehi's great-grandparents were
given title to property outside of Jerusalem at Beit Zayit soon after
their arrival as refugees, but in keeping with the political conditions,
the land was never developed into olive groves, and an estate home
was not built there until after Lehi inherited the land. Lehi's development of Beit Zayit during his lifetime is consistent with both Nibley's
suggestion that Lehi's estate was outside the walls of Jerusalem, and

also Chadwick's evidence suggesting that Assyrian military control of lands outside the walled city until about the time when Lehi reached adulthood and the Assyrian armies were redeployed to the northeastern Assyrian provinces to defend against the rising threat of the Babylonian empire, which would not have permitted Lehi's ancestors to build on that land until about 625 B.C. Lehi's development of Beit Zayit coincides, in this series, with the political changes occurring in the Assyrian control of land near Jerusalem.

Scholars agree that Lehi's great-grandparents fled to Jerusalem; however, Dr. Chadwick's suggestion that Lehi's progenitors left their gold and silver buried in jars on land that was later deeded to Lehi is a departure from other views. His well-documented analysis of Assyrian occupation—which was in decline during Lehi's day and which would have allowed Nephi and his brothers to return to land in the Northern Kingdom to dig up their gold and silver inheritance buried there more than one hundred years earlier and use it to purchase the brass-plate record from Lehi—is a relatively new proposition and a departure from what other scholars suggest. When Lehi received the brass-plate record at his camp in the Valley of Lemuel, the Book of Mormon record suggests that he may have been discovering for the first time his Northern Kingdom heritage and his genealogy, tying him to Joseph who was sold into Egypt (see 1 Ne. 5:4–16). It appears that up until that time Lehi likely believed he was a Jew from the Southern Kingdom of Judah. If that were the case, it is difficult to fully accept Dr. Chadwick's proposition that Lehi had a deed to land inheritance in the Northern Kingdom. He would have had to know about the deed to the land, and that his great-grandparents were refugees—something the Book of Mormon text suggests was not the case. Dr. Chadwick proposes that Lehi could have known about his ties to the Northern Kingdom, but not necessarily his actual genealogy, which he was reading for the first time when he studied the brass record and which accounts for the suggestion that this was new to him. The possibilities are many, and the dramatizations in this novel attempt to portray the account of the gold and silver inheritance left to Lehi and his family based, as closely as possible, on the geo-political forces of the day.

* * * * *

The prophets in both the Northern and Southern Kingdoms of Israel probably paid little attention to the political lines of division, but it is unlikely that all their words are recorded in the scriptures of both nations. From the time of the division of the two kingdoms until the fall of the Northern Kingdom in 721 B.C., the brass plates may well have been the official scripture of the ten tribes. The prophets Zenos, Zenock, Neum, and Ezias appear only to have been recorded on the brass plates (see 1 Ne. 19:10; Hel. 8:20). These were Hebrew prophets known to the Nephites, but their names do not appear in our current Old Testament.

Excavations around Samaria concur with the writings found on a stone tablet left by the son of the conquering king, Sargon II. He claimed to have constructed ramparts of earth, brought up battering rams, and dug tunnels to penetrate the city's fortifications. He also took as prisoners more than two hundred thousand people from the ten tribes, along with their livestock (The Church of Jesus Christ of Latter-day Saints, *Old Testament Student Manual: 1 Kings–Malachi*). During the war, some twenty thousand refugees fled to Jerusalem, doubling the population of the Southern Kingdom's capital city (*Great People of the Bible and How They Lived*). It is possible that both the sword of Joseph and the brass plates found their way to Jerusalem along with what later became Lehi's inheritance. It is not certain if Hoshea, the last king to rule over the Northern Kingdom, escaped during the kingdom's fall, but he and his family may have been part of this vast migration of Jews and could have transported the national treasures to Jerusalem (Daniel N. Rolph, "Prophets, Kings, and Swords: The Sword of Laban and Its Possible Pre-Laban Origins," *Journal of Book of Mormon Studies*, vol. 2, no.1 [Spring 1993], 73).

If Hoshea and his sons did escape to Jerusalem, we do not know if they were given an estate in the Upper City or deeded property. Based on the relative status and wealth of Hoshea's descendants as recorded in the Book of Mormon 120 years later, it is possible that he and his sons were well received by the King of Judah and that they brought with them substantial wealth.

Chapter Twenty-nine

This chapter dramatizes the account of Nephi and his brothers offering their inheritance for Captain Laban's brass plates. The Book of Mormon does not provide details except to record that Captain Laban desired the riches he saw in Nephi's possession and sent his men after Nephi and his brothers in an attempt to confiscate their wealth (see 1 Ne. 3:23–31).

Chapter Thirty

The inspiration for this chapter was drawn from the last chapter of Malachi. Ancient silversmiths waited until a shiny surface formed on the surface of silver indicating that the metal was purified. The prophet Malachi uses the metaphor, likely understood by ancient smiths, to teach that the Messiah, Jesus Christ, through His Atonement, is the purifier of the soul. The metaphor also includes an allusion to the penitent receiving the image of Christ in their countenance, likely meaning that through their efforts and by the grace of God they become disciples of Christ, and their whole being is infused with a Christlike manner. "And he shall sit as a refiner and purifier of silver: and he shall purify the sons of Levi, and purge them as gold and silver, that they may offer unto the Lord an offering in righteousness" (Mal. 3: 3).

Chapter Thirty-two

The Old Testament records numerous references made by the prophet Jeremiah regarding the final gathering to take place in the last days of the earth. Only a few of those references are mentioned in this chapter, including Jeremiah's prophecy that God will have compassion on Israel and gather them again out of the lands where they were driven (see Jer. 12:15) and the metaphorical allusion that God will send fishers and hunters to gather Israel in the last days (see Jer. 16:16). Included among Jeremiah's prophecies is the declaration that in the last days God will make a new covenant with His people, which He will write in their inward parts—likely a reference to the influence of the Holy Ghost as a means of testifying to truth (see Jer. 31:31–32). Joseph Smith Jr. referred to the Book of Mormon as the new covenant (see D&C 84:57), and Latter-day Saints believe that through the influence of the Holy Ghost men and women receive a witness of its truthfulness (see Moro. 10:7).

In this chapter, Baruch inscribes on plates of brass Jeremiah's references to the gathering on the Feast of Trumpets—a holy day on which Israel celebrates, among other things, the future gathering of Israel. The Feast of Trumpets marks Israel's final harvest period in the fall of the year. It is the first feast in a series of three of the holiest feast days in Judaism, which are also referred to as a trio of feasts of ingathering beginning with the Feast of Trumpets, followed ten days later by the Day of Atonement, and ending with the Feast of Tabernacles. Bruce R. McConkie indicates that these high holy days occur during the final harvest period to metaphorically symbolize Christ's final harvest of souls (*The Promised Messiah* [Salt Lake City: Deseret Book Co., 1978], 432–37). These interrelated feasts include the symbolism of the Feast of Trumpets as a time when God remembers His covenants with Israel and is likely the reason the feast day was originally known as the Day of Remembrance *(ha-Zikkaron)* before it became better known as a Jewish New Year *(Rosh Hashannah)*. The term *Zikron* means memorial or remembrance, and according to Hebrew scholars the blowing of trumpets on the Day of Remembrance is in keeping with the definition of *Zikron* "as a sound that will arouse God's remembrance (or judgment) of his people" (Abraham P. Bloch, *The Biblical and Historical Background of the Jewish Holy Days* [New York: KTAV, 1978], 142). Numerous Jewish scholars explain the purpose of the trumpet sound on the Feast of Trumpets as the signal of Israel's redemption from worldwide exile. The Old Testament states, "And it came to pass in the day [the time of regathering] that the great trumpet shall be blown, and they shall come which were ready to perish in the land of Assyria, and the outcasts in the land of Egypt" (Rabbi Nosson Sherman and Rabbi Meir Zlotowitz, *Rosh Hashanah; Its Significance, Laws, and Prayers* [Brooklyn, New York: Mesorah, 1983], 60, 99; Max Artz, *Justice and Mercy: Commentary on the Liturgy of the New Year and the Day of Atonement* [San Francisco: Holt, Rinehart, and Winston, 1963], 21; Snaith, *The Jewish New Year Festival,* 162; Leo Trepp, *The Complete Book of Jewish Observance* [New York: Behrman House and Summit Books, 1980], 95). The prophet Zechariah writes that "The Lord God shall blow the trumpet," and that Ephraim will help raise up God's covenant people, and that those of Israel's blood would return to be part of God's flock (see Zech. 9:13–16). After the Israelites returned from Babylonian bondage, the prophet Ezra gathered them together and read the law to them on the Feast of Trumpets (see Neh. 8:1–2), and they rejoiced when the truth was restored to them. LDS scholar Lenet Hadley Read indicates that this ancient restoration of the law after exile in Babylon, which took place on the Day of Remembrance, may have its latter-day counterpart in the coming forth of the Book of Mormon ("Joseph Smith's Receipt of the Plates and the Isrealite Feast of Trumpets"). Among the ancient readings still used during the celebration of *Rosh Hashannah* is the restoration of Ephraim. The prophecies of the prophet Jeremiah are among the important readings on this feast day, where he calls Ephraim a darling son and says that God will "remember Ephraim" *(zakhor ezkerenu)*. Hebrew religious scholars indicate that Jeremiah's prophecy regarding the remembrance (or restoration) of Ephraim has special significance to the Day of Remembrance, but are uncertain what that significance may be (Artz, *Justice and Mercy*, 146–48). Lenet Hadley Read further suggests in the article referenced above that the part the Book of Mormon plays in restoring knowledge of significant religious covenants to descendents of Ephraim is the connection between remembrance (or restoration) and the Day of Remembrance.

* * * * *

According to the Old Testament, Baruch wrote the prophecies of Jeremiah and read them in the temple. It is unlikely that he read them on the same day that Nephi and his brothers took the brass plates from Captain Laban's treasury; however, the events surrounding Baruch's reading of these prophecies follow the Old Testament account (see Jer. 36). The Old Testament records that Jeremiah told Baruch that due to his incarceration, Baruch must read the prophecies for him in the temple. The scripture also records that it was on a day of fasting, which points to one of the holy days, which includes the Feast of Trumpets (see Jer. 36:6). It was Michaiah who informed the princes of the city of Baruch's reading (see Jer. 36:12–13). Jehudi was sent to bring Baruch to them (see Jer. 36:14), and when they asked him about his scrolls, Baruch told them that he had recorded the writings in ink as they were spoken to him by the prophet Jeremiah (see Jer. 36:17–18).

CHAPTER THIRTY-THREE

It is traditional for Jews to visit the graves of deceased loved ones on *Rosh Hashannah*. Remembrance of family ties is an important outgrowth of the celebration, and it has roots in Malachi's promise that in the last days God would turn the hearts of the children toward the fathers and the hearts of the fathers to the children (see Mal. 4:6).

Most scholars agree that the main theme for *Rosh Hashannah* is remembrance—God's remembrance of His covenants with Israel, and the need for Israel's remembrance of their God (Artz, *Justice and Mercy,* 129; Snaith, *The Jewish New Year Festival,* 162, 172). The prayers offered on the feast day are intended to prepare men and women for the coming Messianic age, and the pleadings include phrases like, "Remember us unto life," and "May our remembrance . . . come before Thee." These prayers invoke the same spirit of covenants made between God and Abraham as well as other ancient patriarchs recorded in the Old Testament. The return covenant blessings from God, which follow Israel's remembrance of their covenants with God, are repeated in prayers offered on the Day of Remembrance and are similar to the words written by the prophet Moroni in the title page of the Book of Mormon, where he stated that one of the two main purposes of the book was "to show unto the remnant of the House of Israel what great things the Lord hath done for their fathers; and that they may know the covenants of the Lord, that they are not cast off forever." As part of the prayers offered on *Rosh Hashannah,* Jews today still read the Old Testament passage, "I will for their sakes remember the covenant of their ancestors, whom I brought forth out of the land of Egypt" (Lev. 26:45).

The Old Testament designates six holy days as times of worship with notable prophetic inference (McConkie, *The Promised Messiah,* 432–37; Lenet Hadley Read, "Symbols of the Harvest," *Ensign,* January 1975, 32–36). The first three—Passover, the barley sheaf offering, and the Feast of Weeks—occur during Israel's first early harvest and appear to contain prophetic reminders for ancient Israelites of the coming death, resurrection, and initial harvest of souls performed by the Messiah or Redeemer of Israel. The prophetic meaning or theme inherent in each of those holy days when juxtaposed with the life of Christ as recorded in the New Testament were fulfilled on the very days those feasts were celebrated.

The final three holy times—Feast of Trumpets, Day of Atonement, and Feast of Tabernacles—occur during Israel's final harvest and also appear to contain prophetic meaning regarding the last days of the earth. The celebration of the Feast of Trumpets, the first of these three final holy times, has four major themes: a time of Israel's final harvest, the Day of Remembrance of God's covenants with Israel, the announcement of revelation or truth, and preparation for God's holiest times with the advent of the Messianic Age. It is interesting to note that since Joseph Smith published the Book of Mormon, it has been the main instrument in the harvest of souls—what is commonly referred to as proselytizing or missionary work.

* * * * *

Joseph Knight was lodging at the Smith home on the night of September 21, 1827, and it is principally in his journal and that of Lucy Smith where the firsthand details of that evening are recorded. Mr. Knight recorded that Joseph Smith Jr. sent his father to scout the Samuel Lawrence property sometime in the afternoon. Mr. Lawrence knew about the plates and Joseph's yearly visits, and had also declared his intentions to interfere. It may have been that Lawrence and others did not anticipate Joseph going to the hill for the plates in the late evening hours leading up to September twenty-second. Whatever the reason, Joseph Smith Sr. returned some time after sundown with nothing to report about preparations at the Lawrence property.

Some time around midnight, Joseph Smith Jr. asked his mother Lucy if she had a chest. She recorded that she immediately knew he wanted to seal away the plates in a safe place, and she was upset for not having one. Joseph told her that "I can do very well for the present without it—be calm—all is right." Moments after their discussion about the chest, Emma came through the kitchen dressed in a bonnet and riding dress. Lucy reported hearing them drive off in Joseph Knight's wagon. It appears that Joseph Knight was not aware of their departure to the hill, but in this chapter he is portrayed as having been present when Joseph and Emma departed. Lucy Smith records that early the next morning, before Joseph and Emma returned from the hill, Joseph Knight believed his horse had been taken by some rogue from the countryside, and Lucy tried to calm him. She said, "Never mind the horse. Mr. Knight does not know all the nooks and corners of the pasture. I will call William; he will bring the horse immediately." Moments later, Mr. Knight discovered that his wagon was missing, and Lucy was successful in delaying him until Joseph returned home.

Joseph Smith did not record any details of what transpired on the hill the night he received the plates, though Joseph Knight and Lucy Smith as well as other contemporaries did record what Joseph told them. In this chapter, Joseph is portrayed as having used the Urim and Thummim to read the title page of the Book of Mormon; however, we have no record if that was actually the case, but we do know that by the time he returned home on the morning of September 22, he had used the Urim and Thummim. He told Joseph Knight that "I can see anything; they are marvelous." Joseph was as animated by his possession of the Urim and Thummim translating device as he was of the golden plates. Lucy was trembling when Joseph returned to the house, concerned that her son had been denied the plates due to disobedience. Joseph told her, "Do not be uneasy mother, all is right—see here, I have a key." He handed her an object hidden beneath a silk cloth. Lucy said she felt "two smooth three cornered diamonds set in glass." She recorded that they were set in bows connected "like old-fashioned spectacles." In reference to the Urim and Thummim, Joseph told Mr. Knight it was "ten times better than I expected." He offered Knight a description of the plates that "were written in characters and I want them translated." Joseph did not bring the plates home that morning. Instead, on his way home from the hill with Emma, he deposited them deep inside an old birch stump.

"I wish also to mention here," Joseph Smith wrote in the *Times and Seasons,* "that the title page of the Book of Mormon is a literal translation, taken from the very last leaf, on the left hand side of the collection or book of plates, which contained the record which has been translated; the language of the whole running the same as all Hebrew writing in general; and that, said title page is not by any means a modern composition either of mine or of any other man's who has lived or does live in this generation" (Joseph Smith Jr., *Times and Seasons,* 3:943). The title page was likely one of the last things written by Moroni before he deposited them in the hill near where

Joseph Smith unearthed them. Daniel Ludlow notes that "virtually all . . . scholars and students of the Book of Mormon who have written commentary about the title page have reached exactly the same two conclusions: (1) the title page was written entirely by Moroni, and (2) Moroni wrote portions of the title page at two different times in his life" (Daniel Ludlow, "The Title Page," in *The Book of Mormon: First Nephi, the Doctrinal Foundation* [BYU: Religious Studies Center, 1988], 28).

CHAPTER THIRTY-FOUR

Nephi recorded that when he was directed by the Spirit to slay Laban, he was given the reasoning that it was "better that one man should perish than that a nation should dwindle and perish in unbelief (see 1 Ne. 4:13). Scholar John Welch points out that five hundred years later, Nephite chief judge and prophet Alma (see Alma 30:47) used a similar justification regarding a divine punishment given Korihor (John W. Welch and law student assistant Heidi Harkness Parker in an article originally published as "Better That One Man Perish," FARMS Update, *Insights,* June 1998, 2; also in Welch and Thorne, eds., *Pressing Forward with the Book of Mormon* [Neal A. Maxwell Institute for Religious Scholarship, 2006], 17–19; also in *Echoes and Evidences of the Book of Mormon* [Neal A. Maxwell Institute for Religious Scholarship, Nov. 2002], 331–87). In the New Testament, the legal concept of one man dying for all members of a group was expressed by the high priest Caiaphas, a member of the political party known as Sadducees (see John 11:50). Legal scholar David Aus in his research regarding the ancient legal precedence of the "death of one for all" indicates that this principle prevailed in legal cases decided by biblical law around 600 B.C. when Lehi and his family lived at Jerusalem (David Aus, "The Death of One for All in John 11:45–54 in Light of Judaic Traditions," *Journal of Semitic Studies,* vol. XLI, no. 2, 340–42). The precedent was likely established when Sheba, deemed a traitor by King David, took refuge in the city Abel where the citizens, rather than allowing their city to be destroyed by the military commander Joab, beheaded Sheba. Both Welch and Aus point to a Jewish Council ruling made in Nephi's day, which points back to this event as pivotal in establishing the legal precedence of the "death of one for all" in the killing of one person in order to preserve the lives of members of an entire group (see 2 Sam. 20). In the case of Jehoiakim, the king of Judah who rebelled against Nebuchadnezzar, the Old Testament records that Nebuchadnezzar went to Antioch and demanded that the Jewish council surrender Jehoiakim or the nation would be destroyed. King Jehoiakim protested, "Can ye sacrifice one life for another?" The council replied, "Thus did your ancestors do to Sheba the son of Bichri." Welch indicates that based on this legal ruling, Jehoiakim was released to Nebuchadnezzar, who took him to Babylon where he was either executed or lived in exile the rest of his life (see 2 Chron. 36:6). Zedekiah became king less than four months later at the time the Book of Mormon account begins (see 1 Ne. 1:4). It is likely that when Nephi recorded his experience regarding his struggle with the Spirit of the Lord justifying the killing of Captain Laban, he was instructed in the legal language of the day—language that would have been familiar to him, telling him that it was "better that one man perish than that a nation should dwindle and perish in unbelief."

* * * * *

Prior to meeting Joseph Smith Jr. or hearing anything about the restored Church, both Brigham Young and Lorenzo Snow recorded seeing a vision of armies marching across the night sky above their homes on September 22, 1823 (Paul Thomas Smith, in "Little Known Eyewitness Accounts of the Coming Forth of the Book of Mormon [American Fork: Covenant Communications, 2000]). Those visions inspired the scene where Jeremiah is depicted seeing a similar vision of the armies of God marching over the earth to gather in Israel for the last time.

CHAPTER THIRTY-FIVE

In this chapter, Sariah's lament to her husband Lehi followed by remorse over her lack of faith in him takes place symbolically on the Day of Atonement. Ten days earlier, on the Day of Remembrance,

Jews believe the Lord makes an initial judgment as to who shall live and who shall die with regard to the salvation of their souls (Louis Jacobs, "Rosh Ha-shanah and Yom Kippur," in Mercia Eliade, ed., *The Encyclopedia of Religion* [New York: Macmillan, 1987], 12:474). Through repentance, prayer, and charity those judgments can be changed up until they are sealed on the Day of Atonement. The interval between these two feasts is called the Days of Awe, with the Day of Atonement being the most awesome. The ten-day period is set aside as a time to return to God and to righteousness and may be symbolic of man's mortal existence as a time of earthly probation reminiscent of the council Alma gave to his son Corianton in the Book of Mormon, telling him that there was a probationary time granted to man to repent and to serve God (see Alma 42: 4, 10).

* * * * *

Religious scholar Sidney B. Sperry points out that after Nephi and his brothers returned from Jerusalem with the brass plates, Lehi examined the records in detail (*Some Problems of Interest Relating to the Brass Plates,* 185–91). He discovered they contained the Pentateuch, or what is also called the five books of Moses, comprising the opening books of the Old Testament. The brass record also included a record of the Jews from the beginning down to Zedekiah's reign. It is likely that the use of the word "beginning" by Lehi is a reference to the constitutional founding of the Israelite nation, which began with the giving of the law at Sinai, since in the previous verse (see 1 Ne. 5:11) Lehi mentions the account of the Creation and Adam and Eve as having been already included in the five Books of Moses. Lehi also found many of Jeremiah's prophecies engraven on the sacred plates and also a genealogy of his family, discovering for the first time that he was a descendant of Joseph who was sold into Egypt, through his son Manasseh (see 1 Ne. 5:14; Alma 10:3). The Book of Mormon records:

> And after they had given thanks unto the God of Israel, my father, Lehi, took the records which were engraven upon the plates of brass, and he did search them from the beginning.

And he beheld that they did contain the five books of
Moses, which gave an account of the creation of the
world, and also of Adam and Eve, who were our first
parents;

And also a record of the Jews from the beginning, even
down to the commencement of the reign of Zedekiah,
king of Judah;

And also the prophecies of the holy prophets, from the
beginning, even down to the commencement of the reign
of Zedekiah; and also many prophecies which have been
spoken by the mouth of Jeremiah.

And it came to pass that my father, Lehi, also found
upon the plates of brass a genealogy of his fathers;
wherefore he knew that he was a descendant of Joseph;
yea, even that Joseph who was the son of Jacob, who was
sold into Egypt, and who was preserved by the hand of
the Lord, that he might preserve his father, Jacob, and
all his household from perishing with famine (1 Ne.
5:10–14).

Nephi recorded that "it was wisdom in the Lord that we should carry
them with us, as we journeyed in the wilderness towards the land of
promise" (1 Ne. 5:22). Lehi and his son Nephi taught continually from
the brass plates in order to "more fully persuade them to believe in the
Lord their Redeemer . . . that which was written by the prophet Isaiah" (1
Ne. 19:23). Nephi transcribed fifteen chapters of Isaiah's prophecies from
the brass plates into his own golden-plate record, which influenced religious thought among the Nephites for centuries (see 1 Ne. 20, 21; 2 Ne.
12–24). The Nephites had the prophetic words of Isaiah regarding the
birth of Christ: "Behold, a virgin shall conceive, and shall bear a son, and
shall call his name Immanuel" (2 Ne. 17:14); "For unto us a child is
born, unto us a son is given, and the government shall be upon his
shoulder; and his name shall be called, Wonderful, Counselor, The
Mighty God, the Everlasting Father, The Prince of Peace" (2 Ne. 19:6).

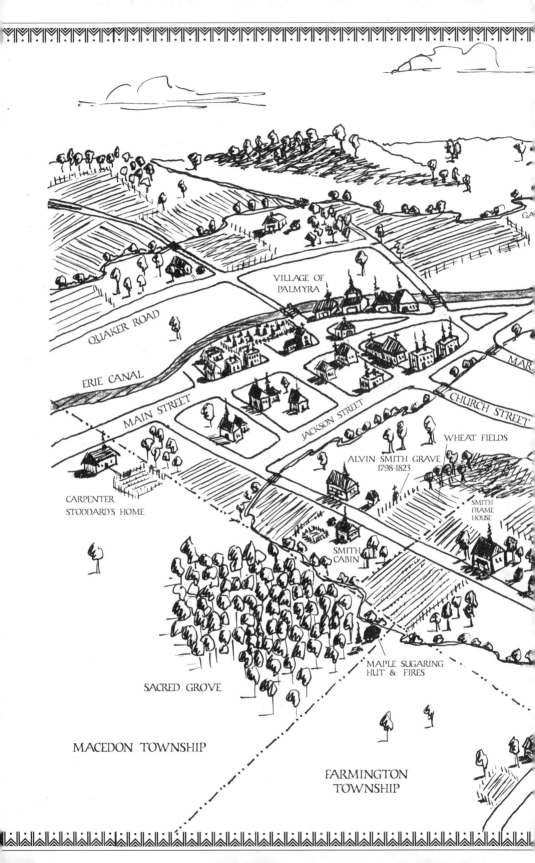

VILLAGE OF
PALMYRA

QUAKER ROAD

ERIE CANAL

MAIN STREET

JACKSON STREET

CHURCH STREET

MAR

GA

CARPENTER
STODDARD'S HOME

ALVIN SMITH GRAVE
1798-1823

WHEAT FIELDS

SMITH
FRAME
HOUSE

SMITH
CABIN

SACRED GROVE

MAPLE SUGARING
HUT & FIRES

MACEDON TOWNSHIP

FARMINGTON
TOWNSHIP